An ancient w

Haven Killian needs help. As the heiress of an ancient organization called the Black Rose, she is charged with keeping alive the line of succession. When she vows to protect a young boy tormented by magic, all she has to go on are rumors of an immortal with the power to save him.

As Battle King of the Undying, Quinn Donovan has the most powerful magic on the planet. Yet, he has waited an eternity to find his lifebond: the one woman destined to be his mate. The moment he meets Haven, he senses she is his. His instincts scream to protect the woman and the boy she guards, and to claim her as his own. But Haven is mortal, and for them to be united, she must become one of the Undying.

Books by Emma Weylin

Undying Hope

Published by Kensington Publishing Corporation

Undying Hope

Emma Weylin

LYRICAL PRESS
Kensington Publishing Corp.
www.kensingtonbooks.com

Lyrical Press books are published by
Kensington Publishing Corp. 119 West 40th Street New York, NY 10018

All Kensington titles, imprints, and distributed lines are available at special
quantity discounts for bulk purchases for sales promotion, premiums, fund-
raising, and educational or institutional use.

To the extent that the image or images on the cover of this book depict a
person or persons, such person or persons are merely models, and are not
intended to portray any character or characters featured in the book.

Special book excerpts or customized printings can also be created to fit
specific needs. For details, write or phone the office of the Kensington
Special Sales Manager:
Kensington Publishing Corp.
119 West 40th Street
New York, NY 10018
Attn. Special Sales Department. Phone: 1-800-221-2647.

Kensington and the K logo Reg. U.S. Pat. & TM Off.
Lyrical Press and the L logo are trademarks of Kensington Publishing Corp.

First Electronic Edition: August 2015
eISBN-13: 978-1-61650-771-8
eISBN-10: 1-61650-771-3

First Print Edition: August 2015
ISBN-13: 978-1-61650-772-5
ISBN-10: 1-61650-772-1

Printed in the United States of America

For my mother, who has always been my biggest fan. Thanks for all your love and support. I love you.

Acknowledgments

Lots of love and thanks to my husband, my girls, and Jennifer McConnell. Without any of you, I would never be able to create worlds or magic and wonder.

Prologue

Roaring power rumbled through Atlantis. Clear, shimmering pools sloshed out of their banks. Crystalline rock fragmented from under perfect mountain waterfalls. Magic of Theron's caliber, bellowing with anger in the water realm, was a rare occurrence.

"Laila!"

She fought the instinct to wilt. Like all pixies of the Avalon realm, her powers had limits. She'd just moved the Undying people on the Gaia realm two thousand years into the future at the behest of Oberon. Destroying one realm while saving another would hinder her cause.

"Laila!" The anguished roar again shook the snowcapped mountains.

She balled her miniature fists, but she knew better than to aggravate Theron further. His power had grown more than even Oberon had predicted. The move had saved many lives, even if the needed action angered Theron.

The next bellow shook the air surrounding her. This time the tip of the eastern mountains started to crumble. Laila blanched. She kept forgetting Theron and his human had reached full maturity.

Laila spread her dragonfly wings, beating them with a blur of speed to carry her up the mountain pass at a rapid pace. It seemed like only yesterday Theron had been a tiny blip of light in the dark pool that had created the essence of the first Undying power source. Fifty-five hundred Gaia, or Earth years, did go by rather quickly when one wasn't watching.

"Do stop," Laila said in soft tones as she came upon Theron, who stood next to the Pool of Sight amidst glistening rainbow grotto crystals. "You'll sink Atlantis."

A deep animal growl emanating from the altered human trembled the ground as the man housing Theron turned on her. Mercury orbs of glowing light were in place of his irises. His lip curled into a snarl. His large, perfect body was strung tight as if prepared for battle. "What did you do?"

Many millennia had passed since Laila feared for her life. Maybe making a creature so strong hadn't been the smartest of ideas... but necessity often had one taking risks they normally wouldn't. Theron was first. His loyalty to her had been unbreakable, but did not extend beyond a mass time teleportation of his people.

"Protected them," she proclaimed.

He pointed at the Pool of Sight, shimmering inside a pure white marble basin. Images of his people flicked across the water as time on Gaia flashed by. Minutes in Atlantis moved like hours on Gaia. "They are lost! They cannot perform their duty. What have you done?"

"Now, Theron." Laila flapped her wings to move her wee size up to eye level with the great power in front of her. "My sister tried to pull a fast one. I had to react, or they'd all be dead."

The mercury swirl of Theron's eyes burned hot. "Send us back!"

"I can't," she said. "Cadeyrn turned out better than either of us hoped. Have faith. I put him where he should find his reward. He will be stronger."

Theron's eyes flicked to the pool. An image of a young woman flashed across the water. Soft elven features graced the woman's face. Her hair was a rich auburn, hanging in loose waves down to her hips. His eyes narrowed on the image in the water. She was worried. There was a boy of his kind with her. Theron's mighty essence stretched beyond barriers he should not have been able to cross to get a feel on the woman—Cadeyrn's lifebond.

His glowing eyes returned to Laila. "I cannot complete my task without Cadeyrn. Pray he comes successfully to his bond to life."

Laila shrank down in size under Theron's angry stare. His eyes bore into her as if he could already have her diminutive heart in his hand. If anything happened to Cadeyrn, no matter how tiny she was, she knew Theron would find a way to bathe in her blood.

Chapter 1

Haven Killian paced the emergency exam room. Once again, Bastian had another of his debilitating headaches. The headaches always came after a fight with another boy. She paused by the bed where he lay in a blissful drug-induced sleep. Pain medication had given needed relief fifteen minutes ago, leaving her to wait for the doctor. She leaned down, touched a kiss to his brow, and lightly cupped the side of his face.

"Oh, my Bastian," she murmured. "How are we ever going to survive this?"

Part of her knew he was one of *them*. One of those beings who appeared like a human on the outside, but wasn't exactly one on the inside. Nor did he resemble anything else in the lore her grandfather had taught her. Marcus Killian, her grandfather, was the leader of a secret organization called the Black Rose. Two thousand years ago, a powerful being known simply as Cadeyrn, had created the organization as a sort of supernatural police force.

Intuition told her help existed somewhere for the boy. He couldn't be one of the nightmares from the stories her grandfather had told her of the creatures out there. Bastian was a sweet and thoughtful boy. At fourteen, he was more considerate than most adults she knew. Even so, he couldn't help his overly aggressive reaction to violence toward someone Bastian perceived as an innocent. With eerie predictability, monstrous headaches assailed him after a fight. The administrators of the school wouldn't—couldn't—understand. Bastian never fought without being provoked.

She'd had no time to find out what triggered him, but it was usually because another boy had a heinous plan for one of the girls in Bastian's class. While she understood those boys were more than likely only saying the crude words that boys sometimes said, the power growing inside of

Bastian hadn't gotten the memo. She was running out of options for his education. This was the third school in as many months from which he'd been expelled.

An archaic organization run by her grandfather hunting her didn't help anything. She was supposed to have married her grandfather's choice in heir. Leadership of the Black Rose would go to her husband. According to her upbringing, an arranged marriage wouldn't be an issue if the supplied groom was someone she could respect and trust. The darkly terrifying Mason was neither. He could make the ground shake. The monster of a man claimed he was Bastian's uncle. Mason claimed his rough treatment of Bastian was his duty. Haven didn't believe either.

When she watched Mason strike Bastian for dropping a pencil, she'd known her existence as a pampered granddaughter of a rich man was over. That same night Haven had cleaned out her personal accounts. She and Bastian had fled the mansion Grandfather used as both a home and headquarters to his global organization that fought against the nastier creatures of the world. Three years of hopping from town to town, school to school, she'd somehow ended up back in Chicago.

The person she needed to help Bastian was rumored to live here. Every clue and every utterance of a shadowy, massive power had led to this city. He masqueraded as a real-estate mogul and entertainment entrepreneur. No matter what she had to do, she would find this Quinn Donovan. There must be a way to make him help Bastian. Bastian couldn't end up like the dark monster, Mason.

A light knock at the door disrupted her thoughts. A cracking voice asked, "Ms. Killian?"

She jerked her head around. "Dr. Livingston. Have you been able to find out anything else?"

The middle aged, balding doctor came into the room. He pulled the door closed, sat down on a rolling stool, and clasped his hands together. "I understand you've declined blood work and any kind of scan. I might be able to help with his headaches, but I am going to be bluntly honest. Sudden behavior changes. Sudden unexplained pain. Those are pointing at a tumor. I can't do any more for him if you won't allow me."

"We can't afford those tests." She didn't lie, but money was not the reason she refused to have them done. Bastian would become a scientist's next experiment if a doctor looked inside of him. "Is there anything else you can do for him without running some kind of scan?"

Doctor Livingston pulled off his glasses, then rubbed at his temples before putting them back on. "I can put you in contact with an organization that gives donations to many families like yours. It's possible to get all of his medical expenses paid for, but you have to fill out the paper work."

Haven closed her eyes and dragged breath into her lungs. "All right," she lied. This emergency room could never be used again. "If you could get me the forms, I'll fill them out."

The doctor smiled as he stood. "We'll find a way to take care of him, Ms. Killian."

She smiled as she nodded. Once he was gone, she pulled on a coat so old it no longer battled the cold and slung her tattered purse over her shoulder. She grabbed Bastian's coat and leaned close to his ear. "You have to wake him up so we can get out of here, but don't hurt him." She rarely talked to the strange power she could feel growing inside of him, but it was sometimes useful when they needed to run.

Bastian groaned, and when his eyes opened, they were flashing molten mercury. Bastian shook his head several times and ground his teeth together. "What's going on?"

"They want to run more tests," she whispered. "We have to go."

Bastian swung his long legs over the edge of the bed. He was already over six feet tall. Even at seven inches shorter than him, she moved close to help him walk while he was still groggy. He staggered a few steps. His eyes glowed, but when he blinked, everything was normal. Haven poked her head out into the hall and then acted as if she was helping Bastian get to the restroom just outside the exam room. A nurse smiled at them before going into another patient's room.

Bastian hunched over as they slipped down the hall and out the door where ambulances brought people in. They ran around the side of the building and waited while Bastian put his coat on. When no one followed them after five minutes, Haven let out a breath.

The snow was falling again.

Bastian put a hand to his stomach. "Can we get something to eat?"

Haven gave him a look, because it seemed all the boy ever did was eat. Bastian ate more than four grown men could eat together, but he didn't seem to gain any weight. She moved in closer to Bastian as frigid winds picked up. The air was ugly cold, even for February. Bastian could go without a coat if she'd let him. She opened her purse. There was just enough money inside that they could stop at a diner on the way back to the shoddy motel they were staying in. "But only one meal, okay?"

Bastian hugged her tight. "Sounds good. What did the doctor say?"

She wrinkled her nose as they headed for the main road that led them to a string of buildings with various stages of failing businesses. "Testing."

"What harm could it do?" He hooked his arm around her, helping to ward off the cold seeping into her bones.

"They could find out you're not human," she whispered. "I have an interview at Fantasia tomorrow. I'll get the job and—"

"What reason would *he* have to help us," Bastian said with a growl.

"Because he just has to," she said, knowing the answer wasn't good, but she didn't have another one. Running from one thing to the next and eluding creatures who seemed to be able to pick up her scent like a bloodhound wasn't getting easier. "That woman said he would help if we offered him payment."

"And what if his expected payment is baby's blood?" Bastian pressed as they turned onto the sidewalk on the main drag.

"Nothing eats baby's blood." She shuddered with the heebie-jeebies. "That's just wrong."

"I get stronger every day," Bastian said with confidence. "Soon I'll be able to protect you from Mason."

Haven hugged him tight but didn't say anything. Bastian's power was like a cup of water to Lake Michigan when compared to Mason. She encouraged Bastian's protective side to keep him from walking down a darker path. She didn't have the knowledge to teach Bastian how to control the power. The Black Rose was closer to finding them. If every grand and pompous claim Grandfather had made about the new creatures was true, she could not figure out why he wanted Mason to lead. There was a streak of evil in him wide enough to make the devil run for cover.

"There," she said when they got closer to the diner. "We'll get dinner and then get back to the motel."

"Right," he said. "And Haven?"

She looked up at him. "Yeah?"

His jaw went tight as he turned his gaze from her. "I'm sorry I got kicked out of school again. I know how important getting an education is to you."

She patted his chest. "It's all right. Your school didn't like our lack of permanent address anyway. We'll find a better one."

He linked his arm with hers and walked toward the diner entrance. "Let's get you out of the cold. I don't want you turning into an ice cube."

She followed him inside, sending a silent prayer skyward that Quinn Donovan would be able to help Bastian. He was her last hope.

* * * *

"You know, we've been in this time for fifty years. You'd think you'd have figured out how to get control of the Black Rose already."

Quinn Donovan gave Nikon a sharp look. It had taken him half a century to get into a position to take back the Black Rose. He didn't want to hurt humans in the process. His people had also needed to gain the knowledge to survive this time without drawing attention from the public. "Shut up. I didn't ask you anything."

The wolf shrugged and then spoke directly into his mind again, *"You seem to be getting comfortable in this time, and I wanted to remind you of your task."*

"I know my responsibilities. You don't have to remind me of anything."

The large black wolf and his mate, a smaller white wolf, followed Donovan through pulsing sound that vibrated through the nightclub he'd owned for the last forty years. The wild animals didn't faze the patrons or employees. The wolves were expected and half of the draw in coming to one of Donovan's establishments. They wanted to see if they could catch a glimpse of both man and beasts. The clubs provided him the money he'd needed to start investing in property in and around Chicago. He'd managed to work himself into being a respected billionaire. Money wasn't something he cared about, but in this strange time and place, it was the only common language. Wealth helped to cover up a hell of a lot of trouble.

Once again, he'd be able to regain control over the Black Rose, an organization he began over two thousand years prior to build a bridge between his people and the humans. When the Book of Avalon had been stolen, the Undying had lost their purpose during the missing centuries from Earth's timeline. They'd landed in a time where humans were making great technological advances. Humans, for all their faults and frailties, always made progress, though most civilizations seemed to have taken a big hit about the time Donovan had lost the book to Kyros.

He shook his head as he walked into his office. He settled his warrior's frame into a soft, black leather executive chair and watched the security system monitors. Nikon curled up on a soft rug in front of a large sofa while Medea snuggled in next to him with her head tucked under Nikon's chin. Nikon had bonded to Donovan at birth as a lifelong companion. Medea was a recent addition. Her charge had perished when the whole of the Undying Nation had suddenly and irrevocably been moved from somewhere around 100 BC to the middle of the twentieth century. She'd taken a liking to Nikon and never left. Their breed was not of this world but of Ashina, Wolf World, and they had been given by Laila to his clan of people to aid them with their fight against darkness.

Donovan had to admit, he liked this time more than his own, but he shuddered when he thought of how old he could be. If he'd already lived over two millennia before he lost the book, and another two had passed since then, he could be old indeed. He shook his head and decided not to think about his true age. He was already weary of his task, but he couldn't give up. His people needed him and so did humans. They were depending on him to fix the mistake.

If losing the book could be fixed.

"You're spinning your thoughts again. Just accept that you're older than dirt, and get over yourself." The cadence of Medea's voice was sensual sweet and never a burden when she suddenly came into his mind, even when she was purposefully being annoying.

Donovan had just shot a glare over his shoulder at the white wolf when the door burst open.

"Sir," a wobbly voice said, and Donovan cringed. He hated the lack of manhood these male humans had.

He bared teeth at Medea before he turned to his employee. "Can I help you?"

The man's brown eyes went wide, and he backed up a pace. "You said to notify you at once if anything happened in the alley. I was just coming back from my break when I heard a scream."

Donovan didn't bother to stop the low growl that rumbled from his massive chest. His eyes flicked to the screen, but even in this world of technology, there were still threats better picked up by ancient methods. He closed his eyes for a moment to let his vast power stretch out, scanning the area outside the club. The fading presence of life was faint. "Call an ambulance," he commanded before he took off through the club, Nikon following closely behind him. Medea would not follow, not while she carried a litter of Ashina wolves. He couldn't hide his now glowing eyes as he stepped out into the chilled air and sniffed. Kyros had been there. The cold stain of an evil presence lingered along with the foul stench. Shadows cloaked him as he walked down the dim alley. He didn't like knowing this was where his employees came on their breaks. He'd have to change the conditions of their outside area. They depended on him for their safety.

Everyone did.

He let out a slow, guarded breath. Perhaps he could kill Kyros, let his brothers find the book, and regain the Black Rose.

He'd lived too long, seen too much. Others could take over and make sure what needed to be done was done. The loss of the book wasn't only his folly, but he knew deep in his soul only he could end Kyros, if any of them could.

His brother, Wolf, could take command of the Black Rose once Donovan controlled it again, and then he'd go on his last hunt. Too many innocent lives were lost to Kyros's obsession with his attempts to create a scenario where Donovan would turn to evil. Donovan would kill Kyros, or die trying. Kyros had the mastery of illusion matched by none, and was the reason he was so damn difficult to track. Then Donovan would simply let himself rest. His body and soul so greatly needed an eternal sleep. His time drew to a close.

He reached the alley's dead end. A woman had been horribly mutilated and was stuffed into a garbage bag filled with her own blood. Donovan didn't react. He never reacted. If he did, he'd lose more of his soul than he already had. There wasn't anything that could be done for her other than put her out of the misery Kyros had inflicted on her. For a moment, he considered calling Riordan, his other brother and a healer, but discarded the thought as blood pooled at his feet. She'd lost too much.

He closed his eyes and filled her mind with warmth and feelings of safety. There was no reason to make her fear impending death. His hand trembled for a moment before he placed it on her. A whisper of words commanded her mind into one last sleep. Donovan sat down next to the dying woman as the whir of sirens broke silence in the distance. His presence would be the last she felt in this realm. When she was gone, he lightly stroked a war-calloused hand down her bloody bottle-blond hair, his head bowed in a silent prayer to whatever god she was going home to.

She'd been alone in the world, a streetwalker trying to make enough money to live. No one would mourn her death, no one would even notice she was gone but him, but he'd keep her close to his heart. She deserved it—all life did.

When the ambulance and police arrived, he was sitting next to the body with his hand shaking as he stroked her hair again, knowing this was the only kind gesture she'd gotten from anyone—even from before her death. He was mute as they collected her body and processed evidence in the alley and on him. He slowly stood up as detectives asked him questions. He didn't bother to wash off the blood before he led them through the club and to his security room. As expected, there was nothing on the videos but a blur of light and horrible screaming from the woman as she was tortured. Detectives started to leave one by one. One whispered to another, "Another burial for the city to pay for."

Donovan's jaw twitched. He knew the girl's name. He knew everything about her from the brief moment his mind had touched hers. "I will pay for her." Then he rose up from his chair, cowering all the men left in the room, and directed them out with one look. The wolves circled around him and pressed up against his legs as he grieved for a woman society had thrown away. Donovan remained standing with his head bowed. When he finished remembering the woman no one else would, he'd go on what he hoped to be his last hunt.

Chapter 2

Snow kept piling up out there. Vinnie, who'd introduced himself as the owner when Haven and Bastian came into the diner, was the only one left. He had offered to let Haven and Bastian stay and keep soaking in the heat while they lingered over coffee and hot chocolate before having to make the mad dash to the motel a few blocks down the road.

"What about cyber school?" Haven asked as she stirred her coffee for the eighteenth time. "You can't get into fights there, and the school can move around with us."

"What about a job?" he countered. "I can pass myself off as an eighteen-year-old."

"But you're not," she said. "All we have to do is get that Donovan guy to help you, and you'll be glad for an education." She tapped the side of his mug. "Drink up. We need to get out of here. I have to be up early tomorrow to get ready for my interview."

"Yes, ma'am," Bastian said.

He would be an easy kid if he didn't have his special issues.

The door chime sounded.

Both she and Bastian glanced toward the door when what appeared to be the devil come to life entered the diner. Blood red, glowing eyes assessed everything. A giant of a man with cropped, black-as-sin hair strolled through the diner, heading for Haven. His eyes roamed down her slight form. "My name is Kyros. I will be murdering you tonight." He gave an eloquent bow. With what seemed like a giant leap, he was across the room, his iron fist clamped around her wrist. "I think you'll do just fine for my purpose." His arm extended and slammed into Bastian's chest, sending him sprawling across the diner. Bastian's head bounced off the corner of a booth before his body slumped to the floor. Kyros leaned down and took a prolonged inhale of her scent, right at her throat. "Yes, you'll do just fine. Ever been used as bait, sweetheart?"

Haven twisted and yanked with desperation to get away from this mad man. "Please, let us go."

His laugh was a gnarled sound of menace. "Do whatever you wish. You're going to die in agony, anyway."

Haven closed her eyes. "*Help.*" She didn't even dare whisper the words, but she projected the word out. While she knew humans couldn't hear her, she hoped someone with enough power to take down this madman would. She tried to smile for him again, hoping she could keep fear out of her eyes and voice. "Would you like a cup of coffee? I am sure Vinnie wouldn't mind."

He yanked her hard against his muscular body, her breasts mashing against his chest. It was all she could do to keep from gagging when his mouth fastened over hers. "You're going to do everything I tell you, sweetheart." The back of his knuckle scraped along her cheek in a gentle manner. "You're going to give me everything I want."

Haven saw Vinnie coming up behind Kyros, and she shook her head in warning, but it was too late. Vinnie swung a pan with hot grease, but Kyros moved lightning fast. He grabbed Vinnie's fist and turned the pan back on him until grease dripped down his arm. Vinnie screamed in agony, and the man holding her only laughed. "Stupid human. Don't think you're going anywhere, sweetheart."

He shoved her down with enough force that she fell back, knocking her head off the counter. She started to crawl toward Bastian. Nothing could happen to him. She'd never forgive herself. It was then she found a treasure. Her hand curled around a broom handle, and she came up swinging. The man caught the handle and brought the broom up, smacking her chin. Her head spun as she staggered backward.

"Stay down, bitch! You're only making it worse for yourself."

Haven slithered to the floor. A silver blade flashed before sinking into Vinnie's throat. Kyros twisted the knife, and when he pulled away, there was a gargle of hot red liquid. Haven shook as blood splattered on her. She yelped when Kyros yanked her to her feet by her hair. The man flicked out his tongue and licked a drop of blood that had settled on her cheek. "I'm not sure which tastes better. You or blood."

She gagged as she struggled to get away from his bruising grip. He laughed the same twisted sound. "Keep struggling, honey. It makes the kill so much sweeter." He let out a vicious growl and lowered his head. Haven closed her eyes and clamped her mouth shut. She wasn't going to be a victim again, no matter what he did to her. She wasn't going to beg him.

A sound like thunder rattled the window glass, and the floor rolled as the diner door was blown open with a surge of raw, savage power. Ketchup bottles and napkin holders vibrated on tabletops. A deep, rumbling voice filled the diner. "Let the woman go."

Kyros stopped his assault. A malicious smile curved his demon mouth, and his eyes glowed an unholy red. His head cocked as if to taunt the man who had walked in. He licked the side of Haven's face. "Your little cry for help wasn't secret after all."

He pulled Haven tight against him and turned to face the most terrifying man Haven had ever seen. Kyros appeared small by comparison. The warrior's muscles rippled and bunched under copper skin. His eyes were aflame with a golden fire. His hair fell over his shoulder in a long, thick braid. His face wasn't pretty by any means, but it was the most beautiful thing Haven had ever seen. The man exuded menace, and his very presence was power and unyielding strength. One idea crept into her terror-filled mind. She and Bastian were going to live because of the mountain standing in front of her.

The warrior stalked toward them. "Let her go. You want me." His voice was a deep, buttery baritone. "You think I somehow stole your book. That I took what you had managed to steal all those years ago. You don't want her. I'm the one you're after."

Kyros's grip loosened, but he didn't let go. "She possesses an orphan. How do you know she's not meirlock? Why will you never let me kill naughty girls?"

Confusion permeated Kyros's voice, and Haven found herself holding her breath, waiting for the warrior to answer.

"You know what she is." He paused, and his gaze flicked to Haven before returning to his adversary. "Dare you risk her belonging to me?"

Her mind was reeling from fear and the danger surrounding her and the strange conversation between the two men. "Please, let me go." She hated her voice when it came out in a whimper.

The warrior's eyes flashed, and one of his powerful arms snaked out, his hand clamping over Kyros's throat. "Let her go. We can end this tonight."

Everything inside of her roiled against the stark words of her savior ending anything tonight. The rational part of her knew this was insane, but the resignation of his tone twisted at her heart. She renewed her struggle to make Kyros let her go. She needed to get to the warrior. Something deep inside of her reached out to him, but Kyros's grip tightened. She cried out as pain shot through her wrist.

The warrior moved. His body was a symphony of motion. Every muscle worked in harmony during the deadly attack. He sprang forward. With one swift motion, he pulled Haven away before colliding with Kyros. The bruising hands left her trembling body, and she stumbled behind the warrior and toward Bastian.

Kyros went flying backward. The window shattered. He skidded across the salt-crusted concrete sidewalk and out into the snow-covered street. He slowly stood while laughing. "A new pawn is added to our game."

A violent swirl of air opened directly behind Kyros. Red and black lightning crackled around the vortex. Kyros gave an eloquent bow. "I look forward to it, Cadeyrn." He stepped back, allowing the twist of angry wind to swallow him.

"Bastian!" Haven turned from the warrior and took one wobbling step toward the boy. A strong arm looped around her before she fell on her face. She shook her head, but that only produced a throbbing. "He's hurt."

"He'll heal in his sleep," the warrior said. "You need to be still so that I may look at your wounds."

She twisted in his hold and then shoved her arms up between them. If her sensibilities were going to remain intact after what she'd just witnessed, he shouldn't be that close. "Who are you?"

"Sit and I will tell you," he said. His tone was final and commanding.

She ground her teeth together, but she sat. "Who are you?"

A half smile curved the corner of a sensual mouth. He bowed low. "I am Quinn Donovan. Might I have the pleasure of your name?"

"No, you're not," she snapped at him. Her head was hurting, Bastian was groaning, and she'd just fallen into a nightmare. "Who are you?"

His glacier blue eyes went fierce. "All right. Then who am I?"

"A figment of my imagination. That man tried to butcher me, and I'm in a hospital somewhere." She took several controlled breaths to calm herself and give herself a chance to listen to her intuition. It kept her away from the Black Rose for the last three years. She curled her lip. That feeling of wanting to crawl into his lap and make his world right grew stronger. "If you *are* Quinn Donovan. I need your help."

"Anything you need, all you have to do is ask," he said.

He had some odd angle he was playing at. He'd just—well—she wasn't exactly sure what that just was. She could hear a hum around him, but full words weren't forming well enough for her to get a handle on them. Quinn appeared to be part of the epic battle her grandfather warned her about, but if her intuition was to be trusted, she wanted to be on Quinn's side. "I need a warm place for me and Bastian to stay. We need food, and he needs medical attention." She paused as she tried to figure out what was going on behind that mask of indifference on his face. "And I need someone to tell me what he is so I can help him with the change he's going through."

"Done, done, done, and done," he said with a gentle voice. "He is an orphaned Undying male child. You are not equipped to handle the type of care and training he will need to survive to full maturity."

"What does that mean?" she snapped as her mama bear hackles raised. "You are not going to take him from me!"

"Wouldn't dream of it," he said with perfect seriousness. "My home has enough room for all of us. I assure you I can be trusted."

She wanted to believe him—to believe herself. Damn Mason for screwing with her. "What are you?"

"I am Undying. Just like the boy. I can take away his pain, and I can teach him how to use the power given to him."

Haven focused on breathing to calm the rising panic. She'd said she was going to demand that Quinn Donovan help her. As crazy as asking for help from a stranger was, she didn't have any other options. They couldn't go back to the emergency room they'd snuck out of to get more pain medicine for Bastian. "We don't do doctors."

"My brother is a healer," Quinn said. "I will call him when you and the boy are secured."

"It might not be—" She took a step forward when Quinn walked over to Bastian and lifted him as if he weighed nothing. "You can't just do that. What if you cause more damage?"

Quinn gave her a fierce look that had her pulling back. "The longer we remain here the better chances we have of being discovered."

"Don't you have one of those wind things?" Haven challenged him.

"Of course," he said, as if trans-dimensional portals were normal. "But then I'd have to leave my Hummer in this neighborhood overnight."

Haven was sure he was joking, but she wasn't in the mood to appreciate the humor. "All right. What about Vinnie?"

Quinn glanced at the dead restaurant owner. His head bowed as raw grief emanated around him. "He'll be given an honorable funeral."

Haven didn't like her lack of choices. While she hoped she could trust Donovan, she still wanted options in case something went wrong. However, no one could tell "no" to a man who could make the ground shake with the force of Quinn's power. She was stuck seeing this out to its end.

Chapter 3

The woman flitted this way and that as she went through the small motel room, gathering items belonging to her and the boy. They'd walked from the diner in the accumulating snow. Bastian had passed out on the bed closest to the door. Donovan had yet to acquire the woman's name, and she still refused to believe he was Quinn Donovan. He could feel tendrils of her delicate, young power assessing him. She stopped in the middle of the room and looked up at him with soulful eyes. "How much of this can I take with us?"

In an instant, he was trapped by the unusual pale green of her irises. Their exotic shape enhanced each emotion as they played in the depths of her eyes. The soft elven features of her face started a stirring low in his gut. His gaze drifted to her mouth—supple lips teased him into taking a step forward to steal a taste. He willed himself to stop the motion. He swallowed hard as his unintended appraisal continued. Her delicate frame swelled and narrowed in all the mouthwatering right places, making him hard. He was positive this woman would look best dressed in only her wavy auburn hair falling down to her hips, built perfect for gripping.

His body shuddered when the *treòir*, his source of power within, made an odd little twitch. A giddy rush flowed through him like a jolt of electricity.

Was she?

No.

A possible greater connection with her wasn't something he could deal with now. She needed help first. He'd sort everything out when he had time and space away from her to think logically. If she was who he thought she might be, his plans to end his days could come to a grinding halt. The entire Undying Nation would become unstable if she was his mate. That needed to be avoided for as long as possible.

He must have stood there for too long staring at her because she backed up a step. Then he forced a smile and grabbed a bag off the bed nearest the door. "Anything you desire you may have."

Her nose wrinkled up even as a smile played in the corner of her eyes. "You're unusual."

"Funny coming from someone without a name," he said as he scanned the room for any odd trinket she may have overlooked.

"Haven," she whispered. "The boy is Bastian." She took the last remaining bag of their meager belongings off the bed. "How do you know you can help him?"

Donovan lifted Bastian over his shoulder and stopped by the door. He glanced out the window to assure the Hummer was still where he'd left it. He had stopped believing in coincidences long ago. Standing here with an Undying child in his arms, and a woman with lifebond magic, was the exact reason fate had him choosing that parking space while he'd been hunting Kyros. His attention went back to Haven. "I am what he is."

She sucked in a sharp breath and slowly nodded. "And what is that exactly?"

"Undying," he repeated for the eighth time since the diner fifteen minutes ago.

She snorted at him. "I don't understand what that means. Something like a meirlock?"

A pulse of *treòir* energy vibrated through the room. "When have you come into contact with a meirlock?"

Her eyes went wide as she stumbled back a step. "I-I'm sorry. I've only heard the term used to describe a man...my grandfather knows."

The room vibrated again. Donovan gritted his teeth in the effort to keep his power from frightening his lifebond further. "Kyros is meirlock. The word literally means lawbreaker."

She studied his face for a long moment. "Why would someone as powerful as you help perfect strangers?"

"Bastian is of my kind," he said choosing his words carefully. "Without an older male to teach him the proper ways of our people, he is destined to be a meirlock and would be marked for death."

Her back went straight as her expression hardened. "He's a good person. There is no need for anyone to mark him for death. He just needs something I don't think I am able to give him."

"Aye," Donovan agreed as he opened the door. "As an older male of our people, it is my responsibility to take the boy in and guide him so our king does not have to give him a death sentence."

"I still don't get why that means you would help us," she said as she moved toward the door. "I am trying to trust you, and I want to believe who you say you are, but I've been searching for Quinn Donovan for nearly two years to help Bastian. How did you suddenly fall in my lap and rescue us from Kyros?"

He closed the motel room door before taking to the Hummer. He settled the boy on the backseat and then joined Haven behind the vehicle. "I heard your call for help and responded before the dragon was able to get here."

Haven waited for him to open the hatch. "Dragons? There are dragons, too?"

"There are several different clans of the Undying. The wolf clan and the dragon clan are but two, though the dragons are the only ones who can shapeshift."

She put her bags into the back as a black wolf ghosted out from between two parked cars.

"Quinn! There's a wolf!"

Donovan opened the back door of the hummer for the wolf to hop inside. "This is Nikon. He is an old friend."

She squeaked. "By your…friend, you're part of the wolf clan?"

"Aye," he said, knowing he was somehow doing this all wrong and not giving her the right information. The more he told her, the more upset she became. "Nikon and Medea would no more harm you than they would their newborn cubs. I understand this is confusing, and more questions come to you than I can answer satisfactorily. Give yourself time. This world you enter is complex."

She puffed out a breath of air before nodding. "Where are you taking us?"

"To my home." He walked her around to the passenger side of the Hummer. Kyros was still out there and regardless of whose lifebond she was, he couldn't risk allowing the meirlock to get a hold of her. "Both of you will be safest there."

"How do I know you are who you claim to be?" She moved to stand in front of the open passenger door.

His hands settled around her waist before he knew what he was doing. Her body slid up the length of his as he lifted her into the passenger seat, sending sparks of heated desire right to his groin. His hands lingered on her waist a moment longer than they should have.

She was panting when he let her go. "I think we just melted snow."

He cocked his head as he worked to figure her out. "I shouldn't have done that."

"I will hurt you if you apologize," she said, and then turned to sit with a stiff back against the seat. She cleared her throat. "The attraction is mutual, and we'd both be childish to deny it." She paused for a moment. "And irresponsible to act until we know each other better. Much, much better."

Now he knew what he was working with. This could get real ugly real fast, or it could be the best thing to happen to him.

"Cool your heels," Nikon counseled him. *"She is still skittish because of the night's fright. Time is best."*

Donovan stepped back from Haven's door and nodded once. "That is probably wise." He closed the door and quickly rounded the Hummer to get into the driver's seat. Nikon and Bastian were on the back seat. Donovan started the Hummer and pulled out. "I need to stop at Tribal. I left Medea there."

Haven shifted in the seat and stared at the side of his face while making that humming sound women often did when they were unsure. "Another exotic pet?"

"Nikon's mate," he said in a soft timber. "She is delicate at the moment, and I didn't want her in danger."

Haven twisted around, facing the back seat. "That's darling, but how do you keep a pack of wolves concealed in the city?"

"There is a woman who will take the cubs when they are old enough," Donovan assured her. "Nikon and Medea often appear to humans as dogs, unless they are in one of my clubs."

"That makes sense, I think," she said and settled against the back of the seat. The tension in her body faded. "You really are Quinn Donovan?"

"Aye," he said and reached into his pocket to pull out his wallet and tossed it at her. "You can take a look and in the glove box as well."

"I don't think…"

"But it is necessary." He briefly made mind-to-mind contact with Medea to let her know to be ready when he pulled up to the back door of the club. "I need for you to trust in me and who I am."

She snorted and then flipped through his wallet before she rummaged through the glove compartment and examined his registration and insurance paperwork. She put all the paperwork back and set his wallet in the cup holder closest to him. "What does your protection cost?"

His brain had to be twitching in his skull. "Excuse me?"

"A woman I spoke to. She told me about the possibility of you. She said you'd help us if we could pay you." Haven twisted her hands in her lap and looked out the passenger window.

He supposed it was best to let those types of rumors circulate, otherwise every being out there with a minor grievance would seek him out to correct their problems and hand him their own responsibilities. "Your ward is of my kind. My responsibility is to raise him to be a warrior. You are, in effect, his mother. It would be cruel to separate the two of you."

"Men don't take on a woman with a child without some kind of expectation," Haven countered. "His food bill in a month is massive. And what the hell do you mean by raise him to be a warrior?"

"I understand," Donovan said, trying to find the right words. "There are already too many chances for him to become what Kyros is. He is Undying and has little choices in what he becomes." He came to a stop at a red light and turned to face her. "We can have centuries of peace, but he has to be ready, and he must learn how to control his power. The best way for him to gain that discipline is to train as one of our warriors. I know you do not understand, but you will."

* * * *

Haven stared at him until the light turned, trying to get the hum of his thoughts to form complete words in her head. "It's green."

She looked out her window again as she tried to process this person who was the man she'd been seeking for months. Only in the last four months had she discovered his name, and then when she'd found out he was a local celebrity, gaining access to him had become more difficult. How lucky for her, all it took was a deadly confrontation with a paranormal psychopath to get him to come to her. He made her body do those tingly things that should not be happening to her with a man she did not know. Bastian didn't need her falling for someone while she had to look after his best interest. Quinn spoke all the right words, but Mason had used all the correct ones as well. But he hadn't exuded any of the warm, safe feeling Donovan threw off in spades. He was disorientating. Like the ninny she was, she gobbled up everything he said like gospel. The ability to trust another person had been what she'd wanted, and like her Grandfather had accused her, she was being a fickle woman. "I don't mean to question everything."

"But you should," he said as he turned onto Michigan Avenue. "I'm not offended."

"You always know the right thing to say." Even when they were odd things like "centuries of peace" and "they were Undying." She could only imagine what it meant. As far as she could remember from Grandfather's stories, only witches and nymphs were immortal.

"I've been alive a long time."

"Do I want to know your age?" she asked softly. "Never mind. I don't. How do you know Bastian is all right? He's been out a long time."

"He is healing," Quinn said as he turned down an alleyway. "I can wake him if you wish."

She chewed the corner of her lip while she thought.

As he brought the car to a stop in a back alley, a door opened, and a very large and hairy man carried out a wolf as white as the snow. He opened the door, and Nikon immediately dropped to the back floorboard, making a soft whining sound as the white wolf scooted toward him until their noses touched. The hairy man closed the back door and waved at Quinn.

He waved back before he pulled out.

"She doesn't like snow?" Haven asked a bit surprised.

"*I love it,*" said a very distinctly feminine voice right in Haven's head. "*My mate seems to think anything wet will make me melt if I have to be subjected to it until my time.*"

Nikon huffed and licked the top of Medea's head. "*Cold paws could give you a chill, and you never know what humans did in the alley.*"

Haven covered her mouth to keep from laughing. She whispered, "Are they always like this?"

"They get worse," Quinn said in a pained tone. "Don't get me wrong. Love is a wonderful thing, but I think some of us are little more gushing with it than others."

"*Laugh it up.*" Nikon said. "*You'll see when it's your turn.*"

Haven shook her head. "I can hear them talking."

"Wonderful," Quinn said, seeming relieved. "Perhaps I won't get roped into girl chat quite as often."

"So you hear them too?"

"Usually," he said.

"*Of course!*" Medea sounded. "*It's rude not to include others in your conversation.*"

"*Unless it's private, and then it's rude to snoop,*" Nikon added in a tone that said someone in the Hummer had a problem with knowing the difference.

Medea nipped at him and then licked the spot she'd nipped.

Haven shook her head, sure they were talking together as she turned her attention back to Quinn. "Bastian?"

"Ah, yes," Quinn murmured as the air around them infused with power.

"What the hell!" Bastian yelled. "Where am I? Where did that asshole go—hey, my head doesn't hurt. Why can't I move?"

"I am Quinn Donovan," Quinn introduced himself. "You are in my car. I have agreed to help you and Haven. Kyros has been run off for now. I thought it best to keep you immovable until I knew how you and your passenger were going to react while I drive on slick roads."

"Let me go," Bastian rudely demanded. He jackknifed upright with a startled cry. He rubbed at the lump at the back of his head. "Thanks. I think. Why doesn't my head hurt?"

"Because your passenger knows it is unable to defeat me," Quinn said in a soft timber.

"Passenger?" Haven and Bastian said at the same time.

"The power growing in him is properly called a *treòir*. It will continue to grow and gain in power until the time of death. As far as I know, no one has aged to the point of its full maturity." Quinn glanced up into the rearview mirror before turning his attention back to the road.

"I thought you couldn't die," Haven said. "Since you're undying and all."

"We can be killed," Quinn said in a somber tone. "The one failsafe we were given when the Originals were created."

"Whoa," Bastian said. "I hear an über history lesson coming on, and I think my head is starting to throb again."

Haven glared over her shoulder at him. "Bastian! This information could be useful to you."

"Leave the boy alone," Quinn said with a chuckle. "It is late, and there was much excitement this evening. A more formal education can wait until both of you have settled."

"But—"

Quinn reached over and wrapped his hand around hers. "As much as you need time to process and figure out the new shift in your world, he does also."

She squeezed his hand. The urge to cry was strong, but there would be time for the release of emotion later. It was difficult to believe she'd finally landed somewhere she and Bastian would be safe.

"We'll be to our destination soon," Quinn murmured.

She kept waiting for Bastian to howl in pain because his headaches were always the worst when she was upset—and he didn't even have to get into a fight to cause them. Quinn, for his part, kept driving one-handed in the middle of a snowstorm while softly stroking her hand and making reassuring noises.

When they pulled into an underground garage, Haven began to get a grasp on her new situation. "Where are we?"

"My home." He pulled into a parking spot right next to the elevator door marked *Building Owner*. "I live on the top floor."

Right. He was supposed to be the richest man in Chicago. "I have an interview at Fantasia tomorrow."

He turned to look at her. "No, you don't."

"Um, yes, I do," she insisted.

"We'll discuss your employment options with one of my businesses once you no longer have a deranged meirlock wanting to kill you," he said in a sweet tone.

Her teeth gritted together. "How am I going to afford—"

"Haven," he snapped at her. "You need to stop and calm down. I will call Mitchel tomorrow morning and let him know you cannot make your interview. If your sincerest desire is to work in one of my clubs, you will, but after you no longer put my employees' lives in danger."

Her mouth dropped open and then snapped shut.

"I need the little puppy's room!" Medea sounded in everyone's mind. *"Now!"*

Quinn scrambled out of the Hummer and opened the back door for her. Medea bounded out, shook her body, and then loped toward the entrance. Nikon hurried after her.

Quinn watched the wolves until they were gone, and then handed Bastian a duffle. "Bastian, you can help me get the bags."

Haven sat frozen. There was just too much all at once, and Quinn was right. She wasn't handling anything well just yet.

Her door opened, and Quinn stood on the other side with his glacier eyes scorching with heat. "You coming?"

"Yeah," she said. "I guess I am."

Quinn helped her down, only this time he didn't let her slide along his body. What a pity. She'd so enjoyed their contact the first time, but it was better he gave her space to get her head back on straight. Quinn and Bastian got the few bags next to the elevator door.

"We'll wait for the wolves," Quinn said, using his body to trap Haven against the wall and block the wind. The heat that radiated from him caused her to grow warmer than was natural in a parking garage this time of year.

When the wolves returned, Quinn pushed a peculiar sequence of buttons before the long ride in the elevator. The door opened into a grand, battle-fortress foyer with huge carved wooden doors flanking either side of the elevator.

"It's"—she paused, not sure she liked post-modern cave warrior—"an interesting choice in décor."

He shrugged. "I've collected this stuff my entire life. I was lucky to be able to find most of it after the time-shift." He dropped the bags next to a closet door. "I only have one guest room," he said in that buttery baritone that left her feeling weak. "The boy can have it. I'll take my office, and you can stay in my room."

"Th-thank you," Haven managed. There should be more questions bubbling out, but she wanted to get a handle on all the new information she had first. Her head was about to explode with the excessive influx of knowledge. "I'm sorry. I—"

"You're exhausted," Quinn said. "No need to apologize. I want everyone settled for the night, and we can figure out everything else in the morning."

"Yes, sir." Bastian led the way into the cavern-like dwelling.

Everything was dark, heavy, and masculine. The style wasn't bad, but it did leave Haven feeling as if she'd just moved into a large cave. A cave with weapons lining the walls. Haven was sure they would give off a pretty flicker of light if there were a fire in the giant stone fireplace that took up all of one wall in the living room. "Don't touch anything," she said to Bastian. "You might get hurt."

"Yes, ma'am," he said respectfully. He stopped when they got to the hallway on the other side of the penthouse and turned to Quinn. "I don't know what I am supposed to do in this situation."

"You need rest first, young Bastian," Quinn said in a stern tone. "You will have time to learn what you must. For now, you need to sleep."

"Thank you, sir." Bastian awkwardly bowed his head. "Which room may I use?"

"The room at the end of the hall."

Bastian bowed his head again. He lifted his backpack over his shoulder and leaned down to kiss Haven's cheek. "Good night. I'll see you in the morning." Then he sauntered off down the hall.

Haven stood there and watched him walk away. She had to remind herself he was getting to be an age where he didn't want someone to tuck him in at night. She waited until the door of the guestroom closed before she turned to face Quinn. "I don't understand. Why is he so accepting of you? He doesn't like men near me."

"His *treòir* has enough of an education to keep an altercation from happening before either of you are ready." Quinn crouched down next to Nikon and gave him a good ear rub with one hand while patting Medea softly with the other. "Bastian has hope. He is still good and recognizes the good in me."

She turned away and cleared her throat. "If you'll just tell me where to go…"

Quinn gave an extra pat before he stood up and snagged her bag out of her hands. "I'll show you."

Haven could only nod. She had no idea what she was doing or how she was supposed to be reacting to anything. He was taking her to his room. Did that mean he was expecting sex?

"No." Nikon said softly only to her. *"He knows you're not handling any of this well."* The wolf padded over to her to offer her support as she followed Quinn through his home.

She stared down at Nikon. He managed to look guilty. *"I can hear what is important for me to hear. Every other thought you have is your own unless you choose to share."*

She wasn't exactly sure how that was supposed to work. Mason had been able to pick up on her thoughts, too, but she had only gotten hums and whispers before meeting the wolves. Her gaze snapped to Quinn's back as he bent down to grab her other bag. She slapped her hand over her eyes. But damn the man had a nice ass, and he could probably hear her thoughts!

The sound of Nikon laughing resonated in her head. *"He is honorable. Even if he was listening to you, he wouldn't mention it."*

Haven stroked her hand down Nikon's back before they started the assent of the stairs. She kept her eyes on her feet so she wouldn't trip up the steps. Which also kept her from checking out Quinn's butt on the way upstairs.

"I am sure he is," was Haven's reply, but it also disappointed her. If the world could be different… She let the thought fall away. Nothing was different. She had Bastian to worry about, and she needed to figure out how she was going to manage to keep herself from getting too wrapped up in the man that was Quinn Donovan.

He opened the door at the top of the stairs and flicked on a light. He stepped back and allowed her to enter the room first. His size made the

Emma Weylin

space in the hall scant, and their bodies brushed against each other. She shivered from the intense heat and quickly darted into the room.

Quinn followed Haven and set the bag down by the bed. He pointed to another door along one wall. "Bathroom is in there, and I'll be downstairs in my office if you need anything. The first door before Bastian's room."

The room was just as dark and cavernous as the rest of his home. Deep blues and warm, dark woods shrouded the room. A California king-sized bed sat in the center of the far wall between two long horizontal windows looking out at Lake Michigan. One tall dresser sat to the right of a wall of closet space. A fluffy dog-style bed big enough for two wolves rested under the left window. Haven did her best to ignore being in his bedroom and turned around to face him. "I haven't thanked you, yet. For helping us."

He smiled. "It wasn't any trouble."

But saving her had been trouble. Kyros had emanated a power vibe that nearly matched Quinn's own. They both had more than Mason. She managed a wobbly smile back. "Thank you, anyway."

"You've been through a lot," Quinn said. There was a flash of a golden glow in his eyes. "You're safe here. I will leave Nikon with you."

"What about Medea?" she whispered. Nikon wound his body around her before he sat at her side. Her hand went to the top of his head.

* * * *

In that moment, Donovan believed she could be his. He swallowed hard, trying to get the lump out of his throat. "She'll stay with me."

His *treòir* stirred at the image presented to them, evoking primal emotions from deep within. His wolf had bonded to a woman. Somehow, he'd missed, or more likely ignored, Haven's connection to him before, but now he could clearly see the link. Nikon would kill any being stupid enough to try to hurt Haven. The thought scared him. He didn't know which way Haven's decision would fall, nor did it matter. His power didn't have much longer to live in the world.

"I will not leave my lifebond so easily," the *treòir* promised in a deadly tone.

Giving up his power wasn't an easy task, but he would do what he had to do. She was human. The only way to make her Undying was a long and painful process that could end up killing her in the end anyway. He wasn't about to put any one through that kind of hell, least of all a woman he was supposed to love with the entirety of his whole self.

"She is mine," the *treòir* snarled at him.

"There is time." Donovan spoke the truth. Giving up his *treòir* was a fatal decision. He'd eventually grow old and die without his power. As much as he knew giving up his *treòir* was best, he also knew his people needed him. Haven would have need of his *treòir* while Kyros still lived.

"You will not give me up!"

He winced with the pain the *treòir* caused. Many centuries had passed since he and the power inside of him struggled for dominance. He put a hand to his temple as he went through the mechanics of keeping the power contained inside. Then Haven was standing next to him. The power faded back but remained closer to the surface than he liked.

"I've done something to aggravate your power thing?"

He opened his eyes, and his body trembled at her closeness. He took a defensive step away from her. "No. I can irritate my *treòir* all on my own."

Her eyes searched his face before she nodded. Her breath faltered before she spoke again. "You don't have to hide anything from me. I might not completely understand, but if there is anything I can do to help you, let me know."

Donovan reached up and touched the tip of a finger to her lips. "I am not your worry. You need rest. I should go." He turned to walk out of the room. He would have escaped, but the *treòir* would not let him.

"She is broken!" the power said with rage bubbling at its core. *"She leaks. Fix her or I will find a way."*

Going back in was a mistake. It was better to flee the room and spend his night fighting with the *treòir* than to look at her, because he knew what he was going to see. The *treòir* snagged control of his body for a brief moment, just long enough to swing his head back around.

Haven stood in the center of his bedroom with tears slipping down her cheeks. Nikon pressed up against her side in an effort to offer comfort. Her delicate body trembled as she turned away from him. Her voice wobbled on the first note, "Good night, Quinn."

"Haven." Her name rolled out with a gritty edge.

She went perfectly still. "Y-yes?"

He moved up behind her. "You're crying."

"I'm fine."

"Look at me."

She hesitated for a moment before she turned around and tilted her head back.

He tried to look impassive, but his arms opened. "Come here."

Emma Weylin

She hesitated again. Those beautiful eyes peered into his, assessing him and his intent before she walked into him. Donovan's arms closed around her as her body curled in against him. The cotton of his shirt became immediately damp with tears. Her slight body kept trembling, but her crying was soft.

"She's leaking more!" The *treòir's* alarm sent pounding through his head.

"She needs this." Donovan kept the response measured. He wasn't about to pretend to understand why women cried after they were safe. He just knew they did. The *treòir* wasn't exactly sure it believed him, but the throbbing headache subsided. He stroked a hand down her silky hair. "Shh. You're all right. I'm right here. I'm not going anywhere."

After a few moments, she finally relaxed against him. Using his power to put her to sleep would have been easier, but Donovan found he couldn't make himself cheat her of his time. She needed to cry first, and he'd be damned if she used any shoulder but his for the rest of her life when she needed one. She was his lifebond. That was the only answer he had for the *treòir's* behavior and the course of emotion hammering through his system.

When the tears stopped, Haven pulled back. Her eyes were rimmed red. "I, um, well, I think I need a shower."

"All right." He tried to get himself to leave, but his body refused to move, and this time the *treòir* wasn't preventing him.

"I will stay with her," Nikon whispered to him. The large black wolf moved to stand guard next to her and nodded toward the door.

His heart constricted. Once again, he was struck by the image of his wolf protecting a woman with more beauty than he could recall to memory. He ran his hand over Nikon's head and then fled the room.

"You ran away from her!" the *treòir* yelled at him.

Donovan ground his teeth together. *"Hell yes! She doesn't need me mauling her while she sleeps."*

Treòir considered his human's words and conceded. *"The sooner we bond to her, the better off we'll be."*

Donovan wasn't sure he agreed. Bonding could be the single most dangerous thing an Undying could face.

Chapter 4

Donovan stalked through the penthouse. He wasn't about to avoid his responsibility to his lifebond. Everything else was the problem. Giving up his *treòir* was shirking on his responsibility as the Cadeyrn of the Undying people. They needed their leader, and they wouldn't be able to survive if he turned into another Kyros. He would also turn into a meirlock if his lifebond died. Only this time, there wouldn't be anyone strong enough to take him out. The Originals hadn't survived the time-shift.

Not one single freaking bonding in the last fifty years since the Undying had arrived in this time. When they needed hope the most, he had to be the one to connect with his lifebond. It had taken him those precious years to settle his people after the cataclysm. A portion of the Undying had survived, the rest were dead or missing. Kyros had touched the Book of Avalon because Donovan had failed. Now, when his people should have the most hope for the future, they were going to lose him.

His choices were to either give up his *treòir* or leave his people to a monster no one would be able to defeat. Neither of which he liked. Giving up his power assured Haven would die at some point of natural causes, regardless if she converted into an Undying or not. Lifebonds did not survive long past the expiration of their mate. Turning into a meirlock was too horrible a fate to even think about.

He made his way into the kitchen to snag a beer out of the refrigerator. He'd have to put grocery shopping on the list of things to do tomorrow—that was if Nikon allowed Haven to cook on the modern contraptions. His ability with the damn things always ended in a spectacular explosion of food and fire with a large mess to clean up. The catastrophes had led to the black wolf banning food that needed to be prepared in any way in the penthouse.

He closed his eyes and leaned against the counter top. Haven changed everything. She should be his hope. His salvation. Damn it, she was. He just had to figure out how to get there. The first step in getting there was talking to his brother. His mind brushed up against his youngest brother's. *"Riordan. You busy?"*

"No. What's up?" The response was groggy, as if he'd just woken the man up.

Donovan paused for a moment to let himself feel what he was about to say. *"I found her. I—I have my lifebond, brother."*

"Your lifebond? You found your lifebond?" The excitement in Riordan's tone couldn't be missed.

Donovan had to smile a little. *"Yes. Get your ass over here because I need a hell of a lot of information I was too young to receive until just a little bit ago."*

Riordan laughed quietly. The joke was customary amongst the males of his kind. There was information they could not obtain until they had their lifebond, no matter what age they achieved. *"Yeah. It's amazing how quickly we come of age. Anything else I need to know before I get there?"*

Donovan waited a beat as he thought. *"Yeah, don't tell anyone else just yet, and I've got a fourteen-year-old Earth Warrior here, too."*

"Got it. I'll be there as soon as I can."

He finished his beer and tossed the bottle into the recycling bin before getting out a package of meat to thaw for the wolves.

Haven's scream from the second floor rattled his teeth. His *treòir's* power spiked, causing the building to shake as he tore off to get upstairs. Nikon was digging at the space under the bathroom door. Before he managed to break the door down, Donovan discovered it was unlocked. He burst into the bathroom to see Haven's willowy frame huddled in the corner of the tub. He carefully pulled open the transparent curtain. "Haven?"

"B-b-blood!" she wailed.

He cocked his head to find where the blood was coming from, and it was then he saw the streak of ungodly pink trailing from her hair down to the drain.

He set his jaw and nodded once. He could do this. He just had to pretend she wasn't naked or wet, and he could do this without turning into a pig. He kicked off his shoes and got in with her, fully clothed. She looked up at him with fear in her eyes, and he reached down and pulled her up.

"Close your eyes," he murmured and was surprised when she did. He did the bare minimum of what was needed to get the blood out of her hair and off her face before he wrapped himself around her. The water ran cold before she shoved away from him and darted out of the tub. She grabbed a towel off the bar and wrapped it around her. Her eyes were wide as she stared up at him. "I was fine."

His brow shot up as his arms folded over his chest. "Really?"

She tightened the terry cloth around her as her head bobbed. "Yes. I like to freak out over blood in the shower alone."

"Right," he said as he took another towel off the bar and wrapped it around her shoulders before he guided her back into the bedroom. He wasn't about to invade her privacy further by rummaging through her belongings, so he plucked one of his own T-shirts from the dresser drawer and pulled it over her head.

She seemed so small and infinitely breakable, standing there blinking up at him while dripping water all over the wood floor. Something inside of him swelled, and the darkness that had been looming over him, threatening to drag him into oblivion, lifted, and once again his life had a purpose. The reprieve from death and doom would only last as long as Haven had breath in her body, but this new feeling was there and pulsed through him.

* * * *

Haven sensed the power shift in the room. The change both calmed and terrified her. A load appeared to have eased off Quinn's shoulders, only to be replaced by something else entirely. She glanced downward, not wanting to process any other odd idea tonight. "You're making a mess of the floor," she said softly.

"Sorry." His tone was strong but gentle, almost tender. She took the towel that had been wrapped around her moments before and got down on the floor to mop up the water. He sauntered back into the bathroom, and Haven made the mistake of looking up when he came back out.

The tightly coiled muscles, the way every part of him worked in unison to make the movement of his body a work of art in motion sent erotic heat spiraling through her. A slow, wicked grin curved his sensual mouth, and he winked at her. "Just returning the favor."

A blush stole across her body, which she imagined began at the tips of her toes and ended at her hairline the way Nathan, the werewolf, had teased her about when she was a child. Her cheeks grew hotter when she remembered how earlier she'd curled naked into his arms. She averted her eyes, trying desperately to wipe the delighted smile from her face. "I think we're getting ahead of ourselves."

"Why?" His voice was a challenge.

Haven waited until she was sure he'd put on pants and then chanced a look at him. "You live forever, and I won't."

The pants he'd chosen were of the black, drawstring variety, slung low on his hips. He crossed the room, dropped down onto the bed, and lifted a brow at her in the irritating way that he did. "Who said I live forever?"

She stood up and dropped the towel on the bathroom floor. "You did. Isn't that what being Undying is all about?"

"I can be killed, and I can choose to grow old and die."

His face was unreadable, but his eyes spoke volumes, making the ground beneath her shift. "But you won't."

"Why not? I've lived too long already."

"You said you protect humans. Who will do it when you are gone?"

He lifted one of his broad shoulders in a shrug. "Bastian and others like him. My brothers. There are more. I am far from the first or the last of the Undying to walk the earth."

She bit her lip. While the thought of him dying threatened to send her into a panic, she had to keep a firm grip on reality, at least the truth she was now living with. She shoved the images in her mind to the side and tried a different tactic. "I don't know you. I've no wish to end up in one of those bad relationships I can't ever escape."

His face flashed dark and violent before his features softened and then went emotionless. "What brought you into that diner?"

She shrugged. "That's not any of your business. You said you'd help Bastian and, for that, I thank you. My personal life is not any of your concern."

His face set with determination. He was off the bed and stalking toward her a moment later. "You live under my roof. You used my water. I have a right to know exactly who is in my home and why she attracted a meirlock."

She walked backward until her back touched the wall. "My grandfather wanted me to marry a meirlock, and I couldn't, not with the way he treated Bastian."

"Did you want to marry him?" Quinn demanded as power began to vibrate the few items on top of the dresser.

She pressed herself into the wall, trying to get away from the darkness seeping out of him. Her pulse quickened. "I kept saying yes no matter how badly I wanted to say no."

His fiery gaze raked over her. "Do you want me?"

"Yes," she managed to say in a whisper. "But it was like this with him, this irresistible draw, one I couldn't ignore, despite all common sense."

Rage made his shoulders shake as he loomed over her. "No, it was different. What you felt for him was something altogether different."

She wanted to turn away from the lethal gaze but couldn't make herself do it. "How do you know?"

He lowered his head until his mouth hovered over hers. "Because I can make you want me as much as I want you. I can plant any thought I wish into that pretty little head of yours and bind you to me forever."

Their breath mingled in an erotic charge of electricity. "How do I know you haven't already?" Haven managed to ask in a whisper.

His voice turned raw, savage. "I'd already be inside you."

She slipped her arms up between them, pushing at his chest, but he refused to budge. "You're too close," she breathed.

The single action of him taking that one step back made her realize his words were true. He did have the power to tie them together the way Mason had tried to bind her to him. It had taken years for her to break the hold, and then only after she'd nearly been killed and Bastian along with her. That night…when she'd taken Bastian and ran. Mason had found them and… Something occurred to her. "How did I get away from him then?"

"I suspect Bastian. He's young, but our *treòir* can do strange things when acting to protect a…" His eyes met hers. "A person we care about."

There had been something else he'd meant to say, but she was afraid to push him. She trembled with emotions she couldn't sort out. "Then what am I feeling for you?"

* * * *

Donovan had no idea what the hell he was doing, but he knew exactly what he wanted. He just didn't know if he had the right to that reward anymore. The best thing would be to take her to his brother, Wolf, until Kyros was taken care of, and then follow his original plan, but dying wasn't sitting well with him anymore. The thought was enough to make his stomach turn. "I don't know, Haven. What are you feeling for me?"

Perfect white teeth toyed with her pouty bottom lip before her eyes met his gaze. "You're a good person."

His voice was a murmur as he turned and walked to the large window overlooking the city below. "I'm glad you think so."

Haven sucked in a breath. "I know things, sometimes." She hesitated for a moment. "I've only been wrong once."

"Were you? Or were you just unable to heed the warning?" He shook his head; the braid swayed with the action. "Don't. I don't need to know. Get some rest. Tomorrow will be busy."

Donovan had to get away from her, and he needed to stay. Keeping the building from flying apart with a fit of epic temper won out. He left without a word and went back into the kitchen for another beer.

"Quinn?" Haven said from the kitchen door.

His shoulders slumped as he turned to face her. "What do you need?"

"To know what I did to make you angry with me," Haven said.

"I'm frustrated," he admitted. "And angry, but not at you. What was the name of the meirlock who proposed to marry you?"

"Mason," she said.

"Earthshaker," Donovan supplied for her, because he knew only one Undying with that name. "Mason Earthshaker. Not very creative, yes, but an apt description. Who is your grandfather?"

She took a tiny step into the kitchen. "M-Marcus Killian. He runs this—"

"Blood of Oberon!" Donovan swore before he could control his temper. "You're a Killian. Damn it!"

Her face paled as she backed away, slamming her shoulder into the doorjamb. "I didn't mean to be a Killian."

He crossed the span of the kitchen in two strides, wrapped his hand around her throbbing shoulder, and closed his eyes. He was no healer like Riordan, but he could attend to minor injuries. His eyes locked onto Haven's. "Marcus Killian is trying to ally my Black Rose with meirlocks?"

She made a humming sound before she twisted away from him. "I guess. I don't know. I was just supposed to be marrying whom he told me to marry."

Donovan was well aware he was making a colossal ass of himself, and Riordan would be here at any moment to drop the news on her that they were going to be mated until his death. He drew in a deep breath and exhaled slowly. "All right. We need to talk."

"I thought that's what we were doing," she said with that doe-eyed look.

"Have a seat," he said and moved out of the way so she could without him hulking over her.

She perched on the edge of a chair. "Yes?"

"The Undying have something called a lifebond," he started.

Her face brightened. "Mason talked about that. He said every one of his people had their own special mate and…" Her eyes went huge as she stood up, knocking the chair over as she backed up, shaking her head. "You're kidding." She laughed in that not quite mentally stable way people had. "Not us. It's just not—"

"Haven," Medea said from the door, speaking in a way all could hear her. *"But he's so loveable and even has a nice welping box already set up for me so that I can have my cubs here, where they will be safe."*

Her eyes dropped to the white wolf before she looked back up at him. "Rejecting you is bad, right?"

"Kind of," Donovan said.

She crossed her arms over her chest and lifted her chin. "Kind of? I've been dealing with a pubescent *treòir* for the last three years. I have had people following me and trying to drag me back to that godforsaken mansion. People have been butchered in front of me, and then you, the person who is supposed to be the answers to all my prayers, just pops into my life with a declaration of forever—and actually means it literally— and you expect me not to be slightly freaked out when you drop this on me? If you're looking for another complete and utter meltdown from me, you're doing a bang up job, pal. There is only so much I can handle in one sitting, and being your predestined soul mate is just…" She stopped talking as she shook her head and righted the chair before sitting down. "You know what? Sure. Why the hell not? At least you don't give me the heebie-jeebies the way Mason did, and I am mildly attracted to you."

"Was that a yes I heard?" the *treòir* asked.

"I have no idea. Let me deal with this." He ignored his power and focused on Haven. He could not handle another meltdown tonight. "My youngest brother is coming. He will fully explain more of this to us and give you your options. You're not stuck with me if you really would rather not have anything to do with me."

Haven rubbed at the shoulder she'd banged into the doorframe. "I am not completely ignorant to how supernatural pairings work. You don't get any more choice in this then I get. We'll figure us out, but I can't take anymore tonight."

He snorted. "And you were the one who was going to have Bastian take in five thousand five hundred years of history tonight."

Her eyes snapped to his face. "You're not that old, are you?"

"No," he said with a chuckle as he pulled out a chair to sit across from her. "Two thousand five hundred."

She gave a small smile. "I always did like older men." She cleared her throat. "Let's just take this slowly, all right?"

"We can do that," he said. "I'd like to speak with Riordan alone when he gets here, and then you can ask him anything you wish."

"When is he going to get here?"

"Any moment."

"I'll just go change and clean up the mess we made. Have Nikon tell me when I can come down."

Donovan gritted his teeth together as he watched her flee the room. Not that he blamed her. He was behaving like a perfect ogre and couldn't manage to get his head on straight enough to form a proper thought.

"He's here," Medea announced just before the elevator door opened.

"Where is she?" Riordan asked as he walked in with Echo, a white wolf trailing behind him. Echo touched her nose to Riordan's hand before she padded into the living room to be with the other wolves.

"Hiding upstairs," Donovan said as he gave the bags a worried glance. "You trust me with food that needs to be heated?"

Riordan laughed at him. "Not likely, but I assume even the kid could manage a breakfast of eggs and bacon, even if the woman cannot."

Donovan's growl was low, bordering on unfriendly. "Thank you for the food. I am sure they will appreciate it in the morning, but I can hurt you. Nadia isn't here to save your ass."

"But you won't," Riordan said with confidence. He set the bags down on the counter and grinned at his brother. "I have information you need. That guarantees my safety."

Donovan started going through bags and putting things into cabinets. "You're enjoying this way too much."

"Possibly," Riordan said. "The first thing you don't do is tell her about your newly developed death wish."

He dragged a hand over his face and slowly counted backward from ten. He was going to have to deal with this from every Undying male within the continental United States and possibly the entire world. Damn it, anyway. "I do not have a death wish!"

"Of course you don't." Riordan pulled out several slabs of butcher-wrapped meat and put them into the freezer for the wolves. "But tell me you've changed your view on a conversion."

"I haven't," Donovan confirmed.

"There you go," Riordan said in a subdued tone. "Death wish."

"I could live for another fifty years," Donovan said with a snarl.

"Right." Sarcasm dripped from the one word. "And every enemy you've ever made is going to ignore the fact you've made yourself helpless."

This topic wasn't going to move anywhere fast. Which was the reason he wasn't going to do anything with his power until his options or time had run out. With a concerted effort, he shoved down his growing ire. "Whatever. I need to know what I'm supposed to do with her."

Riordan settled himself at the kitchen table with a laugh. "Do you really need to have this conversation with me? I thought you had it with father at least two thousand years ago."

He was beginning to wonder if asking Riordan for help was one of his better ideas. Riordan was their paramount healer, but apparently, that distinction didn't stop the bonds of brotherly love—or the need for the younger one to irritate the older one beyond a man's conventional endurance. "I get that," he gritted out. "You've seen the contents of the book while I have not."

"You know basic bonding protocol. Beyond that, if you're going to give up your *treòir*, I am not sure what else you need to know." All of Riordan's previous humor drained away, leaving deep concern. "You need your *treòir* to bond to her in the way of our people. If you still plan to give your power up…" He shrugged. "What is her decision?"

"A tentative yes," Donovan said. "This could get ugly, and I have a child under my roof. If his *treòir* wants to protect her from…" He left it hanging, unsure if he wanted to tell his brother he thought Haven was his lifebond because his power wanted her. If he had access to the Book of the Undying, maybe this would be clearer, but he didn't. The book was gone, and he had to rely on what his brother could tell him.

"Aye, mating can get ugly," Riordan agreed. "What were you going to say?"

"My *treòir*," Donovan murmured. If Haven decided against him, there would be no chance to give up the *treòir* before something far worse than the time-shift or Kyros could happen. His power would go berserk. The carnage would be catastrophic before he spent the energy. Oberon's blood! "You're saying she's mine because of the *treòir*?"

"I'm not saying anything. You've yet to fully accept this bonding. No matter what she decides, you have to also accept it."

His muscles tensed. "She's here. I will not—"

Riordan put up a hand to stop him from talking. "You'll protect her, and you won't physically abandon her. Those are wonderful things, but what if she needs the power in you?"

Donovan grumbled. "And if I kill her in the process? Can you put me down? Can Wolf? Would Memphis or even Maverick have what is needed to put me down before another Kyros is created?"

"So you give up before you've even started?" Riordan countered in an irritatingly calm tone. "You need time with her exactly as you are. That *treòir* is her best chance of survival. No matter what you might think, it wasn't Kyros's *treòir* that killed Helena. Kyros did."

He let out a shuttering breath. Kyros had been his friend a thousand years before the time-shift. Best friends, even, but all of that changed when Helena died. Donovan had disapproved of the bonding, but Kyros insisted he was in love with the woman. Despite all of his objections, Kyros secretly attempted to convert Helena, and the woman died in agony. No Undying had the power to heal the dead, except maybe a bonded male. He paused. He was missing something in the power combination of man and *treòir*. Though he already knew the answer, he needed confirmation for his own peace of mind. "The *treòir* wants her."

A sad, restrained joy filled Riordan's features. "Then she is yours, brother. You have found your lifebond."

Donovan nodded. "I told her you'd give her options after I spoke with you."

"By all means," Riordan said. "Go and get her."

Instead of having a wolf tell her to come down, he went up to the room himself. He knocked before opening the door.

She stopped pacing. "So?"

"According to Riordan, we are, in fact, lifebonds," Donovan said, feeling weird about the whole thing.

She padded over to him. She still had on his shirt, but wore a white tank top underneath, along with a pair of sleep pants. "You mean you didn't know for sure? Mason was very sure that I was his."

He wrapped his hand around hers as he led her down the stairs. "That is how you know the truth. Bonding can be difficult, so there are protocols to follow to assure everyone's safety during the process. Mason should have, at the very least, spoken to another bonded male to get confirmation. You should not be afraid of your lifebond."

She let out a sharp laugh as they entered the kitchen. "What about nervous or intimidated?"

"We," Riordan said, "take that into consideration before any final decisions are made. What was your gut reaction to him upon first seeing him?"

* * * *

Haven stilled and shied away from Riordan. "I didn't mean that in a bad way, he's just—"

"Big," Riordan said for her. "What was your first impression of him?"

"Safe," she said before giving herself a chance to think. "I was sure that he would make Bastian and me safe."

"And what does he do that makes you feel intimidated or nervous?"

She scrunched her nose. "I don't know. He's just… I'm used to giving the proper response at all times, but I am not sure how he will react if I say something he doesn't like."

Riordan gave a brief smile. "So then it's more of a you thing than a him thing?"

"I guess," she snapped. "I am the one who is supposed to be asking questions!"

"And so you are." He hitched a hip up against the counter. "What is your question?"

She looked up at Quinn, trying to see exactly what it was about him that had changed her. She could be skittish and timid, but Quinn didn't seem to want that. He challenged her until she had no choice but to stand up for herself before he'd back off. No. She decided. Quinn didn't want her fear. He wanted someone who could be strong. Well, she had been strong. She needed to get her new situation all figured out and settled in her mind before she could get back to that woman who'd evaded a meirlock for three years and found Bastian the help he desperately needed. Her attention went back to Riordan. "I know werewolf mates get until the next full moon. How long do we have?"

"As long as you need," Riordan said. "Every bonding is different."

A feeling of dread settled over her that if she didn't accept, Quinn would turn into Mason. She'd been able to feel his grief at Vinnie's death. There was this awesome aura of power that surrounded him, but there was also vulnerability there she wasn't sure anyone else cared to notice. "What else do I have to do?"

Riordan grinned. "Enjoy falling in love with your mate."

Love.

That's what she wanted. That she could do. She bit the corner of her lip as she peered at Quinn from the corner of her eye. He was holding his breath, and realization dawned on her. No matter how much power he had in that moment, she had more. The thought was both thrilling and terrifying to know she held so much control. Then she addressed Riordan. "I think you need to go," she said softly. "If he is the man he seems to be, there is no danger of me leaving."

Riordan visibly relaxed. He righted himself and bowed. "Aye, Reannon. It was lovely to meet you. I will follow your wishes."

The brothers exchanged glances, as if they were in silent communication with each other before Riordan walked toward the elevator door. Quinn followed him, and they murmured quietly together before Riordan got into the elevator. Quinn shoved his hands into his pockets. "So."

She wrapped her arms around herself and nodded. "I don't like awkward, so why don't you sit with me on the couch for a little bit?"

His head cocked as if he was trying to figure her out. "We can do that."

"Good," she said and padded over to the large, dark brown couch centered in front of the grand fireplace. "I'm feeling a little bit lost and more than a little afraid. I just *need* for a little while."

Quinn slowly walked toward her and hooked his arm around her when he got to the edge of the couch. He pulled her down with him so she was sitting on his lap. "Then we are equal," he murmured close to her ear. "Sometimes I just *need*, too."

Hesitantly, she reached up and cupped his face in her hand. "Then we can be here for each other for a while."

His eyes dropped to her mouth before going back to her eyes. "We can do that."

The side of her mouth slid up in a half smile. "This is the first time you've agreed to anything since I met you."

"True," he said as his face came closer to hers. "But I want to give you what you need."

There was that moment where their breath mingled, and then their lips touched. Her body shivered deliciously all the way down to her toes as she pressed against him. His arm locked her in place as they explored each other for a solid minute before she pulled back. Her breathing was uneven as she gazed into those glacier eyes, and then she tucked her head up under his chin. They needed to wait. If only for her own sensibilities, but she could stay here with him for as long as he'd let her and soak up that essence around him that made her feel at ease for the first time in a very long time.

Chapter 5

Haven curled into the snuggly, warm male chest and pulled a thick afghan around them. She imagined those friendly talking wolves had brought the blanket to her during the night. Her eyes snapped opened when she realized she wasn't dreaming, and she really had fallen asleep on Quinn's wonderful, beautifully bare chest. Having a mind of their own, her hands came up to run over the chiseled perfection.

The idea of mate would scare away most women, but Haven wasn't so naive. She'd always known she wouldn't have a choice. The next in line to rule the Black Rose would be her mate. For as long as the organization had been around, the elders had arranged the marriages of the men heading the group. If magic had stepped in to help her find a better mate, she wasn't going to complain if he proved he was not like Mason. It was a damn good thing they were supposed to be mates, or she was going to have to have a serious talk with herself about the naughty thoughts flooding her brain.

His hand came up and trapped hers against his beating heart.

"Good morning," he said. The soft cadence of his voice was slightly graveled from sleep. So incredibly sexy.

She blushed when her gaze met his, and she ducked her head. "I guess we got comfortable with each other last night."

He scooted up into a half-seated position but still kept her hand trapped against his heart. He used the tip of two fingers to tilt her chin up. "It's a good thing."

"I come from an old-fashioned family," she said without pulling away from him. "We don't do these things. We have to be respectable at all times."

"Your patriarch also wanted you to marry a meirlock." He leaned forward and kissed the tip of her nose. "You're safe to think every opinion he has is suspect."

She dropped her chin onto his chest and gazed up into his mesmerizing eyes. "What happens when your daughter doesn't marry the man you want her to marry?"

"I will not be the one making the choice," he said, and then frowned. "I'd have to accept a mating even if I didn't like him, or I'd risk her death."

She hid her face. She always managed to make stupid blunders when talking to a man she could imagine being with for the foreseeable future. "I'm sorry, I was just—"

"Asking a valid question," he said, lifting her chin again. "All the ways humans have to pair off are as valid as anything else. I helped the first two Black Rose leaders choose mates for their daughters. That was the way marriage was done then. Today"—he brushed the side of his face along hers. His four-day scruff was silky soft—"I'd make sure she knew the difference between a good man and a bad one and trust that what I taught her was enough to help her find a good mate."

"You do have a unique perspective on this," she said softly. "We are from very different times. Was the past as horrible for women as some say it was?"

Quinn moved on the couch, bringing her with him when he sat upright. "It was horrible and wonderful for everyone, depending on what part of the world you were in and what you aspired to do with your life. Women had their issues while men had others." He gave her a look to curl her toes. "I'd rather we talk about something less heavy this early in the morning." Excitement lit in his eyes. "Please tell me you know how to operate a coffee machine."

She laughed. "You don't?"

"Nikon forbids for me to even boil water," Quinn said. He stood up with her wrapped in one arm, pressed tightly against his chest.

That was the moment she realized how large he was. He held her suspended in the center of the room. The ceiling was easily nine feet, but he could reach up and touch the plaster if he wanted without having to stretch. He had to be seven feet in height, and he was easily twice, maybe three times, as broad as she was. He'd lifted her as if she weighed nothing, and her feet dangled a good foot and a half off the floor. All that size and power and he couldn't make his own coffee? She looped her arms around his neck. "Do I want to know why Nikon forbids you to do it?"

"My last attempt resulted in some singed furs and a minor explosion," he said with a straight face.

She wasn't sure she believed him, but she'd go with it for now. "I can make you coffee. But I do need to get into the kitchen."

"Let's go." He set her down next to the counter. He reached up to the highest cabinet and pulled down the can of ground coffee. "You'll have to explain the coffee smell when the wolves get back or I'll be in trouble. Nikon will piss in my most expensive shoes if I aggravate him enough, not often, but he will."

That brought a laugh as she looked down at Quinn's feet. Any shoe he owned would have to be specially made, so all of them were probably expensive. She grabbed the coffee pot out of the machine to fill it with water. "I'll have to remember that. Do you know where the filters are?"

He reached over her head to pull a box of them down.

"Thank you." She poured the water into the tank of the machine. "Where are they, the wolves I mean?"

"Probably outside." He stretched, touching the ceiling with the flat of his hands and giving her an awesome visual of how all those muscles worked in unison.

Focusing on the task was best if she was going to behave herself. He was adorable as he stood there waiting for her to give him more instructions, but he hogged all the space around her. "Where are the mugs?"

He frowned at her as he crossed the kitchen to get them out of a cabinet that was ridiculous to keep glasses and mugs. She was going to have to rearrange this kitchen for the efficiency of normal-sized people. "How did the wolves get out there?"

"They know the code for the elevator," Donovan said as he brought two mugs over and set them down on the counter.

She nodded. Of course they would know how to do that. Then she playfully pushed him back a few steps. "I need a little bit of space to work." She still had time before Bastian would wake. That boy slept like a stone. "Once it's running, then we can get all snuggly again."

She could feel his eyes on her as she put the filter into the proper place before adding the right amount of coffee grounds. She set everything and switched on the button. As coffee machines went, this was an easy one. She turned around and leaned against the counter. "So the mighty Quinn can't cook anything because his wolves won't let him?"

"Pretty much," Quinn said with a chuckle, though he did rub nervously at the back of his neck.

He had to be doing that on purpose. That chest was to die for, and, thankfully, it was also all hers. Forever wasn't long enough to explore the vastness of his muscles. She cleared her throat. "When was the last time you tried?"

"Thirty years ago," he said. "I keep telling Nikon I need to practice, but he refuses to believe me."

"I see," she said. She thought for a moment on how she could help him. She figured the Undying probably had some special way to educate their children. Bastian couldn't be the only one, and she needed to switch Bastian's school anyway. That would be the perfect time to teach Quinn to cook. "So then while Bastian is in Undying school, you'll be attending cooking classes."

His eyes went wide with worry. "You're kidding, right? Do you have any idea the damage I could do in a cooking school? I could blow up the whole place."

She bit her lip to keep from laughing. She padded over to him and petted her hand down his chest just because he was there and she could touch him. "How about private lessons?"

"Who's the instructor?"

She did her best flirty girl pose and batted her eyes at him. "Me."

A grin spread out over his face. "Sold. When do we start?"

"After I've had two cups." She rested the side of her face against his chest. "Dare I stop to think about what is happening to us?"

* * * *

Donovan wrapped an arm around her and then dropped his chin on top of her head. His whole being felt a little lighter to have that one person who realized he was more than his power and his title. "That depends?"

She tilted her head back to look at him. "On what?"

"If we need to think about magic arranged marriages." He bent down and brushed his mouth over hers. Her lips were soft like silk. His desire to take this mating further was strong and egged on by the *treòir*, but he held his power in check. Spooking her or demanding things that would come in time was pointless and counterproductive, even if having her breasts mashed up against his chest was driving him to distraction.

She rested her head against his solid muscle for a moment before she pulled away and retreated to the coffee maker. "What if I had married Mason?"

The *treòir* twitched. Donovan gritted his teeth as he struggled with its spike of anger. The *treòir* had less understanding of human interactions and didn't always know why he couldn't react in violence toward something that upset him. He leaned back against the L-shaped counter top and studied her for a long moment. "Mason would have been killed, and you'd have been freed to do whatever you want."

She blanched. "That's a bit drastic, don't you think?" She turned and poured coffee into the mugs.

"Being tagged as a meirlock is a death mark. There is no escaping the sentence." He crossed his arms over his chest. This was where the difficult parts of bonding started. Human women didn't find understanding Undying law easy. Mason was an Earth Warrior. No prison in any realm would be able to hold him, and once the *treòir* inside turned down darker paths, there was no bringing it back.

She sucked in a breath. "Bastian!"

Donovan leaned over her and firmly put the mug back on the counter before turning her around to face him. "Bastian is a child. Has he killed anyone in cold blood?"

Her lower lip trembled. "No. He gets into fights sometimes at school. He just got expelled again yesterday because he was trying to protect one of the girls from something stupid one of the other boys said."

Donovan stooped down until he was right at eye level with her. "He only needs a better way to control his *treòir* and some guidance on how to handle those situations."

"You're sure?" she demanded.

"I am."

"Coming in, my lord."

Donovan shook his head when he heard the voice of his Storm Warrior in his head. He refocused on Haven. "I am sure Bastian will be fine. He's only in need of a little fatherly guidance, and we're about to have company."

Her brow furrowed, and then the walls shook as Donovan went to the door that appeared to be nothing more than a closet. When he opened the door, Memphis walked out. "I hate to bother you this early, my lord, but—" Memphis took a step toward Haven and leaned forward as he stared at her for a moment and then took in Donovan's lack of dress and then back to Haven. "She's wearing your shirt."

"Aye," Donovan said, letting out a long sigh. "It's not as it appears, and even if it was—"

"Really?" Memphis grabbed Donovan by both of his shoulders and looked into his face. "She's you're lifebond?"

"I am," Haven said.

Memphis let out a whoop and hugged Donovan tight before stepping back and clearing his throat. "Forgive me," he said more formally to Haven. "I am Memphis Walker. The Cadeyrn's Storm Warrior."

"I will explain later," Donovan said. "Memphis, why are you here?"

"I'll go bother Sloan. I didn't realize you were indisposed." Memphis turned to go back into the wind portal room.

"It's not public yet," Donovan said. Memphis was a man on the list to tell right after he talked to his other brother, Wolf. "You wouldn't be here if the problem wasn't important."

"Aye," Memphis said with a polite bow of his head. "A Caden in Denmark suspects his Cadfael may have done something that requires your judgment. Haldur contacted me."

"That is serious," Donovan said. "Haldur's take?" Memphis didn't have to say anything. The answer was on his face. "All right. Give me two minutes. Make friends with Haven."

* * * *

Haven furrowed her brow at the word Cadeyrn, but she didn't say anything as she watched him leave the room and then turned to give Memphis as friendly a smile as she was capable. The man was huge, not as huge as Quinn, but still huge. Bastian might be on the short side of the Undying height scale, but then, he was only a teenager. She shied back a step. She could feel the power in the man. His was more like Quinn's, but it was better to be wary of things she didn't know. "Where is he going?"

"Denmark," Memphis said, his eyes going to the mugs of steaming coffee on the counter. "He shouldn't be more than half an hour."

"Right, because a trip to Scandinavia is like a hop next door." She turned back to the counter to see if there was sugar anywhere.

"It is when you travel by wind portal."

She stilled and turned back to him. "That wind thing that opened for Kyros... You do it, too?"

Something akin to rage flashed across Memphis's face. "You're not afraid of me, so it wasn't Lazarus you saw last night. What did you see?"

"I saw a vortex of wind with black and red lightning," Haven said with a shudder. "The only meirlock I saw was Kyros."

"And that would have been one of my brother's portals." He shook his head, and then his body relaxed before he grinned at her. "I could show you any part of the world you wish while we wait for Cadeyrn to return."

She didn't know what Cadeyrn meant. There was that word again, but the meaning for the Undying could be vastly different from what it meant for the Black Rose. "Bastian should be waking up soon and I should be here."

"Ah, the boy," Memphis said. "The one who should be here when he wakes would be Maverick."

"Maverick?"

"Aye. Ean Maverick. He is the resident Earth Caden. He will want a look at the boy and, depending on his age, begin training as soon as possible."

"Earth Caden?"

Quinn came back into the room. He stopped by Haven and kissed the top of her head before downing an entire cup of hot coffee. "Excellent."

These men wanted to see if they could make her brain twitch. The man was fully dressed and carried a sword in a scabbard at his hip. A sword! "What are you going to do?"

"Make a judgment for a Caden in Denmark." Quinn's head cocked as his gaze locked onto hers. "If the Cadfael in that region has turned."

"Oh," she said, as she realized he might be going to put down a meirlock Cadfael. "All right. I'll um, start breakfast, I guess."

"Haven."

"No. You can explain everything to me when you get back." She forced a smile. "You need to do whatever it is that you do."

"I can get Sloan," Memphis said. "Though Darius would be better. I believe he has more dealings with those in Denmark."

All these names were flying around, and Haven resigned herself to the fact she'd need to learn all of them. Quinn shook his head. "I need to speak with Wolf before there is a formal announcement. If one of the other Cadfaels show, I'd have to announce that I am bonding. I want to be the one to tell Wolf before giving the Cadfaels an official statement."

"Very well, my lord." Memphis bowed his head before opening the closet door.

Both men walked inside. Quinn stopped and winked at her. "I will be back as soon as I can."

The door closed. The apartment rattled as if a violent wind gust kicked up outside. A second later, Memphis exited the closet.

Haven connected the dots. Memphis opened the portals and not Quinn. She had another question. "Why do you open the portal in there?"

Memphis chuckled. "A strong wind can do a lot of damage to inanimate objects."

"Right," she said. Why hadn't she thought of that? "And he didn't take you with him?"

"Kyros," Memphis said as if the name answered everything.

Maybe it did. "I didn't hear either of you talking about anything." The elevator door opened. When the wolves came in with wet fur from playing in the snow, she understood how Quinn and Memphis had exchanged information. "Never mind. How long have you known Quinn?"

"If you don't mind," Nikon said as he padded up to her and rubbed against the side of her leg. *"Can you get our breakfast? Look on the bottom shelf in the cold box."*

"I'll get it," Memphis said as he went to the refrigerator. "Roughly two thousand years."

"Oh." She needed something to do. "They eat their food raw?"

"It's better for them," Memphis said as he pulled out two packages of wrapped meat. "What do you know about us?"

"Nothing," she admitted after a moment. "Do you want me to help?"

"Do you need to help?" Memphis asked with an edge of humor in his tone.

"I do," she said and moved to the counter space he was using to unwrap the wolves' breakfast. It appeared to be beef chopped up into large, bite-sized chunks. "You wouldn't happen to know where their dishes are, would you?"

Memphis stilled from getting tomorrow's wolf meal out of the freezer and stared at her.

"Just get some plates," Medea said. *"Eating off ceramic won't hurt us."*

"Oh," Haven said. She still felt silly talking to a wolf and knowing she would get an answer. "Would you prefer just having the paper?"

"Cadeyrn is very efficient and doesn't like to wash dishes." Medea rubbed the side of her head against Haven's thigh. *"Eating from a dish would be wonderful."*

Memphis reached over her head, pulled down two plain black plates, and set them on the counter. Haven served the wolves the meat on the floor.

She waited until they started eating before she went back to talking with Memphis. "Why is everything at giant height in this kitchen?"

Memphis chuckled. "Because a giant lives here alone?"

"Good answer," she said. "All right. This is making me nuts. Start pulling things down. I have got to get this kitchen functioning for standard-sized people if I am the only one the wolves are going to let cook."

To her utter surprise, Memphis did exactly as she asked. There weren't many things that needed reorganized, and that had her hunting down a notepad and pen to start making a list. They had enough food to last Bastian one, maybe two meals. She was just putting the last cup into the cabinet next to the sink when the apartment rattled. A moment later, Quinn stepped out. His shirt was torn and the look on his face was heartrending.

Memphis paused.

Haven rushed over to Quinn. Her hand dipped into the hole in his shirt and came out red. "You're bleeding. Memphis call—"

Quinn grabbed her wrist as he handed his sword off to Memphis. "I'll heal."

She studied his face. Part of her knew what he'd done. "He was..."

"Aye," Quinn said. His glacier eyes bore into her. "It had to be done. Like when a werewolf turns. They don't turn back."

That was something she understood from her grandfather. "Is there anything I can do for you?"

"I'll be fine. I'm going to get cleaned up. Stay with Memphis."

Her shoulders slumped as he walked out of the room. "How am I supposed to help him if he won't let me?"

"Go. Even if he won't let you," Memphis said. "I can man the frying pan if needed. Nikon won't kick me out for cooking."

Haven flashed a worried smile before running up to the room after Quinn. She figured she had as much right to be in there as he did since her stuff was there, but she did knock before she entered. A large, arching laceration covered his beautiful chest as he pulled on a clean black T-shirt, but the wound appeared like one that had been mending for a few days.

"I don't need anything right now."

"But maybe I do. What happened? I don't understand." She quietly padded over to the bed and sat down on the corner. She could guess he had to put down one of his own, but she hoped talking about it would help him.

"There is a new Cadfael in Denmark. I had to put down the last one," he said wearily. He sat down on the bed next to her and rested the side of his head on the top of hers. "That part never gets easier. I guess, at least, it doesn't happen very often."

Right, of course he didn't want to talk about this. Haven decided to ask questions about something else to distract him instead. "Cadeyrn, Cadfael, Caden—what do all those terms mean?"

He let out a short laugh as his arm looped around her. "A Caden is like a clan lord, for lack of a better explanation. We have the world divided up into provinces and territories, and the Cadfaels..." He made a face, as if he didn't know what he should be saying next. "We don't exactly rule over them. It's like guarding them and presiding over the Undying who live within their province."

"And your title," Haven whispered, not sure she wanted to know.

He winced. "I preside over the Cadfaels."

"Oh," she said, trying not to let that sink in too deeply. "You're their king."

"Something like that, but not exactly."

She lightly ran her hand down the side of his chest she knew wasn't marked. "Then what, exactly?"

"I help them. I guide them. They are my people. When everything else fails them, I cannot."

The weight settling down on them was tangible. "And you think you failed this Denmark Cadfael? Could he not come to you before he went down the wrong path?"

"Haven, don't—"

"But I will," she snapped as she stood and moved in front of him. "Yeah, I am sure it royally sucks right now, and I'm not going to tell you not to grieve, but you can't let someone else's failing also be yours. Would you have been able to help him if he'd have come to you?"

* * * *

Donovan blinked at her a few times. No one came into his personal space when he wanted to be left alone. They sure as hell wouldn't yell at him not to feel however he wanted to feel after having to put down a meirlock. "It doesn't matter."

"Yes, it does." She stamped her foot and put her fists on her well-curved hips. "You'd help Bastian anyway if I wasn't attached to him. Right?"

"That's different," he said, unsure if he should be amused or pissed off.

"No. The Denmark Cadfael chose not to ask you for help while you could still help him. That is not your fault."

He opened his mouth to protest, but he realized she was right. "I'm trying. This is never easy."

"Nor should it be," she said as her voice went soft. She sat down on his lap and hooked her arms around his neck. "But you should only take on the parts that you had control over."

He looped an arm around her. This was foreign to him. He wasn't used to anyone taking the time to help him muddle through the feeling part of life's darker necessities. "I'll work on it."

She narrowed her eyes on him before she leaned up and kissed his chin. "Good. Are you ready to come back down so I can make breakfast, or did you need more time?"

Donovan opened his mouth as a yowl of pain filled the penthouse.

Haven jumped to her feet and ran out the door. "Bastian!"

When they got downstairs, Bastian was balled up on the dining room floor with his hands wrapped around his head. The wolves were lying on either side of him while Memphis stood off to the side, gritting his teeth together. "Donovan!"

"I've got this." He crouched down next to Bastian and placed a hand on the boy's head. His *treòir* stretched out and easily suppressed the less powerful one. *"It's all right, young one,"* the treòir said to Bastian. *"The Storm will not hurt you or the lifebond. He is here at my behest to aid your power should danger befall us."*

Bastian's *treòir* settled, and Donovan took the opportunity to take a cursory look inside Bastian's head, only to have his worst fears confirmed. He pulled his mind back from Bastian's as he sat on his heels. "Stay down for a few more minutes," Donovan murmured. "That's right. Just breathe in and out slowly."

Memphis let out a breath. "Holy hell. What happened to him?"

"Mason Earthshaker," Donovan said. "I am going to need to take him to Riordan and also have Haven checked out." He scooped Bastian up as he contacted his brother. *"Bastian has scarring from where he ripped out several compulsions on his own. I need for you to look at him now."*

"Bring him," Riordan replied.

"Memphis, I need a portal to Riordan's house."

"Quinn?" Haven's voice shuddered.

"It's all right," he said. "Bastian is fine. I just want some things checked out. Memphis will take you through if you're afraid." He ground his teeth together to suppress a growl. While he knew Bastian needed him more in this moment, he wanted to be there for Haven as she experienced all the newness of his world.

"Put me down," Bastian said weekly. "I can walk."

"I'll take him through the portal," Memphis said. "You should focus on your lifebond."

"I don't need anyone to take me through," Haven said, but she nervously picked at her pinky.

He carefully set Bastian down and waited to make sure he was stable before turning to his mate. "I'd rather you're with me if you're worried."

"But Bastian…"

His brow shot up. "You have people capable and willing to help both of you."

She waited for Bastian to nod. He leaned against Memphis while rubbing the back of his head. "I will be all right. They don't feel the same way Mason did."

She drew in a deep breath. "All right. Let's go. If Riordan can fix his headaches that would be wonderful."

He wrapped his arm around her more for his comfort than for hers. He didn't want to think about the sentence that had to be carried out for the Denmark Cadfael. There were only limited ways for an Undying to be killed. He preferred the one that involved a sword to the one he had to do by hand. With practiced techniques, he shoved aside the horrors of the day and focused on helping Haven through her first portal jump.

"The wolves!" she said when they got into the small room made entirely of tile.

"They are fine alone, and they will guard our home while I am not there," he said.

"You're sure?"

"Absolutely," he said. "Are you ready?"

"No, but Bastian needs a doctor who can actually help him." Her hand curled in a death grip around his. "Let's do this."

Donovan nodded to Memphis.

Haven's mouth dropped open as she watched a tiny tornado form on Memphis's hand. The vortex grew and stretched until Memphis stood it on end. Sparks of violet and silver lightning streaked across the opening large enough to fit a man.

"It's safe," Donovan said. "Memphis, take the boy."

Haven lurched forward when man and boy vanished into the portal. "Quinn!"

"They are safe on the other side. Do you want to walk through or would you prefer a lift?"

She canted her head as she glared up at him. "I'm not sure."

He looped an arm around her bottom and lifted her up, clamping her tight to his body with one arm so they were face to face. "Close your eyes and you'll never know it's happening."

She wrapped her arms around his neck and ducked her face against his cotton-clad chest. "Just go."

Donovan stepped through to the other side. "We're here."

Her eyes popped open as she turned to peek at her new surroundings. "We didn't leave."

"Look at the door."

She did. "Oh. That's not the same."

"No. Everyone has their own symbol. That makes it easier for the Storm warriors to get to where they are going." He set her on her feet. The portal rooms also allowed for lifebonds and children to travel between dwellings without needing a Storm Warrior in the case of danger, but Donovan didn't tell Haven. She was already dealing with a lot. He'd save the lesson for later.

"Right. So, we'll have Riordan look at Bastian, and then we need to talk about things we're going to need."

"You're getting a check-up as well," Donovan said.

"Wait…what? I'm fine," she snapped at him.

"Humor me, woman," Donovan said as Memphis opened the door and led them into Riordan's healing den. The room was washed in calming blues and had Nadia's touch for soft fabrics and comfortable furniture. A set of stairs went up to the main house, and a hall on the other side headed to private examination rooms.

"Where are we?" Haven asked.

"Riordan's healing den. Most of his visitors are more likely to need him in his healer capacity than anything else."

Her hand wrapped tightly around his. "I still don't need a doctor."

"What is causing the worst of Bastian's headaches isn't his *treòir*."

"What? How do you know that?" She moved in front of him and planted her fists on her hips.

He leaned down and kissed her nose. "I was in his head with him to control the *treòir*. There is scarring there from a compulsion Mason had given him at one point. I want you checked for the same thing."

Her eyes went huge. "Oh."

"Exactly," he said, turning around to lead her back into a more private exam area. "Don't fight me, woman."

She snorted at him. "If you say so, man."

Even after the day's traumas, Donovan couldn't help the slight smile curving his mouth. Haven was already making an interesting addition to his long life.

Chapter 6

Donovan dragged Haven out of the exam room when Bastian screamed. She fought hard to get out of his hold. He'd give her that credit. If he'd been human, even with his size, she'd have escaped him and probably done some gnarly damage to his brother.

"Let me go!" she yelled. "He's hurting him!"

He wrapped his arms tightly around her torso and arms and fell back on a couch in the waiting area so he could lock her legs in place with his own. He kept his head back and out of the way to keep her from smacking him in the chin with the back of her head. "Shh," he murmured. "Bastian is going to be just fine." He started a slow rocking in a rhythmic sway and let his power wash around both of them in an attempt to help calm her. "Extracting a faulty compulsion is painful. I am going to have to do that to you."

She stopped fighting him. "What?"

"Mason. He planted thoughts into both of your heads. Bastian managed to root most of it out of his own head, but he wasn't able to get yours without hurting you," Donovan said as calmly as he could, given the situation. It was difficult to hold her down while the *treòir* was actively working against him. The damn thing thought she should be allowed to rip Riordan a new one.

She let out two heavy breaths. "This will make him better?"

"Most of his headaches will be gone. It won't erase all of them because the *treòir* will try to use them to control him for its own bidding."

"Get that thing out of his head," she snapped, but she no longer struggled. "I don't want anything trying to control him."

"Are you calm?"

She jerked, trying to get away from him, but couldn't break free. "Yes!"

"Really?"

She snorted. "As calm as I can be while Riordan is in there torturing him."

Donovan decided against letting her go. "He's not torturing him. He is helping him. Mason's compulsion could set Bastian on the road to becoming a meirlock. The *treòir* is only struggling for dominance. Bastian must win the battle if he is ever to reach maturity."

Her entire body vibrated with rage when Bastian let out one last wrenching scream before there was silence. "Let me go, you son of a bitch!"

"No," he said calmly. "I understand you're angry and confused. To leave the compulsion in there partially intact could get him killed. Like a brain tumor," he said, finally finding the right human jargon to use so she'd understand.

She went limp in his arms. "The doctor thought the same thing."

"Some compulsions are close." He still didn't let her go, though he did rest his chin on her shoulder. "They're more of a metaphysical tumor than a physical one, and the damage is more outreaching if they are done with ill intent."

"Brain surgery would hurt, right? That's what this is. Brain surgery? Why can't Riordan knock him out?" she said with the fierceness of a mama bear.

Donovan tentatively let go of one of her wrists so he could lightly stroke a hand down her silky soft hair. "The procedure must be done while the person is awake."

Bastian came out smiling a moment later, with Riordan close behind. Donovan let Haven go. She sprang up and darted to Bastian, checking over every inch of him.

Bastian flushed with embarrassment. "I feel good. I no longer have a dull ache."

Haven pulled back and looked into Bastian's eyes for several moments before she pulled his face down so she could kiss his forehead and hug him—hard. "I don't care how old you are. I thought he was killing you." She wrapped her arm protectively around Bastian, which was either ridiculous or adorable. Donovan couldn't decide which. Her head lifted high as she gave a tight smile to Riordan. "Thank you. Is there anything else I need to know about his health?"

"Yeah," Riordan said. "How have you managed to afford his protein needs? He could stand to gain a few pounds, but he's in surprisingly excellent health considering you have no knowledge of proper Undying nutrition."

"He's too thin?" She pulled away from Bastian. "I'm so sorry. I—"

Bastian hugged her tight. "We did the best we could. I wasn't starving. I promise."

She reached up and brushed the shaggy hair out of his face. "You should have told me you needed more to eat."

"Haven," Riordan said. "I said a couple of pounds. You did a wonderful job with him, and his *treòir* has attached to you as a mother. You have no idea how much that alone will save him."

Her face went panicked as she turned to look up at Donovan. He stepped in close to her. "You raised him as right as you could. No child can ask for more than that."

"I…" She turned, buried her face against his chest, and then sagged against him. "Would I be asking too much for things to settle down so I have time to process?"

Bastian cleared his throat. "Riordan promised me a three pound steak if I didn't take a break. So, we can go do that if it's all right with *him*." He nodded toward Donovan.

"You may address me as either Quinn or Dov," Donovan said. "Dov seems to be the preferred endearment from the younger members of the clans who know me personally."

A wide grin bloomed over Bastian's face. "All right, Dov. Sir, thank you."

Donovan nodded to him. "You did well and have earned your reward. I will take care of Haven."

"Thank you." Bastian beamed at him. He scampered off to a staircase that led up into the main house.

"I should go with him," Haven said in a subdued tone. "Riordan's wife my not wish to have to deal with an exuberant boy."

"Nadia has a six-hundred-year-old son," Donovan said. "Joseph is still a hand full at times. Sit. Rest. The last twelve hours have been rather exciting for you."

She went over to the couch and sat as her head bobbed. "I have no idea how I am even supposed to begin to process any of this."

He sat down next to her and rubbed her back. "Then take the time you need. We can stay here for a while if that is your wish. As soon as my other brother, Wolf, gets here, the announcement can be made, and I will be at your complete disposal."

* * * *

Haven knew she was being needy, but that was exactly how she felt. The world was spinning wildly out of her control, and she had no way to stop it. Nothing of what was happening made sense, and the blinding need she had to make a mating work with Quinn at all costs was just as confusing. She'd found Bastian's people. He was safe, and he'd be cared for properly. He'd learn how to control the power in him, instead of it controlling him. "I don't know how to do this. Maybe I should just take some time by myself for a little while. I don't know."

He shifted off the couch and crouched down in front of her. There was something in the way he was looking at her that tore at her heart. When he spoke again, his voice was softer, laced with a tinge of desperation. "Just stay with me for a while, Haven, please? You and Bastian. I can and will take care of both of you, and he will need to learn things you know nothing about."

She laced her fingers together in her lap. The lure of a ready-made family was tempting. He seemed so honest, so sincere in his need. "What do you know of the raising of children?"

"I've raised seven of my own kind and countless humans. I can handle Bastian. He's a good kid."

She let out a shuddering breath. He was begging her to stay with him. It was in his eyes, the twist of his mouth. The thought was unsettling. He was her mate. He shouldn't have to do this, but she didn't know how to get her head on straight. Everyone deserved a mate who wasn't a mental case. She rested one hand on his chest. "Why would you do that?"

He caught a strand of her hair in his hand, his fingers twisting in it. His eyes held a great pain when they met hers. "Family, Haven. Those children needed a family. Someone to look up to, someone to count on."

She scooted forward so she could drop her head onto his chest, rest against the solid comfort of his strength. "I'm having a difficult time accepting your motives are entirely pure. I know magical mates exist, but I'm having a difficult time processing that I am one to the most powerful being I've ever come in contact with."

He caught her chin with a crooked finger and lifted her gaze to meet his. "I can promise you now, all I want to do is help both you and Bastian. You can take over my room, and I'll move down to my office. Bastian can have the guest room. I am not expecting anything in return. You can still reject this bonding at any time you wish. Just let me pretend for a little while."

She whispered, "Pretend what?"

He leaned down, his mouth hovering over hers, his voice a bare breath. "I can have my own family and that this can work between us."

His mouth closed over hers. His tongue ran over her lips until she opened up for him. He delved deep, sweeping fire into her. The sensation threaded through her like tiny electrical shocks, making her very skin come alive, burning for him to touch her. She slid her hands up his chest to hook around his neck, pulling herself deeper into his kiss. Damn, the man did know how to kiss. When he pulled back, she was breathless and sagging against him because her knees had turned into butter, and they were both now somehow standing. She gave him an accusing look. "Why did you do that?"

He played with the end of her hair and grinned before he brushed his mouth softly over hers again. "Do you want me to do it again?"

"Yes." She pushed herself back and glared at him. "No, damn it, you've had centuries to learn how to kiss like that. That's not fair."

His laugh was quiet and warming, but his tone husky as he breathed against the length of her neck. "I'd love to show you the other things I've had centuries to learn how to do."

A delicious shutter ran up her spine, and she swatted at him. "You are lethal, Quinn Donovan. Stay on your side of the room." She sidestepped and moved to a safer corner of the waiting room. "You just stay over there where I can keep an eye on you."

His laughter rumbled out. "Woman, you are sinful. Do you realize how tempting you are right now?" He straightened. "I won't hurt you."

She clasped her hands in front of her. "I know you believe that, but it will happen. Sooner or later, you'll leave. If you really can live forever, someday you'll want one of your own kind, or someone younger, who is still pretty."

He was across the room so fast Haven didn't have time to react. His hand looped around her wrist as he crouched down in front of her. "Don't ever think it. What I want right now is here in front of me. I don't know what you're doing to me, woman, but I don't want to let it go. You matter to me. More than you can ever know."

She trembled at the intensity in him. Getting lost in the heat of his eyes was easy. She mentally jerked back away from an awareness she knew wasn't hers, and she actually flinched at the sensation of his emotions. It had hurt him. Her mind raced as she desperately searched for a way he was giving her emotions she wouldn't have without his magic, but she couldn't find it. Panic hit hard. "What are you doing to me?"

"Nothing, my Haven." He shifted closer to her, his voice going softer. "Let me show you something."

"What are you going to show me?"

"How to know if your thoughts are your own or not."

"It's possible to know that?"

He nodded and let go of her wrist, and then held out his hand for hers as he stood. Hesitantly, she slid her hand into his. It was just like with Mason, only this time, her mind wasn't screaming a warning she was compelled to ignore. What had Mason done? She didn't know. Lifting her gaze to meet his, she let out a slow breath. "Now what?"

"Now you have to let me in."

"In where?"

"Your head, Sweetheart. You need to invite me into your thoughts."

"How?"

"Like this."

Haven felt the distinct brush of his mind against hers. He was soft, gentle, but she got the feeling he didn't usually allow someone to know he was there. She squeezed her eyes shut and leaned against him for support as she lowered the mental walls just enough to let him in.

"That wasn't so difficult."

Haven blinked and then smiled up at him. She wasn't sure if it was a good thing or not that his mind touching hers felt comfortable, but this feeling of security was there, and she knew he could see the thought pass through her mind.

"All right, so how do I know the feelings are mine, and not something planted in my head?"

Haven more felt his frown than actually saw it, since she'd buried her face in his chest. *"This might hurt a little, sweetheart, but I need to check something."*

"I trust you." She did feel trust for him. She was most afraid of what he was going to find as he searched through her head. He was careful to keep out of her private thoughts about him, but he scanned quickly and efficiently through her memories. It was a little disconcerting that he was learning so much about her when she didn't know anything about him.

"You will," he promised and continued his search. When he got to where she'd carefully tucked all of her memories of Mason and her grandfather, she went rigid in Quinn's arms and tried to pull away, but he refused to let go. He saw everything—the beatings, the humiliation, the inability to do anything at all without express permission, and the dreaded fear she had of both of them. His chest vibrated, filling the room with a low, violent rumble. *"I almost have it, sweetheart. You're doing well."* He reached deeper into those horrors and pulled out something that Haven knew didn't belong in her head.

Haven struggled against Quinn, to make him let her go and get out of her mind. He held on tight and fought with the compulsion that tried to claw its way back into the crevice of her mind. Her head pounded like she was being stabbed by a thousand ice picks, but Quinn held firm. He pulled the devil out and then crushed it until there wasn't anything left. The pain in her head vanished, and she sagged against him.

Quinn stroked her hair, holding her close to him. *"You're okay, sweetheart. He's gone. He can't hurt you anymore."*

She was afraid to speak, so she didn't. She burrowed into the safe harbor of his arms. *"What was that thing?"*

"The compulsion planted by Mason. He knows he won't be able to control you anymore, but he also knows you are now mine."

The comment was barbaric, but there was something in the way his words flowed through her head that made them more soothing than anything else. "But we just met."

He leaned down, resting his head against hers. *"Then learn who I am. I won't hide anything from you."*

Instinctively, she understood there were things about him that she didn't want to know. Her search through his mind started with last night in the diner. She felt his calm in the face of Kyros's evil. The way Quinn's body had reacted to her despite his wish that it wouldn't. His utter loneliness suffocated him, even when he was with the people he loved and cared about. They knew him, but they never saw him. He was the rock they all leaned on, but no one took the time to see if the foundation was crumbling or not. He didn't blame them. In fact, he was glad they didn't look too close. He needed them safe, able to move from task to task without worry for him. His unwavering grief at the loss of each life he had to take or was taken from him overwhelmed her. The absolute resolve he had to keep the world and everyone safe from harm in a way no one else could. More than that, she saw a man pure of heart, a man who would do and did the most difficult of things for the greater good, willing to risk his own soul so another would not. There was a savage darkness in him, but it was tempered and tamed by his will as hard as diamonds and as unbendable as steel. He carried the world on his shoulders, and he wore the mantle with pride and with the undeniable truth that if he failed, the world would fail with him.

Tears collected in her eyes and shed unabashed down her face. Her breath caught. He was the greatest of men, for all time, and he was utterly alone in the world.

His head was still resting on hers. "Don't cry for me. I accepted my fate long ago."

It was impossible *not* to cry for him. There was no compulsion in her desire for him; everything was true and coming from her. She knew how to check for it now, and she did, just so he would know that she understood. The pads of his thumbs brushed at her tears. "I didn't mean to make you cry. I'm sorry." His arms loosened their hold on her before they fell to his sides.

She went up on her toes and hooked her arms around his neck, pulling him down closer. "I'll pretend with you."

Awe and wonder filled his eyes before he lowered his head. His mouth claimed hers.

"Mine," he demanded.

"Yours." And she meant it. It was as if their minds connected with a double-ended USB cable. They could know what each other was thinking and feeling without having to use words. She would be with him until he no longer wanted her or death found her. She'd touched him in a way no other person had. She didn't need to see everything, only the parts that mattered: that he wanted her, and he would keep his word to never hurt her.

His mouth dragged along her jaw line, his hand slipping up the hem of her shirt, when someone cleared their throat.

"You know," said the graveled drawl. "One of the exam rooms might give you more privacy."

As his head lifted, the growling sound that erupted from Quinn wasn't human. "Haven, darling, I'd like for you to meet the middle brother, Garret Wolf."

Haven turned her head and hopped closer to Quinn. Wolf wasn't quite as large as Quinn, but damn near close. That wasn't what worried her. He had an odd feel to him, and his eyes were an unnatural color brown. "You don't have the same surname?"

Wolf gave a florid bow. "Reannon, it is wonderful to finally meet you. The name was deliberate. Riordan and I share the surname, while Quinn, our public figure, has his own name. I see that you have accepted the bonding process, yes?"

She pressed her back into Quinn and squeaked. There was that "Reannon" word again, but Wolf was too intimidating to ask, and he was already waiting for an answer to another question. "Yes."

"Congratulations." He bowed again, though his tone was mocking. "The Cadeyrn has finally found his Reannon! Our people will be overjoyed."

She managed a wobbly smile. "Thank you."

"You may want to hold on to that," Wolf said as he walked farther into the room. "You have no known Undying kin, which leaves you vulnerable. I will take the responsibility for this bonding." Wolf glared at Quinn when it appeared he would object. "She is my sister now. You do not have the authority to deny me this. She needs a protector until both of you are safely bonded."

"Wolf—" Quinn started.

"My clan," Wolf snapped. "My judgment."

"Stop!" Haven moved between the men. Two tigers fighting would have been less dangerous. "I don't understand."

"He's trying to make putting me down his responsibility should something go wrong, and I go the way of the meirlock," Quinn said coldly.

"If you're king, how do you not have authority to override him?"

"Valid question," Wolf said as he crouched down in front of her. "I am the Wolf Caden of the Heartland Tribe. While Quinn has rule of the Cadfaels, I have rule of our clan. This is a clan matter, and the responsibility should not be given to someone else."

Haven could feel the color running out of her face. A few hours ago, Quinn had ended the life of a turned Cadfael. "But I agreed," she said. "Why are you threatening his life?"

"Precaution," Quinn said. "Sometimes things go wrong in a bonding, and the *treòir* reacts badly."

Wolf's eyes glowed. "You mean like choosing to give up your *treòir* and allowing both of you to wither and die with old age?"

Haven rounded on Quinn. "You said that was a possibility. Not that you were planning on doing it!"

"You don't understand," Quinn roared at her. "Changing you into what I am will kill you."

"You don't know that," Wolf said as a deep, guttural growl vibrated in him. "No one else would be willing to risk your wrath to give our Reannon all needed information."

Haven glared over her shoulder at Wolf before rounding back on Quinn. "You were never planning on changing me?"

"I—" He snarled at his brother. "Get. Out. I will deal with you later." He waited until a smug Wolf ventured back up the stairs before he shifted to sit on the couch and pulled Haven onto his lap. "I've seen many women die in a botched conversion. It is painful and horrible."

While she wanted to be angry with him, there was more worrying him. If she could sort out what was really going on...

"No need to sort."

Her eyes went huge when she heard the voice. It wasn't Quinn exactly, but it could be him. His eyes were glowing an eerie red color and the muscles under them were twitching. Oh dear. *Quinn's power* was talking to her. *"Oh? Why not?"*

A brush of gentle energy flowed through her. *"He'd rather die than see you suffer."*

"And you?" She winced after she asked because Quinn was looking like he was about to explode. *"What do you want?"*

The *treòir* twisted around her and through her in a giddy rush. *"I want to see you live. I want to live. I want him to live."*

She wrapped her arms around Quinn's neck and buried her face in the crook of his neck. He wasn't moving, and she wasn't sure what to make of that. This could be bad. Very, very bad, but this *treòir* was part of Quinn. She wanted to get to know his power. *"What about the suffering?"*

"You will survive, and there are ways to limit the pain. He holds valid fears. Do not discount them, but do not discount me."

Quinn's eyes flashed gold, and the voice and the feeling of his power surrounding her faded. She captured his face and kissed him before he could start bellowing at her. Quinn was afraid of the conversion. That was enough to make her want to find out more before she went off half-cocked and demand he change her into an Undying. She would be wiser to know what she was getting herself into before jumping in. Quinn might also calm down if he knew what to expect.

He broke the kiss as he glared at her with golden glowing eyes. "Never talk to it again!"

She winced but kept a hold of his face. As scary and intimidating as he was, she needed to pull on her big girl panties. All powerful Cadeyrn was not synonymous with tyrannical brute. She'd seen too much of him to ever think that. "I will do what is best for myself and for my mate."

"Haven, you will not—"

"I respect you as Cadeyrn," she interrupted him. "I would appreciate if you started to respect me as your Reannon. We will discuss these things properly." She bit her lower lip and then smiled at him. "Your power was sweet and very gentle. There was nothing for you to worry about."

* * * *

Emma Weylin

Donovan studied her. As his mate, she'd have to come into contact with his power at some point, but damn it, he *knew* how dangerous the *treòir* was if left unchecked. He did not want all of that power accidently getting agitated when she was close. The damage done would be unforgiveable. "It is not safe for you."

A smile threatened the corners of her mouth. She brushed a strand of hair away from his face and kissed his cheek. "How's that headache you get when you need to control him?"

He huffed. "I don't have one."

"Exactly," she said and slipped off his lap. "*He* is not going to hurt me anymore than you would."

Donovan did not like this at all. She should not have any kind of warm and fuzzy feeling toward his *treòir*, but it was there, emanating around her. "You must understand how dangerous my power is."

"And I do," she said as she reached down and wrapped her hand around his before tugging to get him to get up. "But I am not Kyros or any other thing you fight. What reason would *your* power have to harm me?"

"Tell her that I am not accustomed to being let out near delicate women, but I will need practice."

Donovan dragged himself up off the couch as he shook his head. Then he repeated to her what the *treòir* had said. "Do you understand? It's dangerous for you."

She tugged him toward the stairs. "I heard you, but it's not going to squash me into paste. It said it needed practice being gentle. Two very different things."

"Haven!"

"Quinn!" she shot back before he could finish. "Look, I am not asking you to let it out and take control of you for forever. But I am not going to be denied part of you just because you have hang ups."

"Haven," he started again.

She rounded on him from the second step on the stairs. "This is not up for discussion or executive order. I can understand that you need time to process this, and I will give you the time you need, but not forever, pal, unless you plan on doing the conversion. I don't have forever to wait for you to figure yourself out."

She was a vicious fighter. That one shot went right to the quick because it was the truth. There should be a "forever ever after" for them. Immortality was part of what he was, and what she was as an Undying's lifebond. He was still Cadeyrn, and she was not going to worm her way around this just because she had killer curves and enchanting eyes. "I am glad you feel safe enough to tell me exactly what you think, and most matters will be up for debate as needed, but all matters of your safety will be decreed by executive order if necessary."

"Perhaps I should discuss this with my guardian while we bond?"

"Wolf cannot know things about the bonding process yet," he snapped at her. "The knowledge jeopardizes his life."

"Then I will speak with Riordan. He is bonded to his mate, yes?" She crossed her arms over her chest.

"You will not go over my head with this, woman!"

"Man," she said as she wrapped her arms around his neck and leaned forward off the stairs, forcing him to hold her. "Speaking to Riordan will put the matter to rest for now. If he agrees with me, I will give you time to get used to the idea. If he agrees with you, I won't bring conversion up again."

There was no logical defense against that. Riordan was the resident bonding expert, and he'd had the opportunity to read both the *Book of Avalon* before it was lost and the *Book of the Undying* before it had been destroyed.

"*I win,*" the *treòir* said. "*Let the woman do what she feels is needed to protect your life. It's only fair.*"

Since when did his power care about fair? He gave up thinking about it and kissed Haven before going up the stairs to have Riordan tell him he was behaving like a childish ass.

Chapter 7

Haven lost some of her confidence when she went into the kitchen. She smiled for Riordan as she moved away from the door. "Hello." Then she turned to the petite blond woman standing next to him. She had big, bright blue eyes, and her features had an odd pixie-like quality to them. The woman was stunning. The room was the color of honey, and bees were the theme, from the canisters by the sink to the curtain tiebacks. Haven put out her hand. "You must be Nadia. I am—"

"Quinn's lifebond!" the other woman said in a gush as she took Haven's hand and pumped it up and down. "Thank Avalon! Maybe you can talk some sense into him." She pulled her farther into the kitchen. "I have a room set up for Bastian to stay for a while, and I've already talked with Ean Maverick. He'll come and stay with us, too, if that makes you feel better. I am sure there is an extra cell phone around here somewhere so you can call him any time you want, and our door is open any time you want to just peek in to see how he's doing." Nadia tugged Haven toward the delicately decorated living room. "I was going to talk to you about getting Bastian back into school, but he's better off if we don't put pressure on him until after your done bonding. He'll catch up easily enough. Until then, there are plenty of us to keep him entertained and out of trouble."

Haven's mouth dropped open. No one had talked to her about taking Bastian away from her this soon.

Nadia took one look at her face and said something under her breath that sounded suspiciously like a fairy curse. She shot her mate a scathing look before she led her over to the kitchen table. "Sit. I should have realized none of them would have thought to put Bastian some place safer than with a bonding couple. The offer stands whenever you're ready, dear. You and your family are always welcome in my house."

Once the shock wore off, she began to feel at ease in the other woman's presence. The tiny woman was a bundle of pure energy. Nadia moved around the kitchen preparing a kettle to put on the stove and opening a cabinet full of different types of cups. "So what will it be? Tea? Coffee?" She glanced at Quinn grumbling by the doorway. "A shot of vodka? I might even be able to find a big game tranquilizer to slip into his drink." She gave him the sweetest and most plastic smile.

Quinn grumbled louder.

Nadia laughed. Then she was talking to Haven again. "Anything you need, just say the word, and I'll make it happen."

Haven shook her head a few times. "Wow, I…" She laughed nervously. "I have no idea what I am supposed to do." Though, she did feel better when Bastian plopped down next to her with a giant plate of steak.

"How about say thank you and when can the boy move in?"

"Bastian!" she snapped at him. "You are not staying with anyone I don't know."

"Right, like you need an audience while you two, um, bond," Bastian said in only the way a fourteen-year old could.

"Exactly," Quinn said. "You will have complete access to him, and I will show you how to operate the portal room without the aid of Memphis, so you can see Bastian anytime you wish."

Haven needed to deal with one issue at a time. She'd figure out later if sending Bastian to live with someone else for a few days was the right thing to do, when she wasn't so overwhelmed. She made an appeal to Nadia. "What am I supposed to do with him?" She tilted her head toward Quinn. "I have no idea what exactly a bonding couple is supposed to be doing."

Nadia pointed a finger at Quinn. "Say it and I swear I'll zap you. Go take Bastian into the other room and make sure he eats everything before you introduce him to the video game system. I am going to have a heart to heart with my new sister."

"Nadia—" Quinn started.

The air in the kitchen ionized with an electrical charge. "I mean it!" Nadia said. "Shoo. Don't make me do something I'll have to explain to my lifebond."

Haven was up and out of her chair. She was standing in front of Quinn before she knew what she was doing. She liked Nadia already, and she didn't want to have to slap the woman for zapping Quinn.

"Please," she said softly. She reached up and patted Quinn's chest. Her body did an involuntary shudder of pleasure at the feel of his muscles under her hands. She cleared her throat and stepped back. "I need a little bit of sanity in this insane day. Just go with Bastian. It would make me feel better."

He shot Nadia an annoyed glare, and then he let out a dramatic huff of air. "We need to be alone if we are going to bond properly."

"I know, but just think how much easier you'll have it when we are completely alone if I've had a nice chat with *your* sister-in-law." He was a guy. No matter what else he was in the world, she was sure if his male parts thought his chances of getting into her female parts would be made easier in some way, he'd comply.

It worked. He bent down and lightly brushed his mouth along her jaw line. "Don't be too long." He still didn't look happy as he moved toward the door, but then grudgingly jerked his head for Bastian to follow before he left her alone with Nadia.

The tiny woman's eyes went perfectly huge as she stared after Quinn. "Sweet Flora, it is true. You are his lifebond." Then she was at the stove again retrieving the pot of water just as steam puffed from the spout. "I do believe you are the first person in two thousand years who convinced him to do something he didn't want to do."

Haven moved over to the counter next to Nadia. She needed a good relationship with this woman. The feeling ran as bone deep as the need to be connected to Quinn. She and this woman were going to need each other a lot over the course of her lifetime. "You make him sound like an overbearing jackass. Is there anything I can help you with?"

"I've got it," Nadia said. "Just tell me what you like."

"Tea is fine, thank you."

Nadia went for two teacups in the cabinet. "He is an overbearing jackass, but I say that in the most loving way possible." She set the cups on the counter and went to the tea tin in the shape of a blooming rose. "You have questions. I have answers."

Haven's palms started to itch with the guilt of someone else taking care of her needs. She forced herself back to the kitchen table to perch in the chair. She did not like being the only one in a room not doing something. It reminded her too much of her pampered princess days with the Black Rose. "I guess he's afraid to let me talk with his *treòir*. Should I even press that issue?"

Nadia peered through the door leading from the kitchen into the living room. She sat down next her. "Yes, you should, but—"

"Got it," Haven said before the woman could finish. "Don't make him crazy with it. Baby steps."

"Exactly. They are taught to be wary of their power and to always have complete control. In a bonding, things get a little erratic while the *treòir* learns to interact with someone other than its host." Nadia wrapped a hand around hers. "Follow your instincts. There is a part of you that knows you belong with Dov. Listen to your intuition. It is guiding you in the right direction."

"Thank you," Haven said. Having someone she could talk to when everything got weird that wasn't giant and male was wonderful. "Would I be rude if I just wanted to go back to the penthouse? I need to figure out how to make all of this work so it doesn't drive me crazy."

"Not at all," Nadia said with a smile. "I totally understand how crazy bonding is." Nadia stopped Haven before she left the room. "Fall in love with him. It was the one piece of advice I wish my grandmother would have told me when bonding to Riordan. A bonding won't work if you're not in love." Nadia gave her a tight hug. "Call me if you need anything. We'll have forever to chat."

* * * *

Wolf stood in the center of the conference room. He assembled the rest of Quinn's Cadens for a war council. The lodge in the center of the Wolf compound was where he decided to have the meeting that all in attendance thought would never come. Cadeyrn had found his lifebond. The occasion should have the entire Undying Nation exploding in jubilation, but Wolf held off on the good cheer. They could celebrate after the danger passed. Protecting Quinn and Haven while they bonded was his responsibility, and he would not fail them.

Wolf stood at the head of the oak table. "The rumor is true. Quinn Donovan, our Cadeyrn, has his lifebond, and she has agreed to mate with him."

The power vibe in the room kicked up as all of the men and their *treòirs* came to full attention.

Wolf waited a beat. "They will need a constant guard until Kyros is defeated. The woman is not Kyros's target, but she is the most vulnerable out of any of us. Brogan, I want a constant air patrol over the penthouse, and a dragon following them if they decide to leave."

Heath Brogan was the oldest and largest known dragon to survive the time-shift and the Dragon Caden. Brogan nodded once. "I will call in a few other older Cadens from other tribes. I don't want to risk my younger dragons to Kyros."

"Agreed," Wolf said as his attention turned to Maverick. "You're on the ground. The Earth can sometimes hear things before we do, and I want to know there is danger before it happens, if possible."

Ean Maverick, the Earth Caden and the son of the Original Earth Warrior, leaned against the door. "Aye," Maverick said. "The child with them is of Earth, yes?"

Wolf nodded. "If Haven decides, the boy will stay with Nadia until the bonding is completed. Then he will go to you for training."

Wolf worked his shoulders and paced the length of the white-walled room. Standing still made him itch. "Brody." He moved on to the Hunter. "I want you to keep your focus on finding the meirlocks who infiltrated the Black Rose. Haven's mate is to become their next leader, and I want to know all connections between her and the meirlock clan." He was working on a hunch that Kyros was working with the Black Rose. He wanted confirmation before he told Quinn that he suspected Kyros wanted to turn himself into the meirlock version of the Cadeyrn.

The man with no power signature around him was Brody Hunter, Caden of the Hunters. He could track wind over water. If Brody couldn't find it, then it didn't exist. Brody pulled on his chin and then leaned back on the chair. "I've been watching the Black Rose for a few decades. I've yet to feel a meirlock presence at their headquarters."

Wolf crossed his arms over his chest and looked out the window at Riordan's house. He wanted to bring Haven and Quinn here. He and his brother had this discussion a million times over the last fifty years. Quinn was more than the Chicago Pack or the Cadfael of the Undying tribe in America's heartland. He understood Quinn didn't want the other males to think he had preference for his home pack, but there was a reason the ruling packs had gated, compound-like communities. It was an argument for another day. For now, he needed to focus on keeping his brother alive. He turned back to the other men. "Keep watching the Black Rose," he said to Brody. "We're missing something, and I know it's going to come bite me in the ass."

Brody inclined his head.

Wolf moved on to the Storm Caden, Memphis. "We'll need a supply of other realm fruit for after Haven is converted into an Undying."

Memphis nodded. "Sheridan out of New York is already handling it. I want to be close to you if something goes wrong."

"Good," Wolf said. He'd worked closely with these men for the last fifteen hundred years of their lives, and in some cases longer. They knew what each other was thinking, but they still had meetings to make sure everyone knew what was expected of them. "I will keep myself available in case Quinn turns." He clenched his jaw.

The bonds of brotherhood couldn't matter. Before the time-shift, he hadn't worried about who would take out his brother if Quinn turned, but the Originals were gone. The first Undying men were created by a power not of the Earth realm. The youngest of the first seven was over the age of five thousand. They could easily take out any of the men standing in this room should it become necessary, but they went missing when the Undying Nation was pulled through two thousand years of time.

Wolf refused to believe they were dead. If they were, it meant his sister, Fenris's mate, was dead, and he wasn't prepared to cope with the loss.

"Wolf," Riordan, the Caden of Healers, said as he stood up and placed a hand on his shoulder. "Quinn is strong enough to survive this. You're doing everything right."

"Aye, little brother." Riordan hadn't been little for two millennia, but Wolf would forever think of him as such. "I want you to direct all non-life-threatening injuries to Michael. Quinn is going to need you the most. There are things I don't understand about bonding, but you do."

"We've got this," Riordan said. "Just have a little faith."

That was the problem. The last time Wolf had faith, he'd woken up completely healed from injuries that should have killed him. To make the situation worse, he'd been in the middle of a busy highway, having no idea what the giant metal beast with white glowing eyes bearing down on him had been. Now he knew it was a semi-truck, but he wasn't ready to trust the universe again this soon.

* * * *

Her quiet day at home turned into some good old-fashioned retail therapy—with a billion dollar shopping limit. All right, so Quinn hadn't given her the green light to spend every penny he had, but she was starting to think his hummer wasn't going to be large enough to hold everything she'd gotten for the kitchen and for her new wardrobe, not to mention what she'd bought for Bastian. She was with *thee* Quinn Donovan, and part of her couldn't get out of the need-to-look-perfect-in-front-of-the-people attitude she'd grown up with in the Black Rose, even as sheltered as she'd been from its day-to-day operations. Grandfather had insisted she look nothing less than perfect.

"I should be staying with Ean," Bastian said as they entered the food court of the mall.

Ean? Oh, right. That Earth Warrior everyone kept saying Bastian had to be introduced to. Quinn must have said something to him while she'd been in the shower after they got back to the penthouse. She understood if Kyros, or anyone from the Black Rose, found her, things could get dangerous, and it was the responsible, adult thing to do to give him to someone who wasn't in the line of fire. But he was hers. She'd fed him, loved him, and kept him safe all on her own for the last three years. Damn it! And keeping him safe was knowing when to let him go.

She needed to talk to Quinn.

He was loading a fourth round of bags into his Hummer as she assessed which fast food establishment would give Bastian the best nutrition. "Ean has other things to worry about at the moment, I'm sure," she said and tried to keep a smile plastered to her face. "Besides, I need someone who will help keep me sane while I do this Undying bonding thing."

Bastian snorted and stopped in front of the fried chicken stand. "That's why you have the wolves. I'll just be in the way. It will only be like a week."

"You are not eating all that grease," she snapped. "A week? Bonding only takes a week?" Yeah, she kind of got that the speedy way things happened with Mason wasn't how it was supposed to go, but Nadia left her with the impression she would fall in love with her lifebond before the actual bonding happened.

"Give or take, according to Riordan." Bastian made that pleading puppy-dog face he was so good at as he stared at the chicken forlornly. "It's not going to kill me, and I haven't had anything fried in years."

True. A vat of fried chicken for one meal probably wouldn't do anything to harm his astonishing growth. Guilt was a cruel mistress. Did she give into the guilt of handing Bastian's care over to someone else, or him being a *couple* of pounds underweight? She let out a slow huff of breath. "No, but you're going to grow to be roughly the size of a small giant. Good food will help with that."

"Come on, Haven, please." He extended the last word. "How am I ever going to be more than a pole if I can't eat some junk food?"

Another moment of guilt hit her hard, but before she could say anything, Bastian did a cute version of an Undying growl. "Don't go there," he said. "I got the chance to live to find people just like me. You're awesome, and I'd never have gotten here if it wasn't for you."

She wrapped her arm around him. "Oh, my Bastian."

"We're gonna be okay." He wiggled out of her hold, and his expression went embarrassed, his eyes darting around the food court as if he was checking to be sure other kids weren't looking. "You got us to where we needed to be."

"Get the chicken," she said. That boy always seemed to know how to twist up her brain until she had no idea which way was up, and he never meant to do it.

A smile brightened his young face. "Thank you!"

She smiled back at him, despite feeling as if she was still several steps behind where she needed to be for all of this to work.

"Have we decided what we're getting for lunch?" Quinn asked when he was suddenly standing behind her.

"Fried chicken," Haven said while making a face.

Quinn laughed softly as his hand curled over her shoulder. "There are plenty of places to choose from. Why don't I give him some money to get what he wants, and we'll find something more acceptable for your tastes?"

"Mall food isn't exactly in line with—" She snapped her mouth shut. The man had already spent a fortune on her and Bastian today, and even if he was loaded, that didn't mean he needed to take her to some fancy restaurant for lunch. Thinking about the cost was making her lightheaded, but it seemed *her* spending *his* money made Quinn calmer. "How about a burger?"

Quinn's dark brow winged up, but he only nodded. He got out his wallet and handed Bastian an absurd amount of money. "There's an arcade right over there if you're interested," he said to Bastian.

Haven bit her lip. She had to keep telling herself everything would be fine. Quinn would know of trouble before anything happened. Bastian was safe. She was safe. It had to be true, or she wasn't going to survive five seconds without being able to see the kid. Some of her building tension eased when his young face lit into a smile. "Fried chicken and video games? I will behave, and I promise to call the second I feel trouble." He was in line to get his food the next second, leaving Haven and Quinn standing alone in the middle of the food court.

She had no idea how she was supposed to be acting around him yet. He seemed accepting of anything she felt like doing, but Mason started out that way, too. Mason had been overwhelming with how fast he pushed her, but at the moment, she wasn't getting that vibe of dread. She also needed to start listening to her intuition. It had been right about Mason, even if she hadn't been able to act to protect herself. Instinct was probably right about Quinn. "You're good with a burger?" she asked. "There isn't something else you'd prefer?"

His mouth curved in a sexy little half-grin that told her exactly what he'd prefer for lunch—dessert—and she was on the menu. "Burgers are fine. I just need to eat."

She scanned the other establishments and picked out the one that looked like it would have something healthy for her. She wasn't vain about her figure, but she did need to watch what she ate or she would pack on the pounds. She hadn't needed to worry about her weight while they were on the run, but now that she didn't have to skip meals to feed Bastian, it could sneak up on her.

It might provide the excuse she needed to get back into Middle Eastern dancing. She'd owned her own studio and taught classes before Mason. The one thing Grandfather had allowed her to have all for herself. Maybe she'd be able to get Quinn to let her teach again. Dancing was the one joy she'd had while living under the shadow of the Black Rose.

She went for a place that served burgers and tried not to pay attention to how they were being prepared. "This one works. What do you feed the wolves?"

Quinn moved up behind Haven in the line and wrapped his hands around her shoulders. He lowered his head. "Relax. I've taken care of everything."

She made an unlady-like snort. "You keep saying that. You can't take care of everything."

"I can and I do. Stop worrying."

She laughed and leaned back into him. "I'll stop worrying if you stop taking care of everything."

* * * *

Donovan dropped his chin onto her shoulder and took in a long drag of her scent. He loved how she smelled. She didn't cover over her own fragrance with some kind of floral soap—though he was sure his home soon would be filled with the scents that always accompanied a woman— she had this light, feminine earthy aroma that intoxicated him and left him throbbing to get inside of her. "Then I think we've reached an impasse."

"I figured as much." Her tone was disgruntled as they moved forward. "I am going to make you nuts."

"No. You'll give me better priorities," he said before he knew what was going to come out of his mouth.

She slowly turned until they were facing each other. "How so?"

He shrugged. "I'll take care of what you're worried about first. Everything else can wait."

She flashed him a bone-melting smile before she stepped up to order her food. Donovan tripled the order for himself.

They sat in a quieter corner of the mall food court where she was able to see the arcade where Bastian played video games and ate fried chicken like a normal teenage boy. She carefully unwrapped her burger before looking at Donovan. "You're not always going to be able to put me before everyone else."

"Why not? My father did it that way," he said as he set out his meal. "He always said my mother's intuition was the guide he had for leading our people."

Her brow furrowed as her head canted. "Was she ever wrong?"

"What is it?" Concern flooded his system. His teeth gritted together. This hyper-reaction was like being in the middle of an angsty teenage drama with the highs and lows of his emotions because the *treòir* had to add to whatever minor feeling he had in the moment.

"Just something Nadia said. She said I needed to follow my intuition. Maybe there is something to following instincts after all." She bit into her burger. Her eyes closed as pure bliss brightened her face. She swallowed. "You know what? I haven't had a juicy burger in a long time. I know I shouldn't, but this tastes so good." She snagged a fry. "Sorry. What if my intuition is wrong?"

"Then it's wrong," he said while studying her. "The world is imperfect. No one can make all the right decisions all the time."

She giggled. "This coming from you?"

"You've got me. I'm the only one who must be perfect, but only in specific regards. All other times, I am free to make the grand blunders the human species is prone to make."

"So then, there is some human in you?"

"Aye, my mother was a human. Like yourself."

They ate for a little while in silence. He loved watching her. She was peaceful and wanted the world around them to be the same way. As much as he would love to give that to her, complete peace wasn't possible. Pandora had opened her box, and all the ails of the world could not be stuffed back inside because Lilith had destroyed it. The world would always need him.

"So then, human mates are normal for the Undying?" she asked suddenly.

"Aye," he said with a chuckle. "We actually weren't able to discover the reason until this century."

Emma Weylin

She neatly folded the burger wrapper and then stuffed it into the fry box. "That's a little odd."

"Not really. Genetic diversity. That was hardly a topic when the Celts were still living in mud huts."

"Huh. That actually makes sense." They went silent again while Quinn finished his lunch.

Haven leaned over the table. "Bastian thinks he should be staying with Ean Maverick."

"I think that needs to be modified a bit. I think having him stay with Nadia is the best option, and I can have Maverick stay at the compound to start his education," Donovan said, while he cleaned up his side of the table. "Maverick has a unique circumstance that I don't believe would be beneficial for a boy of Bastian's age."

* * * *

"Is he dangerous?" Haven's voice hitched up. There had to be a better way to get through these first few confusing days than to be on a rollercoaster she couldn't get off.

"No." Quinn started stacking everything onto his tray. "Did you study the legends of Mor Ean Corr in high school?'

"No way!" she said in perfect teenaged fashion as she jumped out of her chair with excitement. "He's like one of the greatest Celtic legends ever. It was said that he could make the Earth shake and a forest get up and walk away." She cleared her throat as she sat back down and leaned across the table to whisper. "He's real?"

Quinn laughed. "And you get to meet him. That last tale of Vortigern, the warlock, taking out the clans Ean protected is true. Instead of giving into his *treòir* and leveling all of Britannia, his father, the original and oldest Earth Warrior, showed him how to suppress his emotions completely until he finds his lifebond. Most of the time he's rather good at faking them, but when training Undying males, well, let's just say, he forgets there are moments of compassion needed for our younger generation."

"Oh my," Haven said as she looked over at the arcade to see what Bastian was doing. She winced. Girls. It was only a matter of time before he started to notice them, but they always got him into trouble. "I think we should go get Bastian." She got up and grabbed the tray. "Is there any way to help Ean?"

"Find him his lifebond," Quinn said as he walked over to the garbage can with her. "Until then, we just have to understand he can be a little odd at times and make accommodations for him."

"That's still so sad."

He took the tray from her and threw out the contents before putting it in the receptacle. "He will feel again, and every emotion he couldn't process will come back to him." His gaze went to Bastian. "He will remember his students, and he will feel for them as he should." His attention turned back to her. "That's why we help him now, so he doesn't look back on this time with deep regrets because he was a complete bastard toward everyone he cares for."

"I'm going to need a long time to process all of this," she said.

He leaned down and brushed his mouth along her jaw. "I'll be with you every step of the way."

Her head tilted back as she moved in closer to him. Her gaze met his. "I do think we need time to be alone."

"Brilliant idea." There was much relief in his tone. "You get Bastian, and I'll go pull the car around."

"You're sure? It's cold out there, but we can walk with you."

The look he gave her said there wasn't a way in hell his lifebond was going to be cold for a second longer than was absolutely necessary. "I'm sure, but there is no need for all of us to be cold." Quinn stopped in front of her and bent down to kiss the top of her head. "I'll meet you out front."

"All right." She had a slight pang as she watched him walk away.

This was almost too good to be true. Malls and food courts were a normal, family type thing to do. The dream with Quinn became possible—if anything to do with Quinn could be classified as normal—and she was able to stop being neurotic long enough to get everything making sense in her head. Everything about him was so much larger than life. It was difficult to process how both Quinn and the world existed around him.

He was the Undying Cadeyrn. The king of people so powerful she knew they were capable of killing warlocks. She'd heard of the meirlocks doing it. Quinn wasn't meirlock, but he was Undying, and he was supposed to be their strongest. She let out a slow breath. She was going to be the mate of a man who could be the strongest on Earth.

"Hey, Haven?" Bastian said next to her.

She was startled and, with a slight jump, snapped her head up. Then she forced a smile. Bastian was too young, no matter what he was, to bear the ancient power and the problems with the Black Rose. "Hey, you. We need to get going. Quinn will be waiting out front for us."

Bastian let out a wistful sigh and gave the flashing lights and beeping sounds—and several girls in short skirts—a forlorn look before he shoved a fist full of coins into his pocket and followed her back to the food court. "Dov said he'd get me any game system I want."

Haven arched a brow. "I bet he did. We'll discuss it after we've talked about getting you enrolled in school."

Bastian looked at his feet. "I like that cyber school idea for human information, but I think I want to do what the other Undying kids do."

Haven winced but managed to keep from committing a mortal sin against the teenager—hugging him in public again. "I'm sorry." She should have remembered that. "But we can still talk to Quinn about how to handle your education before we talk about mindless video games."

A flash of unexpected excitement lightened his young face. "Oh, sweet! I'll be trained by one of those guys, won't I? I mean, how cool would that be that I get trained by them!" Then he started with a long list of names she'd never heard before. Quinn and Bastian must have already discussed it while she'd spent hours in the dressing rooms.

Haven put her hand on his shoulder to stop him. She chuckled. "I am glad you're so excited, but I have no idea who half of these people are."

"Don't worry," Bastian said. His movements became quick as he moved forward, bouncing on the balls of his feet. "It would be like learning math from Einstein or astronomy from Galileo. I mean, Maverick is the son of Demek. Demek was the Original Earth Warrior. He could move freaking mountains before the time-shift. I am like the coolest kid ever. Thanks for being Dov's lifebond." He kissed her forehead. Haven was left staring at Bastian as he babbled on and on about exactly what caliber of cool he was going to be.

"Come on, cool kid," Haven said on a dry note. "You can continue to pat yourself on the back for your good fortune while we—" She stopped talking when she felt the unmistakable presence of Mason. She whirled around, looking above the heads of everyone in the crowded food court, and latched on to Bastian's wrist when she saw Mason walking toward her. "We need to run."

"Haven!" Mason's voice boomed out.

No! No! No! This was not happening. If she ran, it was only going to be worse. Mason hadn't liked it when she'd run from him. Her head told her feet to flee because Quinn was waiting for her just outside the sliding glass doors, but they stubbornly remained in place. A violent shiver ran down the course of her body. She shifted her weight to run from the bastard who only wanted to hurt her. He was all blond hair, tawny skin, and blue-eyed gorgeous, but Haven knew better. He was a golden devil.

"You best not run, darlin'." Mason's voice was in her head. His eyes locked on to hers. *"I don't need to be touching you to compel you to do my bidding."*

Chapter 8

Haven wanted to freeze up with the terror icing through her body. She shoved Bastian toward the escalators leading to the exit and Quinn. "Run," she commanded him, but he swung around and planted his gangly body between her and Mason.

Surely Mason wouldn't cause a scene with this many humans around. The large man quickly crossed the food court. He loomed over Bastian.

"Get out of my way, boy."

"No," Bastian snarled.

In a split second, Mason lifted his arm and backhanded Bastian. The boy went stumbling off to the side.

Haven screamed as she lunged forward. Her body connected with Mason's, shoving him back a step. "You leave him alone!"

Mason pushed her back. Haven landed on her butt next to Bastian. Everyone in the food court stopped to stare at them. Haven glanced at the security guard who had lifted his radio to call for backup. Mason shook his head. The guard lowered his radio.

Damn it! She should have known the Black Rose would see her here and report to Mason immediately. Quinn's powerful presence had given her a false sense of security. She scooted close to Bastian and tried to ignore the panic welling up inside of her. Not wanting to give into the rising fear, she squeezed her eyes shut tight and projected out for all she was worth. *"Quinn, Mason is here!"* And she hoped the telepathic communication worked, because she wasn't exactly sure how to make the link with Quinn connect correctly. Then she ignored Mason while she checked Bastian to make sure he was all right.

The boy sat on the floor growling at Mason. "Get away from us."

He crouched down in front of Haven. "Well, well, wife. What do you have to say for yourself?"

"We never made it to the altar," she said. "I am not your wife. Leave us alone."

He reached out to grab her chin when the floor under her started to tremble minutely. Mason's head snapped up. Blazing fear flashed in his eyes as he stumbled backward a step, righting himself to get away from what was coming up behind her.

"Cadeyrn!" Mason said with a snarl.

"I wouldn't touch her if I were you."

The sound of Quinn's voice was chilling. His usual warm, buttery cadence turned cold and brutal. She hooked Bastian's wrist and started scooting backward toward the only safety she had.

Mason's lip curled in a snarl. "She is my lifebond, Cadeyrn. I suggest you check the laws on what exactly my rights with her are."

Quinn knelt down in front of Haven. His gaze moved over the bruise on the right side of Bastian's face. His glacier eyes met with Haven's for one dark moment before the irises flared blood red. Power vibrated the air around them. A gentle hand helped Haven to her feet. "Help the boy," he said. Dark humor twisted the unusual graveled sound of his voice as his attention finally turned to Mason. "Let's see. Haven, do you accept this man as your lifebond?"

Mason growled. "You better answer correctly."

"Of course not—" she started as she helped Bastian up.

Before she could finish and say that Quinn was her lifebond, Quinn put up his hand to silence her. Then he was laughing softly, but the sound held an ominous note. "Now, tell me the truth, Mason." The glow of his eyes flickered from red to gold. "Your lifebond just rejected you. You know what that means. Are you lying about who she is to you?"

Mason's mouth flopped opened and closed several times before his face hardened. "You will not kill me here."

* * * *

"No," Donovan agreed. The only indication of the rage flowing through him was the minor tremble in the floor. Keeping his *treòir* from tearing forth to destroy the monster terrorizing his mate had him shaking with the forces at war in his body. There was only so much he could hold back while standing before the man who knowingly abused *his* Haven. The temptation to rip into this man was great, but he couldn't in front of this many humans. His voice lowered so no one else around them could hear the deadly promise. "You are charged with attempting to steal another male's lifebond. I find you guilty." He stepped closer to Mason. His power pulsed around him with leashed fury. "Your sentence is death."

Donovan leaned forward to snarl right in the other man's face. "I will be coming for you."

They stood there for a long moment before Mason turned and fled. Even Kyros knew better than to do something in such a public place.

He stood poised and ready for battle, should the other male prove stupid, until he could no longer sense him. All that mattered was keeping Haven away from the deadly meirlock. He connected immediately with Memphis. *"I want Mason tracked and brought to me alive."*

"Aye," Memphis responded. *"Brody is already searching for their lair. We thought it might be the Black Rose Mansion, but there are no traces of any meirlock residing there."*

He was quiet for a moment. *"Bring me Mason!"*

"Your will be done." Then Memphis disconnected.

Donovan turned to assess Bastian's injury. The bruise would be easily cured with a quick nap or a flick of Riordan's healing hand. Then he methodically went over every inch of Haven's body without being intrusive. The fear emanating off her made controlling his *treòir* difficult, but she was uninjured. The best way to keep anything untoward from happening again was to get them all the hell out of here.

"The meirlock needs to be killed!" Treòir roared in his mind.

"And we will kill him," Donovan promised. *"But we must make them safe before we can go hunting."*

The *treòir* was only just placated. It wanted Haven now. He willed the colossal power back and into the box meant to keep the world safe from the monster he could become if he gave into the desires of his power.

A security guard met him at the door of the mall. "Sir…"

Donovan caught him by the arm and twisted. He shoved up the man's sleeve to reveal a black rose tattooed on his forearm. "Give Killian a message for me."

The guard trembled while he tried to yank his arm back. "Go to hell."

"I've already been there. I have no desire to visit again." He pulled the man in close. He bared his teeth. "Cadeyrn is pissed off at him."

He let the guard go and shoved him back. The guard scrambled to get out of the way. "The woman—"

"Is no longer his concern."

He collected both Haven and Bastian, and then he moved them through the sliding glass doors and out onto the cold sidewalk. He didn't say one word as he opened the back door for Bastian, and then personally made sure Haven was buckled in the front passenger seat before he went around to the driver's side and got in.

Emma Weylin

Haven was visibly shaking. "Oh my God. He knows I'm here. Quinn, you have to let me go to him. He'll—"

"Shh," he murmured softly as he pulled out into mall traffic. His hand gripped the steering wheel tightly to the point his knuckles turned white. "I know you're afraid, sweetheart. Mason's only hope to hurt me is by hurting you."

"But," she started to protest and stopped herself. "He will try to come after me again."

"Probably," Donovan said. He wasn't going to lie to her, but he hated knowing how much this was going to screw with her head. Mason had never been overly ambitious for power before he'd turned. Donovan wondered if there might be something else behind this bid to rule the Black Rose. There was an angle here he was missing, and he needed to find out what it was.

"Bastian…" Her voice trailed off as she drew in a deep breath and let it out slowly. "He can't be near me. If something happened to him, I'd never forgive myself."

"I can stay with someone else," Bastian said from the back seat. "It's okay. I am not going to think you're abandoning me."

Quinn reached over and wrapped his hand around hers. "I will send him to Nadia. He will be safe in the wolf compound."

* * * *

"Compound?" She knew everything was sending her into a meltdown, but damn it!

"Gated community," Quinn said. "We call it a compound. Not all Undying live that way, but we are wolves and feel most comfortable in a pack. Everyone has their own space, and yet we are close enough to feel comfortable."

"But you live in the city," Haven said. "And in a high rise."

"I am still, as of the moment, unbonded. My *treòir* can make the unbonded women nervous."

She tugged at her bottom lip with her teeth as she shifted on the seat. "That's were Nadia is, right?"

"Yes."

She brushed hair out of her face and tucked it behind her ear. "All right, how much power are we talking about living there?"

"Two ancient males, an Undying fae, several warriors, and a few youths," Quinn said. "Liam and Seth, the Adalwolf twins, can be there quickly if called. It is the safest place on the planet—unless Maverick decides to make a bunker under the earth."

"All right," Haven said as she blew out a breath. "Bastian can stay there for a while. I…" She ground her teeth together and twisted to see Bastian in the back seat. "You're sure you're all right with this?"

"Yeah," he said. "It's not like you'd take me on a honeymoon with you. They are Dov's clan. He says I'll be okay," he said while pointing at his temple.

She settled herself back in her seat and reached over to grab Quinn's hand. She couldn't imagine having to do any of this by herself. "We'll do that. He'll be safe and we can…do what we do."

Quinn squeezed her hand. "It's going to be all right. I won't allow it not to be."

She believed him and let that calm her. Only yesterday, she had thought she'd run out of options, but they kept opening up for her. Possibly it was wrong to want someone to help her, but she needed to have security in her life. Quinn offered that.

Nikon met them in the garage. He yipped and snapped at Quinn's hand as he scrambled to get closer to Haven. *"You let Mason get near her! None of you can leave this place again without me. She could have been hurt! She could have been killed!"*

Haven reached out a trembling hand. "I'm all right. How is Medea?"

Nikon snorted at her. *"My mate is perfectly well. She was safe with me."* He rounded on Quinn and snapped at him. *"The meirlock got too close to her."*

Quinn's brow quirked up. "Careful there, or I am going to think you like her more than me."

Nikon growled low. *"Her life is a little more fragile than yours, and she won't go Godzilla on the city if something happens to you."*

"Touché," Quinn said. "I want to get them inside and settled as quickly as possible. Get the door while Bastian and I start unloading bags."

Nikon stood there staring at Quinn for a long heartbeat before he went over to the elevator and touched his nose to the call button.

Haven ignored Quinn and helped get the piles of bags into the elevator. It was starting to look like everyone and everything wouldn't fit, but they managed to squeeze in. Her breasts were mashed up against Quinn's front as they stood way too close to be comfortable, especially with Bastian in there with them. "You're doing this on purpose," she whispered to him.

Quinn only chuckled. "It was all a diabolical plot."

"You're impossible," she said.

"Agreed." He winked at her as the door opened.

Medea was waiting for everyone. She gave them all a thorough sniff down before she allowed the bags to be carried in. She pranced around Quinn and kept nudging at his hand.

"Are you all right?" Haven asked her as she put the last of the food into the cabinet. Winter did offer the benefit of cold weather. One didn't have to worry about perishables left in the car when your boyfriend decided you needed mall retail therapy.

"You are worried for your foster cub. Your worry is making me nervous."

Haven put the last box away, crouched down next to Medea, and lightly petted her head. "He was all I had, and I was the one he depended on. I feel like I am somehow hurting him by handing him off to someone else."

"He is in safe hands with the Undying fae. Nadia will care well for him, and it is good to expand his pack."

Haven buried her fingers in Medea's fur for a moment before standing up to make sure everything was exactly where she wanted it. "I know that logically. It's the letting go part I'm having trouble with. And what's an Undying fae?"

"A fae is a powerful creature not unlike an elf, though they have different capabilities and are not as long-lived."

Haven nodded. "She went through the conversion then, didn't she? Before she bonded to Riordan?"

"Aye. But she had more difficulty. The fae are closely related to elves. Their bodies must change more before the process is completed."

Haven was ready to ask another question when Quinn came into the room. She patted the top of Medea's head. "We'll talk later. " Then she went to Quinn. "I guess he's ready."

"You can visit him every day if you wish," Quinn said before wrapping his arms around her.

She held him tight for a long moment. "I know. This is just hard for me."

"You can go with him and get him settled in," Quinn offered.

She shook her head and took a step back. "He wants to go on his own, and I need to start letting him."

"All right, then let's do this."

Haven checked Bastian's backpack to make sure he had everything he could need and then handed it back to him. She gave him a tight hug before everyone filed into the portal room.

Quinn showed both of them how to use a pair of stones to open a portal. "It can only link to other places with the same stones and design," he explained. "Whereas Memphis can open a portal anywhere to anyplace."

She gave a wane smiled before she hugged Bastian tight and stepped back from him. "Have fun and remember to call me, all right?"

Bastian bent down and kissed her temple. "You are doing what's good for both of us. No need to feel guilty."

She squeezed his hand and sniffled. "Go, before I change my mind."

Bastian looked at her for a long moment before he stepped through the portal and it closed behind him.

"Quinn!" Her heart plummeted to her feet.

"It works differently than Memphis's," Quinn said. "The design is for emergency safety. It only allows one being through at a time."

She bobbed her head as she walked into him.

His arms enveloped her as the feel of his *treòir* settled around her. Both the man and his power helped her to cope with Bastian growing up.

* * * *

Donovan hung up the phone. He'd transferred all his Undying responsibilities to Sloan of the Pacific Tribe and Darius of the Atlantic Tribe. His dealings with humans had been handed over to his club managers and Wolf until after he was safely bonded. He finally had time to focus all of his attention on Haven.

That was until he got the funny tickle behind his ears he always got right before a lifebond under his roof was about to do something to make his brain hurt.

Wonderful!

His *treòir* always alerted him to the antics of lifebonds before their plans got out of hand. They did the damnedest things in the name of their mate. Only, he hadn't said or done anything to cause Haven worry.

"You better go check on her," the *treòir* said with a slight smug tone Donovan didn't trust at all. *"Wolf did tell her you might give me up."*

"Shit!" He was out of his leather executive-back chair like a shot. There was no telling what Haven might be capable of doing to preserve the life of her mate.

When he threw the door open, Haven leaped at him. He closed his arms around her.

Before he had any chance to figure out what was happening, her legs wrapped around his waist as her body stretched up along his torso. "Hi. Do you know how badly I wanted to do exactly this when I first saw you

Emma Weylin

last night?" Her arms hooked around his neck. Her body pressed tightly against his.

He groaned as he stumbled forward a step. They slammed into the wall across the hall, his arms absorbing the impact, before Quinn was able to regain his equilibrium. Every neuron in his brain was short-circuiting. For the life of him, he couldn't find a word to utter that would come out in a coherent stream of consonants and vowels. His only recourse was to growl at her.

She laughed a soft soothing sound. Then her hips shifted to lock against his. Her tight little body shivered as her eyes dilated. "I get the *feeling* you're happy I did this."

Blood of Oberon! What the hell had gotten into her? Before he'd sent her upstairs, she'd been skittish of the entire process of bonding, and now… Hell, now he wasn't sure he cared why she'd suddenly went from cautious and confused to—to—sex kitten.

She lightly nipped at the hollow of his throat.

He wanted to believe this change in her was because she wanted him. It would be so easy to give into the painful desire making his body throb and strain against the fabric of his jeans. But he couldn't. He used his hips to pin her up against the wall and planted both of his hands on either side of her head. "Haven," he gritted out. He lowered his head in that familiar way and dragged his mouth along her jaw line. "Why?"

She captured his face with her hands and lightly touched her lips to his. "Live in the moment with me, Quinn." She gave him a feather light, tantalizing taste of her lips. "Forget the world for a little while."

"Haven." Her name came out in a rasp of sound. He used his head to tilt hers back to give him access to her throat. "I love how you smell." Her soft hair brushed along his forearms, further inflaming his desire. She was intoxicating. Her scent. The feel of her body pressed against his. The purr in her moan as his mouth moved over hers. It should have been easy to give into her desire, if only for a moment, but there were dangers out there. He needed to keep alert. Her life depended on his strength.

"Quinn," she whispered his name. Her body rippled along the length of him. "I want you."

He groaned. He shifted his hold and trapped the back of her head with one of his hands to hold her exactly where he wanted her. "Need you." He jerked back and growled at her. *Oberon!* He wanted to bury himself inside of her and stay for as long as she'd let him, but something wasn't adding up about Mason. Until he figured it out, her life was in danger. No matter what his needs were, they could wait until she was safe. "Haven."

He dropped his head onto her shoulder. "I—I'm sorry. Memphis isn't the only one who can open portals. I need to be on guard."

She let out a soft little sigh. "No, my Quinn. For once, being on guard is the last thing you need to be."

Chapter 9

Quinn's eyes flared in a blood red glow.

"You moron!" Haven heard a distinctly separate voice roar. *"Our lifebond wanted to mate with us and you denied her? What in the name of Avalon is wrong with you?"*

Quinn's grip on her went painfully tight before he let her go, and she slipped down the wall.

"If Mason is working with a Storm, you'd let lust make her vulnerable to attack?" Quinn's voice snarled back.

Pain ripped through his head, making it feel like his skull was going to split in two. She felt his pain as if it were her own. He wrapped both hands around his head as he sank onto the floor. Every time Bastian had gotten into an altercation with the power growing inside of him, he'd reacted in just this way—only his eyes had glowed silver.

Ha!

She knew what to do. Quinn's power might not listen to her, but at least she might be able to help ease the headache so Quinn wouldn't suffer.

She darted forward and got down close to the floor where Quinn was half curled and now lying on the floor. She shifted around him and gently lifted his head into her lap. His blood red, glowing gaze met hers. She was now dealing with his power. As much as it should make her afraid, it didn't. The *treòir* just needed to back off. "You need to calm down," she said in a stern tone. "I know Quinn was a very bad boy for not having sex with me right this second, but I think it's very sweet he'd deny himself so that I am safe."

The floor under them rumbled. Quinn's eyes flashed between red and gold before they flared gold and then faded back to his usual ice blue. He blinked a few times and then slowly sat up. He rubbed at his temple as he moved around in the hall to prop himself up against the wall. His head cocked, and then a slow smile curved his mouth. "Imagine that," he said in that voice that always made her knees quiver. "You just defeated one of the stronger powers in this world. My head thanks you."

"Defeated?" No. She hadn't meant to do that. "It's all right? I didn't hurt it, did I?"

"He's all right." His usual smooth tones gritty. "He's off sulking."

"Sulking? Your *treòir* is sulking?" Oh, man. The man oozed sex at that moment. She couldn't get over how focused and intense his gaze was on her. She had the distinct urge—no, need—to ask him to take his shirt off. If he kept staring at her like she was the only salvation for his soul, she was going to climb into his lap and demand he sedate the fire burning in her blood.

"Haven," he murmured. "What changed?"

She winced and settled on the opposite wall. "You noticed that, huh?"

"Uh, yeah." He stretched his legs out at an angle across the hall. "I was pretty sure it was going to take a century to get you to trust me."

"My father once told me the Black Rose was started by a man named Cadeyrn." She felt heat infuse her cheeks. "I connected the dots. I'm the heiress to the Black Rose, and it's *your* organization. It only makes sense the universe would throw us together." She looked at him again from under her lashes. "And Nikon said I'm your type."

His laugh was deep and vibrated through her. "I see. So then—"

"Yes," she said quickly and stood up. "I just tried to jump your bones, Mr. Donovan. You are one hot man and you're all mine."

* * * *

Donovan drew in a shuttering breath. He'd never been more terrified in his life. For the first time he could do exactly what Haven wanted him to do and forget the world and its needs. It was something he had never risked before—but he wanted to now. He wanted more than anything to lose himself in her sweet feminine scent and soft curves. He couldn't let himself go that far—not yet. Not when a mistake on his part would cause Haven her life.

Haven turned to face the living room. "Um, well, that is, our food should be here soon. I'll take Nikon and go down to the lobby."

"You want her," the *treòir* said. *"I will guard."*

Donovan shoved up to his feet and gently wrapped his hand around her wrist. "Haven. It's not that I…"

She turned, but her expression was unreadable. "I can… I hear it—him and you—talking. Look, I know what big boys and girls do together, and your desire is obvious." She coughed and covered a smile with her hand. "I just don't know how to react to you denying yourself for my…benefit."

Mason was going to die a slow and painful death. He reached in the door of his office to snag his wallet off the walnut file cabinet. "I'll go down with you. Seven-eighths of what we ordered is mine anyway." He put his hand out for her.

She stared at his hand for so long goose flesh bumped on his skin before she slid her hand into his. "I don't understand. Why? When you don't have to?"

He let go of her hand and hooked his arm around her neck, wishing he could have protected her. "He hurt you." He didn't want details—knew it was better if he never got the details, but he would acknowledge he knew and understood that she'd been mistreated by Mason. "He will never touch you again."

She curled one of her arms around him. "What am I to you?"

"I don't understand the question."

She pulled away from him. Her hand slid down his arm; her fingers entwined with his. "To my grandfather, I am the broodmare who will produce the next Killian heir. To Mason, I am his connection to power. What am I to you?"

"Haven," he murmured her name. "You are my haven." His eyes burned with the double meaning of her name. "My sanctuary... The person I hope I can turn too when I...need."

"Wow. We need to get that food because I swear I'm going to demand you hurt someone if we have to deal with anymore interruptions." Her laugh held a sweet giddy kind of nervous. "How can you say something like that when we barely know each other?"

"You are correct. We need no more interruptions." He tugged her gently toward the door. "I want what my brother has with Nadia." His voice went low and gruff. "I want what my—my parents had. I won't get it if I mistreat you or put a value on you for being anyone other than who you are."

"Careful," she said as she padded behind him on her sock-covered feet toward the elevator. "Keep talking like that and I'll have no choice but to fall in love with you."

He hit the button to call the elevator. He studied her in profile. "Well, then, what am I to you?"

Her face scrunched up in an adorable way as she twisted away from him but didn't let go of his hand. "I don't know. I don't have the same eloquent words you have for me."

"Then what do you want from me?"

Her body stilled. Her eyes closed. The silvery cadence of her voice went dreamy. "I want a man who loves me." Her eyes opened, and she tilted her head to look at him. "That's it. Someone who looks at me and sees Haven, not the Black Rose." The doors slid open. "Quinn, can you love me?"

He nudged her into the space and hit the button for the ground floor. His hand trembled as he reached out and tenderly turned her head so she had to look at him. "Aye. I will love you."

* * * *

Her heart hammered in her chest. No wonder Riordan told Bastian bonding only took a week. When they got down to business, these Undying men really knew how to break down any defense a woman might want to throw at them. "So, teach me how to talk the way the wolves do with each other."

His body tensed. Fear hit his eyes before he physically shook it off. His voice came out in an unsteady rhythm. "No, not here, not right now, Haven, please. I really just don't think I can handle that when we have only a minute or so before we'll be interrupted again."

She bit the corner of her lip in a coy smile. "Oh, right, it would feel the same as when we read each other."

He moved to the other side of the elevator. "I want to be inside of you."

He was too cute. The poor man was in sore need. Boy, was she going to have fun with him. "I think I'd like to try that."

"Haven," he grumbled and then shot out of the elevator when the door opened.

She couldn't hold back the laugh as she followed him into the lobby. "You're making this too easy."

His eyes went hot as they moved over her. "I assure you, just as soon as I get our dinner, things will get much harder."

She canted her head and lowered her voice so the doorman wouldn't hear her. "I don't know. Things look pretty hard from where I'm standing."

"Haven!"

"Mr. Donovan," the man at the front desk said in a respectful tone. "I was just about to call you." He leaned to the side and blinked a few times. "Is that a woman with you?"

"No, Alfred," Donovan said with a straight face.

The older man's expression went annoyed before a smile bloomed over his craggy and wrinkled appearance. "Who is the lucky lady? And I presume she is your lady, since I've never seen you bring a woman in or out before who isn't related to you." Alfred produced a bag with red Chinese symbols from behind the desk and handed it to Donovan.

He took the bag and handed Alfred payment for the meal. "This is my Haven. Haven, this is Alfred."

"It's nice meeting you," Haven said.

"The pleasure is all mine, I'm sure." He winked at her. "Take good care of Mr. Donovan for us. He is a generous man."

"Thank you," Donovan said.

"I will," Haven promised as Donovan herded her back to the elevator. "He seems nice."

"He is," Donovan said and hit the button to call back the elevator. "I wouldn't let any other type of man work here."

"Oh?" Haven stepped into the elevator when the doors opened.

"I have two hundred and fifteen units in this building. Half of them house single women." A hard edge entered his tone as he moved in next to her. "I need to be able to trust the security I have in this building." He stood there looking at the key pad for a moment after the door closed, and then one of his brows winged up. "You know, it just occurred to me. You need the combination and a key." He instructed her on how to unlock access to the top floor and what the combination of buttons were to push. "We'll stop by the hardware store tomorrow to get you your own key."

Haven snorted. "Am I ever going to need one?"

"It's the gesture that counts. You live with me, and you are technically free to come and go as you please."

"Technically? But not really." She had a sinking feeling she wasn't going to like what came out of his mouth next.

"As of the moment? You're on what we call lockdown. You're not permitted to go anywhere without me or one of the other ancient males I've cleared until the threats with Mason and Kyros are eliminated."

That didn't seem quite as horrible as being locked away in Quinn's tower apartment. "And after?"

He shrugged. "Nikon or Medea will accompany you whenever you go out."

"Not even a dog can go with me everywhere." Quinn thought she'd need a bodyguard when not with him. That was probably true, since he was a king of an entire race of people.

His tone was all business. "We already have the kinks worked out. You need to understand that you cannot leave without Nikon or a warrior guarding you, even when the lockdown has been lifted. Your safety depends on it."

"Does this mean I am allowed to open another belly dance studio once Mason is under control?"

He dropped the bag of food. "If that's what you want to do."

"Really? I can have my own studio to teach other people belly dance again?" Excitement bubbled up. She'd give just about anything to have her own studio again. "You'd really let me do that?"

He swallowed hard before he stooped down and picked up the bag of food. "We'll figure out the best way to make it happen after we've bonded."

She crooked a finger at him and motioned for him to come closer. "Come down here where I can kiss you." Quinn dutifully bent down. She kissed his cheek. Then she giggled and turned around in a small victory dance.

Maybe she was silly, but she'd mostly been testing what Quinn would and wouldn't allow her to do. She loved being a girl, and there was nothing more feminine in her mind than her ability to dance. Middle Eastern dance was a celebration of all things female, and Mason had taken it away the second her grandfather wanted her to marry him because he believed Western culture had turned it, like everything else, into a sex act. She was going to get her dancing back without having to fight. "You have no idea how much this means to me."

Quinn cleared his throat and his mouth went crooked. "I think I can guess."

The elevator door opened.

Haven was bouncing on the balls of her feet as she exited. "I promise I'll let you help me find the right building, and I'll listen to whatever security measures you think are needed. You won't regret it."

"Haven." His tone took on a growl.

Her excitement ebbed as she stilled. His eyes were dark, and she got tinges of the anger building inside of him. "Yes?"

He lowered his head so his cheek rested against hers. "I appreciate you taking into account my needs with your chosen profession."

She involuntarily leaned into the heat his body produced. "I love dancing," she whispered. "Mason never allowed me to."

The growl went deeper as he righted himself. "You don't need my permission to live your life. Mates have the responsibility to allow what the other needs to thrive. There is much Mason will pay for. He had no right to take anything away from you."

Then she understood his anger. She lightly touched the side of his face with the tips of her fingers. The way he phrased it made her tingle down

Emma Weylin

to her toes. He wasn't putting the responsibility of their survival squarely on his broad shoulders.

"Maybe not," she murmured. "But I don't want to think about Mason." She went into the apartment. "Can you start a fire in the fireplace?"

"Haven…"

She moved farther into the living room and turned to face him. "I don't care if you're having visions of your own harem dancer or you actually understand what my dancing is for me. You didn't question me, and you didn't act like it was your God given right to control me just because you have a penis and I don't." She bit the corner of her lip and wrung her hands together. "I do get the difference between a good relationship and bad one. I want to focus on what could be the most fantastic relationship of my life instead of the one that nearly destroyed me."

* * * *

Donovan went to the stack of wood near the fireplace and started arranging logs in the large stone structure. It was counterproductive to think about Mason. The knowledge that some animal had abused his mate exploded like a grenade in his gut.

He needed to pull himself out of this tailspin, or he'd end up pissing off Haven in the worst way. There were enough complications. He could already feel the building need to change her into an Undying so he'd never lose her. It wasn't something he wanted to risk, and the more he learned about his mate, the more desperate his need to keep her safe. He shook it off with a growl as he lit the logs to flame the easy way—with magic. He cocked his head. She set up a cozy nest out of pillows and blankets next to the fire place big enough for two.

Donovan realized he needed to let go of micromanaging everything. There were powerful men out there patrolling the area around the building. The Cadfaels of other regions had been brought in. His brothers and the other Cadens were close. He and Haven were as safe as the Undying could make them, and he needed to let that be enough.

He could not wait to see what his woman looked like in nothing but her hair. More than the fire was making him hot as she returned. He pulled off his shirt in reaction and tossed it on the back of the recliner.

She bit the tip of her tongue and then grinned at him. "Now we're getting somewhere." She went to the coffee table where he left the food and set down a pair of plates, utensils, two goblets, and a bottle of wine. When she was facing him again, her gaze moved over his torso. Heat flushed her cheeks. "You sit first."

He lowered his tone. "Anything else need to come off first?"

Her head canted to the side as she assessed the length of him. "Lose the boots." Her eyes met his. "We'll start there."

He sauntered over to the recliner and sat down to take off his boots slowly. He never took his gaze from her face. Then he stood up and tipped his head toward the spot she'd made for them next to the fireplace. "And you want me there."

"Yes."

"Where are you going to be?"

"Just sit." A mysterious smile curved her mouth before she hesitantly went for the bag of food and wine on the coffee table. "I'll be right back. Just—stay there."

He enjoyed the sway of her hips as she walked away from him while he stretched out on the floor, propped up by the pillows she'd arranged. He wasn't sure if it was for his comfort or hers. His body wound tight with anticipation.

"You've done this before," Treòir intoned. *"Why is this taking so long?"*

Donovan dragged a hand over his face and ignored his power. It didn't need to know anything about how to make love to a woman. Besides, he had more important things to worry about.

What the hell was taking *her* so long?

He wanted her. More than he'd ever wanted to be with another woman. If she hadn't instructed him to stay, he'd be up prowling the apartment looking for her. She'd be back. Her intentions vibrated through the penthouse. The woman wanted him.

Before he could let his thoughts pull him away from where his focus was supposed to be, the lights went out. His head jerked to the door between the dining room and living room. He hadn't heard her come back. The lapse of total awareness of his surroundings was totally lost to the sight before him.

There, illuminated by the flicking firelight as it danced and played off the metal surfaces of the weapons hanging on the walls, was Haven. Gone was the teeny shirt that barred him from viewing her slender ribcage. Gone were the pants hiding the exquisite shape of her legs. Her feet were tiny, sexy as hell, and bare. The only scrap of fabric on her body was a wisp of silk and lace between her legs, held on by a flimsy bit of string. Her glorious hair hung down around her, concealing the shape of her body and keeping all but the tiniest peek of her magnificent rounded breasts hidden from his view.

He groaned.

Sweet mother of Oberon! He'd died and somehow managed to find himself in heaven. "Haven?" It wasn't his voice rasping out—or was it?

She padded closer a step. "I—I thought we could start with dessert."

He rose off the floor and walked the distance between them. The tips of his fingers skimmed along her shoulders before he shoved her hair back, revealing those perfect breasts. His head lowered to let his lips trace along her jaw line just before his mouth savagely took hers, but it wasn't enough. He needed to be embedded inside her. With one swift motion he scooped her up into his arms, carried her over to the blankets, and laid her down. He moved his gaze over her body as he followed her. Breaths tore out of him in ragged gasps as he fought to control the burning hunger breaking him apart. Then he was on her. He didn't leave any part of her body untouched. Her body arched up to eagerly meet him. Her hands branded his skin as they moved feather light across his flesh.

"Need to be inside of you." He groaned the words. A heartbeat later, he managed to extract her from the panties without shredding the delicate fabric. Getting his own pants off hadn't fared as well for the leather belt or denim. He froze over her. How he'd found a smidgen of control he didn't know he had, but he was glad for it. She needed gentle. By Oberon's eternal fire he was going to find it for her. He'd lose his sanity if she kept touching him like this. With a deft move, he pinned her arms above her head with one hand. "Don't...touch," he gritted out between tastes of her mouth. "Can't...handle it." His free hand slid over her breasts, down her belly, and to the soft, damp mound at the apex of her legs. "Need you"—his mouth teased a taught nipple—"to come."

Her back arched as he slipped a finger deep in her core. The sound of her pleasure filled his ears and nearly had him coming right then. He shoved another finger inside of her. Her moan turned ragged. He found the sensitized nub in the folds of her sex and flicked the pad of his thumb over it. He let go of her wrists to sit back on his heels to watch her body as she moved to his rhythm in the firelight.

One of her hands fisted in the pillow beside her head, the other in the blanket under her. Her body rippled as she tightened around his fingers.

He used that moment to slide an arm under her hips and position her right at the angle he wanted her in. He used a knee to push her legs farther apart and then impaled her.

The moment her climax shattered through her, Haven's mind brushed against his. He was powerless to stop their consciousnesses from sliding into each other. Donovan felt every mind numbing, sweetly erotic moment of her climax. The shockwaves quivered through them both. His gaze locked onto hers as he sank into her body.

"Haven," he rasped out. His body stilled.

She wrapped her legs around his waist, pulling him in deeper, cradling his hips against hers. One of his hands cupped the back of her head and the other the side of her face. His breathing came out in harsh gasps.

"Let it go," she whispered.

"Can't." Sweat beaded on his brow, his forearms, and along his spine. "I don't want to hurt you."

"You won't."

Her breath caressed along his throat. It was too much of his energy all at once. There was no way she'd be able to survive. Hell! There was no way he was going to survive the essence of Haven tingling along his insides. He'd never felt a woman the way he was feeling her. He'd never given a woman so much of himself. He couldn't keep holding himself back, but he was afraid of what it would do to her. She was so tiny and delicate and perfect. He didn't want anything to cause her pain.

"I want all of you."

The strength he had snapped. He held onto her as tightly as he dared. His body surged into hers. With each thrust, he brought them both closer to shattering and then bound them tighter together again. She seeped into his bones. He knew everything about this woman there was to know. He feared what such a complete and full knowledge of him would do to her. He couldn't stop himself, and it terrified him.

There was that one tortured moment when everything that made up both of them was going to be suspended in that one second of time where, if something didn't explode, they would both perish. Then sweet release ripped through them in a shattering wave of excellence.

Her scream of pleasure lingered in the air.

Donovan was lucid enough to roll to the side before his arms gave out. He puffed for what felt like an eternity, trying to regain his breath. He turned onto his back and pulled Haven up on top of him. It took up the last of the energy he had. Her body was damp and limp above him. "Haven?"

She made a soft, purring sound. "Yeah?"

His jaw worked. They were connected. No longer inside of each other—but still blissfully connected. He relaxed some. "What the hell did you do to me?"

Her head drooped to the side. "The same thing you did to me, I hope."

His arm tightened around her. "You still okay with being trapped with me forever?"

She stuck her tongue out at him and then snuggled in against his chest. "If you don't know what kind of wonderful man you are after living with yourself for the last twenty-five hundred years, I'm not going to tell you."

He barked out a laugh. "I'll take that as a yes."

She kissed his chest. "Fabulous. Now, if you don't mind, I am quite enjoying being all cuddly with you like this. Don't ruin it by worrying. We can analyze it after I wake up."

He found the strength needed to lightly run the tips of his fingers along the column of her spine. "Rest, my sweet Haven."

Within moments, her breathing evened out as her body fully relaxed in his arms. The power of his *treòir* settled around them both in a warm buzz of happy energy. Donovan slipped into sleep without remembering to do a perimeter check.

Chapter 10

Donovan slowly came aware of his surroundings. The fire reduced to glowing embers. Spears of waxing sunlight filtered into the room through slits between the fabric adorning the windows. Nikon's soft snoring was the only sound in the room. Haven's earthy, sweet scent was all around him. Her hair draped over his chest, wrapping him in a softness he adored. Her warm body still snuggled against him.

He felt…rested. The weariness he'd felt bone deep was gone. He shifted into a half-upright position careful not to disturb the woman sleeping on top of him. His arm banded tightly around her as a fierce and lethal protectiveness invaded every molecule of his being.

This much he was expecting, but their joining had been different. Something was unusual. There was supposed to be an intensity, but they'd collided with mind-to-mind contact. All the bits and tendrils for either of them weren't all back in exactly the right places they belonged. He could feel her essence inside of him. The sensation wasn't unpleasant—it actually felt damn good. He'd known his parents were always linked at some level, but he wasn't sure if the inability to disconnect from her was natural.

He needed to contact Riordan. He'd have the answers Donovan wanted. With a quick glance at the wall clock, he sighed. Dawn barely broke the horizon. Nadia wouldn't be happy with this early of an intrusion. Too bad. She'd have to deal.

"Riordan?"

"Everything all right?" The reply was quick, almost as if he'd been waiting for Donovan to contact him.

"Something…weird happened last night." He explained as much as he knew Haven would be comfortable giving another male.

"It might be normal for you, since you're the Cadeyrn," Riordan said after several moments. *"But you know the guidelines. If it doesn't feel evil, then it's probably not."*

Oberon's blood! He never could do anything the easy way, now could he?

"You're sure you've never encountered this with another bonding? Maybe Kenneth mentioned something before the time-shift?" Kenneth was the first Wolf Healer of the Undying. His age easily doubled Donovan's. Something like this had to have happened before. However if there was anyone left alive who would remember or could explain it was another question.

"I have to check my journals. If he did mention something, it will take a while to find," Riordan said.

"All right." Donovan ended the connection. Not all of Riordan's journals survived into this time. A good portion of them were preserved in Brogan's dragon cave, but not all of them.

Haven made a soft moaning sound. Her skin glided against his as she stretched. One of her eyes opened and then the other. A smile graced her face. "It's already morning?"

"Aye." He tried to keep the gravel note out of his voice. Hell. He wanted her, but he wasn't sure sex was the best action to take until he figured out what was going on between them. Connection was good. The inability to completely disconnect might not be.

Her bottom lip poked out in a pout. "Can't you ban morning when I want to stay here with you—just like this for a little while longer?"

He rested his cheek on the top of her head. Haven's body next to his was heaven and hell. When he should be figuring out Mason and the unusual bond he'd forged with her, he was content to stay next to her. "I can't stop the sun from coming up."

She snorted and then tilted her head back. Her mouth was turned up in an impish grin. "So get a morning home on the West Coast and have Memphis open a portal for us."

"You're distracting." He growled the words, but his hand moved lightly across the skin on her back.

She leaned up and took his bottom lip into her mouth before she pushed off his chest to straddle over him. "Excellent." Then she slipped off him to stand. Her hair fell down around her in a beautiful cascade of fiery sunlit waves. "No girl wants her man to be able to easily extract himself from her the morning after." She sashayed over to the recliner. "That would be insulting." Her impish grin went wicked. "I'd make you breakfast in the buff, but since you're worried, I'll take it easy on you today—you might not fare so well tonight." She slipped his shirt over her head and pulled it down before flipping her hair out of the collar. "Re-heated Chinese coming up." She picked up the unused plates off the coffee table and walked out of the living room like she owned the place.

Donovan dragged a hand down his face. He was sweating. A perpetual hard-on was his until the end of time. How was he supposed to concentrate on anything if she was going to walk around naked? The only reason he was able to drag his ass off the floor was because she wasn't in the same room with him anymore. He couldn't ever remember following a woman around like a puppy. He snagged his jeans and huffed when he realized he'd torn the zipper getting out of them last night. He shrugged and just let them ride low on his hips.

"Something's coming!" the *treòir* roared in his head.

His body stilled as he felt a vibration through the air. *Shit!* He was moving by the time the kitchen flashed with a vibrant purple light. Haven screamed as the sound of ceramics crashed on the floor. Donovan ran into the kitchen with the wolves on his heels.

Donovan skidded to a stop at the kitchen door. "Haven, don't move. I don't want you getting cut."

She made a soft whimpering sound as her head bobbed up and down. "There is a tiny purple woman hovering over the counter."

He didn't have to look to know who was invading his home. Laila. Maybe he'd finally be able to get some answers about exactly how and why his people were two thousand years ahead of their time. "Don't talk to her. I'll be right back." It took him seconds to grab his boots and get them on before he was back in the kitchen. His sharp gaze tracked around the room.

Laila was the epitome of a beautiful pixie creature. She had the perfect Tinker Bell hourglass figure with large innocent eyes, sharp, pointed ears and a round angelic face. Dragonfly wings fluttered, keeping her above the counter top at a hover.

He moved slowly and with great precision into the room. He scooped Haven up and sat her on the countertop near the pixie. "I've been trying to contact you for fifty years. What the hell are we doing here? How did we get here? Can we get back? Where are my missing people? Start talking."

Laila huffed at him. She stepped off the side of the counter as her body grew to roughly the size of a ten-year-old girl. Her wings beat faster than the eye could see to keep her hovering. "I don't have time for this. I am dealing with a huge problem in Atlantis right now. If I don't get back to it soon, we won't recover from the cataclysm."

Donovan ran his hands down Haven's legs before he inspected the bottom of her feet to make sure she hadn't stepped on any broken pieces of the plates or been cut by a stray shard. "Then what the hell are you doing here now?"

"Your mother's pendant. Your Reannon needs it. The power inside rightfully belongs to her." Laila held out her diminutive hand with her fist closed and facing down.

Haven reached for the necklace.

Donovan wrapped his large hand around Haven's to keep her from touching the foreign object. He trusted Laila only to an extent. Haven's life was something he would never willingly risk. "Do not accept pixie gifts until you know for sure what they are." He put his other hand out instead.

Laila didn't seem offended by his assessment of her trustworthiness and opened her hand to drop the ancient jewelry into his palm. "You will have to guide her in how to use it. Now I must go."

"Laila wait!" he roared, but the room was already awash with the vibrant purple glow before a light flashed.

Quinn coiled his body tightly around hers. "I think she's gone. Just because they feel gone doesn't mean they are."

Haven drew in several deep breaths before she pushed lightly at his chest.

Another thirty seconds passed before his muscles relaxed and thirty more before he unwound himself from her body. He dropped the necklace on the counter and captured her face between his hands. His mouth took hers with savage possession before he pulled back. "Are you hurt?"

"No," she said on a dreamy sigh. Her pale green eyes fluttered a few times before her gaze focused. "What was that all about?"

He studied her, making sure nothing nefarious had happened before he let her go and went back to the necklace sitting on the countertop a few feet away from her. He turned the silver wolf head pendant and chain over in his hand. He clenched his fist around it. "I believe this belonged to my mother."

"Hello?" She waved at him. "Yeah, hi, um, what's going on?"

He rubbed at the back of his neck and examined the necklace again. "Confirmation you're the Reannon, the Queen of all the Undying. It's yours as soon as I have Maverick and Brogan check it out to make sure it's safe."

She sputtered. "This is real? Quinn, that's—" She dragged in several rapid breaths. If he didn't do something, she was going to hyperventilate.

Donovan moved in front of her. His large hands rested on her hips. He was cheek to cheek with her. "Breathe, baby, breathe. You're all right."

"How can I be the queen?" she demanded. "I haven't balanced a check book in over four years. I kind of caught that yesterday, but you want me to be their queen? Quinn, I am going to die. I can't be their queen!"

Donovan's quandary went exponential. Conversion would kill his Haven. Not converting her into an Undying would eventually lead to her death. Laila didn't lightly gift the kind of power imbued into the stone suspended in the necklace. He absently turned the ring around his right index finger Laila had given him two thousand years ago when he'd acquired Cadeyrn status. All the power once embedded into the ring was now a part of him and a part of his *treòir*. The ring itself was useless except for its sentimental value. The power of Cadeyrn, added to his own and that of the *treòir*, made him the most powerful being currently to walk the Earth.

"You are already their queen," he murmured. "I—I know you're human. I'm sorry." He backed away from her and shoved the necklace into his pocket. Needing to be doing anything else than have this discussion with her, he went to work cleaning up broken plates on the floor.

"Quinn." Her voice hitched up. She slipped off the counter and took a step toward him.

"Don't move!" he roared at her.

She froze. "I know you're afraid."

"You don't know anything!" He reached over and snatched the garbage can from its place and slammed it down on the floor next to where he worked. The metal side cracked.

"Quinn..."

"We are not discussing this."

"Yes," she yelled at him, "we are."

"Haven—"

"I wasn't expecting this," she rushed on. "I reacted badly, but it did bring something up that we need to talk about. Nikon told me you would be difficult to convince to change me."

"He's right." He finished picking up all the large pieces and went to get a broom. "We are not discussing this."

"Why?" She took another step toward him.

He snarled at her. "I told you not to move!"

"If I want to step on bits of broken pottery, that's my business. You will not talk to me this way."

His head lifted and his lip curled. "I am controlling my temper, woman. Do not push me right now."

* * * *

Pushing him was exactly what she needed to do. It was insane, and probably dangerous, but they had to talk about this. The end of her life meant the end of his, and after literally being part of the man last night, in no way would she ever believe Quinn's death was acceptable. "What exactly are you going to do other than bellow at me and try to shake down the building?"

"Haven!" he roared again as the apartment shimmied.

She squeaked and moved back a step against her will. Maybe she wasn't nearly as brave as she thought she was. Quinn was scary as hell when he was yelling like this.

Quinn gritted his teeth together as he doubled over on the floor, his hands clutching his head.

She blew out a breath. His memories were now hers. Quinn had never, not once in his vast years of experience, lashed out at someone in anger he considered unable to defend against his massive physical power.

"Damn idiot," she chided him in a softer tone. She wasn't supposed to talk to the *treòir,* but she had to do something. "You've gone and gotten your power all riled up again." She gingerly worked her way over to him, because getting a tiny bit of pottery stuck in her bare foot wasn't appealing, and got down on the floor next to him. "*Treòir,*" she whispered, "he's upset. Yeah, it's kind of scary to deal with when you compare our size difference, but really, do you honestly think he's going to hurt me?"

"He scared you."

For a moment she had no idea what Quinn was talking about until she realized his eyes had that eerie red glow of the *treòir.* She really wasn't talking to Quinn, but his source of power. She hesitantly put out her hand to stroke the side of his face. "Being yelled at by a man your size is a little scary." She wasn't exactly sure what to say to make this better, but she needed to try. She had no idea exactly what was going on inside of Quinn, though the struggle that she could feel inside of him made her edgy. "Married people argue." She tried a different tactic. Her parents did. Never once had her father hit her mother no matter how bad some of the arguments got. They didn't happen often, but she'd learned two people had to yell at each other sometimes. Shouting didn't mean anyone was going to get hurt. It just meant things were going to be loud for a while.

"It's not always pleasant, and this is something he feels strongly about. I was expecting some yelling."

"He'll kill me to keep from harming you."

"I know he would, and he and I need to work this out. I don't want him—or you—to die any more than either of you want to hurt me." She winced when she realized Quinn had fallen on the dustpan. Trickles of blood trailed down his arm from pieces of the broken plate cut into his arm. "But you did hurt yourself. Come on, let's go get you cleaned and patched while we continue talking about this."

* * * *

Quinn's body trembled as he slowly uncurled himself from the ground and stood up. *Treòir* had absolutely no idea how to handle this. He knew his human, but he'd never had to deal with his human being afraid like this before. The best thing to do was to keep him trapped deep inside where he didn't have to deal with the fear or with the possibility of killing their Haven. He wasn't going to allow a conversion to take her away from them. Keeping the essence of Quinn trapped in the compartment he'd lived in for so long was no easy feat. His head cocked as he assessed the situation. There was still danger to her tender and precious little feet from the broken plates. His hands clamped down around her waist in the next second.

She sucked in a breath. "*Treòir?*"

"Your feet," he said in a tone that didn't sound the same when Quinn used it.

"Oh. Just move me to the doorway, and I'll go get some shoes."

He did exactly as she instructed him. Nikon growled at him as he set her down. She rubbed her sides. "You don't have to hold on so tight next time." She put her hand on Nikon's head. "Stop that. I agree this is weird, but it is what it is. Tell him to go to the powder room, and I'll be right back down to get him patched up."

"*You tell him,*" Nikon said. "*Quinn is already going to skin me for allowing this to happen.*"

"But he doesn't want me talking to his power," Haven said with exasperation in her tone.

"*Yes.*" Nikon did a wolf shrug. "*But his* treòir *likes you, and you were just talking to it.*"

"I'll deal with them, I guess. Just..." She planted her hands on her hips. "You," she said to *Treòir*-Quinn. "Get your ass in the bathroom and wait for me." She stepped closer and looked into his eyes. "Quinn, stop whatever you're doing. I'll get this all worked out, but you're not helping anything by fighting with him."

To *Treòir*'s utter surprise, Quinn stopped struggling. He prowled the back of his mind in much the same way he used to do to Quinn, but making his body follow Haven's command to go into the bathroom was no longer a battle. "Nikon, go with her."

"It's your life," the wolf said and darted up the stairs after Haven.

A few moments later, she had on a fuzzy pair of slippers and was standing next to him in the cramped powder room.

"Let me have a look at your arm," she said in the same silvery tone that had soothed both of them over the last day.

"He can heal himself," *Treòir* said in his gravely tone.

"Then I don't have to worry about infection, but I'd feel better if he wasn't dripping blood all over the place. That has to hurt."

Treòir shrugged. "I guess so."

She shook her head as she opened the cabinet and pulled out a pair of tweezers. She grimaced. "Not that I don't enjoy talking to you, but if I have a chance to save your life, I kind of need to talk to Quinn."

"He'll yell," *Treòir* warned.

"I'm sure he will," she agreed. "But we both know he's not going to hit me." Her eyes went wounded as water collected in them.

Treòir shuttered as a violent flash of her memory tore through him.

There had been no warning. Not even the feel of anger. One moment Haven was begging Mason for her dinner because he enjoyed watching her grovel, and the next she felt the hard sting as the back of his hand connected with the side of her face.

Haven braced her hands on the walls on either side of her. "Whoa, *Treòir*, stop. You'll shake the entire building down."

* * * *

Donovan used the moment to punch back up to the surface. The shaking stopped, and he flattened himself up against the opposite wall. "Haven," he rasped.

She pitched forward, giving him no choice but to catch her. He held on a little tighter than he should have. *Oberon's blood!* This was pure insanity. No wonder lifebonds needed someone hanging around to keep them safe while they bonded. He knew Wolf wouldn't understand. He connected with the one man he knew would. *"Riordan, get your ass here now. Call Memphis if you need, too."* Then he closed off the connection.

"Haven?" he rasped out her name again.

"I'm fine...really, I am...I just..." She wiggled out of his hold. "Let's get your arm cleaned up."

"Riordan will be here in a minute. He can take care of it." His jaw worked for a moment. "Are you all right?"

"Besides my mate freaking out on me and wanting to die, I'm just peachy," she snapped.

"Quinn!" Riordan bellowed when a rattle of wind subsided. "What the hell is going on?"

Haven made a face at him. "You tattled on yourself?"

Donovan worked to keep from yelling so he wouldn't scare her again or make his *treòir* go nuts. "I was twelve years old the last time my power was able to take over like that. Do you have any idea how terrifying it is to be trapped inside your own body? Unable to stop what's going on around you while the part of you that only kills is touching your woman?"

"Quinn!" Riordan bellowed again.

Donovan pushed open the powder room door. "We're in here. Is Memphis with you?"

"Yes. Do you want me to send him away?"

"Not yet. I have something I need checked out. Memphis can take it to Brogan for me." He hooked his arm around Haven as they exited.

Haven shied away from Memphis when they got into the living room. "Sorry," she mumbled and tucked herself up hard against Donovan's side.

"No worries," Memphis said and winked at her. "I understand." Memphis assessed Donovan. The immediate air around Memphis went as icy as his tone. "You have something for me?"

Donovan reached into his pocket and handed him the necklace. "I recently acquired it. Have both Brogan and Maverick take a look before I give it to Haven. I don't want her touching anything possessed with magic until I know she won't be harmed."

Memphis stared down at the item in his hand, and then his gaze snapped to Haven. His sienna eyes streaked with purple lightning. A deep reverent expression softened the hard lines of his face and he bowed deeply. "Reannon. It will be an honor." In the next moment, a spiral of wind twisted around him, and he was gone.

Haven made a squeaking sound even as she relaxed. "See, that kind of thing is just not supposed to happen to me."

"You are my Haven," Donovan said. "He will treat you with more respect and deference than he treats me."

A smile wobbled on her lips. "That's very sweet, but I was talking about how he vanished."

Donovan chuckled. "Memphis doesn't need to open a large portal when he travels alone, unless he's signaling his arrival."

Riordan cleared his throat.

Donovan tensed. "Thanks for coming without the others."

One of Riordan's dark brows winged up. "You sounded upset and confused, not psychotic. I figured one or all three of you were freaking out about something."

"We broached the topic of conversions," Donovan said through clenched teeth.

Riordan winced. "I see. So what happened?"

"He yelled, I wigged, *Treòir* reacted," Haven said.

"That doesn't explain why his arm is bleeding," Riordan said with a true note of concern. "The *treòir* didn't do this to you, did it?"

"No," Haven said quickly. "Some little purple fairy thing showed up to give me the necklace, and I dropped a couple of plates. When *Treòir* reacted, Quinn fell on the floor right in the middle of the mess and cut his arm."

"Don't scare me like that again." Riordan's words came out in a snarl. "I can't save you if your *treòir* is willing to shred you."

"Stop," Haven said. "The goal here is to keep everyone alive and happy." She used an overly cheerful tone. She rubbed at her side. "So why don't we keep the conversation along those lines, shall we?"

"Haven, this could be serious," Riordan said. "A *treòir* would rather kill the man than allow him to harm his lifebond."

She swallowed and put a hand to her stomach. "Yeah, and the man would rather kill the *treòir* than let his lifebond be hurt. I'm not going to say I get it, because I don't, but I can feel Quinn in me. He was yelling and upset. He wasn't going to hurt me, honest. I need to be changed into what he is, but that terrifies him."

"The survival rate isn't high," Riordan said in a somber tone.

"Maybe if I knew exactly what happens during a conversion," Donovan offered.

Riordan blanched. "That would only make it worse."

"How?" Donovan demanded.

"You don't need the details," Riordan said. "If the conversion works, it does, and that's all—"

"The hell that's all I need to know!" he bellowed at his brother. "If you want me to poison the woman with my blood, then you damn well better believe I want to know exactly what happens after that. Why don't our women survive?"

Haven put her hand on his forearm. "We're just talking. There is no need to yell."

He clenched his jaw, but he was no longer shouting. "Riordan, you will tell me."

Riordan paced a few times before he came to stop in front of Donovan. "Haven, why don't you go finish up in the kitchen? Nikon said you'd do the conversion as long as you didn't have to know the details."

She looked between the two brothers before she slowly nodded and hurried off into the kitchen, Nikon right at her heels while Medea stayed with Donovan.

Donovan started picking up the blankets and pillows scattered in front of the fireplace. "It's that bad?"

Riordan helped him with his task. "Her body will have to completely shut down before restarting as Undying."

"No," Donovan said. Riordan made it sound like a simple computer reboot. "You're asking me to kill her."

"Quinn—"

"Don't try to make what I'll be doing sound better than what it actually is. If her body shuts down, she's dead. Now I understand why only twenty-five percent fucking survive. Not even Kenneth could heal death!"

Riordan got right up in Donovan's face. "I did. Nadia lives and she is Undying. Our father did. It's not impossible. You can do this, and Haven will survive."

Donovan ground his teeth together. "Can you guarantee she'll come back?"

"I can't, but—"

"I'm not doing it," he roared. "I am not going to willingly poison her so she can writhe in pain while I watch her die in my arms. I've had to put down too many of our warriors because they killed their own lifebonds. It's not going to happen."

"Helena wasn't Kyros's lifebond, and you know it," Riordan countered.

"Kyros—" He started and then stopped. The apartment shook with the raw anger swirling around him. The man who had once been a brother in arms was now their worst nightmare. "I will be worse than Kyros."

"No," Riordan said. "Kyros's *treòir* would have never left Helena to die like that alone if she'd have been his. Your *treòir* will not let Haven die."

"I can't do this," Donovan said. "I won't do that to Haven. After what she gave me last night…after what we shared. I'm sorry, Riordan. She gave me life. I am not going to take hers away."

Chapter 11

"Quinn?"

Donovan closed his eyes and let her voice wrap around him. The peace that the sound of her voice offered still amazed him. "Yes?"

She padded up behind him and rested her forehead against his back. "It's difficult to do the bonding thing if you're going to avoid me."

He grumbled at the hurt tone. After breakfast, he'd kicked his brother out, then he'd taken refuge in his office. He could lie to himself and say he'd done it to give Haven the space she needed to do whatever women did to get themselves ready for the day, but she was right. He was avoiding her—no, not her—he wanted to be as close to her as possible. He was avoiding having to deal with the fact he wasn't able to give his lifebond what she wanted—what she needed.

Forever.

He turned around from staring out the window as another snow squall fell onto the streets below.

The woman was stunning.

Every time he laid eyes on her, she captivated him. She wore a dress that hugged each delicious curve with soft fabric. The neckline shouldn't have been considered enticing, but his mouth watered anyway. His gaze traveled over her body and down to her waist, then farther down. The skirt of the dress came modestly to just above her knee. Delicate kneecaps were the only skin exposed to him from above knee-high boots. All her glorious hair fell around her, accentuating her beautiful frame. He cupped the side of her face, and lightly brushed the pad of his thumb along her bottom lip. "You should be angry with me."

She moved in closer to him and slipped her arms around his waist. "Would it help if I screamed and cried and acted like a shrew?"

He lowered his head to brush his cheek along the top of her head. He loved the feel of her hair against his skin. "No, not really. I just—

Oberon's blood! I don't know what to do with this. I am failing everyone by not converting you."

She stretched up on her toes to tuck her head up under his chin. "I want you to take me out," she murmured against his skin. "Some place where we can have fun."

His body shivered with the warm caress. "Haven…"

Her arms looped around his neck and held on tighter. "Don't do this to yourself," she whispered. "I asked you to love me, not to live forever."

"If I don't change you, our people lose—"

"Quinn," she said firmly. "Don't focus on what everyone else needs right now. Focus on you." She kissed his stubble. "Focus on me." She pressed her body fully against his. "Focus on us." She ran a finger down the side of his face. "Just because you can't bring yourself to do a planned conversion doesn't mean there is anything wrong with you." She pulled his face closer. "I personally can't find anything wrong with you having issues with doing something to me that will in fact render me dead for a few minutes." She lightly touched her lips to his.

He let his mouth linger on hers, needing the sweet taste of her lips. "When you say it like that, it doesn't sound like a failing."

Her head dropped on his chest, and she made the most adorable growling sound. "Because it's not." She lifted her head and arched one of those delicate brows at him. "Unless you're supposed to find it easy to kill me."

He snarled at her and then jerked back before *treðir* could react. He had enough drama from that part of himself today. "That's not funny."

She let him go and walked to the door with an extra sway of her hips. "It wasn't meant to be. Come on. You're getting dressed and finding some place wonderful to take me today. I'm not going to be trapped inside with Mister Sullen for my entire bonding." Then she vanished through the door.

He was powerless to keep from following her. "I am being an ass. My apologies."

She looked over her shoulder at him. "So make it up to me. I am sure billionaire Quinn Donovan knows many ways to seduce a girl."

"All the best ways are free." He dropped his voice to a suggestive husk.

She turned around to walk backward away from him. A mischievous smile played in her eyes. "Is that so?"

"It is." He stalked forward.

She bit her lower lip and gazed at him from beneath her lashes. It was pure coy feminine seduction. "You promised to love me, Mr. Donovan."

He couldn't remember the last time the need to be inside of a woman outweighed every rational thought he possessed. He reached out and hooked her with his arm, jerked her against the hard length of his body. His head lowered, and he dragged in her scent like it was life-giving oxygen. His hands slipped down to the hem of her dress. His lips brushed against hers once, before he took her mouth the way he wanted it.

Her body arched back. A moan of soft pleasure vibrated in her throat. "Right here."

"Aye." He added an erotic growl to the word. His fingers traced up her thighs, and he stopped before he grinned. "No panties."

"A girl can hope," Haven said. Her leg hooked around his to pull him closer. "You make me want to be a naughty girl, Mr. Donovan."

"I can show you how." His hand slid down her thighs as he went down on his knees on the floor in front of her. "Take the dress off."

She slowly slinked it up over her body, then over her head and tossed it on the floor.

Sweet fire of Oberon! The woman was going to kill him. If there was a reason to be leery of the taking and giving of pleasure, he couldn't remember. His cock was rock hard. She'd planned this, again. He was truly a lucky man.

Then everything became touch, sensation, and pleasure. He hooked one of her divine legs up over his shoulder. He held her balance while he explored her most sensitive parts with his tongue. Damn, did she taste good.

He stopped to fumble with his clothes. She ran her hands over his torso, his arms, his back. Wherever her hands touched branded him with her heat.

He kicked his boots off, and then shoved his pants down. "Haven." He growled her name.

She grinned at him when he pinned her up against the wall. She leaned up and nipped at the hollow of his throat. "Quinn," she moaned. "Need you."

His hands ran over her flesh to grip her hips. He lifted her up and slammed into her.

She locked her legs around his waist and clutched his shoulders as his body moved inside of hers. Her back arched.

Donovan felt her on every level he was able to feel another being. The world melted away. The only two things in existence were the only two that mattered. Haven and himself. His thrusts started out raw, desperate for the release, but his body slowed. He needed to savor the feeling of Haven's body wrapped tightly around his.

He held her head, watching her face and the look in her eyes, needing to see the pleasure his body was giving her. Their emotions slipped and slid together in an erotic dance around them. Each move, each sound, brought them closer and entwined them together in a way from which he never wanted to be separated.

They came together in a primal union. Her body quivered around him. Still joined with her, he sank back down onto the floor in the middle of the hallway. He shoved them back to prop himself against the wall and held her straddled over him.

She let out a soft, little, dreamy sigh and dropped her head on his shoulder. Her finger absently traced along the muscles in his upper arm. "That was wonderful," she murmured with a satisfied hum. "But this doesn't get you out of taking me out."

Donovan curled his body around hers. "I'll take you wherever you want to go."

She giggled. "You're going to spoil me."

"So?" he said. "All queens deserve to be spoiled."

She ducked her head against him. "I guess," she whispered against his chest. "I just want time with you while I can have you all to myself."

He reached over, snagged her dress, and then looped an arm around her bottom. He stood up with her in his arms. "You will always get my time."

* * * *

After a lovely day seeing the Chicago sites, they ended up in one of Quinn's clubs. They walked past the bouncer and right into a wall of deafening sound. His arm went tighter around her as he led her through the barrage of people and straight back to his office where it was quieter. Haven was able to breathe again. "You like all that?"

His mouth went crooked. "It's good for people who don't want to think."

Haven sat down in his enormous executive chair and gave a sad smile. "But you want to think now?"

He picked her up and settled her on his lap. "I want you."

His words were so simple and heartfelt she had to smile.

The office was utilitarian with only a filing cabinet and large desk. Security monitors stood out prominently in the darkened room. "Wow, you can see everything going on in here."

"That's the idea. I have a security room with double the monitors. The people in my club are safe. That's why they come here." A dark shadow passed over his face.

"What is it?"

He leaned his head against hers. "Don't worry about it. I fixed the problem." He pulled back some. "I need to talk to Martin, the manager, but after that, I am at your disposal all night."

Haven bit down on her lip and grinned. "Do you dance?"

A look of horror and then panic crossed his hard features. "You're kidding, right?"

"Uh-huh. I want you to dance with me, Quinn." Her hand slid over his chest, her body pressing closer to his. "I like the way you move."

He groaned and wrapped his hands around her hips, pulling her closer to him. "We don't have to dance for that." His voice was thick and husky.

Haven shifted until she was straddled over him. She bowed up, letting her mouth drag over his and then down his throat. He cupped her bottom and then moved his hands down to her thighs. He slipped his fingers up the shimmering fabric of the dress. Her body grew tight and throbbed with need. Teeth scraped over her exposed flesh. She moaned and dropped her head back, giving him access to her tender pulse point.

* * * *

He took his time, savoring the flavor of her, drinking in her scent. When her hips rocked against his, he slid his hand farther up her dress, his fingers pushing aside the barrier of her panties and sliding into her slick, hot core. She whimpered in ecstasy and moved with the rhythm of his hand. Her hands worked to free him from the confines of his pants. He lifted her up and then brought her down on him. She tightened around him with a sigh. He guided their pace with his hands on her hips, taking them to a quick frenzy.

Donovan held onto the jagged edge, urging Haven over before he let himself follow. There was more power in this joining than there had been before. As she fell against him, spent, he could feel the shift inside her and the calming peace of a decision made.

Her body trembled, a lazy smile on her delicious lips. "I want forever with you, Quinn."

His eyes closed, and he held her close. He didn't move, didn't speak, and allowed her to wrap him in a sense of love and belonging.

He was so lost in her, he'd almost let his guard slip. With a quick jerking motion, he shot his hand up and snatched his suit jacket off the hook. He had it safely wrapped around her hips, covering where they were still joined, when the door opened.

"Someone had better be dead, Martin," Donovan growled before he turned the chair around to face the door.

The dark-haired man stared at him. "You're, sir, I mean, oh dear, I'm sorry. I hadn't realized you were here—a woman. You have a woman in here with you." The man kept stammering, his face growing redder and redder, and Donovan grew more disgruntled.

Haven's laughter filled the room. She sounded embarrassed. "Did you need something?"

Martin lifted his hand, his finger pointing at the file cabinet. "I, um, yes, an employee file, I needed a file. My apologies, Miss, Mr. Donovan, I didn't know you were here." He rummaged through the cabinet, his gaze focused in front of him. He snapped up the file and hurried out of the room, closing the door behind him.

Quinn was still rumbling, and Haven laid a hand on the side of his face. "It's okay. I thought you'd locked the door."

He snorted. "He still should have knocked."

"Maybe, but this is not a killing offence. He just needed a file, and I assume he's allowed, because you're not thinking of killing him because he took it."

He gave a hard stare, the one he knew made his men obey without question. "Haven, that man is going to have fantasies about you tonight."

She laughed at him. "And I will be safely next to you. Stop worrying. You can't police the world's thoughts. I am sure all the sales women at the mall are having naughty fantasies about you right now."

His anger peaked and then began to subside. "I still don't like it."

"No, but this is funny. We were almost caught like a couple of teenagers."

He couldn't stay angry when there was so much joy and life in her. He gently eased her off his lap. "There is a bathroom right over there."

* * * *

She winked at him as she started toward the restroom. "Go deal with your business. I'll find my way to the bar, and when you're done, I want that dance."

Quinn waited until she came out. His arm hooked around her. "I am not letting you out of my sight, woman."

They walked out into the pulse-pounding music, and Donovan escorted her over to the bar. He lifted her up on the barstool and then rested his head against hers. "Be safe. I need you."

"I'm falling for you."

Every other sound in the club faded away. The most goofy, beautiful smile spread across his face. He dipped his head down to give her a long, tender kiss. "Be safe, love. I will be within eye sight."

Haven watched him walk away before she turned to the bartender. He was looking at her with wide eyes and a knowing grin on his face. He glided over to her. "What'll it be?"

"Water is fine, thank you."

He winked at her, grabbed a bottle out of the cooler, and handed it to her. "Never thought I'd see the day Donovan would bring a woman here. You must be something special."

Haven smiled, a little shy. She easily found Quinn in the crowd. He stood at least a head taller than everyone else did. She turned back to the bartender. "Maybe."

Haven settled against the bar while Quinn made his rounds, stopping to talk to people occasionally. His gaze found her frequently, that goofy smile still lighting his rugged face. She absorbed the sights and sounds of the club. It was the best imitation she'd ever seen of a Roman village. The architecture astounded her, and the costumes the servers wore could have stepped out of a history book, but then, she knew that Quinn had probably actually been there himself. She sipped at her water and had fun watching him. Even if he didn't realize, he enjoyed working here, being a part of something normal.

She smiled when Quinn's eyes found her again; then she sat up board straight when his smile faded. His entire body coiled, and then he sprang into action. He was coming at her in a dead run, leaping over the table, people, and chairs in the way. Haven scanned the bar to find a weapon. She knocked the stool over and darted out of the way when Kyros tried to grab her. She snatched a beer bottle from the bar and broke the end. He advanced on her. She cut the side of his face with the jagged edge of the bottle as the bartender came over the counter after him. Kyros wrapped a hand around the bartender's throat and snapped his neck. Haven bolted toward Quinn, who was charging toward her. Kyros caught her arm and twisted it behind her until she dropped her weapon. He yanked her close to him and licked the side of her face. "You taste better with blood, my dear."

Then he pressed something against the side of her throat that pinched. He let her go, and she staggered backward. Donovan crashed into Kyros, sending them both sprawling across the floor. The music stopped. Club employees were herding people away from the chaos. Haven's vision went blurry and the room spun. The floor came up too fast, and everything in her world went black.

* * * *

Donovan didn't have to see Haven fall. He felt the moment she dropped out of consciousness. The power of his *treòir* lashed out, shaking the building as Donovan slammed his fist into Kyros's face with bone shattering force. Kyros's eyes rolled back in his head. The *treòir* wouldn't allow retribution while Haven still breathed. They had to save her. Donovan left Kyros there as he dragged himself to Haven only a few feet from where he'd been. Her body was limp and lifeless on the floor. Soul-shattering grief sliced through him as he collected her into his arms. He closed his eyes, his mind connecting with hers, but there wasn't anything solid for him to hold onto. He was losing her. Her heartbeat was faint, and her breathing was too shallow.

He connected with his brother. *"Riordan, brother, I need you! She's dying!"*

Riordan's response was quick. *"What happened?"*

"I don't know. He injected something into her."

"Poison." Riordan's presence turned calming. *"Do you know what kind?"*

"Get me what was in his hand," Quinn said to the person standing next to him. He didn't know who brought it to him a moment later because all of his focus was on Haven. He studied the air syringe and then twisted it open with one hand and sniffed. *"Bitter Almond."*

"It's cyanide! Get her into your office and lock the door. Now! You don't have much time."

Donovan rose up off the ground with her cradled against his chest. The inside of him threatened to explode, but he held himself together because Haven would need him. He didn't talk to anyone. He made a path to his office with one look and got there as quickly as he could. He closed and locked the door with no explanation to his employees and laid Haven on the couch as gently as he could.

"We're alone," he said to Riordan.

"You're going to have to do a blood exchange. It's the only way to counteract the toxin."

Donovan squeezed his eyes shut and then pulled out the buck knife he always had on him. His hand circled around her wrist and, by sheer force of will, pierced her flesh. Crimson collected at the surface and then pooled before dripping onto the floor. He lifted her wrist to his mouth and drank. Her taste was coppery sweet. When he knew he had enough, he pulled his head back and brushed his thumb over the wound, closing it with a small release of energy. He merged his awareness with hers. Her heart and lungs were starting to shut down from the poison so he breathed for her, letting his heart beat for hers. The cyanide seeped through him, his blood identifying it and neutralizing it. His body shook with pent up anger and soul-blinding fear. The *treòir* raged to get out. When he knew her body could wait no longer, he rolled up his sleeve. He cut his wrist and then put the wound to her lips. "Drink, Haven, sweetheart, drink." His voice sounded hollow and broken to his own ears.

Her tongue swept across his skin in a weak motion. He held her head there, giving her the strength needed to save her life. Gradually, she was able to do it on her own. He pulled away from her when power surged through his body. She whimpered and then went rigid, her mind trapped in a silent scream. His blood caused her this pain, but once wasn't enough to complete the conversion. He crawled up onto the couch and wrapped himself around her, absorbing as much of the pain as he could until her body accepted what was happening. Slowly, the tension eased from her muscles when he could feel a hint of her awareness coming back. She began to breathe on her own, and her heart no longer labored to beat.

Loath to leave her even for a second, he went to the adjoining bathroom so he could clean the blood from his arm, and then brought a washcloth with him to wipe the blood from her face and his own. He threw the cloth into the trashcan and then curled back around her on the couch.

"When will I know if she will make it?" he asked Riordan.

"When she wakes up, she'll be weak and disorientated. You are going to have to tell her what happened."

"I know." He dragged in a breath to help steady his frayed nerves. There was no screaming outside his office. He should check on the humans, but he wouldn't leave Haven. *"I need you and Wolf."*

"We're already here. Brogan alerted us to the problem."

* * * *

Wolf stalked through Coliseum. His senses stretched out to help him find a hint of where Kyros might be. Employees corralled the humans onto the dance floor where Memphis would be able to give them a gentle compulsion to forget what they'd seen.

Kyros was in league with a meirlock Hunter. There was no other way to explain how he or Brogan wouldn't have felt Lazarus opening a portal for Kyros. He sniffed every corner, searched under every table, but he wasn't able to find anything but the air syringe. He didn't need the videos in Quinn's security room to know more than Kyros had been here. The stench of evil was too strong to come from one meirlock.

"Wolf," Ean Maverick said from behind him. "They're gone."

"Aye," Wolf said as he peered under one last table. If Kyros had the use of a Hunter aged enough to cloak a massive amount of power, it would explain why finding the bastard was damn difficult. Wolf righted. The one with a chance to discover another Hunter was Brody. "Take Brody to help you canvas the area again. Ask every rock and blade of grass what it knows."

"Aye, my lord," Ean said and left.

Wolf searched the shadows one last time before joining Memphis. "Were any humans injured?"

"No."

"And you compelled them?"

"I did."

Wolf left Memphis to deal with the humans and non-human employees. The Storm Warrior was the best choice to meddle with human memories without damaging their delicate brain structure. He stopped to speak with Martin.

Quinn's club manager was a werewolf. The burly man sat on a barstool. "I should have known there was trouble. This is my fault, Mr. Wolf. I don't know how to make up for it. An employee lost his life because I failed my job."

Wolf rested his hand on Martin's shoulder. "Quinn missed the evil one's presence. You could not have prevented this." He narrowed his gaze and focused his power. "Once the humans are gone, you will go home and sleep. When you awaken, you will feel sorrow for the tragedy that occurred here tonight, but you will not take blame for anything you did not cause." He released a whisper of power. The compulsion would help Martin cope, but unlike what the meirlocks did to their victims, Wolf's compulsion would not linger and cause the werewolf any problems. He stayed with Martin for a few moments longer before he headed toward the office.

Wolf connected with the dragon, Brogan. *"Keep to the sky. I want to know if anything else changes in this area. Once Quinn and his mate are safe, I will hunt Kyros myself."*

"Aye," Brogan said. *"Let me know if you need anything else."*

"I will," Wolf said, and then ended the connection.

He paused at the office door. Riordan was so much better when it came to dealing with trauma. Wolf's life purpose seemed to be aggravating his older brother. This was not a time to quibble over arcane laws. With a deep breath, Wolf pushed open the door. His jaw tightened. Quinn, in a state of weakness, disturbed him, but he shoved it down. Quinn would be himself again soon if he'd ever pull his head out of his ass long enough to convert his lifebond so he could bond to her.

"Wolf," Riordan said from next to the couch. "We need to get them to the penthouse. Have Memphis open a portal."

"Aye," Wolf said. The sooner Quinn and Haven were safe at the penthouse, the sooner Wolf could go hunting.

Chapter 12

Haven awoke feeling weak, extraordinarily tired, and like a jackhammer had taken up residence in her head. She struggled to sit up and smiled briefly when she made it. She was on the couch in Donovan's living room. Nikon was curled up at her feet.

He lifted his head, his blue eyes meeting hers. *"You are awake!"*

She dragged a hand down her face. "Is that what they call it?" She swung her legs over the side of the couch and stood up on wobbly legs.

Nikon was beside her a moment later, steadying her. *"You should lie back down."*

"I'd love to, but I have to pee."

Quinn entered, a mixture of relief and worry on his face. He crossed the room, lifted her into his arms, and carried her into the bathroom. She swallowed back any modesty and embarrassment she had. She did what she needed to do. Quinn held her steady at the sink so she could wash her hands and brush her teeth. When she was done, he gathered her into his arms and carried her to the couch. He settled her, propping her up with an absurd amount of pillows, and then sat down on the coffee table. He reached forward and brushed a strand of hair out of her face. "How are you feeling?"

She groaned softly. "Like I was hit with a sledge hammer."

Quinn winced. "That will fade now that you're awake."

"What happened?"

He dragged a hand over his face and stared out the window. "Kyros attacked. I chased him off, but..." He snarled and fisted his hands at his sides. "He poisoned you and I had to give you my blood to counteract it."

For one second she wanted to be excited, but Quinn didn't look at all relieved. He appeared pissed. She tugged at her bottom lip with her teeth before saying, "You're not telling me something. What is it?"

His eyes closed tight. "It takes two exchanges of blood to make you Undying."

Haven's eyes went wide, and she scrambled to come up with something—anything—to say to him. "Is that why I hurt so much?"

A dark shadow passed over his face. "Yes."

She slowly nodded, and then panic hit. "Bastian? Nothing happened to him last night?"

He reached out to hold her hand. "He is safe with Nadia and Riordan."

Quinn dragged the other hand over his face and gave her a direct look. "Kyros is out for your blood. You will always be with me or one of my brothers until this is over."

She rubbed at her temples, trying to get the hammering to subside. "Can he kill me as easily if I am what you are?"

"Don't go there. The pain you are feeling now will be a thousand times worse. I am not going to do that to you."

She glared at him. "You need to focus on"—she swallowed hard, never thinking she'd ever say this—"killing Kyros, not worrying about what he's going to try to do to me next. I want you to change me. I can handle it."

"No, and that is final."

Haven blinked back the tears that stung her eyes. "You cannot make this decision by yourself."

He growled at her. "I just did. I have watched women die when a conversion didn't take. It's a horrible, painful way to die."

"Why didn't it work?"

He stood up. "You need to eat. Riordan left soup for you before he left this morning. I'll go try to heat it up." He vanished into the kitchen with Medea right behind him, leaving Haven glaring after them.

"He's not getting away with this," she grumbled at Nikon. "Help me get into the kitchen before he blows it up."

"He won't be happy with me."

"I don't care! He'll have to get through me to get to you."

"It's your head."

She gave the wolf a scathing look. "Just help me." She waited until the large wolf was next to her before she got back up on her wobbly legs. After a few moments, they coordinated their movement.

Haven stood at the kitchen door. Quinn was staring at the microwave as if it was the most foreign thing in the world. Medea lay on the floor at his feet with her paws covering the top of her head. He hit a sequence of buttons, shook his head, hit cancel, and then stared at the paper in front of him before he tried again. "You should be resting."

"With you in control of my kitchen? I don't think so." Nikon moved with her as she went over to where Quinn stood. Medea growled at Nikon before she huffed out of the room. Haven looked at the instructions Riordan left, took a hold of Quinn's hand, and shaped his fingers so he could press the buttons. She showed him which buttons to push, and then had him hit start. The machine came to life with a whirring sound. He tensed as if he was waiting for an explosion and then relaxed when nothing happened.

"Thank you," he said quietly. He turned to look at her. His face was weary and lined with worry. "Can you at least sit?"

"Yes."

He moved to help her, but she shook her head and used Nikon to get herself to the kitchen table. She sat down and turned her gaze to Quinn. He looked so...lost. He was trying to put up walls between them, and it tore at her heart. "You're not alone anymore. Don't cut me out. I can handle this."

The microwave beeped. Quinn went to get the bowl of soup but refused to say anything to her.

"Don't ignore me. This is a big issue, and we need to talk about it."

He brought her the steaming bowl of exotic smelling soup, set it in front of her, and then rummaged through the drawers until he found a spoon. He set that in front of her, too. She played with the spoon between her fingers and stared into the bowl.

"Is there something wrong with it?"

"No, it just needs to cool off. Why won't you talk about this?"

He leaned a hip into the counter, crossing his arms over his chest. "Because I am not going to kill you. I'll die before I put you through that kind of hell. It's bad enough you are in pain now because of my blood."

She dipped the spoon into the broth of the soup and blew. The taste was unusual, but Haven suddenly found herself starving. Willing back the desire to wolf it down, she finished what was on the spoon. He had to know what she was thinking just as much as she was able to pick up on him. "I'd be dead if it wasn't for your blood. Yes, it hurts a little, but it's starting to fade. You are the strongest. Don't you think your *treòir* will make sure I survive?"

"That's not the point."

"Then what is? If you know people who have survived and people who haven't, then there has to be a reason it worked for some and not others. We just have to figure out what it is."

"I am not talking about this with you right now. I almost lost you last night."

"Then when are we going to talk about it? On my deathbed? Be reasonable and talk to me. I might not have centuries on me, but I'm not a child."

"Damn it, I know that, but a conversion is a complicated thing." His powerful shoulders trembled. "I don't know how to bring you back from death."

Haven went perfectly still. "Then ask your brother. Do you not want to spend forever with me?"

His head bowed, and his voice was almost too quiet. "It's not that."

"That's the only other logical thing I can come up with," she yelled.

He started toward her.

"Don't come near me."

He roared at her. "Goddamn it! You haven't the slightest idea of what you are asking for. If something happens, if you don't live through it, I will become what Kyros is, get that and know it."

Chapter 13

The strain building between them wore at Haven during the next few days. After the pain left her, she'd never felt stronger or more alive.

While Quinn avoided her, Nikon had become her constant companion. *"You need to find something to occupy yourself. You're going to wear out the baseboards if you keep washing them."*

Haven sat back on her heels and tilted her head as she looked at the gleaming wood. "I have no idea what to do with myself. My life was never my own. I've always been told what to do and when to do it. I don't remember what I did for fun anymore."

"Yes, you do. Was there some kind of dance you did?"

Haven laughed as she remembered Quinn had said she'd be allowed to open up a studio again. Now was not the time to broach that topic with him. "I think Quinn is under enough stress at the moment."

"It will do the old man some good."

"He'll insist on being there for every class I teach. I'm not sure that would be fair to the students. He can be kind of intimidating, I think."

The wolf snorted. *"You think? The man is a terror, but he will do it for you."*

She bit her lip, imagining what Quinn's reaction would be, and decided the only way to get the full vision would be to actually ask him. No—she'd demand it. Or at least have him take her someplace she could dance. "Come on. If he has an adverse reaction, you can distract him while I make a quick getaway."

"Thanks." The tone was dry, but Nikon did rise to follow her into Quinn's home office. *"Don't forget I am expecting cubs any day."*

Haven gave Nikon a reassuring pat on the head. He had to know she'd never do anything to put him in danger. They ventured down to Quinn's office where Medea was laying on her side under Quinn's desk. He looked so alone, sitting there going over papers. Haven slipped into the room with him and slid her arms around his massive shoulders. He went completely still. "What do you need?"

"For you to stop being grumpy. I am perfectly okay."

He swiveled in the chair and pulled her into his lap. "You're angry with me."

His forlorn expression broke her heart. "No, I just need you to believe in me, believe in us."

"I do. I swear I am trying with everything in me to find a way to risk you."

Her fingers moved feather light over the lines of his face. "Then I will give you the time you need."

His mouth brushed over hers, some of the worry easing from his face. "You wanted something when you came in. What can I do for you?"

She gave an impish smile, complete with batting her eyelashes. "I need to get out of here for a while. I was thinking of trying another one of your clubs—one with belly dancing."

His look of shocked bemusement followed by searing heat was well worth it. "You want me to take you someplace where you can publicly seduce me?"

She laughed. "I already know how to do that. I just need to brush up on my skills. It's been a while since I've had a chance to really dance."

His growl was low and dark and brought a smile to Haven's face like nothing else could. He'd been so hopeless the past few days. She was glad to have sparked another emotion in him. "All right, but we do this my way. My club Tribal."

"Oooh, I haven't been to Tribal, yet. When can we go?"

His arctic eyes blazed gold at her. "You are trying to explode my head, aren't you?"

She smiled innocently. "Whatever do you mean? I just like going places with you. Besides, I am Quinn Donovan's fiancée. You should want to show me off."

"I do want to show you off, woman, but Kyros has already tried to kill you twice. I am not going to make you an open target."

"Then you're just going to have to stay right by my side. I want to go out with you, and you still owe me a dance."

"I can't dance to save my own life."

She slipped off his lap and captured his wrist, tugging him with her. "Nonsense. Everyone can slow dance."

"You are no good for me. I'll dance with you, but I don't want to hear one word when we both look like fools."

* * * *

Her laughter was a soothing balm. He loved to watch her move. The sway in her hips, the little feminine gestures she did without knowing. If anyone thought he was the one who held the power in the relationship, they were wrong. Haven could spellbind him with one look from those pale green eyes. She held all the strength and command he'd spent centuries acquiring, honing into the fine-bladed weapon of destruction in the palm of her delicate hand. If she only knew the power she wielded. For her, he'd tear apart the world, and for her, he'd find a way to mend it.

They had just gotten to the bottom step when the penthouse rattled. Wolf and Memphis's presence filled his senses. Donovan redirected them into the kitchen as the portal room door opened.

"My lord," Memphis said as he dragged Wolf out with him. "He wanted to come here first. I will get Riordan and stay with Nadia and the boy." A small tornado twisted around the man, shaking the appliances, and he vanished from sight.

"Haven, get the first aid kit," Donovan said as he stooped down to help Wolf to his feet.

The building rattled again just before Riordan stepped into the kitchen with his white wolf, Echo, in tow. Haven ran to get the kit.

"What happened?" Donovan asked as he eased Wolf into a chair in the kitchen.

Wolf's clothes had been ripped opened from one end to the other. Scrapes and lacerations covered every part of his exposed skin. His voice was easy, almost light. "Your quarry has a den, brother."

Donovan took out his buck knife and started to cut away at the threads of cloth still stuck to each other. "And you decided to check it out on your own?"

"You need to see to our Reannon," he said, as if the explanation made all the sense in the world. "I took Brogan and Hunter with me."

"What else did you find out?" At least Wolf was allowing the other Cadens to help him. Donovan kept his emotions and voice controlled as he continued his work while Riordan healed Wolf's mangled leg. Wolf and Riordan meant more to him than he was able to put words to, and guilt sliced through him when one of them was hurt.

"He has been amassing your army. Kind of like the good old days. He's going to send them after you. Many human lives will be lost."

"My army?" Donovan demanded. "Cut the cryptic crap."

"Black Rose. It appears Mason was not acting on his own."

Donovan stilled and then cursed. Of course. Kyros wanted to win. He was attempting to recreate the Undying structure and alliances in a dark mirror reflection, with himself as Cadeyrn at the top. "How many follow him?"

"A thousand at my last count," Wolf said. "I sent the Hunter to help ferret out information."

Brody Hunter was perfect for the task. He could mask his power and appear human to all, including Kyros, as long as Kyros didn't recognize him.

"We cannot kill that many humans. Human authorities would notice," Donovan said, pulling at the stubble on his face.

"I wouldn't worry over much," Wolf drawled. "Kyros always uses his charisma to build the quickest, stupidest army."

"Stupid doesn't make an army any less dangerous, and it's not the warriors that are the problem you need to worry about. It's the general. Kyros was always a good general, one of the best."

"Then you need to be very worried. He's planning an attack, and I can guarantee you the woman is at the heart of his plans."

Donovan went still. "Wolf." His voice was a growled warning.

"He plans to try to convert her." Wolf tried to stand up to get into his brother's face, but Riordan pushed him back down to keep working on a nasty gouge in Wolf's upper thigh. "If he gets his hands on her, you know the death she faces."

Donovan swung his arm as he turned to pace, barely missing Riordan's head with the blade still in his hand. He stopped short when he saw Haven standing in the door. The white box of medical supplies clutched in her hands fell to the ground and scattered across the floor. Donovan took a step toward her, but she coiled, ready to run. With two quick steps, he had her caged in his arms. "I won't let him do that to you. You are safe. I promise."

Her eyes closed, and she buried her face in his chest. "He can't do it if you've already changed me, Quinn."

"She speaks truth," the *treòir* said deep in his mind. They were both right, but he could not—would not—risk her that way. "I will stop him before it gets to that point."

Her whole body trembled as she extracted herself from his arms and stooped to clean up the medical supplies. She righted herself, carried the box over to the table, set it down next to Wolf, and turned to look at Quinn. "We will talk about this later. Your brother needs attention."

Riordan pointed to the door. Donovan clenched his jaw. Wolf's health came before arguments. A savage growl rumbled from him as he stalked from the room. He walked into the main hall, his eyes going over his battle regalia from an ancient era long past. His hand lifted to touch the hilt of his sword. Countless had died under that blade when he was in a battle rage. He carefully pulled it off its mount on the wall and tested the weight in his hand. Perfectly balanced, the ultimate killing weapon. He stepped into the living room to swing the sword a few times. He closed his eyes. He could see the battlefields all shifting and merging into one. The chilling ring of metal against metal as men fought in deadly combat for their very lives to defeat an enemy.

The feud with Kyros had to end. He carefully put the weapon back on the wall mounting. He caressed the soft leather of the garb, and then he turned to see Riordan and his Haven working together to patch Wolf up enough to get him into bed. She needed to be safe. He wouldn't allow Kyros to kill her. All of his power meant nothing without her. What was the point if he couldn't protect the one thing that mattered in all his long, lonely centuries? His mind was made up. He knew what he had to do. He walked back into the kitchen. He pulled Haven into him and brushed a strand of hair out of her face. He bent down and claimed her mouth with his.

"I love you," he whispered and then left her standing there as he walked out to go hunting.

* * * *

Haven started to follow him, but Wolf whipped his hand out and caught her wrist. "He'll be okay, Reannon. He just has to see for himself."

"See what?" She watched some of the less extensive wounds heal and then fade as if nothing had happened, the same way the scar on Quinn's chest hadn't lasted a day. "Look at you! Is he going to come back to me like this?"

Wolf laughed quietly and then let out a sharp hiss when Riordan nudged his arm. Riordan stood up and regarded Haven with the same predator eyes his brother had. "Kyros has been trying to kill him for a thousand years. He won't get himself killed this night."

She closed her eyes and sank into one of the empty chairs. She stayed there for a moment before she abruptly stood, went to the refrigerator, and pulled out four chunks of meat. "I know Echo, but I don't know the gray one."

"He is Apollo," Wolf said as he cocked his head to watch her with his ever-glowing eyes. "You do not have to feed them."

"Yes, I do. Donovan gave Bastian to Nadia and has left me with nothing to care for, since Nikon takes care of Medea and himself. I don't know what to do with myself."

A light hand rested on her shoulder. The presence of Riordan was nothing like Quinn's or Wolf's. He was calming, soothing in everything that he did, from the way that he spoke to how he moved. "Your worry for him is to be expected, but Quinn has not survived as long as he has by being reckless. It can take him years, sometimes centuries, to make up his mind about something, but once he does, he is immovable."

"Or seconds," she whispered. She went to turn the oven on low. "I know you don't like overly cooked meat, but I didn't know we were going to have company. It's not all completely thawed. I'll make the meat as rare as I can." She took the freezer wrapping off, put the steak into a pan, and placed it in the oven.

"Um, I can make up Bastian's room for Wolf to stay tonight. He can heal himself like Quinn can?"

"Yes," Riordan said, his eyes fading into a brilliant blue.

"All right, I will be right back, and I'll find something of Quinn's for Wolf to wear. Should we clean him up more?"

Wolf growled. "I can bathe myself, woman. Stop worrying."

Haven shot him a look full of daggers. "I will stop worrying when you stop trying to get yourself mangled while helping me." She stormed off down the hall, muttering to herself about male stupidity. Nikon was close to her heels.

"Medea is with him in mind," Nikon said. *"The dark one is not going to battle."*

"It sure seemed like he was. He said he loves me, and then he just left, just like that." Her bottom lip started to quiver, and she willed back the tears that wanted to come as she went into Bastian's room, stripped the bed, and then put the new sheets on. Nikon was silent for a time.

"He has only been in this civilized world fifty years, young heart. He doesn't always respond the way you might think he would."

She tucked the pillows into place, gathered the bedding off the floor, and took it into the laundry room. "He's actually more civilized than I'd expect him to be. I've shared his deepest thoughts. I have no misconceptions about what he is."

"Yet you still want to be with him."

Haven stuffed everything into the washer, started the laundry, and then went up to the bedroom. "I love him, Nikon. God help me, I do. It makes no sense in my head, and I know so much better than to let anything happen this fast, but he's Quinn. I've never met anyone like him."

"And you will never meet another. He is part warrior and part savior. He keeps the very gates of hell closed."

Haven went back to the kitchen and checked on the meat for something to do with her hands. It was still cold in some places, so she put the pan back in and then took a seat at the table. "Then how can I convince him? He's terrified the same thing will happen to us that happened to Kyros and Helena."

Wolf shifted his golden gaze to Riordan. "After Echo has been fed, I think you're wife needs you."

Riordan studied Wolf, and he slowly nodded. "Very well, as long as you haven't hidden any wounds from me, I will go home, but you cannot rest until Quinn has returned."

Wolf's eyes glowed. "I know."

* * * *

Haven didn't like being alone with Wolf. Apollo was friendly enough, but Wolf made her shiver. There was something cold and animalistic about him. While Quinn had compassion, Wolf seemed to have none, which frightened her. He was in the living room in one of Quinn's over-sized recliners. His eyes were closed, and Haven let out a breath. She grabbed a blanket, figuring Quinn could make him move later if necessary, and went to place the afghan over him. His glowing eyes snapped open. He caught her by the wrist, pulled her on top of him, and clamped her in place with an arm banded around her. They were face to face. "You want my brother to live?"

"Yes." Her voice quivered.

"Would you die for him?"

"Yes."

The smile of a predator spread across his face. He pulled her hand closer to him and then placed the necklace the pixie had given Quinn into her hand. "It will give you the ability to disconnect from him…along with enhancing your natural talents. Always wear it."

"Why would I want to do that?" she asked in a shaking voice.

"It's difficult to be a properly mysterious woman when he can read all of your thoughts."

She jerked to get off him, but he wasn't ready to let her go. He placed a small, unadorned knife into her other hand. "Make sure he is near when you do it. He will not let you die."

Then he let her up. "Practice using the necklace. Nikon can instruct you." His eyes closed, and his arm dropped over the arm of the recliner to scratch at Apollo's ears as he settled his large frame.

Haven stared at the knife in her hand and then slowly went to the bedroom on the second floor.

* * * *

The woman was dead. Body parts sprawled over a snow-covered rooftop. Donovan had been too late to save another one. A burning rage simmered in his gut. There would be yet another body for the city to clean up, and they would get another anonymous donation to cover the expenses. This game with Kyros had to end. Too many innocents were losing their lives. Their battle had always been about them, but he couldn't allow Kyros's evil to touch Haven. Kyros knew the real value of a lifebond. They bound to their mate for life. Not to the humdrum of every day existence, but to the essence of living. To happiness. To contentment. To the things that make waking up each day worth the fight. Donovan would make a promise with the devil to assure Haven's survival as a human.

The air moved around him. He stood up and braced himself for the impact. A swirling vortex cracked opened with the orb of black and red lightning around it. Kyros came out in a rush and knocked Donovan forward, his head bouncing off the side of the building. Donovan wiped the blood from his face and then willed the flow to stop as he turned around to face his enemy.

Kyros chuckled. His arms crossed over his chest, and his legs spread in a power stance. "You always cared too much, Cadeyrn."

"And you too little," Donovan said while being careful of the emotion in his voice. "This ends now."

Kyros made a tisking sound. "It ends when I say it does."

"You don't have the power to—"

"Don't I?" Kyros taunted. "Then why haven't you bothered to kill me yet?"

Donovan fisted his hand. "What do you want from me?"

"To win. I thought you'd have figured that out by now."

Donovan studied the man he had once called a friend. They circled around each other in a steady, predatory stalk. If Haven had been converted, giving up his power wouldn't be an option, but since she wasn't Undying, there was one thing he could do to keep Kyros from forcing her to drink his blood. "I will not convert Haven. I must give up my power."

Kyros froze. "You would never—"

"But I will," Donovan cut him off. "You of all people should know what a real lifebond means. You've already won. All you have to do is outlive me."

Kyros's eyes flashed a demon red. "Then give it up now."

There was an odd note to his voice that Donovan couldn't quite figure out. He decided to play the meirlock's game for a little longer. "I need to make the preparations for it."

"Then do it. I give you until midnight tomorrow."

Donovan gave a low growl, enough to make the ground under him tremble. "Or what?"

A sick smile slithered across Kyros' face. "Haven will suffer the same fate as Helena."

He had no choice but to agree. Haven would not go through that as long as he had blood in his veins. "So be it."

Kyros stared at him for a moment in shock before he started to back away. "Do I have your word?"

"You have it."

A vortex of wind spiraled around Kyros with Lazarus's signature black and red lightning. In the next heartbeat, Kyros was gone.

"Bargained for my death!" the treòir roared in his mind. *"You have killed her!"*

"I am giving her the human life she was to live," Donovan shouted. The one law the Undying had that all of magickind had to abide was to preserve the life of a lifebond. The only loophole was giving up the *treòir,* enabling the woman to live out her natural lifespan. "You cannot destroy me before this until Kyros is dead."

"You win for now, human," his power said. *"Once this threat is over, you will not fare so well."*

Donovan didn't bother to argue. He'd deal with *treòir* in the morning light. For now, he'd stay with the body until the authorities arrived, and then he needed to get back to Haven.

* * * *

The front door closed, and Haven was off the bed and flying down the stairs. She hit Quinn at full force, knocking them down the last few steps. He steadied both of them, and his arms went tight around her. "Haven, sweetheart, what's wrong, are you okay?"

"I'm scared, that's all." She winced when she saw the gash over his eye. "What did you do? You're hurt." She looped her hand around three of his fingers and tugged him up the stairs.

"I'm fine. I just had to go check some things out. It's a small cut, nothing to worry about."

Haven pulled him into the bedroom and checked every inch of him before she dragged him into the bathroom so she could clean out the wound. "What did you find out?"

"Kyros is connected to your grandfather and to Mason."

Her heart clenched. "That makes him more dangerous, doesn't it? He is going to try to kill us?"

"Yes, but I won't let that happen. Once he's dead, I will take control of the Black Rose. It will be what was meant to be."

Chapter 14

Donovan woke with Haven curled into his side. She was so small and delicate beside him. Her silky hair was splayed out over the pillow, the early morning sun catching the highlights of fire. He let his fingers tangle in her hair and watched her sleep. He needed to go out again today. He needed ti get the athame made of an alloy found only on Avalon that would allow him to give up the *treòir*… But something was off with her. He traced his finger along the chain of the necklace his mother once wore. Wolf must have given it to her. She'd managed to close part of herself off from him when they'd been so entwined. She was hiding something, and that scared him down to his core. He must have damaged her in some way when he gave her his blood. That had to be what she was hiding from him. The only reason Donovan could think Wolf would give her the pendant before he could do it himself.

Haven opened her eyes and then reached out to sooth the furrow in his brow. "What's wrong?"

"Are you okay? Any lingering effects from the exchange?"

She shifted and braced herself against his chest. "No, I feel fine, why?"

"I just had to ask. You know you can tell me anything, right?"

She got out of bed. "Yes."

"Stay here with me for a while?"

"I—I need to fix breakfast for Wolf. Those injuries were pretty bad, and he could use the nourishment."

Donovan propped himself up on his elbow and watched her as she got dressed. "Did he scare you?"

She went still, and her gaze went to the floor. "No. He's just a little more intense than you are."

"We've led different lives." He got out of bed and closed the distance between them. "You're sure you're all right?"

Her smile didn't reach her eyes. "You worry too much. I am fine. Pancakes or waffles?"

"Waffles." He brushed the back of his hand over her jaw. Everything was changing again, and he worried she wouldn't want him if he gave up his power. "We'll figure this all out."

Her gaze narrowed on him. "What did you do last night?"

"Nothing that can't be undone," he said quietly, praying it was true. A pact with evil wasn't binding by Undying law, but that didn't stop the destruction Kyros could cause if Donovan didn't uphold his end. "Wolf is waiting for his breakfast. I'll be down in a minute."

Haven searched his face. "You talked to him, didn't you?"

He traced his finger down her collarbone and over the pendant before his gaze met hers. "Don't do this. Not now."

"Damn it, Quinn! What did you do? I have a right to know. Remember that I can feel what you feel. Why do you feel guilty?"

"Wolf is hungry."

"When you're ready to treat me like an adult, I'll be down stairs." She stormed out of the room and made sure to stomp as loud as she could as she went down the stairs.

Donovan dragged a hand over his face. This was why he needed to be able to disconnect from her. No matter how hard he tried to block her from the things he did, she always seemed to slip right through his defenses. How the hell couldn't he slip through hers?

"You've never endured what she has, dark one." Nikon uncurled himself from the extra-large dog bed he shared with Medea. *"You've always had the power to destroy your tormentors. She is more wounded than you've allowed yourself to believe."*

"This is a defense because of Mason?"

"I believe so. She and I have had a lot of time to get to know one another in the last few days.

Donovan winced at the reproach in the wolf's tone. *"But I've seen all of that. Why would she hide that from me?"*

"You're seeing it through your eyes." Nikon lightly nosed at Medea to wake her. *"For as much as her torment enrages you, and I know Mason will not meet a good end from the blade of your sword, you have not seen it through her eyes. You have the power and strength to stop that kind of treatment from happening to you. Haven had no other choice but to lie down and be beaten."*

Donovan stood in the middle of the room as he worked it over. Helpless was the first word that came to mind, but he knew that wasn't true. Haven didn't think of herself as helpless. His jaw twitched. *"What does she think she's protecting me from?"*

"I would not be a good confidant if I told you, now would I?"

"If she's in danger, you had better tell me."

"She's in no more danger than you are because of what you did last night."

Terror gripped his chest, and he doubled over with it. He'd made a pact with Kyros to buy some time. Wolf was here. He should have been watching her. He couldn't fathom what she might have been able to do, but she wouldn't understand how to make a pact with evil. "Nikon, what did she do?"

"That is something you will have to ask her. Do not make the changes yet, dark one. You may need your power still."

Kyros had given him until the end of the day. He didn't bother to get dressed; he jogged down the steps in his sweatpants and bare feet. He found Haven in the kitchen. He blew out an explosive breath. "Haven, I know something is wrong, and you have to tell me what it is."

"Not until you tell me what you did last night." She finished mixing the batter for the waffles and then turned on the burner to warm a pan for the bacon sitting on a plate on the counter.

"Goddamn it, woman, this is not acceptable."

"You're right; it's not." She slammed the pan down onto the burner. "But here we are, seeing who's going to be the most stubborn."

Nikon said he needed to see things through Haven's eyes. He was going to be a bastard. But then, he'd always been one. He slammed his fist onto the table, making Haven jump. His eyes flared gold, and he growled dark and dangerous at her. "You will tell me, woman, or things will not go well for you."

She stopped what she was doing and turned to look at him. "This is not acceptable behavior, and you know it. Think of the fear you have for me right now, and that's exactly how I feel for you."

"I cannot feel your fear!" His voice rose a level. "I can't protect you if I don't know what's going on."

"Damn you, what did you do? Did you make some kind of bargain with Kyros for me?"

His jaw tightened.

A look of horror marred her features. "You did. Take it back. You can't do that. I will not risk your life any more than you'll risk mine."

"I already told you I would die for you," he roared at her. "I am not going to let him hurt you. You have no idea what it would do to you to be forced to drink the blood of a male who is not your mate." He forced his tone to go softer. "Please, you have to believe that."

"What was the deal?" she demanded as she pointed the spatula at him.

He squared his shoulders. There had never been more fear in him than in this moment, not even when having to recount some action or another to a council of the Originals. "I let my power go."

First, there was fear, and then anger flashed across her face before she settled on horror. "You can't do that."

"To save your life, you're damn right I will!"

"When do you have to do this by?"

"Tonight."

"Damn you! I am going to take a shower and don't you dare follow me." She left everything cooking in the kitchen and ran up the stairs.

Donovan went to go after her, but Wolf walked into the kitchen. "Let her go, brother. Sometimes you just need to let them be upset."

"What the hell would you know about it?"

Wolf shrugged. "That's what Riordan says about Nadia, so I figured it has to be true."

Donovan glared at the ceiling, listening for her sounds as she moved around up there. She was pacing in the bedroom. "I should go up. She's not handling this well."

"At least help me figure out how to turn this stuff off so nothing burns."

Donovan grumbled, "You get two minutes."

* * * *

Haven covered her face with her hands. This needed to happen. It was just a little bit of pain. It couldn't be worse than anything Mason had done to her. She walked over to the nightstand and pulled out the knife. Her hands trembled.

Quinn couldn't give up his *treòir*. She needed him too much. The world needed him too much.

Kyros would be an unstoppable monster, and Quinn would be able to do nothing about it.

There wasn't much time before Quinn came up to check on her. She had to have the deed done before he got there. She went into the bathroom and locked the door. It would hold him for all of two seconds, but she needed that time to build up her courage. She turned the water on in the tub. She'd planned to do a little Internet research on the most effective way to cut herself, but now there wasn't any time.

A sob escaped her. She didn't want to die. No matter how bad life got, she knew there was always something to hold on to, and Quinn was a pretty big something. The exact reason she had to make him convert her. Quinn wouldn't allow her to die. She trusted him that much. Now it was time to keep him with the living and with the power he was born to possess.

Which way was she supposed to cut, horizontal or vertical? She studied her wrist and decided the most damage would be vertical. She needed blood loss, a lot of blood loss. She got into the tub with her clothes on and pressed the knife to her flesh. Her hands were shaking too badly. She wanted a clean cut, something easy for Quinn to heal.

Images of Quinn and Bastian flooded her mind, and then an image of Kyros and what he could do to the world if Quinn wasn't there to stop him. She took several deep breaths and held the knife over her wrist with a steady hand. If she was an Undying, then Quinn would have no choice but to remain one as well. With a will she hadn't known she'd had, Haven sliced through the flesh of her wrist. She bit down on her lip, drawing blood, to stop her scream of agony. The blood flowed red and warm down her arm, but there wasn't enough yet. She pulled the blade across the savage wound again, cutting deeper, nicking bone. She dropped the knife into the tub and let her injured arm fall into the water. The warm water helped to draw out her blood.

Quinn's footfalls were coming up the steps. Damn it! She leaned forward and turned on the shower. She needed more time. She could feel the blood seeping out of her body, but it wasn't enough yet. Just a little more time.

Quinn knocked on the door. "Haven, can I come in?"

"No." Did her voice shake? God, she hoped it didn't. Not yet. He couldn't come in yet.

"Damn it, Haven, this isn't helping anything. What's done is done."

Sleepiness settled through her, and she fought the urge to clamp her other hand over her wrist. Maybe she needed to cut the other one, too. She nodded and moved to get the knife from the bottom of the tub. "I don't want to talk to you right now."

Her voice was weak. He was going to come in. She curled her hand around the knife, but the ligaments and tendons she'd damaged refused to let her get a good grasp, and the knife fell into the tub, making a loud clang as it hit the bottom.

"Haven, what are you doing in there?"

"Go away." The words came out as a whisper as she slid farther into the tub. She blinked several times, trying to keep herself from slipping into sleep, but the blood loss and the hot water were making it impossible.

Panic rose and her natural instincts to fight for her life swelled up inside of her. "Quinn!"

* * * *

The wall Haven had built up between them suddenly crumbled, and all Donovan could see in her mind was red, too much red, and a thought that *he* wasn't going to get in there in time. He grabbed the doorknob, and when it wouldn't turn, he put his shoulder to the door. The power of the *treòir* welled up at the same time and splintered the door on the hinge. The sight that greeted him would forever haunt him. The shower curtain was wide open as the hot water streamed down over her limp body. The tub was filling up with red water. With one leap, he was across the room. He pulled her body out of the tub and found the bone-deep slash on her left arm from her wrist to the inner part of her elbow. "Oh my God, Haven, what have you done."

He grabbed a towel and pressed it to the wound, but there was no way of telling how much blood she'd lost because of all the water. "Wolf!"

Without being commanded, the *treòir* stretched out to stem the flow of her blood. He went deep inside of her, reaching for her heartbeat and breathing. They were there, but far too weak.

"No, no, no!" He let out an anguished roar, shaking the entire building as the ground beneath quaked. "You are not leaving me this easily." Without thought or hesitation, he lifted her wrist to his mouth and took in her blood, as much as he needed for his body to process before he gave her any of his. He didn't care how much pain she'd be in, she was going to live so he could throttle her himself. He pulled his buck knife and slashed open his own wrist and then pressed it to her mouth, his other hand cupping the back of her head, lifting her up to make it easier for her to drink.

He had to help her ingest the blood. She wasn't getting strong enough on her own, though he was able to feel her desire to stay alive. He touched her arm to seal the wound, healing it enough so she wouldn't die. Later, Riordan could fix the damage she'd done to herself. He forced her to keep drinking, and when he would have stopped, the power of his *treòir* took hold and kept her drinking a few drops more. Her eyes flew open, and the scream that tore from her ripped through Donovan. Her body convulsed and bounced off the tile floor. He curled around her. There was no turning back.

Her body jerked and twitched as if she was having a grand mal seizure. He cradled her head against his chest so she wouldn't hurt herself. A slow burn spread through her body and flared into a searing heat. She let out scream after ragged scream, and Donovan held onto her, body, mind, and soul. He was not going to lose her. He absorbed as much of her pain as he could, trying to make the conversion bearable. He didn't know how, but he dragged them both to the tub and pulled her in with him, hoping the now cold water would ease some of the pain. An eternity passed as he kept himself locked around her, feeling everything she was, enduring the pain with her. He couldn't do anything less when he was the one who'd caused it. He was still breathing for her, his heart beating with hers.

Then everything stopped—the fire, the muscles spasms—there was nothing. If he hadn't been controlling her vital functions himself, she would be dead. The grief tore across his soul. He would stay until she spent every ounce of his energy.

Then she wheezed in her own breath, and her heart jumped in her chest. Her body shuddered, and a blinding pain shot through her before she went limp against him. A vicious shiver rattled her teeth.

Wolf calmly walked over and turned off the water. The eerie glow of Wolf's eyes dimly lit the bathroom. "Do you need help?"

It took several moments for Donovan to find his voice. "She's freezing. We need to get her dry and warm."

Donovan rose with her from the tub as quickly and as gently as he could. He peeled her wet clothes off and wrapped her in towels Wolf had gotten for him. He could feel the burn still in her body, but she was clinging to life. He would bear her pain for as long as she needed. He lifted her and took her into the bedroom before he laid her down. Wolf handed him another towel. Only then did he realize he was soaking wet. He stripped his sweat pants and wrapped the towel around him. He wrung as much water out of his hair as possible, and then got onto the bed with Haven. She was still shivering, and her muscles twitched occasionally. She was far too pale. "She needs more blood."

Wolf nodded. "I'll call Riordan. He'll know what to do."

"Thank you." Donovan curled around Haven and pulled the blankets over both of them. She was alive, just barely, but he could throttle her himself now. He ran his hand through her wet hair and murmured to her in his ancient language. Mostly nonsense, but the words seemed to calm her. How was she dealing with this pain piercing through her? He didn't know, but he was going to help her.

Somewhere in the back of his mind, he knew he'd never be able to keep his pact with Kyros now. Even without bonding, with Haven now Undying, her life was linked to his. Giving up his *treòir* would be handing her a death sentence. He shoved it out of his mind. Haven was his focus.

How could he have missed this? How could she have blocked something this huge from him?

Fear coiled around him. The *treòir* settled over them like a warm blanket. His home rattled as was typical of Memphis's arrival, and then the penthouse began to fill with the presence of amassing *treòir*s. The other North American Cadfaels were arriving, and they were quickly followed by Donovan's own Cadens. He curled tight around Haven as her body shivered. When he knew Wolf had enough power assembled to keep them safe, guilt slammed into him hard, gnawing at his gut. This was his fault, and there was nothing anyone could say or do to convince him otherwise.

* * * *

Donovan woke to a throbbing pain in his entire body. Haven rested peacefully, snuggled against his side. The image of her dying in the bathroom flashed through his mind, and he jerked away from her. He winced when her arm flopped against the mattress. With the greatest of care, he moved her arm to a more comfortable position and slipped out of the bed. He stared down at her. Haven. His beautiful Haven had tried to kill herself.

His jaw ticked. The power of the *treòir* seemed to swirl in the air around her. As long as Haven was unconscious, his power's awareness would remain with her. He shook his head and, not caring he was an absolute mess, walked out of the bedroom. Someone had replaced the bathroom door. Possibly one of the men he could feel congregating on the first floor of the penthouse. He descended the stairs in a slow stalk. The heads of the strongest men on the planet turned to assess him.

All the Heartland Cadens were assembled. Memphis stood near the window, the air around him ionized in preparation to open a portal at a moment's notice. Maverick leaned against the opposite wall, the only one who didn't seemed affected by the events of the last twenty-four hours. His green gaze assessed Donovan, promising death if he spoke the wrong words.

Brody, the Hunter, wore an impassive expression, but Donovan knew him. There was a slight tension in the other man's stance, belying his worry. Next to Brody was Brogan. The dragon showed in his eyes. Donovan's brothers stood close to the staircase.

All six of his Cadens stood at attention when they saw him. Each one bowed his head in turn. Wolf was the first to step forward. "How is she?"

"Healing," Donovan said. "Kyros?"

Brody stepped forward. "I've tracked him to a mansion the Black Rose uses as headquarters. Lazarus is with him."

Donovan had figured Lazarus, Memphis's twin brother, worked with Kyros. Brody was the only one here with the ability to cloak his power. He could get in with the humans and less powerful of magickind without notice and discover secrets. "Anything to report?"

"I'm sorry, my lord." Brody's body tensed. "Kyros is well guarded."

Donovan nodded. "Wolf. Riordan. I need both of you here." He shifted his gaze to Maverick. "I want you on the ground."

Maverick gave a slight, respectful nod of his head. "Aye, my lord."

"I will take the air," Brogan said.

Donovan didn't miss the excitement in the other man's eyes. It wasn't often he had the time to allow his dragon the freedom of flight. "Thank you." His attention when to Memphis and Brody. "Keep an eye on Kyros until I work out a plan."

They gave a nod.

"And Brody, keep a leash on Memphis." Donovan trusted his Cadens with his life, and he knew them too well. He could not lose his Storm Warrior. Memphis and Lazarus were too evenly matched to foretell the outcome of a battle between the two.

"Of course," Brody said. "Have you need of anything else?"

Riordan cleared his throat. "The usual."

Half a smile cracked Memphis's hard expression. "Aye." He and Brody turned to go to the portal room.

Donovan let out a breath. Haven would need the magic of Riordan's conversion soup—as the others liked to call it. Memphis could get the other realm ingredients.

Maverick and Brogan left for their posts, leaving Donovan alone with his brothers and their wolves.

Riordan moved up beside him. "You should go back to bed."

Donovan snarled. "She tried to kill herself."

"Use your head," Wolf snapped. "She did no such thing."

"No," Donovan said in a tone leaving no room for argument. He didn't want to contemplate any other reason Haven would have taken a knife to her own flesh.

Chapter 15

When Haven awoke, she knew she was in Quinn's bed. She expected all kinds of awful pain, but other than stiffness and a slight headache, there was nothing. She groaned and sat up. Nikon was next to her in the dimly lit room, and there was a tall, dark figure sitting next to the bed. The man wasn't Quinn. Her voice came out in a croak. "Where is he?"

"He's out. He'll be back in a few hours." Riordan leaned forward.

"Did it work?"

"You arc Undying, and Quinn has not given up his power." Riordan's face was stern, and Haven winced at the reproach in his tone.

"Where is he?"

"He needed to take care of a few things." Riordan's tone went so soft Haven had to lean forward to hear him. "He didn't want to be here when you woke up."

"He didn't?" She closed her eyes as a different kind of pain sliced through her. Well, what had she expected? For him to accept what happened and move on as if nothing changed? She willed back the worst of the heartache. "How long have I been out?"

"Two days. Quinn made sure you slept through the worst part."

Of course he would. He was still Quinn, no matter how pissed off he was. With a sigh, she shoved back the blankets and swung her legs over the side of the bed. Her arm refused to be helpful as she struggled to get herself into a standing position. She'd probably have very limited use of that arm for eternity, but she'd already accepted that. Nikon was next to her, guiding her into the bathroom. She stopped at the door and turned to Riordan. "I am going to get myself cleaned up and ready to leave, and then you are taking me to Quinn. I have to talk to him."

"No, you still need to take it easy, and I still need to fix your arm."

Her face twisted. "Don't bother."

Then she went into the bathroom, closing the door behind her. Taking a shower and preparing for her day took four times longer than it usually did without the use of her left arm. She promised herself that she would get adept at being normal. Her arm was worth Quinn's life, no matter what anyone else said. When she came out of the bathroom an hour later, another fifteen minutes passed while she figured out how to get dressed, and the tying of shoelaces was impossible, so she settled for a pair of slip-ons instead.

Nikon went down the stairs with her, pressing her close to the wall to keep her steady. "At least I still have you," she said quietly.

"You will always have me, young heart. My task has always been to protect his heart."

Haven gave the wolf a peculiar look and then shook her head. "Have you eaten?"

"I am a wolf. I can go a few days without if I need to."

"Nikon!" She crossed the dining room and went into the kitchen. She did her best to ignore Riordan and rebuffed his offers of help as she unpackaged the thawed meat and put it onto a plate to serve it to her wolf. She decided that Nikon was no longer Quinn's, but hers. It had to be the reason he had two, because she needed her own. Then she warmed her own bowl of soup. She continued to ignore Riordan while she ate. When she began to rise to put the bowl into the sink, he stopped her and put a sling over her shoulder, settling her arm inside.

"If you are not going to let me fix it yet, then you should at least take care not to damage yourself more. Quinn is going to insist that I heal you."

She sniffed. "He can insist all he wants, but that doesn't mean I'm going to allow you to heal me. I can handle the consequences of my own actions." But she did keep the sling on because it relieved the throbbing in her hand. Riordan arched a brow at her in a way strikingly similar to Quinn. She rolled her eyes. "Can I have Nadia's phone number? I need to talk to Bastian."

Riordan handed her his cell phone with the number displayed. She quickly memorized the number and then dialed.

"Memphis," answered the quiet voice of the Storm Warrior.

"Can I talk to Bastian?"

"Of course."

A moment later, Bastian's anxious voice filled her ears. "Haven! Are you okay? I heard what happened. You survived."

Her voice was soft. "Yes, Bastian, I did. Are you okay? You've been eating properly?"

He took the tone of a disgruntled teen. "Yes, Mom, I'm fine. I've been worried about you, though."

She'd smiled when he called her "Mom," but was glad he wasn't there to see how upset she was. She was careful to keep her tone light. "I'll come and see you in the next day or two. I miss you."

They spent the next half hour on the phone. Haven deftly dodged his questions about exactly what had happened while she extracted every bit of information she could about how he was really doing. By the time the call ended, she was worried Bastian might try to do something rash, like sneak out of the house to come and see her. She sighed. After waiting a few minutes and then calling again, she gave Riordan his cell phone back "It's been a few hours. Why isn't Quinn back yet?"

"He'll be here. Stop worrying."

But she was worried. She'd ruined everything that had been between them with her one act, but she couldn't have let him commit a slow suicide, not for any reason. She blew out a puff of air and absently buried her hand in Nikon's soft fur, needing a small measure of comfort. "He's angry."

"Aye. What else did you expect? He believes you tried to end yourself. Wolf and I haven't been able to convince him otherwise."

She nodded and sank down onto the kitchen chair. "What is Kyros going to do now that Quinn hasn't changed?"

"We are still working on that," Riordan said. "We have several of the more powerful males of other provinces in the city, including our nephews, helping to keep an eye on the humans."

She drew in a sharp breath. Riordan wouldn't tell her if Kyros went on a rampage through the city. Everyone seemed to think she was too delicate to handle the truth. If Kyros killed, those deaths would be on her hands.

"No, he makes his own choices," Nikon said. *"You cannot take the blame for what an insane Undying does. He would make those kills anyway, and if you'd not forced Quinn's hand, there would be no one left to stop him."*

Haven didn't exactly want Riordan listening to her side of the conversation. *"And I do understand that, I think, but Quinn said he made a pact. What are the ramifications of him breaking it?"*

The wolf turned his gaze on hers. *"If Kyros wasn't insane, it would mean the dark one's death, but since Kyros is one of the hunted, the only danger is any retribution Kyros would take. Which, considering his power, could be substantial."*

She closed her eyes and let out a breath. She should have thought of all the people Kyros could hurt because of what she'd done. *"What are the consequences for what I did that no one is telling me about?"*

Nikon nuzzled her hand. *"There are six Cadfaels with their Caden teams in the city. So far, no one has reported a death, but Kyros is trying to punish the dark one for not giving up his power."*

Haven drew in a calming breath. She was going to have to trust Wolf had known this would happen and that the Undying would be able to protect innocent people from the choice she'd had to make. *"There is a lot I need to learn about being an Undying, isn't there?"*

"Yes, but you have many around you who will help you, and Wolf has prepared a gift for you."

"Wolf? Gift?"

The sound of wolf laughter filled her mind. *"He will arrive before Quinn. He may seem odd to you, but he has always been practical and feels that knowledge is paramount in avoiding tragedy... And I think he's developed a bit of a soft spot for you."*

Haven knitted her brows together. Wolf didn't seem the type to have a soft spot for anyone. Quinn's absence weighed heavily on her, and she began to wonder exactly how large a rift she'd created between them. She had tried several times to reach out to him, wherever he was, but he kept his defenses firmly in place and didn't even respond to her plea for him to at least acknowledge her. Nikon nuzzled his nose into her hand. *"Do not despair, young heart. Quinn is the strongest of his kind. He will not allow himself to fail."*

Haven knew that, but she also knew he considered what she'd done his own failure. She left Riordan in the kitchen and wandered through the penthouse. She nearly jumped out of her skin when a hand came down over her shoulder while she was studying Quinn's battle regalia. She whirled around and stared up at Wolf. "Oh, it's you."

His expression was unreadable and his face hard. He handed her a gift-wrapped package. She had to snap it in close to her chest to prevent the book from falling. It was heavy, like some kind of book. She chewed on her lip for a moment before, went into the living room and sat down, awkwardly putting the gift on the coffee table so she could unwrap it.

Both of Quinn's brothers and several wolves followed to watch her. Medea came to rest at her feet. Haven patted her head before she peeled back the beautiful paper and found a leather bound book with a strange

Emma Weylin

symbol carved into the cover. She turned to the heading page. Neat
script writing filled the beautiful gold-leaf pages. It was a manual. She
beamed at Wolf as she started flipping through the book. There was a
section on their laws, one on their rituals, a section about different kinds
of supernatural beings, one on magic, and another on history. There was
countless other information filling nearly a thousand pages. All the basic
material she would need to start her new life. "Thank you."

"My pleasure, little sister."

"Who wrote it?"

"I did," Wolf replied. "I have several copies. We cannot be too careful
with our families."

Her hand ran over the cover. "Thank you, Wolf. I love it."

His face flashed into an odd expression before turning back to stone.
"You are welcome. Now, you will let Riordan fix your arm."

"Shouldn't I have healed when I became Undying?" she asked after
thinking for a moment.

Riordan sighed. "If Quinn wouldn't have sealed the wound, then yes,
but when he did it to stop the bleeding, it tricked your body into thinking
you already healed."

"No," she said without hesitation. She would accept the consequences
of the choices she'd made.

"Quinn is having enough trouble accepting this. He will not handle a
reminder of what happened every time he looks at you."

She sneered at him. "It doesn't matter, because he's not here to see
me."

"You are being ridiculous. You already hurt yourself. Don't add to it by
refusing help," Wolf said.

Her mouth dropped open. She then growled at him. "You are the one
who gave me the knife! What I did after the fact is my own business."

He smirked. "Impressive first growl. But you want to start lower in
your chest to make it more intimidating." His expression sobered. "I will
hold you down and force you."

He did not just try to give her a growling lesson while she was arguing
with him. A moment passed before her brain recalibrated to the point she
could reply. "You wouldn't."

"Wanna bet?"

His eyes flared red, and she scooted away from him on the couch. "You
can't make me do this." She appealed to Riordan. "Can he?"

"I agree with him. Quinn is in a delicate state, and you could easily
push him over the edge right now."

"The edge of what?"

"Sanity."

She squeezed her eyes shut and let out a slow breath. It was all Wolf's fault. She had no problem blaming the frightening warrior, because if he hadn't given her that knife, she would have never thought of cutting herself. She let out an explosive breath and just looked up at the men. That wasn't fair. Wolf had given her a way to override Quinn's decision. One that would have ultimately killed him. True, Wolf had given her the knife, but she'd cut herself. They'd both had done what was needed to save Quinn's life. Quinn would live, and both she and Wolf shared the blame. Haven set her jaw. "How bad is this going to hurt?"

Neither one answered. Wolf took the book, escorted her back to the master bedroom, and sat her down on the bed. She glared at him, but allowed Riordan to move her where he needed her so that he could begin the process of fixing her arm.

Haven wasn't a violent person by nature, but she wanted to find something, anything hard to hit Riordan over the head with. Wolf stood in the corner of the room, his predatory eyes unblinking as the healer focused on fixing the massive damage she'd done to her arm. The muscles, ligaments, and tendons weren't so bad, nor was the repair process for the blood vessels running the length of her arm, but the tedious work of repairing dying nerves sent sparks of white hot electricity though her arm and into the rest of her body, making already sore muscles jump and twitch. After what seemed like hours, Riordan sat back, sweat drenching his brow, and smiled. "It's done. You're all better."

Her face went crooked. "That doesn't seem right." She flexed her arm and worked her fingers. Things felt tight, but everything worked properly. "Shouldn't there be some kind of consequences for what I did?"

Riordan had an amused look on his face. "And you wish to add an eternity of being disabled to what you've already suffered?"

She frowned. "Well, no, but still. I did it to myself."

"Yes, but your reasons were unselfish. I've seen many a stronger man unable to defend what is his when another inflicted the wound, but you, Haven, you were able to do this to yourself for the sole purpose of saving another life." He gave a low, courtly bow. "My brother could not have found a better lifebond than you, Reannon."

Haven lowered her head, having no idea how to respond. Wolf stirred in the corner. "Let her rest, brother. Quinn will be home soon, and Haven still has a fight ahead of her."

The two men made a sweep through the bedroom, gathering up all sharp items or anything else Haven could use to harm herself, from Quinn's ties to shoelaces. She let out an indignant squawk. "I am not going to kill myself."

"I know that, little sister, but Quinn is not yet of the faithful." Wolf placed her book about the Undying next to her on the bed. "Rest, he will be home soon, and then you can convince him."

Nikon glided through the door and hopped into the bed next to her. Riordan nodded before he left, and then Wolf followed him, closing and locking the door behind him.

"So now I am on suicide watch. Great!"

Nikon dropped his head into her lap. *"Relax. Quinn is about an hour out. Rest, read a little, and be ready to show him there is one alive who can be more stubborn than him."*

"How is Medea? She seems a little subdued today."

"She grows closer to her time. It is natural."

Haven grumbled, fluffed her pillows, settled against the headboard, and pulled the book into her lap. She flipped through the pages and stopped at a section referencing the Mortis. Humanoid zombie-like creatures created with black magic spells that scaled walls like a spider and wouldn't die, no matter how many pieces they were hacked into. She grimaced and decided history might be a better place to start. She flipped through the pages, skimming until she found an entire section devoted to Quinn, to the Cadeyrn. The name meant Battle King in ancient Undying, and it wasn't something Wolf had bound into the book because Quinn was her lifebond. He was the most important male of their people. She sat upright and placed the book on the bed. She found the comfort of Nikon's fur as she became absorbed in the long history of the man she loved.

* * * *

Donovan's mind had reacted violently when he found Wolf's knife in the bathtub, and he had to get himself out of the penthouse before he'd done something unforgiveable—like kill Wolf. Donovan knew his brother had put the idea into the woman's head.

He knew she'd had a lot of insecurities and fears, but he'd never thought she was capable of taking her own life. He wasn't in the proper state of mind to pass judgment against his brother. Part of him was elated he wouldn't have to give up the *treòir*. Another part of him was terrified soul deep at what Haven unleashed inside of him.

He wanted to stay in denial.

The elevator door slid open. It was quiet. Maverick was out patrolling the city on foot while Brogan was still perched on top of the building. Riordan was in the kitchen cleaning dishes, and Wolf was lounged across the couch in the living room. A low rumbling began in Donovan's chest. He still wanted to kill his brother, but now wasn't the time. He would need Wolf to kill Kyros, then, his brother would suffer for what he'd put into Haven's head.

"Where is she?"

"Locked in your room. Don't worry. We left her with Nikon and removed anything she could use to hurt herself."

Donovan didn't like that Wolf's statement made him feel a tiny bit better. "I will deal with you later." He took off his coat and hung it in the closet before he took the stairs two at a time. He stopped at the door and stared at the knob. Would he need to break the door down to get to her? Would she be half-dead when he entered the room? If she was, could she be saved this time? He shoved all that out of his mind and reached above the door molding for the key. After unlocking the door, he replaced the key and silently went into the room.

His body and mind stilled when he saw her. Her hair was draped around her as she sat hunched over a leather bound book. Her hand tightened in Nikon's fur. "That's so sad. Did this really happen?"

She bit her bottom lip, and then her head snapped up, her pale eyes wide as she looked at him. Her voice unsteady. "Hi."

He nodded but didn't move closer. "Haven."

She pushed the book away from her and moved to the edge of the bed, her eyes never leaving his face. "How was your day?"

"I had to work. You can't expect me to be able to stay with you every second of every day."

She stilled and lowered her head. "I was just asking how your day was. I haven't seen you in a while."

The muscles in his jaw contracted. "You've been a sleep for a while. Do you hurt at all?"

Her lower jaw trembled. "Only a little sore. Riordan fixed my arm, under threat of Wolf holding me down."

Donovan's heart twisted in his chest. "You didn't want him to heal your arm the rest of the way? Why?"

"I did it to myself. I can't expect anyone to fix my consequences for me."

His hands burned with the need to reach out to her, to touch her and sooth the new hurt he could feel growing inside of her, but he was afraid of the damage his mind could do to hers. "You should have talked to me."

"You'd already given up. You were giving into what Kyros wanted." She got off the bed but didn't go to him. She went to the window and looked out. "I love you. I'm sorry I hurt you."

Dark and savage emotions reared. His voice came out as a snarl. "You tried to kill yourself. If I hadn't gotten to you when I did—"

"We'd both be dead. I know." Her shoulders rounded. "Did I break us?"

"Why didn't you talk to me?"

She caught her breath. "That's not an answer."

"I can't trust that you are safe even with yourself."

"You said you love me. Is that still true?" Her voice was so soft and so full of despair that his heart twisted again.

"I don't know what I feel right now."

She let out a slow, shuddering breath. She quietly went to the bed, collected her book, walked a wide circle around him, and left him standing in the room.

Nikon bared his fangs as he hopped off the bed and advanced on Donovan. The wolf circled him. A low rumbling coming from deep within. *"You wound her unjustly, Cadeyrn. You do not understand what she overcame to sacrifice herself for you."*

"What are you talking about?"

"Speak to her with an open mind. Her reasons were just and not against the laws of your kind. Her actions were of love. Do not dishonor her, or my allegiance to you is finished."

Donovan moved his hand in time to avoid Nikon's vicious snap of sharp fangs. Then the wolf trotted after her.

Medea nuzzled his hand. *"You are wounded, but so is your heart. Go and speak with her while I go and speak with mine."*

Donovan rubbed Medea's ear as he stood there for a long moment, and then with a heavy sigh, he changed into something more comfortable and went to go find Haven. She was sitting at the kitchen table. The book was open. Her brow furrowed in an adorable way as she studied the contents. His voice was a soft whisper. "What are you reading?"

She didn't look at him. "A book Wolf wrote about the Undying. Dinner is started. I'll let you know when it's done."

"Where are my brothers?"

"They left. Riordan will be by tomorrow to take me to see Bastian."

He kept his voice soft. "I can take you."

She shook her head and finally looked at him with a soul-deep sadness in her eyes. "I know you have things to take care of, and he said he didn't mind."

He sat down across from her. He sought to find some kind of numbness from the twisting in his gut, but he wasn't going to leave her alone. Not in the kitchen with so many knives within easy reach. He stretched across the table and ran a finger over the top of the book pages. It was the closest he could bring himself to touching her. "So, he actually did write a book. Learn anything interesting?"

Her pale eyes met his. "He has over a hundred pages on you."

"Does he? That's…interesting."

She smiled faintly, but it didn't touch her eyes. "Actually it is, and a lot of it is heartbreaking. You saved the life of two young Undying Dragons, even after their father killed yours."

"Aye," he said softly.

Haven's smile went a little wider. "But you love them, anyway. You saved their lives. They would be the same kind of monster as Kyros if it wasn't for you."

The tension in his body eased. "Kale can be a problem child at times."

"That may be, but you took in the children of your enemy, even after he killed your parents. Not many men would do that." Her eyes were filled with so much love and compassion that he had to look away. She let out a soft breath.

"It wasn't their fault their father went mad. I couldn't take it out on them. Kane was just a baby."

"Quinn, why are you defending this like you did something wrong?"

The tips of their fingers touched, and he jerked back.

"What is it?"

He grimaced. "You tried to kill yourself! Why? I would have left you alone if you'd have asked."

Her mouth dropped open, and then she took several deep breaths before she reached over and lightly ran a finger over his. "I wasn't trying to kill myself. I never expected to die."

He clamped his hand down over hers. "What are you talking about?"

Fear registered on her face. "You said if I was Undying and you weren't, you'd find a way to make me change you because you'd have to protect me forever. I thought… Damn it! Quinn, I thought if I was dying, you wouldn't have a choice, and then you wouldn't give up your power, your life. You'd taken away my ability to convince you over time."

His eyes flared a deep and golden umber, and he caught a hold of her wrist, clamping down with so much force she was afraid he was going to snap the bone. She tugged, but his grip only went tighter, pulling her up and onto the table. "You manipulated me. Goddamn it, woman!"

Instead of closing herself off from him, Haven projected a raw fear that ripped through her because of him. Her voice was a whisper. "You're hurting me."

He let go, and she sank back into her chair. She took a deep breath and slowly let it out. Carefully, she closed the book and then stood up. "Is there a way to change me back? You can choose to grow old. Can I do the same?"

His growl was a savage snarl, his teeth bared. "I am not letting you take this back, woman! Not after the hell you put us both through because of it."

She didn't back down from him. Her chin lifted, and her eyes met his with a fire of their own. "I survived it. Maybe not because of my own strength, but because you wouldn't let me die. That has to mean something. I am your lifebond. You don't have to like what I did, but please don't shut me out because you are angry with me."

He was prowling the kitchen now as rage boiled inside of him. Donovan knew her arguments made sense, and it's exactly what he would have done if the situation was reversed. He caused this. He killed her. She'd been dead in his arms, and the only thing that had brought her back was his unwillingness to let her go. Every wall, every carefully constructed cage for the power within he'd created vanished, and he struggled to control it. He couldn't hurt her, couldn't be what destroyed her. If he did, there would be no coming back for him. "In all my life no one has ever once defied me the way you do. No one has ever been able to make me do anything against my will. My will is what rules us and binds us to our laws. You carelessly threw it away on a whim for immortality."

Her face drained of all color, and she cast her gaze to the floor. "I think I need to be alone for a little while." She went to the oven and turned it off. "I'll finish your dinner later." Then she walked out of the room.

Donovan dropped onto the chair. Goddamn it. She wasn't Helena, and he wasn't Kyros. Instead of owning the fact his inaction had caused her to harm herself, he accused her of the same thing Helena had done because Kyros thought she was his mate. Helena had wanted immortality, and she'd wanted Kyros to convert her.

Haven's footfalls paced the length of the bedroom before she went into the bathroom. Fear clawed through him, and he was in motion in the next instant. He didn't even stop to see if it was locked. He put a shoulder into it and broke the freshly mended door off its hinges. He'd have preferred the sight that greeted him to have been the same as the one he walked into days before, but instead, he found her curled into the corner, her arms wrapped around her knees, which were pulled in tight to her chest. Medea sat close to her, trying to offer comfort Haven wouldn't accept. Haven's head was bowed and her shoulders rounded. Her tiny body was wracked by savage sobs.

With two quick strides, he was in front of her. He crouched down and started to reach for a strand of her hair and then let his arm fall to his side as he realized he didn't have a right. His voice was subdued, more like his own. "I'm sorry. I don't know why I said that."

She grew still. Her voice shook. "Go away, Quinn. I want to be alone for a while, please."

"Damn it! I'm a bloody bastard. I caused you to kill yourself. And it's making me crazy."

Haven's eyes were swollen and red from crying. "I'm not dead."

"No, but you were. There were a couple of minutes that I was alone in the tub. It was just me breathing for both of us."

"I died?" The realization showed in her eyes. "My God."

His voice cracked. "Yes."

She scrambled into him, knocking him backward. His arms banded tightly around her as she cried, "I'm sorry, Quinn, so sorry."

The *treòir* within faded back into the corner of his mind. Anger still bubbled in its core, but it was content to let her scent, the softness of her skin, the way her hair brushed fire across his flesh sooth the man for now.

The beat of her heart sounded loudly in his ears and brought the sting of tears to his eyes. She was alive, and he wasn't trapped in some fantasy his mind had concocted to keep himself from totally losing his sanity.

Chapter 16

"What have I done?" she whispered.

Donovan held her close to his chest as the madness faded back, and he was finally able to think clearly again. Being able to feel her helped tremendously. He wasn't safe to be around her, at least not alone. He knew all the dangers. The *treòir* had been unlocked in the moment of Haven's death, and he didn't know if he could control the power again, not even with her sweet scent enveloping his senses, the feel of her skin touching his. The *treòir* was quiet for now, but raged at what Donovan had done to his lifebond. At how careless he'd been to her feelings and her own need to save his life. If Donovan didn't regain control, the *treòir* would claim her for itself, and Haven would be trapped in a nightmare far worse than anything Mason could have done to her. He carefully lifted her with him as he stood and carried her into the bedroom. He set her down on the bed and took several steps back from her. "It's not your fault. I should have listened to you and trusted myself. The only one to blame is me."

Haven squeezed her eyes shut. "I'm the one who didn't—"

"Don't. You're in danger here. You are my lifebond, and even as I fight the *treòir,* it wants possession of you. To control you in a way I can't even begin to explain."

She opened her eyes, so much love and trust showing in them that it tore at his heart, ripped at his insides. The *treòir* wanted to rear up and devour what hurt her, but Donovan shoved it back once more. She slipped off the bed. "I did this to you. Let me help you. Let me find a way to make this right."

Donovan couldn't stop her hand sliding under the hem of his shirt, her touch branding his skin. He let out a dark rumble, knowing this was the least safe activity for them to be doing. He stepped back and groaned.

Haven's eyes went round. He was afraid of her. No, he was afraid *for* her.

She canted her head to the side. "Very well, then, I want you to take me out. I want to be with you, but if we can't do that here, then take me to one of your clubs. You have four, and I've only been to Coliseum."

That was safe. Being near helpless humans would make it easier for him to control the *treòir*—as long as Kyros didn't show up. "All right, do you want to go to Tribal, Pharaoh, or Fantasia?"

* * * *

Swallowing hard, Haven made up her mind to do this. The other horrible things that had happened the last few times they ventured out of the apartment couldn't happen this time. Quinn had an army of men walking the city streets. There was a way to help him, and she needed to focus on what would get Quinn captivated.

She mentally went through the new clothes she had, and nothing seemed to work for what she was planning to do. Once again, they had that wonderful connection where it was difficult to tell who was who, but she was learning to use Rowan's necklace to help her keep an air of mystery with Quinn. She glanced at the clock. It was still early enough they could get to a boutique and then make it to Fantasia before it was too late to really enjoy themselves. She'd heard that while Tribal did have belly dancers, Fantasia did, too, but they let the audience participate in the show. She turned a sweet, innocent smile up to him. "I need a new dress."

"Fine, let's go." Then he bellowed, "Nikon, you are coming with." He started toward the door and looked over his shoulder at Haven. "Where are we going?"

"Fantasia."

He froze and turned to look at her. "You wanted to go to Tribal the other night." His voice was tight, almost pleading.

She grinned at him and pushed him out the door. "Of course I did, but this is today, and I want to go to Fantasia today. It will be fun, and we need to hurry if I am going to spend enough of your money to get myself a knockout outfit and make all the men's heads turn."

"I am a danger to others." His voice was strained.

She nodded as she tugged him down the stairs. "Yes, Quinn, I know." He thought he was dangerous, but she knew better. Neither Quinn, nor his power, would do anything that would prevent them from having their lifebond. "I was thinking something in green. I look dynamite in the right color green, and maybe something backless, with those thin little spaghetti straps with a flowing skirt on it or something with slits in the side." She batted her eyes at him. "What do you think?"

* * * *

His head was going to explode, right into a bloody mess on the floor, but he'd be damned, the fucking *treòir* was amused with what she was planning. He growled when she stopped and turned to look at him. "You're not going to wear that, are you? Go change and I will clean up the kitchen real quick."

He was so stunned that the *treòir* inside of him had stopped rumbling that he couldn't do anything other than what Haven had asked. When he got back downstairs, she was already dressed to combat the cold and was waiting for him by the door with Nikon at her side. Her smile was beautiful, excited, and made his heart do a flip.

She made an erotic sound with her throat. "I expect more than just the men's head will be turning tonight, my Quinn." Then she slipped her hand into his and allowed him to guide her down to the Hummer.

When they got to the boutique she wanted, Haven appeared shocked when Donovan insisted that Nikon go in with them. "You're not going to let me into the dressing room with you, so he's coming with us."

"He's a wolf. You can't explain him away as a seeing-eye-dog." Her hand went protectively on top of Nikon's head. "That would be insulting to try to do so."

The heaviness on his shoulders lifted a smidgen. "No, but he does have his companion dog papers, and I have the right harness in the back."

"You're serious?" She narrowed her eyes at him. "What breed did you say he was?"

"Husky-Newfoundland mix." He opened the glove compartment, flipped through a stack of papers, and then handed her the right ones.

Her name was on them as the person who needed the companion animal. Her brow furrowed. "Why is my name on these?"

"I had the papers made a few days ago. I don't need a wolf to follow me around to make sure some dark and evil thing isn't going to carry me off into the night. I already had the papers because that makes it easier to take him places when I need to, but they like to have a name on them."

She gave him an accusing look. "So you put mine on there."

"I am sure it would be nice to have Nikon around if Kyros showed up while you were shopping."

Her mouth dropped open. "You're not coming in with me?"

"No, I have something else I need to get."

"Okay. How do I put the harness on him?"

They got out of the car, and Quinn showed her how to put the harness on Nikon, take it off, and had her practice a few times. He pointed out the modifications Wolf had made so that if the wolf needed to, he could be free of the contraption in seconds. "Get whatever you want, and I'll be back in a while. I'll let you know when I am on my way."

She was still grumbling about how insulting it was to call Nikon a dog as she stuffed the papers into her purse. "All right, and I'll let you know if I'm done before you get back. What's my budget?"

"Get whatever you think you need. I'll have bank cards with your name sent, and we'll go to see my lawyer tomorrow to get my will redrafted."

Her eyes snapped to his. "Will?"

He went over to her and brushed a kiss on her forehead, which seemed to please the *treòir*, and then took a step back. "I need to look human. Humans change wills as they move through the stages of life."

"Oh, okay." She kept giving him that wounded look, as if he was going to drop dead on the ground at any moment.

He gently pushed her toward the door, making sure she was holding on to Nikon's harness properly. They got strange looks as they went, and Donovan turned to her. "Stay in this store. If you need me, call me our way, all right. Brogan is out there close as well. It's faster, and I'll see what we can do about getting you a cell phone tomorrow."

"You're doing it again."

"What?"

"Spending too much money on me."

This time he leaned and brushed his mouth over hers and let his fingers play with a strand of her hair. "Humor me, my lifebond. It will make me feel better."

Her brow furrowed. "Does this mean we are something like married?"

"Not yet. It just means that you have to accept my need to provide for you everything you need and everything you want." He closed his eyes to keep her from seeing his struggle with the *treòir* as he said the words. "I love you, Haven. We will make this work between us, forever."

She brushed her fingers down the side of his face, and he opened his eyes. "I love you, Quinn, all of you. I'll meet you back here in a while, okay?"

He stood there, leaning his head against hers for a long moment before he slowly turned and walked away.

* * * *

The plan was simple. Prove to Quinn he was in control of himself no matter what else happened around them. She could feel the presence of what she thought was a dragon, and she was starting to be able to notice Wolf when he was close. Now that she was Undying, the only thing preventing her and Quinn from bonding was his inability to trust his *treòir*. Quinn seemed to feel better after spending money on her, so she'd factored that into the plan. Now she needed to swallow back her hang-ups with extravagance and enjoy getting ready to show Quinn he wasn't the menace to society he thought he was. Haven blew out a breath as she patted Nikon's head. "*Okay, you have to help me find something to spin his head off his shoulders.*"

"*You do know how dangerous he is, right? Those red eyes of his are not a very good sign at all.*"

"*He's Quinn, and every part of him is Quinn no matter what issue he is having. I said I accepted him and everything about him, and I meant it.*"

"*Then you just may save him yet. Come. I smell a pretty lady, and she might be able to help you with human fashion far better than I could.*"

Haven let the wolf guide her through the store to the woman at the perfume counter. Nikon backed up and flattened his ears, then moved forward slowly, his nose twitching. "*She's dying to do something called a Cinderella make over. I'm not sure what that means, but you can ask her.*"

Haven smiled and then caught the attention of the woman at the counter. Her nametag read *Donna*. "Excuse me, I have this really important date tonight, and I have no idea what to pick out for it. Can you help me?"

The woman flicked a glance at her. When she saw the wolf, her eyes went huge. "Is that what I think he is?"

Haven's smile went sweet. "This is Nikon. He's a companion dog. I am seeing this man, Quinn Donovan, and we're going to his club, Fantasia, tonight, and I have no idea where to even begin, and we are leaving from here, so I kind of need to get everything here."

"Quinn Donovan? Hang on just a second." She picked up the phone and hit a few numbers. "Hey, I need help! There is a woman here who has a date with Quinn Donovan." She paused. "Yes way, and she needs our help." She hung up the phone and beamed at Haven. "Okay, the first thing you need is a dress, so let's get your coat off to see what kind of figure we are dealing with."

Haven took off her coat and put it onto the counter. The woman inspected her and smiled. "Okay, Fantasia is a fantasy-themed club, and they have this awesome Middle Eastern Dance show. Is that something you would want to be a part of?"

"I dance some."

The woman gave her an impish wink. "Then we need to find you something that will show off your belly and make Donovan drool."

Several more sales girls flocked the area, and before Haven knew what was happening, she was in the dressing room and modeling dress after dress until they decided on a shimmering Kelly-green dress that bared her stomach and dipped low in the front. The skirt was long and flowed around her just the way she liked, the one side with a slit up to the hip. They found a darling pair of silver high-heeled shoes that wrapped around her ankles. Then the women herded her to the counter for a complete makeover. One of the girls played with her hair and then decided to leave it down for the exotic dancer effect they were going for. Then, they all stepped back to admire their work.

They stuffed her clothes into a shopping bag. Donna was babbling excited at her. "You should get a full length coat, too, just so it will be a total surprise when you get to the club with him, and a few bracelets, and some kind of necklace, too."

Haven groaned. It physically hurt to not look at any of the price tags, but she needed to do this. Quinn needed to see that she trusted him completely, even if he was having difficulty with his dark side. To prove herself, she had to let him take care of her, which, for some strange male reason, equated into him spending money. She couldn't believe that he would turn into anything like Kyros, not when she was here to pull him back. "All right, whatever you ladies think."

They added a set of wrist bangles to each arm that worked perfectly with the shoes, but Haven firmly declined a necklace. Rowan's wolf head pendant was beautiful and not something she was willing to take off just yet. Then they took her back to the dressing room for the mirror. Haven stared at her reflection and almost demanded they take everything back. The person looking back at her was some sexy vixen, but she was glowing.

Her voice was shy. "Do you think he'll like this?"

"Haven, honey, Quinn Donovan would be a fool not to fall madly in love with you," Donna said as she helped her back into the full-length suede coat that covered her down to her toes.

"I'll have to take your word for it."

Donna blinked and looked confused for a moment, then brushed it off. "I'll give you a sample of perfume to take with you."

"Tell her no," Nikon said.

"What? Why?"

"Quinn likes how you naturally smell, and so do I. Please don't add any more offensive orders to my poor nose tonight. I think you may have to bandage it when we get home. Besides, that smelly stuff has been upsetting Medea's belly."

Haven couldn't help the laugh, and Donna just shook her head at her. "Thank you, Donna, but I won't need the perfume."

"Okay, but it can only help you."

"I'm sure, but my companion has a sensitive nose."

"Oh, right. Okay, well I'll just get this all rung up for you, and I'll meet you over at the counter." Donna took a collection of tags over to the counter to do just that.

Haven pulled herself away from the mirror and closed her eyes. "*Quinn?*"

"*Are you okay? I can be there in two minutes.*"

"*I'm fine. I have everything I need. I just need to pay for it.*"

"*I'll be there in a few minutes.*"

"*Thank you.*"

"*Haven?*"

"*Yes.*"

"*I love you.*"

Her heart warmed. He was starting to sound like himself again. Her plan seemed to be working. She didn't need retail therapy. He did.

* * * *

Donovan walked back into the boutique and found Haven shrouded in a huge coat that covered everything but her face. She grinned at him. "Well, how do I look?"

A gaggle of women peered at them from over the clothing racks. He lifted a brow, and several of them gasped and backed away. Haven only tsked at him. "You are scaring people, again. Now, I've done what you asked, and I promise I didn't even look at one price tag, but it hurt, pal, it really hurt."

He chuckled. "I'm sure you'll find a way to live." He went over to the counter and paid the bill.

His hand cupped around her waist as he led her back to the car. He leaned down and murmured against her ear. "You look happy, and your new coat is beautiful. Am I going to find jeans and a T-shirt under that?"

She laughed. "You just might, but you're not going to find out until we get there."

He loved her laugh. It calmed and soothed both him and the darkness fighting to get free. He helped her into the passenger seat and then took the harness off Nikon. A short while later they were at the club. Haven made him stop before he could whisk her into his office again as she turned in a slow circle. His other clubs had been designed to mimic ancient civilizations he'd witnessed firsthand, but Fantasia was a creation all his own. It was what he thought a fairy glade would look like in Avalon with twinkling lights and floral garlands draped between pillars.

"This place is wonderful. Why do you live in a cave?"

He put his hand to his heart as if he'd been hit with a fatal wound. "Ouch, Haven. If you don't like it, we'll redecorate."

"Only if we start with the bathroom, if that's all right with you."

"Perfect. All right, I am curious to see what my money bought for you to seduce me."

She giggled and slowly undid all the buttons on the coat and then shrugged out of it. He swallowed hard as his cock went hard. "You're going to give this old man heart failure. I swear it."

She laughed again. "Not if I only stand here, I won't. You owe me a dance, and before we get sidetracked by anything else, you are going to give it to me."

He leaned down and nibbled at her throat. "Are you sure? I have to work with some of these people. I can't have them laughing at me whenever they see me."

She bit down on her lip and grinned at him. "I told you anyone could slow dance."

"But the beat isn't slow. It's for the dancers on the floor."

* * * *

"Then I'll just have to teach you," she said as she curled her hand around his. She tugged him to the dance floor. She loved the Middle Eastern Dance, and seeing so many people attempting it was lovely. The beat was just right for a sultry shake of the hips. Dancing was like riding a bicycle for her.

The first song was to get used to the movements again. When the next song began, the patrons cheered, and everyone crowded the dance floor. She locked her gaze on Quinn's as she allowed her body to start to sway with the tantric rhythm. This was for Quinn. Her body moved with the pulse of the beat, brushing against his solid body with light, feminine motions. The music, the atmosphere, and the man transported her to another time, another place, and she danced with her soul. She didn't stop until the music did. She smiled at the carnal lust in Quinn's eyes. His hands clamped on her hips, and he pulled her into his arms, claiming her mouth.

"And the winner for this round is…. The woman lip locked with the boss in the center of the dance floor."

Haven's body was flushed with heated desire. Quinn dropped his head against hers and growled quietly. "I am going to fire him."

"Would the pretty lady like to come up and collect her prize?"

Haven grinned at Quinn. "No, you're not. You're going to be a good sport about this. What's the prize?"

"I have no idea. Usually it's a free drink or a free ticket to get in."

"Then I'll just have to decline," she said sweetly and tugged him along behind her as she went to the DJ booth.

The young man was grinning at Quinn with humorous intent in his eyes before his gaze went to Haven. "My, my, what a lovely winner we have here. What do you think we should give her?"

The crowd started shouting things out. Anything from a free drink to one man offering her a night of his services for free. Haven placed a hand on Quinn's chest when he growled. "Do behave," she whispered when saw the flecks of red in his eyes. "Both of you. I am having fun."

* * * *

To Donovan's astonishment, the *treòir* backed off, but they both agreed that glaring the man back into his place was in the bounds of behaving.

The DJ cleared his throat in a dramatic way. "I think that we should leave it to our overprotective host to bestow a gift on the lovely lady."

The crowd applauded their approval. Donovan gave Gary, the DJ, a look that could melt stone, and then his grin went wicked. He took Haven's hand. This was perfect. A dragon out of the Pacific tribe had finished just in time. He shifted a glance at Gary. "You asked for it."

Then Haven became the only thing he could see. She would be bound to him and his *treòir* for an eternity. Though he was terrified of hurting her, but without her, the *treòir* would take over him completely, and the man that he was would be no more. Haven had given much for this moment, and she deserved something special for her troubles. Both of his giant hands clasped around her tiny ones, and he pulled her in to him. He didn't notice the DJ until he was in close with his microphone. But all he wanted was his lifebond to know how much he needed her. He dropped down onto his knees in front of her.

"Haven Killian, from the first moment I saw you, I knew my life would never be the same without you. Every part of me is in love with every part of you. I know we come from two different worlds, but I need you with me, forever and always. Haven, will you marry me?"

Haven's face lit up as tears collected in her eyes, her head bobbing before she could say any words, a hand covering her mouth. She closed her eyes and smiled as she wrapped herself around him. "I love you, Quinn. I will marry you. I want to be with you forever and always."

The crowd cheered and then started to chant. "Ring, ring, ring."

Donovan laughed as he slid a hand into his pocket, pulled out a tiny purple box, and opened it. Haven's face flashed amazement, and she beamed at him as she gently took the ring out and slid it on to her finger. He breathed against her ear. "Woman, you are mine."

She laughed quietly before her mouth yielded to him. The crowd went wild.

"All right, all right, I think we should give the happy couple some space and start the next contest, though I can't promise as good a prize as what Miss Haven received." He winked at her. Donovan ushered her off stage and away from the DJ booth toward his office.

* * * *

"I need something to drink first," Haven said and pulled him to the bar instead. "A water is fine," she told the bartender. She moved in close to Quinn and was glad when Nikon pressed into her leg. While she tried to pretend she was handling the traumatic events, she had no wish to repeat them. The bartender gave her the water and served Quinn the glass of bourbon he ordered. Quinn gave him a large tip, and Haven settled onto his lap. She couldn't stop looking at everything disguised as a magical fairy glade. "Do I even want to know where you've seen this place before?"

He shifted her in his lap, and then placed his hand over his heart. "Here, I've seen it here, but I didn't realize until tonight that this place is real. It lives in you. You are magic, woman."

She laid her head on his chest in a way that she could keep looking at everything. The club was beautiful, from the walls to the fairy lights that glittered to the secret grottos with tables and happy people all around them. Quinn had created a fairytale. Here and there were paintings that added to the illusion of this magical place, but the paintings were of warriors, standing as silent sentinels over the patrons, making it safe for all who entered. She'd seen all those faces in the men who guarded them during this eventful bonding.

The one above the bar was a life-sized painting of Quinn. He was in his full battle regalia, the same on display in the penthouse. His brow and chest gleamed with sweat, and he had the very same look as when Mason had scared her in the mall—a man determined to keep the gates of hell closed and those around him from the dangers only he could hold back. She studied the painting. The likeness was uncanny. She shifted in his lap. But there was something that wasn't quite right. His eyes. They did have their golden umber flame, but there were tiny flecks of red in them. She furrowed her brow as she sipped at the water. "Who's the artist?"

"Emily Hopkins. I'll introduce you. She and I get along fairly well, if she'd ever learn to lock a door."

Haven laughed. "Maybe she does it to drive you crazy? I would, if I didn't think you'd throttle me for attempting."

He nibbled at her throat. "I don't want to talk about paintings. I want to talk about being buried deep inside of you."

She leaned back into him but couldn't take her eyes off his in the painting. "Does she know what you are?"

He rested his chin on the top of her head. "No, she's human."

"Did you stand for the painting? In your battle regalia?"

"No, Emily sees things as they really are. I think she is one of fairy sight. I've thought about telling her, but it could be dicey with how humans view another who sees magic, and she already believes she is a little crazy."

"As they really are," Haven echoed. She leaned forward to get a closer look at the eyes of the painting. Yes, Quinn's *treòir*, the red flecks of the power within, were there. It was a part of him, like the sword in his hand, his thick hair twisted into a braid and hanging over his shoulder. It was as much a part of him as Nikon at his side or her being his lifebond. "Quinn, we need to go home. I need to look something up in the book Wolf gave me."

"Now?" He sounded disgruntled. She could feel why when she settled her bottom in his lap, and his hard-on pressed against the back of her thigh.

"Yes, now. I'll make it up to you once I look it up. I promise."

He let out a long-suffering sigh. "All right, woman, you want to go home, we go home, but we share a bed tonight."

She turned, grinned at him, and then leaned up and kissed his chin. "I need to be a good lifebond. There are just things I don't know yet, and you and all your stubborn glory would try to protect me from them."

His brow furrowed. "What is it?"

"It's just a thought, but I have to check something first before I tell you."

"All right," he said with that mournful note of a man who knew he was going to be denied.

Chapter 17

Haven flipped the book open the second she was able. She turned to the page where Wolf explained in great detail how the *treòir* of the Undying male worked. She skimmed over the information, taking in every word. The power was a part of them since birth but didn't activate until they hit puberty. They always struggled to keep it from taking control of the body and mind. If that happened, they would turn into the same kind of monster Kyros was, locked in a hell where there was never enough blood to quench their thirst. Then it would slowly consume them until they started hunting the innocent to get what they craved. But the book didn't give a reason for why someone with fairy sight would see a mix of color in Quinn's eyes. She closed the book in frustration. Nothing told her why or how the sides of Quinn would combined.

There were a couple things that made the long, lonely fight bearable. One was to find a lifebond, and the other was death. She closed her eyes to see the painting over the bar again, and then she looked at Quinn who was hovering over her. Her mouth dropped open. "How long have you been with your *treòir* this close to the surface?"

He huffed. "As long as I can remember."

"And you let it out to make the kill, don't you?"

His face twitched and went dark. "Always."

He closed his eyes as he pulled Haven into his memory. The battle was still fresh in his mind, unable to be dulled by the passage of time. Back to a time in his youth. To when his father was still Cadeyrn.

A storm raged far above in a turbulent sky, sending down a torrent that could not quench the hell fires licking the stone walls. A fire that burned so hot it reduced the stone to ash. Only the fire of the dragon clan could burn that hot. Screams drowned out the battle sounds raging below. For untold centuries, the clan of the dragon and that of the wolf had worked together to insure the safety of their people. Directing them, commanding them, helping them, and leading them. It had all been wiped out in one night of madness. The dragon Caden of the Cadeyrn had turned, but it should have been an impossibility. His lifebond should have prevented it, should have kept the change from happening. But no one could have foretold of the woman's untimely death.

There was a river of blood, human and Undying. So much death, the air was rank with it. The children. It was the only thought in his mind. Someone had to save the children from this blood bath. Swiftly, Quinn moved through the great halls of his ancestral home, calling his brother to him, the one who bore the name of their clan.

His mother stood guard over the door that led to the safe room for the women and children, the warriors all around her fallen. Her life was fading as she used her essence to keep the children locked inside a room in the belly of the citadel, protecting them from the fires as they raged. He reached out to aid her, adding his strength to hers, but it was to no avail. He was too late. By the time he reached the door, she, too, was lost to the senseless slaughter.

"Father." *His mind reached out.*

"I know, my son." *Despair was thick in his tone.* "Do not let her death be in vain. Protect them."

He fought the fires with his own magic, but he was not strong enough. The power of the dragon was too great. The beast of legend flapped its wings, sending waves of gale force winds whipping through the citadel. Quinn was unable to stand up against it. In the distance was the call of the wolf. The pack was coming to help them. "No." *He warned Nikon and the other Ashina wolves of the pack.* "Call them back. We are doomed. Do not let your pack be killed."

"We are coming." *Nikon, the strongest of the pack, responded.*

Quinn's strength was failing as he fought the unholy blaze. The whispers in his mind grew louder. The one he'd been taught to keep locked inside at all costs. It called to him, enticed him with long life and a power that would be unmatched. The children—they would die if he couldn't stop this. Fire kissed the soles of his boots. Frantic screams ripped through him. For all the power and might of the Wolf Clan, it was no match for that of a Dragon with a slain mate. Quinn wished his father were with him, knew that his father would be able to stop the fires, but he wasn't there. With his lifebond, Quinn's mother, gone, there was no hope for them. Soon Joseph would join the dragon in its destruction. Still, the voice of the treòir *within called to him. Promised to stop the fires, to conquer the dragon with a fire so hot he could melt stone. The door made of granite protecting the women and children started to melt. Pulsing liquid rock puddled on the floor. Quinn called out for his brother again, but there was no answer. He was trapped, his body broken. Quinn was alone.*

May the gods forgive him! He reached out to the whisper, giving in to the tempting words, and allowed his own treòir *to fill him. At once he was able to reach out to a mountain pass, and with the aid of an Earth Warrior, bring down a flash flood. Then, with the aid of a Storm Warrior, Quinn was able to make the air around the women and children so cold that the fire choked and died. They were now locked in a room surrounded by ice, and Quinn's eyes burned with the dark power within.*

He ran up the stairs to the main hall where his father confronted the power of the dragon. His father's gaze turned to him. "Protect them, my son." *He slipped the sacred ring from his finger and threw it into the rubble. Mighty Joseph, the Cadeyrn of all the Undying people, threw down his weapons and spread his arms open wide.* "You took her from me. You took her from our sons and from our people. I will not become you. Take me!" *The dragon landed over top of him and consumed him.*

The treòir *inside of Quinn raged hot and violent. Quinn ran directly at the dragon, picked up his father's sword, and skidded across the stone, plunging the blade deep into the belly. The dragon screamed its pain and rage. The form flickered and then faded into a black nothingness. Quinn lifted his head, his gaze narrowing on his prey. He might be an ancient, but Quinn knew with his new power, he'd be able to defeat him.*

"Quinn!" *Came the voice of his youngest brother, Riordan, not yet six years in life.* "Quinn, the water is coming in. I can't hold it back."

The treòir *raged to kill the enemy, but Riordan's voice called to him again.* "Quinn, the other children are afraid. Are we going to die?"

It was a battle Quinn expected to lose, but he held on tight to the image of his young brother, and with everything that was inside of him, he pushed the darkness back into the tiny corner of his mind so that it was only whispering to him again. "No, little brother, you will not die."

He broke eye contact with the monster dragon and ran back to help the children survive. The ice was melting all around them, and the room was filling up. Again, he knew he could not save them with his power alone, and once again, he let the treòir *consume him, knowing that once his people were safe, he'd be able to put it back into its cage.*

Quinn's body trembled. His grip was brutal and bruising, but Haven wasn't going to let this happen to him, not to her Quinn. She didn't mask the fear that tingled along her spine, but she wasn't going to give into it either. "I won't leave you."

The laugh that rumbled from him was dark and not entirely his own. He lifted her up and brought her down hard on the kitchen countertop. He forced her legs apart and stepped between them. One hand slid under the skirt of her dress and the other was possessive on her breast. "You do not need to fear me."

"I do not fear my lifebond. You will not hurt me."

His teeth scraped against her throat, nipping, pinching her tender flesh. She drew in a sharp breath, and he smiled. "I am your bond, not the man."

She leaned up and flicked her tongue over his pulse point. "You are part of Quinn and are part of what makes him my lifebond. You've a duty to protect me above all things."

"He is pathetic and weak and would have allowed you to die. We bond now." To prove it, he ripped the front of her dress apart and bent his head down, his teeth scraping across a nipple.

She curled her fingers into his hair, holding his head to her breast. She whispered, "You cannot take what I freely give you."

The grip he had on her arm grew tighter and tighter until Haven had no choice but to cry out for fear he would snap a bone. His eyes were a mix of gold and red flame when his hold loosened. Haven slipped her mind into Quinn's.

The landscape was black and foreboding. She could feel the two distinct presences, one of unfailing compassion and duty, the other of power and control. They swirled around her, fighting for dominance, and it frightened her, but she pushed forward, seeking something she could hold on to, something solid in his mind, the image he held of himself. Two figures formed. One of the man Haven knew, who was tall, brooding, and beautiful with eyes of a golden fire. The other was of an ancient warrior, poised and ready for battle, the darkness glowing red in his eyes. She stood between them and could feel the menace as if it was a third, altogether different, entity.

"You cannot do this," she whispered.

The dark Quinn laughed. "She knows I will take you, my brother."

"Not while I have breath in me," the golden-eyed one said as he moved with jungle cat grace, putting his essence between Haven and the threat.

"You will get her killed and us. You are weak with your compassion. I would not allow such things. Kyros would already be dead."

Haven slipped herself between the two Quinn's in his mind. She didn't look at either one of them. "I need you both."

The dark Quinn wavered. "That is not possible."

"I cannot survive the way you wish of me, as a slave to your whims and desires. What makes me would fade into a place of nothingness that I've no wish to go back to." Then she addressed the other Quinn. "The world is far more dangerous than I ever imagined, and I need you safe. He protects the heart of you, the part of you I need to survive." She moved back so she could look at both of them. "I need both of you to survive. Can't you see that? If one defeats the other, I die too."

The *treòir* roared his anger. Haven crouched down and covered her ears with her hands at the horrific sound.

Quinn's voice sounded. "Is this what you want for her? Cowering in fear of you when she willingly gave up her life for you?"

The *treòir* rumbled and prowled the space like a caged animal. "This cannot be. She should only need the strongest, the one that will destroy everything that threatens her."

"She is our lifebond. She needs safety, yes, but she needs to be loved, cherished for who and what she is. She brings laughter to us. Even you were willing to allow her antics at the club."

The *treòir* growled at him and then stopped all motion. "I have damaged her. You must fix it." Then the apparition evaporated back into Quinn's mind.

* * * *

Donovan was alone in his head again. His hand curled around Haven's bared midsection. He let go of her but didn't back up, because if he did, she'd fall to the floor. She lay there as still as death for a moment and then slowly sat up. Dark shadows were along her rib cage and belly. She shook her head and then rubbed at the bruising on her sides. When her eyes met his, she said, "I think I understand a little better."

He set her on her feet as gently as he could and went to the freezer to get some ice. She'd heal relatively quickly on her own, but he wasn't going to touch her, not after what just happened. The thought of her hurting made his head ache and the *treòir* twitch. "I'm calling Wolf. You are to lock yourself in my office and do not come out for any reason."

She took the ice from him and held it in her hand. "He didn't mean to," she pleaded. "It was an accident."

He took a step back from her. "Haven, I don't like your excuses for what I did."

She shrugged. "I've been beaten before, Quinn, and that's not what was happening here. Your *treòir* is just as possessive and protective as you are. It was just holding on a little too tight." She frowned. "He doesn't

understand emotions, I don't think. Like he leaves that up to you so he can
deal with other things. How often do you converse with him?"

She set the ice in the sink.

He growled at her. "Goddamn it. My body is where that thing lives,
and I can't control it anymore. I hurt you."

She let out a sigh. "So heal me. The bruise is small and doesn't even
hurt. I just startled your power when I slipped into your mind."

Donovan reached out and lightly touched the darkening shadows on
her ribs and belly. They vanished with a small release of his energy. "I
don't like you explaining this away. You are staying in my office. The
room's reinforced so that I can't break in. Well, so that an Undying can't,
which amounts to the same thing. You will be safe there, and I am calling
Wolf to come and get you."

"You can't do that. Your *treòir* is already attached to me, and it will
hurt you if you send me away, and you already know what I am capable
of if I think your life is in danger."

His head shattered into a million pieces. Images of her lifeless body
in the tub assaulted him, and his eyes flared at the thought. "So you're
going to bind yourself to an eternity of things like this happening? That's
not acceptable."

"Learn to work with him. He's right. I saw what happened with your
parents. Your *treòir* gave you the power to save those children, and he
was the one who drove out the dragon, but you took care of the aftermath.
And you took up the mantel for our people. He is part of you more than
you will admit, and you have to learn to live with him and work with him.
It's the only way you are ever going to find peace."

"But it hurt you, Haven. I hurt you. A small bruise this time. What's
it going to be next time? A broken arm and blood? I can't live with this.
Even if you've allowed Mason to condition you for abuse, I will not let
myself be what hurts you."

Haven went completely still at Mason's name and then looked up at
Quinn with hurt and defiance. "I know what abuse is, and I will not have
you telling me that I cannot help you with this fight. If your *treòir* gets
control, then we are both dead, but if you let me help you, together we
can find a way to control him for all time. I could feel you fighting for
me, to keep him from hurting me. That is not abuse. Mason never did that.
He just let his *treòir* have its way with me whenever the whim struck it."

His stomach twisted. "I can't hurt you."

"I won this argument the last time. Do you really want to live through
what I will do to protect you the way you protect me?"

He snarled. "This isn't funny. I could kill you without thought."

Her hands covered her face, and she shook her head. "No, you can't. Mason never could, though he'd came close a couple times. I don't think the *treòir* in and of itself is at all evil. I think the good or bad comes from the person who possesses it."

"Then how is Kyros evil now when he wasn't before?" he countered.

"The same reason humans who never seemed bad before suddenly do horrible things. The mind can only handle so much. Obviously, he really did care about Helena. Watching her die snapped something in him and probably in his *treòir*, too."

He took in a deep breath and let it out slowly. "We can discuss this more in a little bit. I need you to go change."

Haven glanced down and her face crumpled. "Damn, I really liked this dress, too. Maybe I can fix it." She looked up at him with an innocent face. "Can you get me a sewing machine, one with all the cool things on it? I love sewing things."

He crossed his arms over his chest. "I don't like this. Go put something else on, and we can finish this. Me and my *treòir* are going to pop a vein if we have to keep thinking about how the top was ruined."

"Touchy, aren't we?" She sashayed toward the door and then looked over her shoulder. "Keep him close. I may have some questions for him when I get back."

Donovan leaned against the counter, his shoulders trembling once she was out of sight. "Goddamn it," he swore to himself.

"I didn't mean to hurt her. Thank you for fixing her." The *treòir* seemed contrite.

"I must have finally lost my fucking mind." Since Haven and the *treòir* agreed that she needed the damn thing, he decided to try talking to it like he would anyone else. "Fuck it. I shouldn't have to fix her. She should have been perfectly safe with me. She is *my* lifebond."

"She is ours."

"Fine, whatever, but she can't be near me if you are going to hurt her."

"She's not upset. Why are you?" There was real confusion in the tone.

"Because I outweigh her by two-hundred pounds of muscle, because it would be easy enough for me to snap her neck and not even realize I did, because hitting a woman is just wrong for any reason. And I can't believe I am talking to myself like this."

"Maybe we should. She's tied your hands in getting rid of me, so maybe we do need to learn to coexist in peace."

"What are you anyway?"

"*I am a* treòir. *I am the power and the darkness that allows you to be what you are without destroying your soul. I am you.*"

"Then why have our people not told our unbonded males what to expect?"

"*Because we are dangerous. Only a lifebond can truly tame us. Haven's only partly right. Something inside of Kyros's* treòir *snapped and took over. The man you once knew is trapped in there, unable to stop the horror he is creating.*"

Donovan shuddered because he just had the experience and never wanted to go through that again. "Why can only the lifebond tame you?"

"*That is a little more complicated to explain in terms your mind would be able to understand. I know you wonder why she is your bond, and all I can tell you is that it is because I am attracted to her. There is something like me inside of her, but it is different. I am the warrior, the protector, and I will destroy anything I know that will cause her harm, but she tempers me and forces me to look at the world through your eyes. I still rile against being confined, and I will fight you for all eternity to be free, but I now see your compassion through her. I understand the need to be part of the world in a way that will not cause harm to others.*"

Haven came back into the room dressed in an over-sized T-shirt. He forced himself to be aware of the *treòir* and how he reacted to her without being confined. "*You will give me complete control of my body while I do this.*"

"*Yes, my brother.*"

A playful grin lit Haven's face. "I see you have been doing this without me. Care to share?"

He dragged a hand over his face. "Sit."

She shook her head. "I need something to eat, and you probably do, too. I should get the wolves fed. Medea should not be skipping meals at this point, no matter the reason." She turned to the refrigerator and bent over, the hem of her shirt sliding up, giving Donovan a wonderful view of her legs as they just started to round into her ass.

"We've agreed on a truce of sorts."

"That's wonderful. How'd that happen?"

"He likes you," he said.

Haven laughed as she pulled out the lasagna she'd started earlier, put it back into the oven, and turned it on. "Of course he does—he's you."

"That's what it said." He grabbed a couple of plates and set them on the counter.

Haven winced. "He's part of you, but acting independently of you. He can do things against your will. He's you and he's not, so I still win the argument about you not being the one who hurt me."

His brain twitched at her logic. "If he hurts you again, I swear by all that is holy I am locking you in my office, and you are not coming out for all eternity."

"So now he's a *he* instead of an *it*? I think there might be some progress. Can I talk to him?"

"Woman, you're making my head hurt."

"Stop being such a baby. He's not going to hurt me. I know you don't believe that, but he's part of you. This is that whole practice thing, and why I should have been talking to him all along."

It disturbed him greatly that not only had she said his own words, but the words of the *treòir*, as well. She also wasn't afraid of him. He knew what she'd suffered at the hands of Mason's *treòir*, and yet, she wasn't afraid of his. He let out a long sigh. "I have no idea how to do this, and I already feel certifiable for talking to something residing in my head." He was not going to confess that he did occasionally upon necessity. The relationship with one's *treòir* was an interesting experience and the reason why finding boys like Bastian was vitally important. They needed a father figure to teach them how to control their power. There wasn't enough known about the *treòir* and how it related to the ones who turned meirlock to allow the younger, unbonded males to have more information other than to keep it under control. "Sure, ask your questions, and I will tell you his answer."

She beamed at him. "Thank you." She went over to the drawer where the note pads were and snagged a pen and paper. "Is there a way for you two to completely merge together as one?"

"I cannot do it for you. This is something you must discover on your own, or it won't work. I wish I could help you more, but I would also like to survive this."

"He can't tell me, but he said I can figure it out on my own." He let out a breath, glad Haven wasn't trying to talk to the *treòir.*

Her face scrunched up at him. "That's not helpful." She wrote that down and then tapped her pen against the pad of paper. "All right, can you promise me that there will never be another incident like we had earlier? As much as I know it wasn't Quinn, I still don't like being afraid, and I didn't appreciate the bruises." She gave Quinn a look. "Even if that faint of a bruise could happen while having sex."

Donovan blinked at her. Her eyes bore right into his with her reproach directed at the *treòir*. The *treòir* snarled quietly in his mind and then went remorseful. *"She will not fear you or me again. I give her my word that I shall not harm her, nor shall I use you to harm her in any way again. I will learn this word you call gentleness."*

"He gives you his word that you shall not be harmed again."

Haven studied him when her head canted to the side. "Good. I can't be afraid when I am with you." She chewed on her lip and then absently drew an ancient symbol on the paper. She opened her mouth to say something when there was a loud crash in the hall, and then the building shook.

Donovan shot across the room, taking Haven off her chair and covering her body with his own as weapons fell from the walls. Pots and pans danced in the cabinets until they'd worked themselves out to crash on the floor. Haven stayed curled under him until everything went quiet.

Donovan unfurled himself from her. His hands moved over her, checking for wounds, his mind probing to be sure, and then he cupped her face. "Are you all right?"

"I think so. Where are the wolves?" She slipped out from under him and darted out of the kitchen, calling their names. He was several paces behind her when she stopped at the entrance to the hall that led to the first floor bedrooms and let out a wail. Then she lunged forward, landing on the floor next to Nikon's still body covering Medea. Crimson spread out from under him and a blade that Donovan knew didn't belong to him stuck out from his side, right where Medea's belly would have been pierced had Nikon not been there.

"No, Nikon, please, you can't die on me." Haven curled herself around her friend and glowed with a healing ability she didn't know how to control, keeping the animal away from death's door.

"Don't let her do this. It will kill her."

"Goddamn it, I can't let him die on her. Riordan!" He broadcasted his trouble to the entire Heartland tribe.

The *treòir* faded back as his brother's voice sounded in his mind. *"What's going on?"*

"Kyros is here in my building, and Nikon is dying. Haven's holding on to him. Get your ass here now!"

There was a long moment of silence. *"Let* him *help you, brother. Memphis has portals opened all over the city. We're coming in."*

The *treòir* hissed. *"I cannot let either of you do this. The animal's life is not worth hers."*

"But she thinks it is. Understand, please!"

There was turmoil in his head, but his body was moving under the *treòir*'s direction. His hand spread over the wolf's fur. *"Like you did with Haven. Just enough. We need to have power enough to protect them should Kyros come back."*

Donovan did as he was told, and then his body was moving again, extracting Haven from the wolf. When he spoke, his voice was a strange mix of his voice and the *treòir*'s. "Do not touch him again. He will live, but you must be safe. Kyros is here."

"I won't leave him."

Donovan snarled, taking over. "Damn it. Get your ass into my office now." He lifted Nikon, carried him into the office, and set him onto the couch. Medea whined in that heartrending way wolves had as she put her head near her mate's.

"Thank you, dark one."

Nikon whimpered softly. *"She hurt herself again. Help her, not me, you fool."*

Donovan was in the hall with Haven a second later. She was weak since she'd used too much energy, but he'd have to deal with that later. He scooped her up and set her down on the floor next to Medea where she'd be able to see and touch Nikon. "Stay." Then he left the room before he closed and locked the door. He slipped the key under the door so only Haven could control who went in.

"We cannot fight him here," the *treòir* said. *"This is your home, and I will not have any more harmful memories for our lifebond. Draw him out and let your brothers chase him off. Once the animal and our mate are safe, then we will go hunting."*

Donovan didn't question the *treòir*. He'd have come up with the same thing on his own. He allowed himself to connect further with the *treòir* within. He always did when there was danger.

Chapter 18

Haven curled around Nikon and reached out to put a hand on Medea. She couldn't imagine how terrified Medea would have been to have Nikon brought down like that. She prayed Quinn would come back to her. She had no idea why he thought this room was safe, but he seemed to believe it, so here is where she would stay with her wolves. She felt weak, like she'd just run a decathlon and then climbed Mt. Kilimanjaro. Breathing was an effort, but she wasn't going to allow herself to slip into sleep while Nikon was hanging between life and death. She knew she couldn't help Quinn, but she could help her wolf and comfort his mate. It was an eternity before she heard a knock at the door. She slid off the couch and scooted across the floor, unable to stand up. "Who's there?"

"Wolf. Quinn sent me to get you."

She closed her eyes, trying to think. The man sounded and felt like Wolf, but she wasn't really sure she should trust anything at the moment. "How do I know it's you?"

"Because I told you to kill yourself, little sister."

She puffed out a breath and looked to Medea.

"It is Wolf," Medea said as she went over to the key and used her nose to slip it under the door.

A second later the door burst open and Wolf stood there, filling up the frame. His eyes blazed a golden umber. "What did you do to yourself?"

She growled at him from the floor. "I tried to save my wolf. You should put magic lessons in that book of yours."

Echo and Apollo moved past Wolf to Nikon, who lay still on the couch. Their noses touched, and the three of them began to glow in a soft purple light. When the light faded, Nikon hopped down and stretched and then shook his massive body. Nikon turned and licked where the wound had been. He nuzzled his mate before going to Haven and sitting down next to her. He dropped his head onto her shoulder. *"Get lessons on magic control before trying it again. A total loss of energy is a loss of life."*

Haven rested her head on his. "I couldn't let you die."

Wolf crouched down in front of her. "You can talk to the wolf later. My job is to get you out of here right now." He didn't wait for her to respond. He just lifted her and took her to the bedroom. He deposited her on the bed and rummaged through the drawers, tossing pants and socks at her. "Get dressed."

Haven just stared at him.

"Do you need me to help you?"

She groaned and with great effort summoned the energy to dress herself. Having Quinn help her was one thing, but Wolf was an altogether different matter. He still scared her for one, and for the other, he still had some kind of *treòir* trapped inside of him that didn't find her amusing. "Where is Quinn?"

"He is alive. Don't worry. He won't let himself be killed."

"I know that, but sometimes things just happen. I wasn't expecting an earthquake in the middle of Chicago. This isn't a seismically active area and hasn't ever been." She scooted off the bed and took tiny, slow steps over to the closet to get a pair of shoes. She sat down on the floor to conserve energy once she was there.

"He's over two thousand years old. I think he can take care of himself."

She snorted. "Right, and you're all confused about the *treòir*."

His eyes sharpened on her. "What are you talking about?"

She grinned at him. "I've talked to Quinn's. He likes me quite a bit, and they have a tentative truce."

"We'll talk about this once I get you safe." He stooped down and lifted her off the floor.

Haven couldn't relax against him. She wasn't comfortable being this close to Wolf, though she was starting to wonder if she'd spend half of eternity with her feet never touching the ground. He carried her down the steps and to the portal room where one of Memphis's portals spun open.

"Don't forget my book and the note pad. I'm working on something."

He growled low, sounding just like Nikon, but did grab what she'd asked for before he threw her coat at her and swung back around to the portal. She managed to put it on without asking for help, and a second later, he had her in his arms again, carrying her into the room, wolves at his heels.

"The wolves are very close to all of you," she said once they were on the other side.

"They are bonded to us. We are of the Wolf Clan."

"I read a little bit about it. You are a good storyteller."

His face twitched. "They aren't stories."

"No, but the way you tell history is like curling up with a good horror novel."

"Horror?"

"It's all very interesting and absorbing, but a lot of it is scary with the perspective that it all happened."

"Aye, little sister, every story was real." He wrapped his body around her like a shield as he stepped out of the portal room to where they'd gone. "I live in the Clan lodge. It's small, but it serves me well enough."

So this was the exterior of the compound. She'd never seen it, since she'd always traveled to and from Nadia's house via a portal. It was a long street with several modern houses on either side. A large building rested at the end of a cul-de-sac. Woodlands surrounded the lot, and a large iron gate sat between two stone walls. The walls disappeared behind the trees.

She was exhausted and wanted nothing more than to find somewhere to sleep for the next week. Worry for Quinn kept her from finding oblivion. She reached out for him with her mind, needing to know what was happening to him.

"I am fine. Stay with Wolf. I will come to you when I know Kyros is back in his lair for the night."

"I worry about you."

"I know. Be safe. We have much to talk about once you have rested."

She winced. *"You could have warned me before I used magic."*

"Yes, but I seem to remember discussing something just as important."

The tension in her shoulders eased. *"I love you."*

"I love you, too, my Haven. Rest. I will be with you soon."

* * * *

Donovan broke contact with her. He was keenly aware that his fight against the *treòir* over the centuries might have been a senseless one.

"Do not think that, my brother. Power and control are addictive things."

Donovan nodded his agreement as he crouched low to the ground. As soon as he'd known Haven was clear of the building, he'd had it evacuated of every resident. He stalked the halls. Dragons soared the skies. He looked out a window at the end of a corridor and wondered what it would be like to be human and unable to see through the illusions dragons built around themselves to keep from being seen. He wasn't sure he'd be able to cope in a world where he didn't see at least one dragon circling in the distance. He knew exactly what had caused the quake.

Maverick came in close to him. His eyes were a glow of swirling mercury. "The building is secured. I saw the vortex from the ground, but I did not feel them. There is rumor an aged Hunter joined their ranks."

"Aye," Donovan said. "I still want you to check the building's structural stability before you allow anyone in. Kyros is trying to recreate us, I think. Be on the lookout for an Earth Warrior on par with you."

"Of course, my lord." Maverick pressed the button to the elevator that would take him down into the basement.

Only after making contact with all the men he had in the area did he go to seek out Riordan.

They met in the front lobby of the building.

The two brothers stood off to the side where the crowd of residents had gathered for warmth. Donovan's tone was light, belying the turmoil he was still in. "Is there anything you would like to tell me?"

Riordan shrugged. "I am sure you are getting the information you need."

"But how much of that information can be shared without an adverse effect?"

"Do not tempt nature. There are reasons for the way things are."

Donovan wasn't so sure. "How much is natural law and how much is superstition?"

"You cannot understand what you speak of yet. Your process is not complete."

"No, but I have more control and more hope than I have had in two thousand years. You were just a child the first time I allowed the power of the *treòir* out, and he likes Haven."

Riordan gave a knowing smile. "It is a bit disconcerting to discover that. I thought I was going to go mad when I found out mine wanted Nadia for himself, but it is exactly what makes Haven your lifebond. Keeping us ignorant of some things is more for the protection of clans than it is for the benefit of the men. Only a small percentage of us live to be ancients. The rest…"

Donovan bowed his head. The rest were either killed in battle or killed for becoming a meirlock. "Aye. So this is the contents of the Undying book that was revealed to all bonding males? Because the threat of them turning—"

"Is no longer there, provided she is his true lifebond."

Donovan understood. They lost a great many men in battle, and bondings were just as fragile. The chances of surviving went up with age, but too many Undying found their bond to life while still in their warrior years. "Haven seems to think I must make friends and work with him."

"Yes," Riordan said. "You need to become one with him. There is no other way, and a bond between you and Haven will not take until the merge has happened."

"He said I need to discover how to make that work on my own," Donovan said. It wasn't that he didn't trust Haven, but he was leery of accepting everything the *treòir* said at face value. His power didn't understand the workings of the world and tried to do things in ways that weren't always according to Undying law.

"Yes," Riordan said. "That is the part about bonding the males cannot know about. We need to keep the men leery of their *treòir* until they can be trusted to handle the power of a merge." He looked at Donovan. "We cannot risk more Undying like the one that destroyed our parents. They cannot merge until there is something to keep them grounded in life."

"I understand." The dragon went insane when his mate had been killed while he'd been away dispatching a warlock. Joseph hadn't allowed himself to live long enough to turn into that kind of monster after Rowan fell. "We will discuss this at length once I have completed the process."

"That would be a good idea and maybe have Wolf create a book, like the one of old, for the males once he has completed the process."

Donovan's heart suffered. He still didn't know what had happened to Wolf to make him so odd, but the man was still his brother, and Fenris, the Original Undying Wolf Cadfael, had drilled it into his head that as long as Wolf followed the laws, his lifebond could still save him. He had hope they could still find her. "Aye, I will talk to him about it."

"Your Cadens work well together," Riordan reminded him. "You're supposed to be on vacation."

Donovan sighed. "I know." His jaw started to work. He needed to get back to Haven. He knew Wolf would take care of her, but he didn't like her being afraid or worried about him, but these people putting their lives on the line were still his.

Riordan sensed his unease. "Go. I will take care of things here."

He didn't ask if he was sure. He turned and started the walk to the back alley that would take him to where Memphis would be able to open a portal for him. Only then did the *treòir* completely disconnect from his awareness, satisfied their lifebond had not been forgotten.

* * * *

The way Wolf kept his home amazed Donovan. He knew his brother made enough money for a comfortable home, but Wolf insisted on living in a one-room apartment above the Wolf Lodge with one threadbare over-sized chair and a mattress on the floor in the bedroom. The rest of his dwelling had boxes stacked against the walls, and in the corner was a table with pages and pages, piled nearly to the eight-foot ceiling with a tiny space for him to sit and work by the only light in the main area focused over the table.

But then, Wolf had been unusual for a long time. For many centuries, Donovan had believed his brother had given up his emotions in the same way as Ean had done, only to find that he had not. He was part deadly warrior and part philosopher. The odd mix, even for their kind, helped Wolf keep the *treòir* locked inside, so Donovan didn't pry. They stood in the small living room, looking at each other. Wolf's deep voice rumbled out. "She is in the bedroom. I put her to sleep when we arrived."

"Brother," Donovan started.

"Take my room for the night. I have hunting to do." Just like that, Wolf was gone.

Donovan shook his head and went to the bedroom door. She was curled into Nikon with Medea on the wolf's other side, Apollo resting at her feet. The silver wolf lifted his head and then glided out of the room on silent paws. Donovan looked at her for a long time, watching the slow rise and fall of her chest as she breathed. The *treòir* was watching her, too.

"What kind of magic does she have? She is making me feel...strange."

Donovan's mouth curved. "It's called love. We are supposed to feel this way for our lifebond," he said in a soft tone.

"This love thing is dangerous. You should limit it."

"Not likely." He was mildly amused. *"One moment of love is worth an eternity of hell."*

"Perhaps, but it makes your thinking unclear."

"Isn't that what you are for? To make sure I don't fuck this up any more than we already have?"

Now there was humor in the tone. *"So now I am acceptable to you."*

"I never said I had all the answers. We will need to talk more before I let a merge happen. I need to know some things that might help our kind."

"Then we talk now."

"No, now we hold Haven and be thankful she was not harmed." Donovan tugged his shirt over his head and kicked off his shoes before tossing everything into the corner of the room barely big enough for the king-sized mattress on the floor. He knelt down and moved in next to

Haven, his arms pulling her close to him. The wolves left the room a moment later. Donovan stroked the soft tresses of her hair, needing the silkiness against his rough hands. He breathed in her sweet scent, letting it wash through him, calming him.

* * * *

The *treòir* grew still in Quinn's mind. This was all too confusing. For centuries, the man had pitted their wills, neither one ever claiming complete victory over the other. Now, with the lifebond at stake, the man was simply willing to compromise, give in just enough to calm the rage within the *treòir*, to let it free from the darkest corners of the mind to share in a being they both found enticing and enchanting.

Haven's eyes fluttered and then opened. Her face lit with a lazy, half-sleepy smile. She was beautiful, all the more so when staunch concern filled her pale eyes. She was fully awake in the next moment. Her hands moved over Quinn, touching every part of him to make sure he hadn't been injured. Her hair draped over his chest, causing his skin to tingle with fire as the tips brushed against him. The *treòir* didn't understand the reaction. Always before, when the man found a woman to sedate the needs of the male body, the *treòir* would use the time to sleep. It was of no importance to him. He knew this woman was different, as their physical connection seemed just as important as the mental.

The *treòir* decided now would be the time to share in the experience. Lust was a powerful motivator. Quinn's body reacted to the mere sight of Haven above him. Her eyes never left his face as she pulled her shirt off, and immediately, Quinn's hands palmed her soft, firm breasts, molding them into his hands, letting his thumbs brush over the taught nipples. The tiny erotic sounds that came from her throat as her head dropped back brought Quinn to full arousal.

The *treòir* urged him to take her right then, but he refused. *"Gentle,"* Quinn intoned. Then he showed the *treòir* how to love Haven the way Quinn knew she needed to be loved. His hands moved over her flesh, taking in the softness, feeling every part of her, memorizing every curve, every sensitive spot. His hands were light as they moved over her, taking his pleasure from what he was giving her.

Haven's responses both delighted and awakened the *treòir*. He crept closer to the surface of Quinn's mind, wanting to feel what he was feeling. Needing to watch her body shiver as he touched her, needing to see the love in her eyes, the complete trust she had for Quinn, for them. It both awed and terrified the *treòir*. He'd been so cruel to her, so willing to enforce his total dominance over her, but here, now, even as she was above Quinn, she was giving herself to him. She offered her body for his pleasure, for his comfort. Her hands stroked and inflamed him, bringing a boil of desire to Quinn's blood, and the *treòir* couldn't understand why he hadn't already thrust himself into her, staking his claim.

"Not yet. This is just the beginning," Quinn counseled him. The *treòir* started to retreat when Haven's body convulsed after Quinn buried his fingers deep into her body.

"Stop." The tone was high alarm, almost panicked. *"You're hurting her."*

Quinn laughed quietly in his mind. *"She is as far from hurt as a woman can be."* He looped his arm around Haven and gently turned her onto her back. He hooked his fingers into her pants and slid them off her still quivering body. His mouth was nestled into the apex of her legs a moment later. Her hips came up off the mattress, her hand tangling in his hair, pulling his head closer. He let out a soft, possessive growl as his tongue licked over her before he pushed it into her soft core.

"What are you doing to her? She's screaming!"

"Isn't it great?" Quinn said with a lazy drawl, loving how her body moved against his, wiggling a small protest, even as she urged his head closer.

The *treòir* was shocked, appalled, but Haven's reaction to this crude behavior was the most astonishing of all. She was enjoying this strange assault Quinn was delivering to her tiny body, begging him for more, urging him to go faster, and taking her farther away from him. He reached out, gripping her mind and pulling her back, afraid that Quinn was doing something truly horrible to her, but all he found was her opening up further to Quinn, to them, giving herself over to him.

Her body did the strange convulsion again, and the *treòir* was afraid Quinn was doing something terribly wrong. Quinn laughed at him again. *"No, I am doing everything exactly right. That will teach you to sleep during the good parts of life."*

The *treòir* never felt anxiety before, but he felt it now, and he resented Quinn for the lesson, but crept even closer to the surface when Quinn finally shed his own pants. He kissed his way up her flat belly, spending a long time letting his mouth tease each of her breasts before he positioned himself over her. He then sank into her hot, soft core. Her reaction was instant. Her hips moved up to meet his with urgent demand. Her hands blazed feather light over his skin, bringing sparks of flame with them. Her body moved with his, giving him all of herself in a way the *treòir* couldn't comprehend. The way their bodies entwined was beautiful. He watched her face through Quinn's eyes with a single-minded fascination, each sound she made sending sparks of fire through his blood, demanding he bury himself so deep inside of her, she'd never get him out, and she didn't want him to.

She was connected to him—body, mind, and soul. Everything she offered up freely for his taking, and Quinn demanded she give him more. He filled her with long pulse-pounding strokes. Each one bringing her closer and closer to a soul-shattering climax, his hips thrusting into her. She met his pace, her body arching off the mattress, sounds of sweet ecstasy escaping her throat.

The *treòir* was rocked down to his very foundation when both Haven and Quinn released the madness building inside of them. It was a powerful, intoxicating force, and he felt a surge of magic like he'd never felt before pour through him, through them both, binding them closer together, bringing them closer to being one.

Quinn held himself above Haven, his massive shoulders trembling. He brushed damp hair away from her face. Her eyes shined bright with love and trust. She bit her lip and smiled in a coy way. Her arm looped around his shoulder, and she pulled herself up to bury her face in his chest. He rolled to his side, drawing her closer. He brushed his mouth over hers in a tender kiss. "I love you, my sweet Haven."

She moaned in a deliciously lazy way. "And I love you."

"Sleep, my love."

The *treòir* put power into those words, knowing her still quivering body needed rest. He stayed close as Haven's breathing evened out, and she settled into a warm, restful sleep.

"What the hell was that?"

Quinn Chuckled. *"It is called making love."*

"Still strange. How could you make her scream like that?"

"Humans call it an orgasm. They are quite pleasurable and stress relieving." Quinn's tone was light, full of laughter.

"You're making fun of me."

"Why yes, I am."

"That's a dangerous thing to do."

"Maybe, but are you really going to do something to upset her when she's so relaxed?"

The *treòir* growled low. *"No, but you knew that already."*

He receded back into his corner all on his own to sulk and think over what had just occurred, leaving Quinn free to let his mind wander on its own. The man was still stroking Haven's hair when he, too, gave into the need for restful sleep.

* * * *

The next day Haven discovered the mess in the penthouse. She groaned. The lasagna had burned, filling the entire place with smoke. Luckily, one of the maintenance men had thought to check on Quinn after the inspectors let everyone back into the building. They had turned the oven off and opened a window. Pots and pans littered the kitchen. Plates and other dishes were shattered on the floor. Weapons of every kind were scattered throughout, and there was a dark red congealed pool of blood in the middle of the hallway. Her breath shuddered out and her knees wobbled. She braced herself on the doorjamb leading into the hall and then forced it all back. Quinn was in his office, making phone calls. Haven decided to leave everything and went to take a shower and get changed into something different before she was ready to tackle the clean-up.

Nikon followed her around, keeping a close eye on her.

"I'm not going to break." She pulled her hair into a ponytail.

"No, but you have suffered trauma. The dark one wants me to keep a close eye on you."

She made a face as she carefully tossed broken crockery into the trashcan. "When doesn't he want someone to have a close eye on me?" She shook her head, not needing an answer. "All of this stuff is going to have to be replaced."

Quinn had quietly come into the room. "We'll go shopping soon. We'll start making this place into what you want it."

She wrinkled her nose at him. "I'm kind of getting used to the whole caveman style you've got going. It's better than Wolf's Neanderthal-man look, anyway. Maybe we can add some flowers so everyone knows you've captured your mate."

He snorted at her humor. "I'd rather line the walls with erotic photos of you."

She gave an indignant squawk. "See? Caveman!"

Quinn pulled her up to her feet and wrapped his arms around her. "I have some people coming to clean this place up. I don't want you touching things, and you are not allowed near the hall until that's been taken care of. What do you say we go for that cell phone and go get the will redrafted?"

"You're too good to me." She turned her face into him for a moment. "I need to see Bastian. Can you take me, please?"

"Of course, sweetheart, I should have known you'd want to see him. We'll take him with us. You need some time with him."

"Thank you." She hugged him tight. "How's your passenger?"

He let out a hearty laugh. "Apparently, how I can make your body move for me confuses him. He's been hiding since last night."

"Seriously? The big, bad wolf is afraid of sex? That's just... I don't know what, but it's just." She laughed quietly, then let out a sigh as she surveyed the kitchen again. "You're sure you want to pay people to clean this? I can do it."

He snorted. "And deny someone their livelihood?"

She growled at him. The sound coming out of her still startled her, but it was stress relieving. "That's not fair. I try not to spend all of your hard earned money, and you keep finding ways for me to."

He leaned down and kissed the tip of her nose. "I love you. Please, don't ever change. I need you just as you are."

Her insides warmed as delight streaked through her, but she kept glaring at him. "Not even a billion dollars can last forever."

"Yes it can, as long as I keep making money." He guided her toward the coat closet. "And he and I both agree that you don't need any more harmful memories of our home."

"Well," she said with slight sarcasm, "then I really do have no hope of winning the argument if you both actually agree on something. Do I need to worry about lightning or a meteor trying to strike us?"

He helped her with her coat and then put on his own. "Maybe, so you'd better stay close."

She laughed. "You can't stop a meteor, can you?"

He shrugged. "I've never tried before, but I'm sure I'd find a way if it was aimed at you."

Haven shook her head. He was Quinn, and he would find a way if it was a threat to her. The thought humbled her and frightened her. He was so gentle and tender with her when the *treòir* was in check, but she knew at his core was a violence so strong, there would always be parts of him that were broken. She suffered for him, it and made her more determined than ever to protect him, as much as he protected her. This was love, and she'd always wanted it, but never once had she'd ever thought she'd find it. Yet here she was, willing to give everything to the most powerful man she'd ever known or could ever know. He needed her, and for Haven, that made them equals. She'd never be as physically or magically as strong as he was. She'd never be able to provide for a family the way he could, but it was in the softening lines of his face, the way the world lifted off his shoulders just a little when he looked at her that told her everything she needed to know.

She did bring a lot to this relationship. She brought him laughter, love, and life. She gave herself to him willingly, and her return gift was his love and undying devotion. It was something she'd never expected, but knew she'd never be able to live without again.

She wrapped her arm around his waist and rested her head against his bicep as they walked to the elevator, Nikon ghosting her footsteps. "All right, we'll go spend your money and see what other trouble we can get ourselves into."

He growled quietly at her. "That's not funny."

She bit her lip. "But it's true. Every time we leave the house, something happens that scares the hell out of me."

His face twitched and went dark. "Then I will just have to fix that."

She winced because he'd do just that. Nothing in her world was supposed to make her upset, and she knew Quinn had the power to bring down mountains so her world was right.

Chapter 19

Bastian was looking at her with a big, owl-like stare. His eyes were unblinking as he assessed her, and for the first time she was able to see the Undying in him. He was already filling out in ways that told Haven he was going to have considerable height and mass on him. He wouldn't be nearly as big as Quinn—she didn't think anyone, human or Undying, could be that big—but Bastian definitely would have the sheer size the males of the race seemed to have. Not that she'd met that many Undying, but from Mason to Memphis, they were all incredibly large.

It had her thinking about what her own children would be like, if the girls would have size like the men did, or if they would take after her. She went still when she realized she was thinking about kids. She'd wanted her own before she'd met Mason, but then after, her only thoughts of children were to keep Bastian safe.

"What're you thinking about?" Bastian asked when he finally broke his gaze and dug into the huge serving of cheese fries in front of him.

Haven blinked and flushed a little. "Uh, nothing. How ya been? Do you like Nadia and Riordan?"

Bastian gave her one of those arched-brow looks that Haven knew was an Undying trait. "Yeah, they're cool, but I miss you."

She wiped at the tear that suddenly formed in the corner of her eye. "I know, sweetie. I miss you too."

He grimaced at the word "sweetie." "Haven, what if my friends were here?"

She rolled her eyes and sighed. "I knew it was going to happen. Sooner or later I was going to become uncool."

He snorted. "You'll always be cool, but a guy has to have a reputation, and you can't go around calling me sweetie." He shuddered in an over-dramatic teen way. "Why don't you call me bruiser or something like that?"

Haven sighed. "All right, bruiser, eat your lunch. We have things to do today."

"Oh, like what?"

"Quinn needs to see his lawyer. We are going to check out one of the cyber schools we talked about, and Quinn wants to spend some money on us." She made a face. "It makes him feel needed." Then she gave Bastian a critical look. "I think you're growing out of your clothes again. I swear you've grown three inches since last week."

Bastian nodded as he started to shovel more of his cheese-drenched fries into his mouth. His face went black when a total stranger sat down next to Haven and put his arm around her. Her insides froze. She peeled his fingers off of her, pushed him away, and stopped Bastian from reacting with a stern look. She turned to the man next to her. "Can I help you?"

His face was bright, and there was something wrong with his eyes, as if he wasn't completely there. His head bobbed up and down. "You're a pretty lady."

"Thank you. If you don't mind, this is a private table."

He just smiled at her and went to put his arm around her again. Nikon rumbled low and dangerous under the table. He was curled up at her feet. The man didn't seem at all perturbed at the wolf's warning. "You're a pretty lady," the man repeated, as if it gave him every right in the world to be there. "A beauty like you should live forever."

Haven scooted closer to the wall, trying to get away from the man. "Thank you, but please leave. I don't know you."

His face didn't falter. Instead, he slid closer to her. Bastian came over the table, his hand curling around the man's throat, and tossed a man who had fifty pounds on him out of the booth. Everyone in the restaurant turned to see what was going on. The man sprang to his feet. The stupid, vacant smile was still on his face, but his eyes filled with terror as he took off, shoving people out of his way as he bolted out the door. Haven reached out and grabbed Bastian before he could take off after the man.

"Quinn! Something strange just happened here."

"I'm on my way."

The manager came over just as Haven got Bastian back into the booth and turned her attention to calming Nikon down. "Ma'am, are you all right? Is that animal dangerous?"

"What? Oh no, he just doesn't like me being upset. He'll settle out."

Nikon responded with one last ferocious growl and then took the bite of burger Haven offered him under the table.

"Would you like for me to call the police?"

Emma Weylin

Haven shook her head. "What would I tell them? And he didn't stick around."

Bastian's face was still dark as he stared in the spot where the man had vanished from view. "I don't like this. When's Dov going to get here?"

"He's on his way."

* * * *

Donovan walked into the restaurant, his entire presence filling up every inch of the space. The *treòir* was on full alert, and for the first time, keeping his power in check wasn't a struggle. He was coiled tight, ready to spring. Haven appeared harassed as she spoke with a manager. Her eyes would flick to Bastian, who was looking like a caged tiger waiting for his opening to strike, and Nikon, who was perched under the table, ready to lunge. Everyone's focus was on Haven, and he could feel her anxiety. "What happened?"

The six-foot-four manager had to tilt his head back to look at Donovan's face. He took a step back, intimidated. "Someone was bothering the lady, and I am trying to urge her to report him."

"There was something wrong with that man, and I don't know if a police officer would be safe handling him," Haven said into his mind.

"Humor the manager. I'll take care of it."

She relaxed and took refuge under his shoulder. He said for all to hear, "Sweetheart, you should report this. Odd behavior can be a precursor to violence."

"All right."

Donovan contacted Brody to track the strange man. The man could pose no threat, but with Kyros still out there, everything was suspect. They waited in the restaurant for the police to arrive. Donovan stood guard over Haven as she answered the officer's questions. He couldn't wait to have control of the Black Rose. Dealing with human authorities would become exponentially easier. This was the exact reason he'd set up the organization all those years ago. He wouldn't have to worry this officer would be injured if the strange man turned out to be something a human shouldn't handle.

Haven blew out an explosive breath when the officer walked away. "See? You can't take me anywhere. I am going to become a hermit. I swear."

He wrapped his arm around her and pulled her in close. "I'll fix this." He looked at Bastian. "And you, young man, we need to have a talk."

Bastian squared his shoulders and puffed up. "That freak had his arm around her. No way in hell was I going to let him get away with that."

Donovan put a hand on Bastian's shoulder. "I understand, and I am thankful you were here to protect her, but there are better ways of dealing with these things when humans are involved."

"Oh." Bastian's face took on a goofy expression at the praise from the older man, and then he nodded. "I'll do better next time."

"Of course you will." Donovan then ushered them out onto the sidewalk.

Haven held tight to Nikon's harness, her head resting on Donovan's bicep as they walked. "Did you get to finish what you were doing?"

"Yes. Now we go do the dreaded shopping," he said with a measure of humor.

She waited for him to tell her. When he didn't, she nudged him with an elbow. "Well?"

He shrugged. "I was working."

Her eyes narrowed on him and then went wide before she whispered, "You were killing something."

He kept his voice low. "I was planning what should be done with the Kyros situation."

Haven took a step away and studied him. She bit down on her lip. "Do I need to worry you're going off to get yourself killed?"

He wrapped his arm around her. "You're Undying. You die if I do. I'm not going to let that happen."

Her brow furrowed as she took up her place next to him. "That strange man. Could he have been Kyros trying to distract you?"

"Of course it is, but it won't work."

"You are so full of yourself," she said.

He laughed quietly and dipped his head down to brush his mouth up her neck. "I'd rather you be full of me."

Chapter 20

Donovan wasn't ready for this, but it had to be done. Three days after the strange man incident in the restaurant with Haven, he finally got the report that operatives from the Black Rose were scoping out the building. All they needed to do was get Haven down to the parking level. She was vital to making the plan work, and that pissed him the hell off, but it made sense. Killian and Kyros both would use Haven to get to him if given a chance. He was a generous man. He'd give the people what they wanted. Though, they'd probably regret the consequences.

"Quinn!" Her voice went shrill as two men came out from behind pillars as soon as the elevator doors opened.

His arm went tight around her to keep her pinned against his side. His tone was calm, but the cadence was lethal. "You're all right. I think it's time I met your family."

She shivered, playing the distressed mate to perfection. "No. Call Memphis. You can't meet my grandfather. This is a set up."

The two men moved in closer. One was human and the other was a marrok werewolf.

"Ms. Killian," the marrok said. "We've come to take you home."

"No," she said. "And it's Mrs. Donovan."

The two men paused and looked at each other before they both assessed Donovan. The marrok stepped back. His lip curled as his eyes turned the golden yellow of the wolf. "Mr. Killian desires to speak with both of you."

Donovan evaluated the men standing in front of him. They were only following orders. The human was confused beyond belief, but the marrok sensed what Donovan really was and fear wafted around him. "Your guns are useless here. If one goes off, both of you will be dead in the next second." Then he lowered his head so his mouth was close to Haven's ear, but his gaze never left the men posing a danger. "We should go see your grandfather. The sooner he understands I am your mate, the easier it will be for me to gain control of the Black Rose."

"I don't want to see him," she said, her voice cracking. "I am happy here with you. I don't need to go back there."

"Aye, sweetheart, I know, but I must speak with your patriarch. I will have Memphis and the others on standby should the need for them become necessary."

"Quinn." Her voice trembled. She reached up with her free hand and wrapped it around his. "I don't want to do this."

"I know. I will make this up to you. I promise, but this is one of those things I must deal with."

"I don't want to do this," she whispered.

He petted her hair and kissed the top of her head. "You will not be hurt."

"Can you prove he's your mate," the marrok asked in his growly voice.

Her face crumpled as she shook her head. "I—I don't know how to prove it. He—Nathan, please, you know me. I don't fear him. That has to mean something to you."

The ground under Donovan's feet began to tremble with a precise measure of released power. "You are unduly stressing my mate. If this continues, I will be forced to react."

The human lifted his gun. "I don't know what you are, but whatever you're doing needs to stop."

Donovan snarled low. "Put down the gun, human. This does not have to get violent."

"Listen to him," the marrok said. "He's the same thing Mason is. He's not something we want to fuck with."

"Not the same!" Haven yelled. She was shaking so badly that the trembling ground could have been caused by her. "Mason is evil. Please, Nathan, you understand mates. I am Quinn Donovan's mate."

"I cannot go against orders," Nathan said as he moved slowly over to the human and took the gun away from him. "Your grandfather wants both of you brought to him."

"Then he shall get us," Donovan said.

"Quinn!" She protested the way they'd practiced. All of his attention and focus was on the two men with weapons. She pressed her back up against Quinn. "Please, my grandfather will—"

"The longer things are left open between the Black Rose and I, the longer your life is in danger. I assure you by the time I am done with your grandfather he will be pleased with your choice of mate."

Emma Weylin

* * * *

Haven didn't like this alpha male crap one bit. But this hell needed to end. Fear bubbled up despite her wish it wouldn't. "You've contacted Memphis?"

"My men are already assembled and awaiting my instructions." The usual velvety baritone chords of Quinn's voice were now cold and brutal.

He was no longer the man she was in love with, but the same warrior who'd frightened Mason in the mall, the same one that banished Kyros from the diner. As much as she didn't want to do this, she also needed to trust Quinn. He would never do anything to put her life in danger, and her life was forever connected to his.

"He knows other meirlocks. I don't know their names, but I know there is more than just Mason," Haven said.

"Aye. I know who they are," Quinn said.

Wolf said it would take two Undying to kill Quinn if they could sneak up on him. While she knew she didn't have to keep reminding Quinn of the other meirlocks, she did it anyway. Quinn could have more information than she had, but she needed to tell him everything she could.

She squeezed her eyes shut and buried her face against Quinn's side. "I don't want to be trapped with Mason or Kyros. You have to live through this."

"The end of the world will come before I allow either of them to touch you."

The tremble of the ground and the fiery glow of Quinn's eyes said he'd bring about the end if needed.

* * * *

"At least your mother was intelligent enough to wait until after you were born before she fornicated with other men," Marcus Killian snarled when Haven walked into the grand foyer of the mansion. The large turn-of-the-century building had been headquarters for the last forty-five years when Marcus took over the organization at his father's death.

Haven flinched at his words. His eyes flicked over her. Outwardly, she was every inch the Killian he'd raised her to be, but it didn't make her any less afraid of her grandfather. Marcus only lifted one silver-white brow at her. "Mason has been worried sick over your whereabouts only to find you've been carting with playboys."

"You will apologize," Quinn said with a low warning rumble. "I frankly couldn't care less if you are an old human. You will respect my mate."

Marcus chuckled. "You will not threaten me in my own home. Many thanks for bringing my granddaughter home. You may go."

"Perhaps I should introduce myself. I am Quinn Donovan. I am the Cadeyrn of the Undying People." His eyes flared with a holy golden fire. "You have insulted my mate after you used your position in my organization to bring about the abuse of a lifebond. I suggest you hold your tongue and think hard before you open your mouth again."

"Why of course," Marcus said in mock apologetic tones. "You are the very man who disappeared on us over two-thousand years ago."

"Grandfather," Haven interjected in a respectful tone. "Mr. Donovan is exactly who he says he is. I've…shared his thoughts. He speaks the truth."

"You expect me to believe an adulteress?" Marcus demanded.

Haven flinched again. "I cannot commit any such thing when I was never Mason's wife."

"Haven, dear heart, I may be old, but do not think me the fool. You can choose whomever you wish to warm your bed, but the men will only accept Mason as their leader, and they will only accept a legitimate heir in the future. Mason is your only choice."

Haven refused to cry in front of her grandfather. He was being hateful on purpose, trying to get her to react—trying to get Quinn to react. She couldn't let the situation devolve. Her back straightened and her chin lifted. "I acknowledge Quinn Donovan as the same Cadeyrn who founded the Black Rose. He is the rightful leader."

"This is why there is a line of succession," Marcus explained loudly for all the men lining the foyer to hear. "We cannot have leadership change each time a woman gets fickle about her bed partner."

"My mother was faithful to my father," Haven said coolly. "I do understand you couldn't keep my grandmother faithful to you, but do not pass on your failing to me or my father. Your own coldness is what drove her away from you. Quinn is my mate. Accept him or don't, but if he does not control the Black Rose, I will allow it and Mason to fall."

"Mason," Marcus murmured, taking a step forward, using a cane for support. "He understands the need the world has to keep this organization powerful and operational. He will bring it back to heel. Those who've faltered of late will respond to his power."

* * * *

Donovan subtly put a hand on Haven's shoulder and pulled her in close to him as Mason entered the room. He had the look of a man who'd just shagged the king's wife. His bow was florid. "My lord, Cadeyrn. How lovely to see you again. Hand over my lifebond."

"My judgment on you is already passed," Donovan said in a calm, deadly tone. "You should explain to Marcus exactly what it means when an Undying lifebond rejects her mate."

"There is that pesky compulsion thing I've already explained to him," Mason said. "The real Cadeyrn, Kyros, has assured Mr. Killian that he will make his granddaughter safe from you."

Then Donovan knew the piece he'd been missing. In an instant, he had a complete picture of his surroundings. He knew where every being of magic stood. He knew which ones were human. He knew where every possible weapon lay and exactly where and how to position his body to keep Haven away from the pending altercation. "Care to test the real power of the Cadeyrn?"

Worry clouded on Mason's face. "She must be tested for a compulsion by the Cadeyrn."

"Already done," Donovan countered. "And I found none. She is *my* lifebond, meirlock. You dare touch her. You will find death."

"Kyros!" Mason's voice boomed out in the marble foyer.

There was a flash of red and black streaked lightning as the portal split open. Out walked two men. Kyros held the same sheer massive size and physical power Donovan had, and the other—

"Memphis," Haven's voice rang out in fear. "No!" Her little body backed in tight against Donovan. "He can't be."

"Shh." He moved his hand feather light down the length of her hair. "Call for him, love. Memphis will come for his Reannon."

"Memphis," she said again, only this time it was whispered in disbelief.

Another portal sparked open with shots of silver and purple lightning that flashed directly in front of Haven and Donovan. Memphis was the first to step out followed by Wolf and Riordan. Ean Maverick came next and the rest of the Cadens.

"Maverick," Donovan said. "Make sure no one can leave this room until I am ready to let them."

Maverick poised himself in a stance that looked like he was praying. Then one fist slid against his other open palm. He brought the fist up and then slammed it down into the marble floor. The shockwave vibrated the massive hall. The marble stretched and groaned before it grew up from the floor like stalagmites on a cave floor to block the doors and windows.

"Brogan," Donovan said in a calm tone. "My mate is frightened. I believe your dragon takes great delight in making lifebonds safe. Indulge him."

Brogan waited until the rock formations were in place. He glanced at Haven. His mouth turned up in a shy smile even as his eyes went reptilian. "Stand back, my lady," he said in a soft timber. "The dragon is not pleased."

* * * *

Haven made a small sound and fully moved herself behind Quinn. Brogan moved forward. His head cocked to the side as he assessed the Memphis look-a-like and Kyros. "You frightened our Reannon," he said. "Yet you do not run. Curious." His body shimmered, and in the next instant where the man stood was now a dragon, his wings stretched out the full expanse of the twenty-foot foyer. A mighty roar shook the building down to its foundation. Every being of non-Undying descent scurried to the blocked doors and huddled there in the protective alcoves forming around them, including Marcus. Maverick knelt on the floor with his hands pressed against the cool marble, whispering to the stone.

Haven ducked her head against Quinn's back. Wolf and Riordan moved as one to flank their brother, effectively boxing her in a circle of their protective power. She realized Quinn was playing with Grandfather. Showing the old man who was in charge. They were giving a systematic and blatant show of power.

"You think these games will frighten me," Kyros taunted.

"No," Quinn said in a weary tone. "I expect the games are far from over. Brogan. Guard my mate." Quinn pulled his shirt up over his head and handed it back to Haven before he stepped forward. Brogan's dragon shimmered, and his formed changed until he was once again in human form, and then automatically took his place in the defensive position in front of Haven. She peeked around Brogan to see what Quinn was going to do.

Quinn put out his hand. Memphis lifted his. A rope of lightning whipped out across the room to coil around one of the many swords on the wall. The lightning snapped back, tossing the long-bladed weapon at Quinn. Haven whimpered and tried to rush forward but Wolf looped his arm around her. "No, little sister."

Quinn caught the sword. He worked his shoulders and swung the long blade a few times. A low growl rumbled from him, filling the room with his ire. "Is this not what you wanted? To challenge for the true status of Cadeyrn?"

The blood-red fire glow of an insane *treòir* took over Kyros's eyes. "This isn't over. You converted her." Then he hissed, "Lazarus!"

The Memphis look-a-like put out his palm. Tornado force winds whipped out in a vortex to form the portal. Kyros and Mason jumped through, and then Lazarus followed, the portal snapping shut behind them.

"Memphis! Brody!" Donovan's voice shook the walls. "I want Mason back here. Alive. Now."

"Lazarus?" Memphis demanded in a hopeful tone.

"Will be protected," Donovan said. "Bring me the Earth meirlock only. Do not risk yourself against more power. We deal with Mason, and then we will hunt Kyros and his clan."

"Aye," Memphis gritted through his teeth. "Brody."

Brody joined Memphis where Lazarus's portal had closed. He shut his eyes and tilted his face. His body moved in the soft rhythmic sway of the power flow. His nose worked, and his head cocked this way and that before his eyes opened again. His gaze locked on Memphis. The portal ripped open, and Brody dove through. A few seconds later, he came back, falling backward with Mason kicking and screaming to get out of Brody's deadly embrace. Memphis ground his teeth together as he worked to close the portal, either Storm Warrior able to overpower the other. "Damn it, Donovan. Help me!"

Quinn slashed his hand through the portal, and the gaping hole to another place vaporized. In the next second, the air of the foyer ionized with an electrical charge. The essence of Donovan's *treòir* infused the charge, making it stronger, sealing off the room from any disturbance. Haven finally, blissfully felt safe.

Quinn handed the sword to Memphis. He turned to where Brody held Mason pinned to the ground. "Let him up."

Brody let Mason go. He staggered up to his feet. "Kyros! Lazarus!" he bellowed.

Brody moved over to where Haven stood in the center of a bubbling cauldron of pissed off and angry power. Oddly, it was the safest she'd ever felt in the entirety of her life. Mason stood quivering in terror several feet away from Donovan. He bellowed for his friends again and again, but no portals opened this time.

Donovan let out a disgusted sigh. "Maverick, settle the room. Brody, bring me Marcus. Wolf hold Mason here."

The unnatural stalagmites melted back into the floor as if they'd never been there. Brody helped the aged man with surprising gentleness cross the expanse of the room. Wolf stood beside Quinn with all his power aimed and vibrating around Mason.

Haven had no idea what she was supposed to be doing. Riordan stood beside her. "Mason has been sentenced to death," he explained in a low murmur. "Killing an Undying is not an easy or pleasant task, but must be done."

"I—I don't understand," Marcus said.

"Haven." Quinn's voice drowned out all others. "Come here."

She hesitated for a moment before she slowly walked across the foyer, the heels of her boots unnaturally loud as she went. "Y-yes?"

"I know what you know," he said in the soft and easy timber she so loved about his voice. "What this man did to you..." He didn't finish. "It is against Undying law for any male to touch a lifebond other than his own."

She was able to easily understand the law because of her connection to Quinn. The law wasn't something arbitrarily put into place because of some patriarchal nonsense. It was there to protect the woman from being used, to protect her from being abused, and to keep the men from senselessly fighting over a woman who didn't want them. Mason willfully broke the law to gain power. He'd damaged her in the process. She was Quinn's mate. Even if he wasn't the Cadeyrn, his duty was to end Mason's life. She swallowed hard. Mason had known the consequences before he'd set about trying to make her his wife. He'd known the law and he'd broken it. "I understand now."

"I merit out the sentences I pass," Quinn said in a low tone. "You are not required to be here for his execution."

"Our connection," she whispered. "I'd be here, anyway."

"The pendant you wear will help give you the protection you need. Wolf will be able to show you what to do."

She let out a soft breath of relief. On impulse, she reached out and touched her fingers to Mason's cheek. She snatched her hand back as if she'd been burned. In that one touch, she knew. Mason would have killed her and Quinn, and all the people he protected would have died along with her.

Quinn's arms were around her in the next heartbeat. She let out a sob and stood rigidly in his arms. She didn't want Mason or Grandfather to see her cry. Every frightening and awesome thing she just witnessed spun wildly in her mind.

"Quinn." His name gritted out between her teeth. She would not look weak in front of her people.

"Breathe, baby, breathe." His deep baritone resonated through her whole body from the mind-to-mind contact. Her body shuddered, and

then she felt calm. Quinn's composure saturated every part of her. She took a moment to dab under her eyes in the safety of Quinn's arms. "I would like to be here when you address my grandfather, but I..." She drew in a deep breath. Knowing Quinn was going to put down an evil being and watching it were two different things. "While you address Mason, I believe it is in our best interest if I see if several items I had to leave behind are still there."

"I agree," he said. "I will have Riordan and Wolf assist you."

"Thank you." She extracted herself from him and then laced her fingers tight with his. After another moment, she was ready to face Grandfather again. He stood several paces away from Mason. Brody loomed over him as prison guard and protector. The old man appeared frail and aged when he'd never seemed that way before. Haven bit her lip. "Quinn is Cadeyrn. The Black Rose belongs to him. I am his mate. I'd have allowed this organization fall into ruin, but because of Quinn, I decided it should be saved for the good it can still do. Mason is evil. I don't know where or how you lost your ability to see those things, but this organization is no longer your concern." She took a step closer to him and, on a hunch, she gently laid her hand on his forearm. She got another shuttering flash of intent. Her hand went tighter around the pendent. Her grandfather wasn't evil, just a bitter old misguided shell of the man he could have been. There were still some less twisted parts of him that did care about her, but he was too blinded by power lust to do anything good with it.

"Pass your judgment." Quinn's voice was in her head. *"You need experience in doing this."*

Her back straightened and her chin lifted. If she stopped to think about what she was doing, she never would be able to subject another person to her will. She had to go with the knowledge that if she was wrong, Quinn would help her correct it, and she wouldn't look like an idiot. "You are to retire and live out your life away from a lure of power you cannot handle."

"The Reannon has passed the sentence," Donovan's voice boomed out. "Do you have anything to say?" His penetrating gaze bore into Marcus.

Killian bowed his head. "How can I trust your power isn't what we fight against?"

"I allowed Haven to show you her mercy. Had I passed judgment on you, you would share Mason's fate."

"She is a woman." Marcus sounded confused. "Why would you allow her any say?"

"Her life was the one most affected by you. If she can find it in her heart to show you the compassion you did not show her, I am inclined to follow her instincts." He took a menacing step toward Marcus. "Of course, if you prefer for me to embarrass her and rescind her judgment, I'll be overjoyed to pass my own."

Marcus turned his head. "That won't be necessary."

"I figured as much." His voice boomed out again. "The sentence stands. Marcus Killian is barred from any and all beings who possess or practice magic until his death."

"Quinn," Haven said through her connection with him. *"Did I do it wrong?"*

He touched his hand to the small of her back and bent so he was cheek to cheek with her. *"The punishment suited the crime. His intention was not your death. I will not put you in a position where you are responsible for ending another's life."* He brushed a kiss on the top of her head. "Go with my brothers to retrieve your belongings. I will finish up here, and then we shall end the threat that is Kyros."

She squeezed his hand and gave a wane smile. "Thank you."

Donovan tilted her face up to his and touched his lips to hers. "Go. I will find you when I am done here." He stepped back from her. "Wolf. Riordan. Go with her. *And Wolf, hold Mason until Haven is at a safe distance."*

Wolf moved in next to Haven. "I know some of the pendant's secrets, little sister," he said. "May I assist?"

Haven looked to Donovan. He nodded once. She walked over to Wolf.

His gaze sharpened on the pendant near her throat. "It is beautiful on you, Reannon. Let me show you how to reverse the shield of the connection."

Haven's gaze fluttered to Mason and back to Wolf. "That is probably a good idea." She wrung her hands together. "Is it difficult?"

"Not at all." Wolf lightly touched Haven's elbow. Then he was inside her head with her as he showed her how to use the power in the pendent to block her open connection to Quinn.

A few moments passed, and then Quinn's voice boomed out. "Wolf!"

Wolf smirked over his shoulder. He guided Haven toward the main staircase.

She stumbled a step. Not being able to feel Quinn's irritation with his brother had her internal alarms going off.

"You're okay," Wolf said in her mind, and then he showed her how to fine tune the connection block to let a trickle of Quinn's awareness

seep in. "I had to test the shield. Remember to never sever the connection entirely. That could have catastrophic consequences."

"Thank you."

He inclined his head. "My pleasure, little sister." He put his arm out and Haven took it, allowing him to lead her out of the foyer. Riordan was close behind them.

She looked over her shoulder at Donovan just as they reached the door leading into the mansion. *"I'll be waiting for you."*

* * * *

"I will come for you." He could see the worry in her eyes.

Donovan turned to face the man who abused his Haven. He stalked to where Mason stood. He felt the moment when Wolf's ability to hold a man frozen released.

Mason staggered back a step with a whimper and sank to his knees. "My lord, I was compelled," he begged. "Kyros made me!"

Donovan already knew the truth. He had to systematically sift through the memories of a man to find truth or compulsion. Haven would have felt the compulsion with her new gifts. She was to assist and help guide him in the decisions he had to make. He worked on hard logic. At times, it took longer for him to come to a decision than what Haven would be able to feel with an intention. Mason intended to kill a lifebond. Still, he couldn't ignore the accusation. Even if it was only to stay in accordance with the laws. "You understand this means I get free access to your mind?"

"Please, a man can be compelled by more than a compulsion," Mason begged. "He threatened what was left of my clan! He promised to kill them and turn Bastian. You have to believe me!"

"Then I read you," Donovan said without sympathy. "If you continue to refuse, I will carry out your sentence."

Mason licked his lips and moved back. He formed a fist. "Show mercy." Then he slammed his fist into the marble floor.

The marble cracked and bulged up as it rolled toward Donovan. *Treòir* reared up as Donovan unleashed the power. The shockwave stopped the ground ripple even as the mansion rocked on its foundation, effectively blocking the ancient Earth Warrior's attack. It shoved Mason backward, slamming him into the wall. Donovan advanced on him, making a tisking sound. "I suppose Kyros compelled you to try to kill just now, too." He crouched down and wrapped his hand around Mason's neck to haul him up to his feet. "For my own peace of mind, I will get the knowledge I want."

He wasn't gentle when his mind connected with Mason. The sweep was swift, brutal, and seeking only one thing. The compulsion. When there wasn't one, Donovan let Mason go. "The sentence stands."

Donovan tossed away the sword. There were several ways to kill an Undying. One was the removal of his head. It was the swiftest and most painless way to go. Another was the complete loss of blood or energy. Those could be relatively painless, depending on the circumstance. The last was heart removal.

Donovan's gaze locked on Mason's. He curled a lip. The power flowing through him caused the room to rumble. "She is my lifebond!"

Mason was screaming before Donovan shoved his hand up into the meirlock's chest cavity. He glided his arm through tissue and blood to find the organ he wanted. He wrapped his hand around Mason's heart. He twisted and yanked it out. Mason stared down at his heart in Donovan's hand before he collapsed on the ground, his blood pooling onto the white marble. Donovan dropped the heart onto the body.

"Brogan," he ordered. "Clean this up." He shook off the excess blood on his arm. He pointed at Marcus. "Get him out of here." He found Nathan, the marrok, among those brave enough to still be in the foyer. Donovan walked over to him. "Kyros is not going to give up this place or Haven easily. Even as we speak, he and his men are working to tear down our defenses. I will keep the battle contained to this place. If there are any within these walls worth saving, I suggest you evacuate them."

Nathan's eyes went huge before he took off running down the hall, bellowing for everyone to get out of the building.

Chapter 21

Wolf was on edge. He did not like Riordan here with the other Cadens. They were risking too much having their healer here. If the unthinkable happened and Quinn was injured, they'd need Riordan to save him. He stood rigid by the door of Haven's old bedchamber. Power warred in the air itself. All the safeguards they had surrounding Haven had kept her safe. They only kept the power of a meirlock clan at bay for a short time. This place his queen once called home would be no more by sunrise. Power contracted around him, and he gritted his teeth together as he fought to keep the air from opening up with a portal powered by Memphis's dark twin. Donovan was almost here. Then they could allow the darkness that was Kyros to enter, and they would defeat him and his minions for all time.

Haven stilled in the center of the room. She turned to Wolf. "I…" She let out a soft breath. "Maybe it would be best if we just left. I don't—"

The building shook.

Pain seared across Wolf's chest as he dropped to his knees. He ground his teeth together as he staggered up to his feet and lunged for her. His hand wrapped around her wrist just as a portal cracked open under her feet. He yanked her backward, pulling her away from Kyros as he entered into the room. In one motion, he shoved her behind him and drew his broad sword.

"Get her out of here!" he bellowed at Riordan as the head of a red dragon shoved his head through the portal hole. Wolf threw every ounce of power he had into keeping it closed. His muscles flexed. This was no young dragonling easily held at bay by his will. The dragon's mouth opened as all the oxygen was drawn out of the room. This son of a bitch wasn't going to take away his brother's lifebond while there was still breath left in him. Apollo growled and crouched, ready to attack the ancient meirlock dragon. Wolf aimed his sword and charged.

* * * *

Haven screamed when white-hot flames billowed out the bedroom door. Riordan snatched her away from it and shoved her toward the stairs. "We need to move."

"Wolf," she said.

A horrible agony-filled wail rose up over the flame.

"He'll need you!" Haven shouted above the roar of fire.

"Aye," Riordan agreed as he grabbed her wrist and dragged her toward the stairs. "Quinn needs you more."

"He's your brother!" Haven said, even as she staggered along the wall leading to the spiral staircase to the foyer.

"This is not the first dragon he's faced." Riordan's voice was clipped and worried. "Once you are with Quinn, I will go back for Wolf."

The entire building rumbled again. Shouts and screams echoed around the mansion as the lights went out. Riordan moved in close to her. "Shh. Stay still. Lazarus…"

Black and red streaks of lightning split open the air just before the stairs.

"Oh, fuck," Riordan muttered under his breath as he pulled out an impressive set of machete knives. "Run!"

"But—"

"Fucking run!"

She ran. Riordan was not prone to using expletives or yelling. The dragon roared as she ran past the bedroom toward the back staircase that would take her to the lower level. The building shook. She couldn't see anything. The hall grew longer and longer until she wasn't able to find her own way. When there was suddenly no floor under her, a scream strangled in her throat before she fell into black nothingness.

A hand of steel wrapped around her wrist before she hit anything solid. Pain tore through her shoulder as the sudden jerking stop. Light illuminated around Kyros as he snarled violently at her before he hurled her across the floor. She bounced and skidded into the wall. She lay against the cold stone, oblivious to the shiver of fear as she tried to shake the ringing out of her head.

"He's already changed you!"

When she didn't respond, he stalked toward her, crouched next to her, and slapped her in the face. "I am talking to you!"

She pressed a hand to her forehead and then glared up at him. Her ears still rang. "Of course. He's my lifebond." His eyes glowed red, but before he could say anything, she continued, "You are disgusting and a monster."

He grabbed a fist full of hair and yanked her to her feet. He tore the front of her shirt in half. "If I can't torture him one way, I'll find another way."

She kicked him in his shin. He grunted as he brought up his hand. She braced for the blow and rolled over the ground as it sent her sprawling across the floor. She was up and running in the next instant, but the door that had been there suddenly vanished.

"It's really there," she spat out and closed her eyes as she ran directly at what appeared to be a stone wall. She put her hands up just before she would hit rock and stumbled a little when she went through the illusion. Hope rushed through her. She didn't know where she was going, but she would keep running from him until the end of time if necessary. The maze of moving walls and vanishing light made this deadly game of keep-away more difficult. She'd managed to redirect his attention from everything else to chase her around the mansion. It would have been funny, because she felt like she was trapped in some B-rated horror flick, but she knew that she could end up dead—or worse, with Kyros for an eternity.

* * * *

Wolf staggered out of the charred remains of the bedroom. Kyros had Haven. He could feel it in his bones. There was no other reason for the dragon to fall back and allow him to live. The ends of his hair still smoked, and his boots were warmer than was comfortable, but once again, he had Apollo to thank for not becoming a meirlock dragon's barbecue snack.

"Riordan!" he bellowed. "Rior—"

He stilled in the hall when he saw Quinn crouched down next to their youngest brother.

Quinn's head snapped up. "Where is Haven?"

Wolf closed his eyes before he squared his shoulders and walked over to where Riordan lay. The clans would need their great healer no matter what happened here tonight. "*Memphis, open the portal for all Cadfaels. We are going to need all the power we can get.*"

"*What's happening?*" Memphis demanded.

"*Cadeyrn will turn.*"

"I asked you a question," Quinn roared at him. "Where is she?"

Wolf stared at his brother's glowing eyes. "Kyros has her." He flung himself forward, covering Riordan with his body. He curled around Riordan as power erupted around Quinn. The building rocked on its foundation as glass everywhere shattered.

Quinn grabbed his head, but the power expanded out of him in a flashing wave with the concussive force of a bomb. He doubled over with a horrific yowl, and all the power that had turned to angry energy sucked back into him. His hands flexed as he slowly stood up with the red of the eyes of a *treòir* gone mad.

Wolf threw his sword down the hall and, predictably, a power-mad Quinn ran after it and then vanished into the darkness.

A portal created by Memphis opened up.

Wolf shoved to his feet. "We need to get the humans to safety."

"Cadeyrn?" Brody demanded as he came out of the portal.

Wolf stared in the direction Quinn had vanished. "Only Reannon can save any of us now."

* * * *

The ground jumped and rumbled under her feet. Stones dislodged themselves and came spraying down around her. The earth shook again, and Haven looked up when crystal clinked together overhead, only to see a chandelier falling toward her. She opened her mouth as the scream started to rush out, but a blur shot across the room, scooping her body up and crushing her into a hard, corded male chest. The chandelier crashed to the floor and fractured right at her rescuer's back, his body shielding her from the debris. She pushed at his chest and bit down on the hand that tried to wrap over her mouth. She was dropped to her feet, both of her hands caught in an iron grip. Rough breathing hissed in her ear. The tone was a quiet menace. "Bite me again, woman, and I may just decide to bite you back."

Relief flooded her, and she let out a small, involuntary whimper. The hands around her wrists loosened, and she turned around to look up into Quinn's face. His eyes were a blood-red glow, and she curled herself into the solid safety and warmth of his chest. "You came!"

* * * *

The *treòir* stood there frozen and confused. The waves of abating fear and her love for this body washed over him. The *treòir* blinked several times, not understanding what she wanted or how she could not be terrified of him. She'd seen the monster burning in him. Her slender arms wrapped around him, pulling her trembling body in closer. He lifted his arm hesitantly, and then he looped it around her. A feeling of awe and wonder enveloped him.

He bent down, her scent filling his lungs, the one that always made Quinn weak in his knees. His chin brushed over the top of her head, her soft hair breathing life into his skin, and suddenly it made sense why Quinn craved to run his fingers through the silkiness. He could feel her softness, the warming of her skin touching his. Never in his long existence had the *treòir* been able to smell or feel what Quinn had. He tilted her face up to meet his. His large hand trembled with fear of hurting her if he inadvertently used too much force to make her look at him. Then he dipped his head down to taste her, just one, small taste. When his mouth brushed against hers, her lips sent hot, molten desire through him, and he shook with the need to bury himself deep inside of her. Senses he'd never known before had come to breathtaking life. He didn't know if it was because of her or because he'd defeated Quinn that he felt such things. His heart twisted in his chest, and emotions he didn't like clawed at his gut in reaction.

Haven pulled back, her eyes searching his face. "I love you."

"I killed him. I am not what you seek."

Her delicate hand reached up to touch the side of his face. "You are him, and you stand before me. I love you."

"I am only the *treòir*. You've seen my eyes."

Her hand shook, but she didn't take it or her gaze away from his face. "Oh, my love, you are the warrior who protects the heart of us both."

A minute tremble touched his shoulders. She hadn't called him a meirlock, the traitor to their kind. He couldn't sense fear in her, but there was pride and love and trust in her pale eyes. She named him the warrior, the protector, not a monster. But he was. Quinn was trapped deep inside. He felt the despair Quinn felt that he was so close to his Haven, yet unable to hold her, to touch her. He growled low and pushed her back from him. "It is done, Haven. I will take you to Quinn's brother, and then I will defeat Kyros. After that—"

"No!" she screamed. "You won't do this. You are not a monster. Quinn is inside of you. He is part of you. You have only taken over for a little while, protecting him from this madness."

He cupped her face with his hands. "I am sorry."

Quinn's voice was quiet and yearning. *"Please, brother, we are the same. I would tear the world apart for her just as you would."*

He closed his eyes. What was this feeling swelling in his chest, making it ache? How could this be happening to him? He was too powerful, too... evil to be allowed near Haven, but Quinn wasn't. Reluctantly, he began to fade back. He could do this. He was a savage, and Haven, his lifebond, had no business being cradled in his arms. The man, Quinn, who deserved her love, should get the look of adoration and trust. Not him, not when he had fought so hard to be set free to run a rampage over everything living in his path to get to her. But Haven... His sweet, stubborn Haven was all the things he was not: gracious, full of life, and laughter. She was the heart of him, and he was supposed to be the warrior, the protector of her heart, of Quinn. If he stayed, he would only destroy them both.

Quinn rushed forward when he was released from the cage deep within himself. His need to get to the forefront before Kyros found them tucked beneath a crumbling staircase was great. The *treòir* was close to him, and he made the decision of his lifetime. Quinn swept up the *treòir*, and dragged it to the surface with him. The *treòir* roared its anger. "*Accept my sacrifice!*"

"*She needs us both. She needs us as one.*" Quinn held out his hand to the *treòir*, to his power and his ability to be a savage monster. His glowing red eyes stared at that hand for what seemed an eternity. Then the *treòir* lifted its head, a cold, savage smile curling its lips.

* * * *

Fear ripped through her when the light in his eyes went out. Not even the ice of their usual color flickered in the darkness. They were soulless black voids. Had it happened? Had the *treòir* won? Was her Quinn gone forever? He wasn't moving, barely even breathing. They couldn't stay tucked under the stairs forever. Kyros was coming. She could sense him as the walls in the room began to shift. Torch fires lit, and the echo of his footfalls filled the room. She pressed herself into Quinn. "Don't you do this. I swear, I will do something you will regret if it's the only way I can bring you back!" As if to prove the point, she slipped a dagger out of its sheath at his hip.

His hand snapped up with a speed she hadn't seen coming. His fingers curled around her wrist with bruising strength as he plucked the knife from her hand. He closed his eyes, and when he opened them, they were a flaming golden umber with deep flecks of blood-red fire burning at the centers.

Quinn's hungry gaze raked over her. His face twitched and went firm. His hand glided over her, the tips of his fingers touching each bruise and each wound. He released the healing energy.

She made a face. "Do not look at me like that. Nothing happened. Nothing like *that*, anyway."

"Good." He sheathed the knife and pulled a broadsword. His head came up, and he narrowed his eyes in the darkness. "Time to go."

Haven pressed herself into his back. The connection to him washed over her as their thoughts were shared once more. He checked the room before he brought them out from behind the stairs. Guiding them around the shattered chandelier, he murmured, "Don't look at anything. I will get us out of here. His illusions are strong, and I don't want you reacting to anything that's not really there."

She took a sharp intake of breath, and then she squeaked. "Quinn!" She shuttered behind him and pressed herself more tightly against him. "I don't even know how to get out of here. How are you going to find our way out?"

"I'm just good like that." There was humor in his tone, but she did not appreciate it at the moment.

The merge had happened. Quinn was different. Calmer, more in control, and the glint of the monstrous predator that was always just below the surface was now his entire presence. It soothed the fears rolling around in her belly. She'd known that Quinn would come for her in one form or another, but this man in front of her was one she was not wholly familiar with. He allowed her to easily slip into his mind. He was Quinn and he was *treòir*. All the strength of each one to dispel the weaknesses of the other. He was stronger, more confident, and the power that flowed through him was awesome and frightening. Haven breathed easier.

He led them swiftly and easily through the twisting labyrinth, as if he could see what walls were really there and which ones were not. Haven was running to keep up with his pace, but she would not fall behind, nor would she slow him down. The feeling of Kyros was getting weaker, and she was beginning to hope this wretched night would soon be over.

The corridor became alive with dark motion that appeared human but wasn't. Haven could feel the evil exuding from the creatures. They were walking the hall and moving in strange, spider-like ways as they crawled along the walls and ceiling toward them. Coming from the direction Quinn wanted to go.

"Mortis," Quinn hissed. "Haven, sweetheart?" His tone was light with a lace of warning.

She was trying to breathe as she made out the spidery creatures in the shadows. She started to back away, but Quinn held her tight to his back. "What?"

"I need you to trust me."

"You know I do." But the tone of his voice had been slightly manic, giving her no choice but to ask, "Why?"

A low grumble sounded deep in his chest. "Because where we want to go is on the other side to avoid Kyros. We're going through them."

She gulped. "What? Why?"

"Wolf is that way." He backed her up a few paces as he let go of her. "Stay as close to me as you can." He pulled his dagger and started forward.

She inched behind him. Nikon ghosted up next to them, snarling and snapping as they walked past twitching body parts.

"Where did you—"

"Memphis," the wolf said in her head just before snapping a white bone in two. *"You're not the only ones who can demand Memphis open a portal."*

Her eyes were huge as she watched the slaughter, but she knew if Quinn weren't doing this, they'd both be dead. These things were everything evil, and they were loyal to Kyros. She shoved back the hysteria that wanted to come.

One dismembered arm reached up to grab her ankle, but she kicked it and then had to duck when Quinn pivoted and swung his strong arm, slicing the hand off, before he turned back to focus on the creatures crawling all around them. They got to a balcony that overlooked the grand foyer, but the stairs were now a pile of crumbled stone. Two men fought with the deadly mortis, one using steel weapons, the other a torch. The hideous things shrieked as they burst into smoky flame and stopped moving. She recognized Wolf and Brody. She closed her eyes and another measure of her fear faded back. Wolf turned the blade in his hand and drove it into another of the awful beings.

"Wolf!" Quinn bellowed.

His brother turned to look, his face hard, his eyes glowing.

Quinn lifted Haven up and over the rail. "Catch!"

She stifled the scream when he dropped her. Wolf caught her with seemingly no effort. She was shaking so badly her teeth rattled when he set her on her feet. Her breathing was labored, and it was a struggle to keep herself upright. She glared up at Quinn still on the upper level. When this was over, they were going to have a very long talk about him warning her before he did those kinds of things.

Her heart dropped into her toes and then slammed up into her throat when Quinn leaped over the railing. He landed right in front of her, in a low, predatory crouch. He rose up from the ground like a majestic ancient warrior. Everything about him was calm, controlled, and deadly. Wolf slid his body in between Haven and Quinn, and she was only vaguely aware that Nikon had leaped off the balcony into Brody's arms. Everything inside of her coiled tight when she realized what Wolf was going to do. She darted around him and planted herself between the two brothers.

Wolf's face went into a dark frown, his eyes blazing in holy gold. "Move."

She went desperate. "He's not what you think he is."

His lip curled into a sneer as he studied his brother.

Quinn's tone was calm. "Do not think you can take me. I am not what you fear."

Wolf's eyes flickered over him, and then a genuine smiled curved his mouth. Haven's eyes went huge as a shadowy figure came up behind him. "Wolf!"

Nonchalantly, he spun his blade and rammed it into the stomach of a Mortis. The foul creature slid off the back of the sword. As the blade left its body, Brody touched a torch to the Mortis, and it burst into smoky flames. Haven turned into Quinn as its death squeal reverberated through her. Then everything went quiet.

Quinn's hand ran over her back, and he tilted her face to look at him. "You are going with Wolf. I will come back, but I can't have you in here while I take care of Kyros."

Wolf already had a hand curled around her upper arm. She planted her feet. "No, you can't make me do this. I won't leave you."

Quinn's expression was stern. "Yes, you will." Then he went completely still. The dark creatures scurried back as the torches lit all around them. A low, rumbling laugh filled the room. Quinn, Wolf, and Brody surrounded her. Their bodies faced out as they tried to determine where he was coming from.

Kyros materialized from the shadows. "You can't take her anywhere. I challenge you for your lifebond."

"Your challenge is nothing to me."

"But we are the same once again, Cadeyrn."

Quinn's eyes flashed. "You have broken all the laws of our kind. I pass my judgment. The sentence is death."

Fear flickered across Kyros's face and then settled into a deep rage. He stalked forward. "You have no right to condemn me. We are the same!"

Quinn's muscles rippled and bunched under his skin. He poised for battle. Wolf pulled her back. She struggled and then went still. Fear gripped her belly, but she had to trust Quinn would defeat him. He'd already done the impossible, and now, she knew he could do it once more. Other Undying warriors surrounded them. Some she recognized, but others she didn't. Power surged in the room, making the air around them spark and sizzle. All the illusions dropped away, leaving the main hall a shamble of crumpled stone. Two torches lit the area with an eerie light as the two men circled each other.

Quinn's voice rumbled out. "I am the Cadeyrn. We are not the same and you have threatened the woman I love, my lifebond. There will be no mercy."

Quinn was moving before the last words were out of his mouth. The two were locked in a deadly combat worthy of the ancient Roman Coliseum. Neither man was willing to yield to the other. She winced with each blow Quinn took. It should have been impossible for either of them to survive the punishment they were giving to each other. She let out a strangled cry when Kyros's sword slashed across Quinn's chest, but he only let out a rumbling laugh. "Is this the best you can do?"

The ground under them started to rumble and shake, but Maverick knelt down and placed his hand on the ground in a gentle, almost loving manner. The ground groaned and then fell silent.

* * * *

"You cannot use outside help!" Kyros shrieked.

Donovan stalked forward, his gaze never leaving the demon eyes. His voice was a quiet menace. "You were right. I was unable to defeat the *treòir* in me. Nor did I allow him to consume me."

Kyros hit Donovan with the full force of his mind. Twisted scenes of Haven looking up at Kyros with love filled his mind. He fought against them, but it brought him to a stumbling halt. He knew they were false, but he couldn't get the images out of his head the way Kyros showed her body being abused and used by Kyros. He growled though the pain in his head as he fought to clear his vision. Kyros was the master of illusions, but Donovan knew Haven would have never let him touch her like that, not while there was still breath in him. The hold Kyros had on him was beginning to slip, so he switched tactics.

Haven's wail of soul-shattering grief ripped through him like not even a burning sword could. He merged his mind with hers, but she tried to reject him. He pushed forward to see what she was seeing. His body was broken on the ground. His heart smashed and lying in a bloody heap on top of him. Kyros wasn't able to make pain affect Donovan directly, but through Haven, he was able to bring the warrior to his knees. With a mighty roar, he forced himself up as Kyros's sword stroked downward. Donovan blocked the attack with his own sword, and then with his other arm, he rammed his fist into Kyros's chest. The images assaulting his Haven vanished. His arm moved up through blood and organs for his hand to wrap around the heart. Kyros's eyes went wide with shock. He looked down at the arm sticking out of him and then back at Donovan's face. His eyes flickered and then extinguished into a chocolate brown.

A wave of relief and bliss washed over his face as he fell to his knees. Donovan went down with him. The grief that threatened to consume him was great, but he steeled himself and yanked down and out. A hushed silence fell into the room.

Donovan stood and moved back a pace. "Be at peace, brother."

Kyros fell face-first into the soot-covered stone. His heart beat once and then twice in Donovan's hand before it beat no more. Donovan bowed his head for the man Kyros had once been, for his brother in battle and his best friend. He gently laid Kyros's heart on his body.

A ragged sob tore out of Haven as she ripped herself from Wolf's grasp and ran to Donovan. She slammed into him. He wrapped a non-blood drenched arm around Haven and buried his face in her hair.

The men gathered around them. Brogan knelt and lightly touched Kyros, setting the body to flame. She had lost all color and looked so small and delicate standing in a protective half circle of the males.

Scraping started along the walls. He hissed, "Mortis. Everyone out!"

Donovan let Wolf take her, hefting her up over his shoulder as they all ran out and down the mass of stairs that had led to the front entrance. "Maverick," Donovan bellowed. "Seal them in."

Hunter pulled off his shirt and handed it to Donovan so he could clean off the worst of the blood before he went to take Haven from his brother. Her body shook with pent up emotion. She leaned into him and watched Maverick with unblinking eyes. The Earth Warrior drove his fist into the bottom stone step. The focused shockwave sped up the stairs and exploded the door into a pile of rubble. Haven drew in a sharp breath and Donovan whispered the command. Brogan's body shimmered into his dragon form and took to the air. He circled what was left of the Black Rose Mansion, setting every square inch on fire.

Chapter 22

A breath shuddered out of Haven. She could handle this. She turned from where a real, live, dragon filled the night sky, breathing fire. She was not going to question how or why they didn't have the air force here trying to shoot Brogan down. There was probably some answer to explain it all, but for now she focused on other, more important things. "Riordan?"

"I'm here," he said, coming up behind them.

She twisted around and closed her eyes. "I can't send you back to Nadia looking like—"

"Shh," Wolf said as he moved in closer. "He's a healer. Nadia will never know he broke a nail."

The three huge men closed in on her in a massive group hug.

She sagged against Quinn and willed the tears not to come. "What about everyone who had been inside?"

"The others got them out," Wolf assured her. "Everyone who should be alive is alive."

At this point she was beyond caring if he was just trying to make her feel better or if what he was saying was true. She sniffled. "I want to go now. Can we go now or did you need to stay?"

He brushed the back of his knuckles down the side of her face. "I have to take care of one last thing." He lifted his head. "Bring me the werewolf Nathan."

"I will," Memphis said from somewhere behind Haven.

Several moments passed before Nathan's voice stammered, "You wanted to see me?"

"Aye," Quinn said. He turned Haven in his arms so she was also looking at Nathan. "How many of your men here tonight survived?"

Nathan wore a stunned expression. He blinked a few times and then shook his head. "All who didn't turn into Mortis."

"Good," Donovan said. "Can you find your men shelter for the night?"

"Most of them have their own homes." Nathan's voice grew steadier. "Those who do not can stay with my pack until other arrangements can be made."

"Good," Quinn said. He gingerly moved Haven behind him and stepped up in front of Nathan. "I need a man your men will trust to ease the transition from Marcus's authority to mine."

Nathan snorted. "I don't think there will be any opposition. Not after what we just witnessed." He took Quinn's hand in a hearty handshake. "Thank you. I was at a loss of how to correct the damage Marcus was doing."

Quinn hooked his arm around Haven and pulled her up next to him. "It is no longer your worry. I will leave the others to aid you in the cleanup and make sure your people have safe lodging for the night."

"This part we can do," Nathan said with a strained laugh. "We were trained to clean up after supernatural disasters, though we've never had one so large before."

"My men will help," Quinn assured. "Now, I have a mate who needs my care."

"Of course," Nathan said. "Again, thank you."

Quinn nodded and turned. He lightly brushed a stray strand away from Haven's face as he bent down to kiss her before lifting her into his arms. "Home." He brushed his mouth against hers once more. "Memphis."

In the next moment, the portal to home opened up. Quinn bellowed, "Nikon! We're leaving."

Tears were already running down her face before the portal closed. Mason was gone. Her grandfather no longer controlled the Black Rose. Kyros could never hunt her again, and yet, here she was curled up in Quinn's arms like a sobbing ninny. At the moment, she was grateful she had to consciously think about having the shield up to not feel her connection to Quinn. She was absolutely sure she'd go mental if she didn't have the strong hum of his presence warming her from the inside, even as he held her.

He shifted her in his arms to open the door of his portal room closet. Haven latched onto him tighter. Crying was ridiculous. Really, it was. The danger was over, but the stupid tears kept coming, and what was worse, she was now shaking.

Nikon pranced around Quinn. *"She doesn't go anywhere without me,"* he lectured. *"She is too important to lose. I will not have anything happen to her where I cannot rip out throats if needed. Medea will be able to guard our den soon. You are not to take her away from me again. It will not go well for you if I have to call Memphis to open a portal for me again."*

"Aye," Quinn murmured. "Help me figure out how to make a cup of tea without blowing up the kitchen."

"Haven?" Nikon pleaded. *"You can't be that bad that he has to use modern cooking appliances."*

She sniffled and hid her face against the tawny skin of Quinn's bare chest. She must have left his shirt at the mansion. "I'm fine," she mumbled. "I don't know what's wrong with me."

"Shh," Quinn murmured low against her ear. He sat her on the countertop and stroked her hair for a moment before he pulled back to give her a critical look. "All right. Nadia dishes out tea like it's a magic elixir when people are upset. I think she sent some of what she uses with Riordan the other night. Just talk me through this."

"I can do it," she said softly. "Making tea is not that difficult."

One of his dark brows arched up close to his hairline. "Of course it is." He made it sound like making a pot of tea was the most impossible task in the world. "I can stop earthquakes, but a tiny cup of tea eludes me completely."

She giggled nervously, despite herself. She remembered the rumble that had shaken the mansion under her feet, and how it had suddenly stopped when she'd felt her Quinn's *treòir* fill the entire building. "I thought Ean stopped that first one."

"An Earth Warrior is not nearly as impressive as when I do it." He went to the sink to wash off his arms and torso before going to the stovetop and picking up the kettle sitting on the back burner. "Okay. This is about as far as my knowledge of this goes."

"You need to fill it with water, but not too full or it will boil over."

He clunked around in the kitchen. At first, he didn't add in enough water; then he over filled the pot, and then he took to letting a few drops of water drip into the sink until the water level was just right.

He grinned at her with triumph. "Now what?"

She was laughing as his antics kept her mind off what had happened. "You have to turn the burner on, preferably a back burner."

"Uh oh. This is when things might get dangerous. I might have to barricade you in the living room for safety—of course the bedroom is farther away." He winked at her. "You're probably safer there."

"Hmm, I bet you think so. I can do this myself."

"Yes, yes," he agreed placidly. "Medea keeps telling me I need to at least learn how to boil water. Now seems like a good time to me."

Haven slipped off the counter and went over to the front of the stove. "All right, then let's teach you how all this really works." She gave him the remedial course on how to get the gas burners to work and then made him practice a few times before she let him turn on the back burner. "Great. Now you have to put the kettle on top of the flames."

His face was perfectly straight. "You're sure? That seems dangerous to me."

"How else is the water supposed to heat if you don't put it on the burner?"

He shrugged. He put his hand under the kettle bottom and the lines of his face creased with concentration. She felt the buzz of power stirring, and he murmured a few words. Several moments later there was steam coming out of the kettle spout. Quinn put the kettle on the front burner and turned off the back one. "Faster and safer."

She reached out to put her hand near the kettle. Sure enough, there was real heat coming off. "How did you do that? Can I do that?"

"You probably can now." The laughter in his eyes faded. "Creating a spark is a pretty standard Undying trait. It's nowhere near what a dragon can do with fire, but it does keep us warm and helps dispose of…things."

She shuttered at what those *things* could be. Then she crinkled her brow in confusion. "If you can heat the water like that, then why did you go to the trouble to learn how to use the stove?"

He reached up and lightly trailed the pad of his thumb down the side of her cheek. His voice went deep and buttery. "I needed to see you smile. I love the sound of your laugh."

After everything they'd been through, he just wanted her to smile. Haven's heart melted. The stupid tears collected again. She captured his hand and held his palm to her cheek. Whether the reason she could feel him so completely came from her newfound power of the necklace or the growing connection between them, Haven didn't know, nor did she care. His purpose was as solid and pure as the man's heart. She placed her other hand over his heart. The sniffle couldn't be helped, nor the tear slipping down her cheek, but she could smile for him. She wanted to smile for him. She wanted to more than just smile for this man. His intentions for her were clear, be it their connection or the necklace, she was able to feel it. He wanted her happy above all things. "You are a wonderful man. All I am in love with all of you."

His eyes searched her face, and his mind brushed against hers for a brief moment, leaving behind a tingling warm sensation. He got down on his knees in front of her, clasping her tiny hands in his massive ones. The man was so large that even on his knees, Haven was just barely taller than he was. There was a sweet nervousness about him, and his voice was a whispered plea. "Give yourself to me."

She knew exactly what he wanted because of the book Wolf had given her, and because she wanted it, too. She knew her smile was shaky, but the swell of emotion in her was making it difficult to think straight. "To you, my lifebond, you are my heart, my soul, my life, in your hands I trust all that is me. I will be what sooths you and keeps you whole. That is the promise I give to you. I give you all that I am, trusting myself in your safe keeping."

* * * *

Donovan's shoulders were trembling again as he looked into those pale green eyes with so much love and so much trust. He loved this woman with every fiber of his being, and this day, she would be forever his. "To you, my lifebond, you are my heart, my soul, my life, in your hands I trust all that is me. I give you my strength, my courage, and all the power within me to keep you safe and whole. You will always be in my care. I take all that you offer to cherish and hold forever."

He swept her up into his arms. The power surged within them both, binding them together for all time. It was a sweet mingling of light and dark, of souls coming together as one. He fastened his mouth to hers, needing her sweet taste, needing for them to be joined in all ways. He carried her up the stairs and carefully stripped her of her shirt after he laid her on the bed. He shed his pants before he climbed next to her while she wiggled out of her pants. His whole body covered hers. He took his time, enjoying her as he worked her into heated velvet under him. When he sank into her soft core, finally he was completely whole.

Epilogue

Two Months Later

Something was wrong with Haven. He could sense her discomfort, but she wasn't talking to him. Donovan prowled his office as his stomach clenched and twisted. Hell, she'd gone to see Riordan alone. That could only mean her health was in jeopardy in some way. For the life of him, he couldn't figure out what. The Undying couldn't get the illnesses that humans did. When he heard the door open, he tore through the penthouse and was standing next to her when she shed a spring sweater and hung it in the closet.

She appeared as if she wasn't feeling well. Damn it, the woman's skin was nearly green, and she didn't smell the same, either. She dropped her purse onto the entry table. She went up on her toes and kissed his cheek. "How was your day?"

He put a hand up against the wall when she tried to walk past him. "Haven, what the hell is wrong? Why aren't you talking to me?"

She winced, and then she really did turn a shade of green as she put a hand over her mouth. She whispered, "I need the bathroom, now."

Alarmed, he moved out of her way and followed her as she ran to the downstairs powder room. She threw up the lid of the toilet and emptied the contents of her stomach. Flushed, she sat back onto the cool tile. She was up and washing her mouth before he even had a chance to react.

"Goddamn it, woman, you will tell me what's wrong with you!"

She turned and lifted a brow at him. "Nothing is wrong with me." Then she glided past him and went into the kitchen to start a pot of water to make herself some tea. She ignored him while she sat down at the table and started to go over Bastian's homework while the kid played video games in the living room.

He dragged a hand through his hair, seriously thinking of pulling it all out. She was nervous, that much he could get, and she was worried and excited and terrified of telling him something. She shut off the contact whenever he'd get that far. He sat down in the chair next to her and pulled her into his lap. He ignored her squawk of protest and brushed a silken strand out of her face. Their gazes locked. "You can tell me anything, sweetheart."

She closed her eyes and opened her mouth, but nothing came out, and then she promptly burst into tears. That produced a loud rumbling from under the kitchen table where Nikon had settled after they had gotten home.

"Shut up," Donovan snapped at the wolf.

He rested his head on Haven's, now truly terrified of what she was going to tell him. "Sweetheart, just tell me. I promise I won't be angry." He brushed at her tears.

Her bottom lip trembled and she curled into him. "You're going to be a father. I'm pregnant."

Everything inside of him went still. He was going to be a father. His Haven was going to give him a child, his own child with Haven as the mother. His eyes were suddenly damp, and he tried to blink the tears back. He stared down at her in complete awe. Even with his great strength, he found it almost impossible to lift his hand to lightly caress her still flat belly. He brushed his mind against the baby's. Just a tentative, gentle sweep, afraid of hurting the life inside of her.

He gathered her into his arms and nearly crushed her too him. Tears rolled down his rugged face. "Thank you, Haven, thank you so much."

She reached up and brushed the tears from his cheeks. "I love you, my Quinn."

He rested his head against the top of her head, taking in her pregnant scent and letting it flow through his lungs. Haven, his sweet Haven, who had already given him life, was now going to give him the one thing he never thought he would have—a child of his own. Love swelled for her, and he knew his Haven was worth the two thousand years he'd waited for her.

Meet the author

Emma Weylin fell in love with the written word as a child. She loves to create her own worlds full of magic and wonder. One of her favorite things is populating those worlds with interesting and true-to-life characters who experience everything from epic love and heartrending battles to seriously silly or embarrassing "duh" moments. She believes love can and does conquer all things. When she's not writing, she enjoys her family and has a copious yarn addiction. For more please visit her at www.emmaweylin.com.

If you enjoyed UNDYING HOPE be sure not to miss A.S. Feinchel's

DECEPTION

When Demons threaten Regency London, only a Lady can stop them.

Lillian Dellacourt is beautiful, refined and absolutely lethal. She's also the most feared and merciless demon hunter in The Company. She's come a long way from the penniless seamstress's daughter sold to the highest bidder, and it wasn't by trusting a man, let alone an exiled Marquis with more on his mind than slaying the hellspawn…

For Dorian Lambert, Marquis de Montalembert, being sent to keep track of Lillian is no mean task. He's wanted the fiery vixen since he first heard of her five years ago. But wooing the lady while fighting the demon uprising is no easy feat, especially when the lady's tongue is as sharp as the Japanese *sai* blades she favors for eviscerating the spawn of hell.

These two will have to learn to trust each other fast, because the demon master is back, and he's planning to turn Edinburgh into a living hell…

Read on for a special excerpt!

A Lyrical e-book on sale now.

Chapter 1

Gripping the chair arms to keep herself seated, Lillian fought an urge to leave and never set foot inside Castle Brendaligh again.

It had been a demoralizing battle and they had lost, but they had lived. They had done all they could, but still the demon master had ascended into man's world.

"You failed and we are all likely to die because of it. I hold every person at this table responsible for the state of England. You have ruined us." Lord Clayton's voice grated on Lillian's nerves.

Accounts of the battle were clear. Nearly everyone in the room had risked their lives trying to disrupt the ascension, not to mention keep the earl's daughter, Belinda, from becoming a demon sacrifice. Making such a show of ferocious reprimands insulted their brave and selfless efforts. If not for the fact that he was her best friend's father, she might have indulged her desire to pull a *sai* blade from her boot and slice his throat.

As if Lord Clayton, the Earl of Shafton, needed to attract more attention, he waved his hands. "You had one mission, to keep the master from entering our world. All you had to do was kill one demon, but you failed. You should all be shot for treason. Treason!"

His bright red face gave her hope his heart might fail and save her the trouble of killing him.

Other hunters at the table murmured, but no one spoke out.

"Everyone in this room is to blame. You had the perfect opportunity to end this mess. Now the master is free of his realm and living in ours. It's only a matter of time before he is strong enough to destroy everything we hold dear. When your families are killed mercilessly, will you sit here so unrepentant about failing in your duty?"

"Father, really." Belinda Thurston rolled her eyes.

Lillian missed Reece's steadying presence. Reece might have even been able to stop his lordship's tirade with a few quick-witted remarks.

Her partner had nearly died, and now lay upstairs recovering from demon poisoning.

"Don't you roll your eyes at me, Belinda. You are equally to blame. You were with the master for days and made no attempt to destroy him."

Gabriel, Belinda's husband, bristled. It was of course a ridiculous statement. The Earl of Tullering was not used to public abuse of his family. "Just a minute, my lord. You are out of order. Belinda was in no position to defeat the demon master. The information she gathered will be very helpful in our eventual victory."

Shafton pointed a fat finger. "I do not want to hear about information that will take years to decipher. You, Tullering, are by far the most culpable. You and that woman"—he pointed at Lillian—"made a conscious choice not to destroy the master."

Lillian reached toward her boot and let the hard steel of her *sai* blade handle bring her comfort. One second and Shafton's head could be rolling down the long table and land in Drake Cullum's lap.

Besides Shafton, Drake and his assistant, Dorian Lambert, were the only ones present who had not been at the battle. Their leader, Drake, had attended to assign new orders to the hunters.

Shafton said, "You could have destroyed the beast as it rose and was weakened. I know you had the opportunity, but you chose to save yourself. It was selfish and stupid."

Lillian could kill him and no one would be able to stop her. Of course, there were always consequences when dealing with men in power. She'd lose her home within The Company. Yet another arrogant earl would not take her from her rightful place. She was in control. It was nothing like her youth and the titled man who'd ruined her life.

Belinda said, "They saved my life, Father."

"It was the wrong choice, Belinda. You might have cost us our one chance to stop this." Shafton narrowed his eyes on Lillian.

Lillian said, "I can imagine your pleasure if we had allowed your only child to become the master's sacrifice. Perhaps we should have stood by and watched until the master, with his full power rose, from the depths of hell and destroyed us all. As it is, Reece Foxjohn is still recovering from battle and the rest of us might have been sucked into the demon's realm. But by all means, my lord, go on and tell us how you know we willfully failed on our mission. I do not recall your life being in danger that day at Fatum Manor. You were safely tucked away in your castle while the rest of us faced death or worse."

"You are out of order, Dellacourt." Shafton said her name as if it were a curse.

Lillian wasn't sure when she had stood up, but clutching the leather wrapped steel, she rounded the table toward the earl. "If you have something you want to say about my abilities, my lord, I suggest you do so. I will be happy to display them for you, and we can evaluate them together."

"Miss Dellacourt." A warning came from the other end of the table.

"You were not there. You cannot know if we could have destroyed the master. As far as I'm concerned, we made the only choice possible under the circumstances. Maybe if your intelligence had supplied us with the location of the gateway before the master had grown so powerful, we might have been able to seal him in."

"How dare you imply that I failed in some way? You who completely disregard orders at will."

She had only ever hated one man the way she despised Shafton, and he too was an earl. At least that one was dead. Steeling her nerves, she slid the *sai* blade through the pocket cut in her skirt. "You speak of orders that were selfish and almost succeeded in getting your own family killed."

"You have no right to question me or my motives." To his credit, he faced her and stared her in the eye.

"I have every right when you point your fat finger at me."

"Who do you think you are? I know where you come from Lillian Dellacourt. I know what you are."

Drake Cullum pounded the table. "Shafton, that will do." The demon hunters' leader stood rigid, narrow-eyed. He was formidable when he was calm, but enraging him was never a good idea. He was furious now.

Had she gone too far? The idea she might have overstepped her bounds with Cullum was enough to make her relax the grip on her blade. Lillian turned and stormed from the dining room.

Shafton yelled something about not having dismissed her from the meeting.

Once in the hallway, she pulled her second blade and turned to go back in and finish what she'd started. It would be nothing to remove his pompous head from his shoulders.

Cullum stood in the doorway. He smiled at her and closed the door, barring her reentry.

Had she ever seen him smile before? No instance came to mind. She stomped toward the front entrance. She'd leave the damn castle, get her carriage, and ride like the devil back to London. Yet the one person in the world she could really talk to was a resident of Brendaligh. Holding her full skirts with both hands, she sprinted up the curved grand staircase.

Brendaligh, the Earl of Shafton's Scottish holding, boasted fine marble floors, crystal chandeliers, and expensive draping. To the casual observer, the entry looked like any other wealthy man's country home, but upon closer inspection, they would find the bedchambers rather bare and the ballroom fitted for mock combat sessions. Instead of fancy draperies, shields and weapons hung on the walls. He'd converted the estate from its former grandeur into a school for demon hunter training. Of course, in Lillian's opinion, it was also the earl's way of shirking his responsibilities to his family.

His wife and daughter had never been to the Scottish castle until Belinda's life was in jeopardy, and she descended on her father unannounced to verify his part in the demons' desire to capture and kill her. Before that, the earl had hidden his knowledge of any hunting activity and made excuses to remain in Scotland.

At the top of the stairs, she turned right, then entered a small salon, set up as a kind of hospital. A strange little demon's poison had turned a strapping man into the withered soul sitting in a wingback chair near the window.

Her heart tightened painfully. It took willpower not to clutch her chest.

Reece Foxjohn had been her constant companion for the last five years. His handsome face showed strain where there had always been joy. His bright blue eyes had dimmed.

Elizabeth Smyth picked up the untouched food tray from the table beside Reece, whispered something to him, and turned toward the door. Slimmer from her hunter training, she looked up and smiled. "Miss Lillian, I'm so happy to see you."

Reece turned sad eyes toward Lillian.

She put on her best grin for his sake. She wanted to detect his joy at seeing her, but nothing in his expression indicated he was happy she'd come. He returned his attention to whatever was outside the window.

"It's good to see you, Lizzy. You should just call me Lillian. No need for formality here."

"Thank you, Lillian." Lizzy blushed, but her brown eyes were sharp and direct.

"How are your studies going?"

"Very well. I've never enjoyed anything more in my life. I know there will be danger, but it is still better than scrubbing pots." She'd been a scullery maid in a wealthy home before the hunters rescued her from a ritual sacrifice in London.

"I'm glad your finding your time here well spent."

"Oh yes, Miss—um, Lillian." She appeared far fitter than when she'd joined the demon hunters, her waist small, even beneath her voluminous dress.

Lillian wanted to learn more about Elizabeth Smyth. "You'll get used to it. It takes time to shuck the old ways. Then you'll have to learn when to act the part again. It won't be easy going into society once you get used to the equality of our little group."

Lizzy glanced away, then back. "I imagine it will be another challenge, which I had not counted on."

"I'm sure you will be up to it. How is your patient doing?"

Lizzy studied the floor. "He's not my patient. Dr. Barns has that privilege. Whatever poisoned him left him very weak. His shoulder has healed and he is getting stronger, but he still refuses to eat much. He's been leached several times, and the leeches die from the poison in his blood. I think that must mean they are successfully drawing it out, and he is getting better."

"I hope you're right." Lillian kept her voice low so Reece couldn't hear the doubt in her tone.

"He is so much better than when he first came from Edinburgh. He is a strong man, a fact he seems to have forgotten. Once he remembers, his recovery will go quickly."

"I can see you are the perfect person to nurse him."

"It is the least I can do. If not for you and Reece, I might not be here today. I would have died on that altar, and who knows what plans the master had for my soul."

"You owe us nothing, but I'm glad you are here to help with his recovery. I don't know how you find the time while training to become a hunter."

Lizzy glanced at the clock on the mantle. "Oh my, speaking of time, I must get his tray down to the kitchen and get to my combat class. If you'll excuse me?"

"Of course."

She turned to leave, but stopped. "I almost forgot to tell you. Mei Lin asked me to give you her regrets that she is not here to see you."

"I heard she has already been sent on her first assignment." The strong willed Oriental girl had been a hellion when Lillian found her. It was impressive that after only a few months training she was ready for assignment.

"Yes. She is remarkable."

"Do you know where they sent her?"

"I'm afraid not. I'm not even sure Mei knew where she was headed."

Lillian didn't like the sound of that, but there was little she could do. Drake Cullum knew what he was doing. "She will do well, no matter where she has gone. You had better get to class."

After a bob, Lizzy scurried out of the room.

"Hello, Reece." She sat across from him on a small settee.

Dark wood wainscoting and rich draperies darkened the room. Three beds had been set up, but at the moment, only Reece occupied the space. Other wounded hunters had been treated here rather than carting them all the way to London.

Hunched in a dark blue robe, Reese stared outside. Fog rolled in and a light drizzle added to the gloom. "How are you, Lilly?"

"I came to complain and bristle about the meeting I've just walked out of, but I can see you are not in the mood for my foul temper."

He turned his head, and a hint of a smile lit his face. "I always love to see that fiery temper of yours, my sweet. Nothing gives me more pleasure."

"Lies. Many things give you far more pleasure. In fact, I'm surprised that lovely young woman who just carted your uneaten tray out of here is not under your spell. There was a time when a girl like Lizzy would have brought a smile to your face."

He frowned and the glint went out of his eyes. "She is a sweet thing, but that time has passed."

"She looked at you as if you were the sun and the moon. Why don't you court her?"

His stare returned to the window. "Those days have passed, Lilly. I am not the same man anymore. Lizzy deserves a man who can take care of her."

"I think she is well on her way to taking care of herself and you as well."

He shrugged. "Then a man who will fight alongside her."

"You will fight again, my dearest."

He shook his head. His malaise was worse than expected. The short, hairy pravus demon had damaged him more than sword or fist injuries ever had.

The hunters had first encountered the harmless looking demons at the Fatum Manor battle. Pravus climbed walls and ceilings like spiders on a web, and had almost cost Reece his life.

She shivered against the memory of that terrible night. She should have come sooner. Perhaps she should have brought Reece to The Company sponsored hospital in London to recover. She'd thought the castle comforts offered a better place to regain his strength. All the youthful recruits should have bolstered his spirits. "I spoke to Dr. Barns not a week ago, and she told me you were recovering nicely from your injuries. Why don't we go and watch the students practice their combat training? It will cheer you."

Dr. Emily Barns made the long trek once a month if there was a need. It was time The Company invested in a second doctor. Lillian had a feeling the wounded would be increasing in the short term.

His chest lifted as he sighed deeply. "I would rather not. Tell me why you were in such a fit of temper when you came in here?"

She paced the carpet. "I nearly cut the head off of our host in the meeting downstairs. I imagined his bulbous crown rolling down the table and landing in Cullum's lap. He is insufferable, going on and on about how we have jeopardized all of England because we chose to save Belinda. The fact that he didn't provide us with enough information to destroy, or even trap, the master never entered into his tirade."

"Do you think that could be why he's going overboard with blaming us? Is he covering up his failure?"

Lillian saw fear behind the earl's bluster, fear that needed an explanation. "I think it's more than that, Reece. He's hiding something. We saved his daughter's life, and he is completely ungrateful for our effort. In fact, he accused Belinda of negligence for not singlehandedly killing the master while she was imprisoned in the Fatum dungeon."

"He did not." Reece's voice rose, and he scowled.

"I know he is hiding something, and I intend to find out what it is."

Reece's attention returned to the window. "Would not your time be better spent finding the master and destroying him?"

Lillian knelt in front of Reece's chair and took his hands.

He looked down at her with tired eyes.

"I know that seems like the thing to do, but if I find him, how do I kill him? I don't even know if it's possible to kill the master. Is he even alive? Does he bleed? In my belly, I know whatever Shafton is hiding is a clue to how to win this war."

"Wouldn't he be eager to tell us something that might help us defeat these demons?"

"I don't know. He is a proud man, too proud. Look at how he endangered Belinda to keep his secrets. I don't trust him."

Reece kissed her forehead. "You have the best instincts of anyone I've ever seen, my sweet. If you are sure discovery of Shafton's deception will better our cause, then I support your quest. I only wish I had the strength to accompany you."

"Thank you." If Reece supported her, she could go hunting information with a clear conscience. Her gut told her she was on the right track. The earl's anger was out of proportion with the facts, and there had to be a reason for it. She hugged Reece.

His arms came around her, and he patted her back.

She longed for his strength but settled for the light comfort.

"You are my dearest friend, Lilly. Never doubt I am on your side."

She pulled away and looked him in the eye. "It's not that I doubt you. I'm unsure of this path because it's not in line with headquarters' orders. I was told to stay here and wait for a partner to be assigned to me. I've never disobeyed reasonable orders before, Reece. What if Cullum tosses me from the demon hunters? Where would I go?"

A man cleared his throat behind her.

Startled, she turned.

Belinda and Gabriel stood inside the doorway.

Embarrassed, Lillian rose brushed out her skirts and pulled her shoulders back.

Gabriel closed the door behind them and ushered his lovely wife forward. A bump preceded Belinda's normally athletic figure, evidencing the coming of the couple's first child.

"We did not mean to eavesdrop, but since we overheard the last of your concerns, I have something to add." Gabriel Thurston had been a soldier in the king's army and fought bravely in France. He'd survived capture and imprisonment only to come home to London and find Belinda, his fiancée, altered from the sweet girl he'd left behind. The earl had taken a leap of faith to join them on a hunt and afterward join The Company.

How any depth of feeling survived the madness of a hunter's daily life was beyond explanation. Demons brought nothing but death and mayhem with them, yet they had found beauty in the midst of disaster.

Lillian straightened her spine. "Say your piece, my lord."

"My name is Gabriel, as you well know, Lillian, since you have called me by that name on many occasions." He flashed a crooked smile. "I speak for my wife and myself when I say, should the demon hunters ever be foolish enough to dismiss you, you shall always have a place with us. I could not work for an organization that showed you disrespect after all you have given to this cause."

Her vision clouded and her throat clogged. "Perhaps you should know what I'm about to do before you make such a blanket statement."

Belinda stepped in front of Lillian. A smile lit her eyes, and she brushed blond hair back from her forehead. "It makes no difference to us, Lilly. We are confident whatever mission you choose will always be for the cause of good. If you need our help, you have only to ask and we are at your service. I would be dead now, or worse, living in the hell of the demon realm if you had not risked your life to help save me."

Lillian took her hands. "I appreciate the thought very much, Belinda, but you might not feel that way if you knew."

Gabriel said, "You underestimate our powers of deduction if you think we cannot recognize Shafton has something to do with whatever you intend."

"He's your family. I do not want to put more strain on your relationship with your father, Belinda. You have just become reacquainted." Even though they were not her blood, they were the only family she knew. She didn't want to lose them, but some things were more important than what she wanted.

A deep frown marred Belinda's pretty face. "My father overreacted in the dining room. Everyone at the table saw it. I hope my father is not so foolish as to harm the hunters or England, but my relationship with him is tentative at best. We shall stand behind you no matter the outcome."

Tears spilled and she dashed them away. "It means the world to me to hear you say that. Still, you should stay clear of this. It will be better for everyone."

"Are you certain you will be all right working alone? Belinda is not up to a mission, but I could accompany you." Gabriel's training as a soldier made his offer tempting. He struck an imposing figure and could get into places she would have trouble.

If her instincts were off, the fallout could be catastrophic. She wouldn't risk her friends. "I honestly believe it better if you were not involved. The family connection will

Made in the USA
Middletown, DE
04 September 2015